Praise for Blooming All Over:

"Even the most goyische reader will get a kick out of Arnold's novel... As simple and scrumptious as one of Bloom's Heat-'N'-Eat entrees. Memorable!"
— *Publishers Weekly*

"*Blooming All Over* is a story that will stay with you long after you read it... This book will be loved by everyone, no matter what kind of food you like."
— *Romance Reviews Today*

Blooming All Over

Judith Arnold

Story Plant Books by Judith Arnold

Love in Bloom's
Full Bloom

This is a work of fiction. Names, characters, places, and incidents either are the product of the author's imagination or are used fictitiously. Any resemblance to actual events, locales, organizations, or persons living or dead, is entirely coincidental and beyond the intent of either the author or the publisher.

The Story Plant
Studio Digital CT, LLC
PO Box 4331
Stamford, CT 06907

Story Plant hardcover ISBN-13: 978-1-61188-296-4
Fiction Studio Books E-book ISBN-13: 978-1-945839-47-4

Visit our website at www.TheStoryPlant.com

For information, address The Story Plant.

First Story Plant printing: June 2020
Printed in the United States of America

To my boys,
Ted, Fred, and Greg
with love

The Bloom's Bulletin
Written and edited by
Susie Bloom

A fellow addicted to knishes
Found at Bloom's, all the food was de-
licious.
He bought bagels, a blintz,
And some stuffed cabbage, since
Bloom's cuisine fulfills all of his wishes!

Welcome to the May 14th edition of the *Bloom's Bulletin*, which is jam-packed with tasty tidbits, recipes and—of course!—news about sales and specials throughout the store. Bloom's has become the most famous kosher-style food emporium not just on Manhattan's Upper West Side but all over the world by fulfilling our customers' wishes.

All over the world? Yes, indeed. Jay Bloom is the director of Bloom's Internet and Mail-Order Services, which distributes Bloom's Seder-In-A-Box, a package containing matzo, gefilte fish, horseradish, *charoseth*, chicken soup with matzo balls, salt, and *Haggadahs*—just add wine and serve. According to Jay, by mid-April, the store had filled Seder-In-A-Box orders from thirty-seven states and fifteen foreign countries, among them Finland, Japan, South Africa, New Zealand, Bolivia and...are you ready?...the research station at the

South Pole! Yes, Bloom's has extended its reach into Antarctica. When an order arrived from the McMurdo Station on Ross Island, Bloom's was able to get four Seder-In-A-Boxes prepared and ready for delivery by the New York Air National Guard, which serves the U.S. Antarctic Program. The Seders arrived in time for the holiday, along with two complimentary bottles of Passover wine, Bloom's gift to the intrepid researchers who live and work at the South Pole. Good *yontif!*

Feeling bleu?
French cheeses are specially priced all this week at Bloom's. Camembert, Port Salut, Brie, Roquefort—come on in, buy some cheese and keep the change!

Did you know...
The word "schmaltzy," which is used to describe music or a story that's overly sentimental, is derived from the Yiddish word *schmaltz*, which means congealed fat. In Ida Bloom's day, chicken schmaltz spread on a slice of dark pumpernickel was considered a gourmet treat. Now, the mere thought of it is enough to give most people heartburn. If you're in the mood for schmaltz, listening to Rachmaninoff is a whole lot healthier.

Employee Profile:
Who's that tall-blond-and-handsome fellow standing behind the bagel counter? None other than Casey Gordon, co-manager of the bagels department. Casey studied at the Culinary Institute of America before transferring to St. John's University, where he earned a degree in English. Ask nicely, and he might just recite a little Shakespeare while he counts a dozen sesame seed bagels into a bag for you.

Since joining the Bloom's staff three years ago, Casey has put his culinary school experience to work by designing a variety of new flavors of bagels. Thanks to him, Bloom's sells pesto bagels, cranberry bagels, apple-cinnamon bagels, and sour-yogurt bagels along with the standard plain, egg, garlic and poppy-seed varieties. "Some flavors rotate in and out," Casey says. "Some are interesting experiments that just don't click. Others become very popular, so we make them a permanent addition to our inventory." Among those that didn't "click" he mentioned curry bagels and banana cream bagels. His most recent surprise hit? Dill pickle bagels, which customers seem to love.

When he's not dreaming up sensational new bagel flavors, Casey says he likes to play basketball, analyze movies, and spend time with his girlfriend. What's her favorite kind of bagel? "Egg," Casey reports. "But she's adventurous. She'll try anything."

Wise Words from Bloom's founder Ida Bloom: "There's a reason for everything, but some reasons are stupid."

On sale this week: pita crisps, all varieties of blintzes, smoked sable and more. Turn the page for details!

Chapter One

Susie could have been using this time to contemplate the course of her life. Instead, she was driving a truck—which was a lot more fun.

It wasn't so much a truck as a van on steroids. The rear seats had been removed, leaving a vast cargo space in the back. The front seat was elevated, the windshield broad, and the steering wheel as big as a bicycle tire. She and her sister had rented the van from a downtown outfit called Truck-A-Buck, which specialized in cheap rates and vehicles that looked as if they kissed bumpers with slutty abandon. Among the van's special features were an ashtray crammed with chewing gum wrappers, a crack in the passenger's side mirror, mysterious streaks of dark red paint—or maybe it was blood—staining the driver's side door, and an aroma of gasoline with notes of Lysol and barbecue sauce permeating the interior.

Susie loved the idea that she, a member of the Bloom family, a poet, a Bennington College alumna, the Bloom's newsletter writer/editor—a position which came with the fancy title of "creative director"—and a sometime pizzeria waitress, was driving a truck. It felt right.

It felt more right than mentally rehashing the conversation she'd had last night with Casey, when he'd asked her to move in with him.

Casey was wonderful, she adored him, he was without a doubt the sweetest, hottest, smartest guy she'd ever hooked up with. But merely thinking about living with him caused her soul to break out in hives. So she decided not to think about it. She thought instead about inching her way through the ooze of traffic on the West Side Highway, wishing she were actually driving across the North American continent behind the wheel of an eighteen-wheeler packed with freight of incalculable value—gold ingots or high-tech machines or cartons of Ghirardelli semi-sweet chocolate.

It would be a lot easier to imagine if Grandma Ida weren't riding shotgun beside her.

"You're driving too fast," Grandma Ida said. She sat strapped into her seat, her arthritic hands clenched in her lap, her hair so black it looked like a blob of licorice glued to her skull. Someone ought to talk to her about her stylist's lack of skill with hair color. Someone *had* talked to her about it: Susie and her sister Julia had both mentioned to their grandmother that perhaps a new coiffure was in order, one that matched her face. Grandma Ida was eighty-nine years old, and for eighty-nine she looked amazingly good. But even if her face hadn't been laced with lines, her eyes slightly faded and the skin of her neck pleated like an accordion, the ink-jet hair wouldn't work. She needed a softer style with variations in the color, some silver mixed in, some gray. Something that looked as if it might have actually sprouted from a human scalp.

Grandma Ida should have gone in the car with Sondra, Julia, and Joffe. All four of them could have fit comfortably in the Toyota Camry Joffe had borrowed from his brother, and Susie could have driven the van up to Cornell University solo. She could have blasted Ben Harper and Ani DiFranco through the van's admittedly feeble-looking speakers and sung along at vocal-cord-popping volume.

Of all the configurations the family might have sorted themselves into for their journey, assigning Grandma Ida to the van rather than the car had made the least sense. Climbing into the high-riding vehicle had been as big a challenge for her as scaling Everest might be for an aging Sherpa. The seats were stiff and unforgiving, and the smell could upset an elderly woman's delicate constitution. But Susie's mother had wanted to ride in the car so she could discuss Julia and Joffe's wedding plans during the trip, and everyone except for Susie felt Susie should not have to make the four-hour drive to Ithaca alone.

For a person who shared a tiny one-bedroom walk-up with two other women, four hours alone would be a luxury. Of course, if Susie moved in with Casey, she wouldn't have to share the tiny one-bedroom walk-up with Anna and Caitlin anymore.

No. She wasn't moving in with Casey. He lived in Queens, for God's sake.

"You're driving too fast," Grandma Ida said again.

"I'm driving three miles an hour," Susie retorted. "It's impossible to drive too fast on the West Side Highway."

"You're going faster than three miles an hour. You think I can't tell? You think I don't know from cars?"

Yes, Susie almost answered. "This is a van, not a car."

"It's too big. Who needs all this room?"

"Adam does. He's graduating from college. He's got four years' worth of junk he has to move out of his dorm room."

"Junk? You rented this van so he can move junk?"

"He doesn't think it's junk," Susie explained.

"What is he, an idiot? All that money for a fan-cy-schmancy education, and he wants to move junk," Grandma Ida muttered. "Where is he going to put the junk?"

"In Mom's apartment. And then he'll take it with him when he leaves for graduate school in September."

"Graduate school." Grandma Ida sniffed disdain-fully. "Where's he going again? That place with the chickens?"

"Purdue," Susie told her. "And it has nothing to do with chickens. It isn't even spelled the way the chicken company spells it."

"Purdue." Grandma Ida sniffed again. "I never heard from Purdue. It's out in the middle of nowhere, right?"

"Indiana."

"That's what I thought. Who needs graduate school, anyway? I never went to college, and I made a life for myself. My Isaac, he never even finished high school, but he knew how to sell knishes. You don't need graduate school with Indians to know how to sell knishes."

"True—and if Adam wanted to sell knishes, he wouldn't have applied to graduate school," Su-sie pointed out. "He doesn't want to sell knishes. He wants to get a Ph.D. in mathematics and become a col-lege professor."

"He should consider sales. You and Julia work at the store. It wouldn't kill Adam to work at the store, too."

"Julia's the president of the store. I'm only a part-time consultant." Julia had given Susie that fancy ti-tle—creative director—in an effort to entice her into a full-time job with the family enterprise. But she refused to give up her waitressing at Nico's. Keeping the waitressing job reminded her of her roots—or, more accurately, helped her to escape her roots.

"I don't know why you want to sell food downtown and not in your own family's store," Grandma Ida muttered.

Susie sighed. If she was going to have to listen to the old lady rant all the way to Cornell, it was going to be a very long drive.

"As for Adam," Grandma Ida continued, clearly warming up, "Isaac and I never got Ph.D.'s. We never even got Ph.A's or Ph.B's. And we built the biggest delicatessen in the world."

Susie knew she ought to keep her mouth shut, just nod and smile and let Grandma Ida run at the mouth. But she couldn't help herself. "Bloom's is not the biggest deli in the world."

"The biggest good deli. We started with my parents' push cart—they were selling knishes from the cart, in all kinds of weather, you shouldn't know from standing in the rain on a cold day in November and trying to sell knishes..."

Susie braced herself for the entire up-by-the-bootstraps saga. She'd heard it enough times to be able to recite it verbatim. Her lips moved, shaping Grandma Ida's words as the older woman spoke them.

"Just a cart on Upper Broadway, that was all it was until Isaac and I moved the store indoors. And it grew, and we expanded, first to the storefront on one side of us, then to the storefront on the other side, until we took up the whole block. I did the books, but your grandfather—" she wagged her index finger at Susie for emphasis "—he knew how to sell. Borscht, gefilte fish, bagels, stuffed derma—if it was edible, he could sell it. Chicken soup. I didn't think we'd do so well with the chicken soup, but people got sick, they came into Bloom's and Isaac would sell them chicken soup. And before you know it, they'd be feeling better."

"Right," Susie said wearily.

"Adam wants to be a doctor? Your grandfather Isaac was a doctor without college. People came in sick, he sold them chicken soup and they went home and got well. Without college he did this. Who could afford college? We were too busy working."

"I know."

"So, your brother is going to the chicken school out there with the Indians to get a doctor degree, and your sister is marrying that reporter. And what are you doing with your life, Susie?"

"Right now, what I'm doing with my life is driving you to Cornell so we can see Adam graduate." *And I'm listening to you—for which I deserve a medal.*

"You're a waitress. All that education, and you work as a waitress."

"I work for Bloom's, Grandma. You know that."

"Once a week."

"More than once a week. I write and edit the *Bloom's Bulletin*. That takes a lot of time."

"It's an advertising circular."

"It's a newsletter with ads mixed in. Julia hired me to write it because I'm a good writer. And I redesigned the store windows, too, and spruced up the interior." And she wasn't going to do a damned thing more for the store. Enough was enough.

From the time she was old enough to daydream about what she wanted to be when she grew up, she'd resisted working at Bloom's. Her father had been the president of the company until his death two years ago, and the store had been the pulsing heart of his existence. Her mother had worked side by side with him, and now she was working side by side with Julia, whom Grandma Ida had named president of the company last year. Her father's brother, Uncle Jay, ran the store's on-line business and its mail-order program. Enough Blooms had been sucked into the place. Susie preferred to live her own life, a life that had nothing to do with borscht, gefilte fish, bagels, stuffed derma or any of the hundreds of other items that filled Bloom's shelves: breads, gourmet coffees, overpriced olive oil, cookies and kugel, cheese and chopped liver, and a spectacular array of kitchen tchochkes—potato peelers, garlic presses, melon ballers, pepper mills, vegetable steamers and egg timers.

She just wanted to live downtown, go to poetry slams, stay up late drinking wine, have mind-blowing sex when the opportunity arose—and not make a capital-C Commitment, or do capital-S Something with her life. She just wanted to be herself and enjoy each day. Was that so much to ask for?

Apparently, if you were a Bloom, it was.

o

Adam felt Tash stir against him. "You're not asleep?" she asked.

"No."

"You always fall asleep after."

"No, I don't." He knew he sounded gruff, but now wasn't a good time for her to complain about their sex life. As far as he knew, that sex life was about to end. Sex, pot, music, freedom—every fun activity he'd indulged in over the past four years would become taboo starting tomorrow. College graduation was supposed to be a joyous event, but in his case, graduation doomed him to spend the next three muggy, dreary summer months in his mother's Upper West Side apartment, where he was sure that bringing a woman to his room and firing up even the skinniest little joint would create a family crisis so huge, World War II would seem like a minor tiff in comparison.

He loved his family. But he loved them a hell of a lot more when they were two hundred miles away.

"Thinking about tomorrow?" Tash asked.

"Thinking about the day after tomorrow." Tomorrow was commencement. He'd don his cap and gown, pose for photos, grab his diploma, load up the van Susie and Julia had rented and travel back to New York City. The day after tomorrow he'd wake up in his mother's apartment.

Shit.

"It won't be so bad," Tash assured him. She stretched, and he tried not to stare at her body. She wasn't fat, just solid, with lots of firm curves and dimpled knees. She ate a lot and didn't care what she weighed.

That was what he liked best about her: she didn't care. She didn't care about impressing people. She didn't care about high fashion. She didn't care about being graceful or elegant or loved, or any of the things every other girl he knew cared about. She did care about the decimation of old-growth forests and the exploitation of Third-World laborers. She could get a little sanctimonious when she launched into one of her diatribes about eight-year-olds stitching soccer balls in Bangladesh for ten cents a day—or maybe it was ten-year-olds stitching soccer balls in Bangladesh for eight cents a day. Adam listened to her harangues, but they tended to bleed together in his mind.

So she was passionate about that stuff. Why shouldn't she be? Her mother worked for Planned Parenthood and her father published a socialist newspaper, and they'd named her Natasha. She'd told Adam how they used to sing her to sleep with Woody Guthrie and early U-2 songs and explicate her bedtime stories for their political subtexts. "'Little Red Riding Hood' is about the exploitation of the proletariat," her father would instruct her. "The wolf represents capitalism. When he devours her grandmother, it's like management devouring the laborers."

Adam didn't agree with her about everything. He didn't disagree with her about everything, either. Mostly he let her rant and then had sex with her. And he didn't always fall asleep after. Usually, but not always.

In a matter of hours, his mother, his grandmother, his sisters and his future brother-in-law were going to drive onto the Cornell campus and bring his sex life to a crashing halt. He'd have one more night with Tash, and then he'd graduate and return to New York City with them.

Shit.

"I'm going to miss you," he confessed, tangling his fingers into the frizzy brown curls that churned around Tash's face.

"It's just for the summer. In September, you'll go to Purdue, and I'll find meaningful work in Indiana, and we'll be together again."

"What kind of meaningful work? They don't have old-growth forests in Indiana, do they?"

"I'll find something," Tash promised. "I'm sure there are downtrodden people in Indiana. They live in Indiana, after all. By definition they must be downtrodden."

He wasn't sure that made sense, but he let it go.

"So, is your mother going to be bringing bags of bagels with her?" she asked.

He'd told Tash about Bloom's. Growing up in Seattle, she'd visited New York City once, but she'd never heard of Bloom's until Adam had mentioned it to her. He found this bizarre. Everyone in the world had heard of Bloom's. Tourists from Belgium, Brunei and Botswana visited the store and posed for photos outside its main entrance, holding kosher salamis. People from Yonkers and Massapequa and Bayonne showed up at the store at seven a.m. Sunday morning to shop for the brunch they'd be eating later that same day. A few years ago, a New York City guidebook had labeled Bloom's "the eighth wonder of the world, and the wonder with the most cholesterol."

But like so much else, Tash didn't care about cholesterol or wonders of the world. And she sure didn't care about kosher salami. She was a vegetarian—almost a vegan, but she couldn't bring herself to give up cheese omelets, a fact that caused her some remorse but not enough to switch to granola for breakfast. Adam had described to her the variety of cheeses and meats sold at the deli, the mile-high corned-beef sandwiches, the smoked fish, the stuffed cabbage. "I don't think I'll ever set foot in there," she'd said.

Adam gazed at her now. She was lying on her back, her head resting on his shoulder and her voluptuous breasts flattened against her chest like mounds of dough. Her skin was pale, her fingernails short, her nose a pudgy button at the center of her face. She wasn't what you'd call beautiful, but she looked warm and natural, at home with herself.

He really liked her. He adored her passion, her confidence, her laugh and those big breasts, as well as her big hips and her thick thighs and her enthusiasm for sex—and her access to free birth control, thanks to her mother's job at Planned Parenthood. But he couldn't picture himself spending the rest of his life with a woman who wouldn't enter Bloom's. Not that he shopped at Bloom's himself, not that he made a habit of eating the gourmet kosher-style delicacies the store sold, but Bloom's was his legacy.

"My mother won't bring bagels," he said. "Even if she did, they'd be frozen bagels from the supermarket down the street. She never eats Bloom's food."

"Why not? Doesn't she own the place?"

"My grandmother owns it. I think," he added. He wasn't too clear on the Bloom's corporate hierarchy. "My mother works there. So does my Uncle Jay. My sister Julia is the president. My other sister Susie does freelance work there."

"Freelance deli work?"

"I don't exactly know what she does," he admitted. One of the blessings of attending college two hundred miles away from home was that he didn't have to be on top of such things.

"And they buy their food at a supermarket down the street? Why?"

"Because they're crazy?" He shrugged, jostling Tash's head. "They do what they do. I don't know. I don't live with them."

"When are they going to get here?"

"They said they were leaving New York City around nine." He craned his neck to peer past Tash at the clock radio on the windowsill. A little past noon. Shit. "I've got to shower and get dressed," he said, shoving himself up to sit.

His dorm room looked alien to him. The walls were bare, his posters of Josie and the Pussycats, Zippy the Pinhead and Sequoia National Park—that last one a birthday present from Tash—rolled inside cardboard tubes. His stereo speakers were nestled into molded foam in-

side the carton they had come in, his printer packed into
another carton and his laptop stashed in a canvas computer bag. More cartons held his clothing, his books, his
Frisbee, his video of his freshman year roommate hurling
after an all-night beer-pong tournament, the smiley-face
eraser he always tucked into his pocket when he was taking an exam, and other essential mementos of the past
four years. He hadn't dealt with his rug yet, and the bed
linens wouldn't get stripped until tomorrow. In his closet hung his rented cap and gown and the Cornell T-shirt
and khakis he planned to wear underneath.

The room wasn't his anymore. Tomorrow he
would be evicted, exiled to New York City. He should
have lined up a summer job in Indiana—or in Seattle,
with Tash. Maybe she could have found him employment sitting in a tree for three months, protecting it
from the chain saws of lumber companies. But that
probably wouldn't pay well, and besides, his mother
would kill him if he didn't spend the summer at home.
His father had died two years ago, and his mother kept
reminding him that he was now the man of the family.

Actually, Adam suspected that his sister Julia was
the man of the family, even if she was a woman. She
was the oldest, the big success story, the lawyer who'd
taken over Bloom's and increased its profits. And now
she was engaged to a hotshot columnist from *Gotham
Magazine*. Let her be the top dog; Adam would be just
as happy sitting in a tree for the summer, especially if
someone paid him to do it.

Then again, he'd survived last summer in New
York. He'd devoted six weeks of the summer to bagging
groceries at Bloom's—Julia had pleaded with him, and
he'd had nothing better to do. He and Tash had been
sort of together before last summer, but not *together*
together, so he hadn't missed her that much.

This summer... Hell, he didn't want to have to bag groceries again. He was a goddamn Cornell graduate, ready to begin work on his Ph.D. in mathematics. He wanted to do something interesting, something profound. Something like what he'd been doing the past four years in college—studying hard, sleeping, sleeping with women, listening to alt-rock, and getting stoned every now and then.

"My parents won't be getting here until five o'clock," Tash said, shoving a dense mass of hair back from her face. "Time zones and all. They're probably going to fall asleep the minute they check into their hotel room."

"Lucky you." His family wouldn't be drowsy when they arrived. They'd be full of energy. They'd demand a campus tour. They'd argue, hug him mercilessly, force him to pose for photos and argue some more. "You may as well get dressed too," he suggested. "You can hang around with my family until your parents get here."

"I've still got some packing to do. But I would like to meet your family. I bet your mother will be carrying a bag of bagels."

"I already told you..." Unwilling to repeat himself, he let the thought drop. Tash would probably never understand that Blooms didn't eat food from Bloom's. He wasn't sure he understood it, himself. His mother always used to insist that the store's food was for selling to others and that if the family ate it, they'd be consuming their profits.

Maybe things were different with Julia at the helm. Maybe *she'd* be the one who arrived in Ithaca carrying a bag of bagels. Her fiancé loved Bloom's food. Maybe he'd make her bring bagels. As if she'd ever do anything just because someone made her do it.

Tash socked him in the arm, leaving an aching spot just below his shoulder. "Chill, Adam. It's graduation. You're supposed to be happy."

"Yeah, right." He faked a smile. "See how happy I am?"

She socked him in the arm again, in exactly the same place. She packed a wallop; he didn't have to worry about her ever getting mugged. "I can't wait to meet your family," she said, swinging out of the bed. "I bet they're lots of fun."

Yeah, right.

But they were the only family he had, and in about an hour they would be descending upon him like the plague of frogs upon the Egyptians at *Pesach*. Unlike the Egyptians, at least, he wouldn't be subjected to a blood sacrifice.

Doing without sex and weed for the summer was almost as bad.

Chapter Two

Julia's head felt like an egg with hairline cracks running through the shell, thanks to having spent the past four hours trapped in a car with her mother, who refused to talk about anything other than how utterly wonderful a wedding at the Plaza Hotel would be—"Remember your cousin Travis's bar mitzvah? That's the kind of wedding I want for my firstborn. Remember those little portobello quiche hors d'oeuvres? To die for. Ron, have you ever been to an affair at the Plaza? Trust me, I know what I'm talking about..." Just one tiny push, one jarring motion and the shell would shatter, allowing Julia's runny yolk of a brain to spill out.

So she was not in the right frame of mind to deal with a hassle at the hotel. Not a minor hassle, either. A hassle tricky enough to scramble her brain and serve it on a platter with a side of hash browns.

She'd been looking forward to this trip. She was proud of her baby brother. Adam had survived four years at an Ivy League university, undaunted by the trauma of their father's death during his sophomore year, and she'd just wanted to come to Ithaca and kvell over his achievement. She'd been excited about the prospect of spending a couple of days out of the city with Ron, including him in this outing because she already thought of him as family, even if they weren't married yet. She hadn't even objected to the car arrangements, although she'd known her mother would spend the entire drive talking about the wedding.

No matter what her mother said, no matter how good the portobello quiche hors d'oeuvres were, she and Ron were not getting married at the Plaza. She was the president of Bloom's, and her wedding was going to be catered by Bloom's—not just to show loyalty to and confidence in the business she ran but because Bloom's food was delicious, and even the Plaza's portobello quiche hors d'oeuvres couldn't compete with mini-blinis and potato "latkettes" from Bloom's. In the year since she'd taken the helm of Bloom's, the catering service had expanded significantly, and she had every intention of contributing to that expansion by hiring the service to feed her wedding guests. Since the Plaza Hotel wouldn't let her bring in her own caterer, the Plaza Hotel was out.

The Plaza Hotel was also miles away. The Ithaca Manor Inn was her current problem. Actually, Grandma Ida was her problem.

Julia had reserved two rooms. She'd made the reservations nearly a year ago—she'd had to reserve rooms far in advance for commencement weekend—and at the time, she'd figured she and Susie would share one room and their mother and Grandma Ida would share the other. Then Ron had suggested joining them, and of course she knew the weekend would be greatly improved if he was a part of it, especially because he was able to borrow his brother Ira's car for the trip. Susie had generously offered to sleep on a rollaway in the room with Sondra and Grandma Ida so Julia and Ron could have a room to themselves. Everything had been worked out. The plan had been sealed by Julia's Visa card. Two rooms awaited them.

"But you're not married to him," Grandma Ida squawked, her voice echoing in the hotel's atrium lobby, causing several guests emerging from the dining room to turn and stare. No doubt they were trying to decide who the unmarried hussy among the group was.

"We have only two rooms, Grandma Ida," Julia said, lowering her voice and glaring at the too-attentive registration clerk. "We worked this all out last winter. You and Mom and Susie will share one room. Ron and I will share the other."

"What?" Grandma Ida chose this moment to become hard of hearing. "What did you say?"

"I said, we're divvying up the rooms so you can stay with Mom and Susie."

"You're not married. Make the reporter get a separate room."

"We have no more rooms," the clerk said helpfully. "It's commencement weekend. We've been booked solid since last summer."

"Then he'll use one room and the four of us will share the other room," Grandma Ida resolved, sweeping her hand in a circle to indicate the four Bloom women. Her gold bangle bracelets clanked against one another. That metallic noise was enough to widen the fissures in Julia's eggshell skull.

"We can't have four people in one room," Susie objected. "That's even more crowded than my apartment in New York."

Julia looked at her mother, who shrugged. The four-hour drive—and her four-hour oration on the glories of the Plaza Hotel—seemed to have worn her out. Her hair was flat, her lipstick clotted into vertical lines across her lower lip and her sunglasses rode low on her tiny nose. "You're her favorite," she muttered, motioning with her head toward Grandma Ida. "You deal with her."

Julia knew she was her grandmother's favorite. It wasn't fair, but somehow she'd been cursed with that designation. She glanced at Ron—whom her Grandma Ida was generally quite fond of—but he only sent her a half-baked smile and became engrossed in the framed street map of Ithaca that hung above the registration counter.

"Grandma," Julia began, praying her head would remain intact, "Ron and I are getting married next year. We're engaged. We're going to spend the rest of our lives together. We can share a room for one night."

"What am I, stupid? A man and a woman share a hotel room, they've got only one thing on their mind."

"Adam's graduation," Julia said. Ron glanced toward her, his hazel eyes glittering with amusement and disbelief. He nearly always had only one thing on his mind, and it wasn't Adam's graduation.

All right, so Ron Joffe was the sexiest man Julia had ever known. If the hotel situation went as planned, she would not be thinking about Adam's graduation when they retired to their room for the night. Unlike Ron, she occasionally did have other things on her mind even when she was in his presence—not often, but more often than he did. She could sit with him over breakfast and discuss the profit margins on Bloom's Heat-'N'-Eat entrees and be thinking about nothing but the fact that the spinach loaf sold better than the kasha varnishkes. When she raised her concerns, he always provided cogent observations. He was the business columnist for *Gotham Magazine* and had an MBA, so he knew more about business than she did, although she knew more about spinach loaf and kasha varnishkes. Yet even when he was making his cogent observations, he was usually running his foot up and down her leg, or nudging her knees apart with his toe. He might think the kasha varnishkes would sell better if the gravy was less salty, but he was also obviously thinking about what he and Julia had been doing in bed a half-hour earlier, and what they could be doing now instead of discussing kasha varnishkes, and what they might wind up doing if his foot progressed any further up her thigh.

"I wasn't born yesterday," Grandma Ida bellowed, her rattly voice bouncing off the tile floor. Anyone looking at her would know this was true. Dressed in a navy blue twill skirt, a dowdy cotton blouse and orthopedic sandals, with her gnarled hands and her creased face and her flagrantly black hair, she did not resemble a newborn. "I watch TV. I know what men and women do in hotel rooms."

"How about if I stay in the room with Julia and Joffe?" Susie suggested. "I can chaperone."

Julia rolled her eyes. Ron laughed. Grandma Ida failed to share their amusement. "What, *two* of my granddaughters sharing a room with a man they're not married to? *Oy, vey ist mir.*" She dramatically pressed a fisted hand against her chest, as if the shock of Susie's words was enough to trigger a coronary.

"Okay, look," Ron interjected, stepping into the breach just seconds before Julia's head exploded. "You and Susie can share the room. Your mother and grandmother can share the other room."

"What about you?" Julia asked.

"Does Adam have a sleeping bag? I'll sleep on the floor in his dorm room."

Julia gazed up into Ron's eyes. He would sleep on his not-yet brother-in-law's floor to keep her head intact. No wonder she loved him. "You don't mind doing that?"

"Of course I mind. But it's better than having Ida stroke out."

A stroke, a coronary—obviously Ron shared Julia's concern about her grandmother's health. "It's really not her business."

"In case you hadn't noticed," Ron murmured, "everything is her business."

"Check us in, Julia," her mother said. "I want to unpack and freshen up. The sooner we're settled in, the sooner we can go over to the campus."

"Can we get some lunch?" Susie asked. "I'm starving."

Julia tried to catch her sister's eye. Susie seemed punkier than usual, her short hair sticking up in dark tufts and her eyes rimmed with black liner and exhaustion. As usual, she wore black—black shorts, a black tank top and black sandals that exposed the butterfly tattooed onto her ankle. Her cheeks appeared gaunt. Julia wondered whether she'd lost some weight. Hard to believe someone who worked days at Bloom's and several evenings a week at a pizzeria, and who was involved with Casey Gordon, the bagel maestro of Bloom's, could lose weight.

She'd been so excited when they'd picked up the rented van yesterday afternoon. She'd yammered the whole ride downtown in the subway about how she was going to pretend to be a trucker, about how she'd seen a movie on TV once about a bunch of cross-country truckers talking to each other on CB radios, shouting, "Breaker, breaker!" "I don't know what that means," Susie had confessed, "but I want to drive in a truck and shout, 'Breaker, breaker! Ten-forty!'"

So now she'd driven two hundred miles in the van—albeit without a CB to shout "Breaker, breaker" into—and she looked piqued. Wan. Distracted. Thin.

Julia knew her sister well enough to sense when something was bugging her. Maybe it was just as well that Ron—her fiancé, her best friend, her red-hot lover—would be shacking up with Adam at the dorm tonight. Susie was bugged, and as the Bloom in charge of fixing everything, Julia was going to have to debug her.

"All right," she relented, turning to the nosy registration clerk and doing her best to cow him with a steely stare. "We're ready to check into our rooms now."

Chapter Three

Susie stared at her reflection in the mirror above the sink. The fluorescent ceiling fixture shed a milky light, and a warp in the silvered glass created an odd ripple in her face's reflection. She looked like someone whose nose was literally out of joint.

"Are you all right?" Julia called in from the bedroom.

How could she be all right when her hair was such a disaster? She'd had the window of the van open for the second half of the drive—the air conditioner had chosen to conk out somewhere around Middletown—and the wind had restyled her hair into a shape not far removed from a feather duster. The breeze hadn't budged Grandma Ida's hair, of course.

Not that Susie envied the immovable object that was her grandmother's coiffure, but really, when you spent a fortune for a decent haircut, you ought to look good even after being blasted by a hundred miles of hot highway gusts. Susie had been patronizing an expensive salon for a year now. One good haircut and she'd committed herself to Racine—she had no idea why it was called that, since it had nothing to do with either the French playwright or the Wisconsin city. She'd come to understand that any salon with a single-word name charged twice as much as a salon with a two-word name, like Snip City, where she used to get her hair cut years ago. Julia had always said she could do a better job with a hedge pruner than the Snip City stylists did with their scissors, but the cuts had been cheap. Racine's haircuts were exorbitantly priced, but Susie was making enough between Bloom's and Nico's that she could afford them.

She wondered why she'd had so little hesitation about making a commitment to a hairdresser when she couldn't bring herself to make a commitment to Casey.

Damn it, she *had* made a commitment to Casey. She hadn't slept with anyone else since she'd started seeing him, which was more of a commitment than she'd ever made to any other man. Why couldn't he be satisfied with that? Why was he pushing her to move in with him?

Probably because the subway ride from Forest Hills to SoHo was a bitch and a half. She ought to stop worrying about the forever-after implications; Casey had in all likelihood asked her to move in with him because he was sick of the IRT.

"Susie?"

She abandoned the bathroom for the bedroom. "That bathroom is gross. The walls are green. They made my complexion look like barf."

As Julia stared intently at her, she fleetingly resembled their father—the dark, probing eyes, the narrow nose, the skeptical curve of her mouth. Ben Bloom had always looked skeptical, as if he didn't really believe Susie had gotten an A on her math test—he'd been right, she'd lied about the grade—or he doubted that Julia had memorized Shelley's *Ozymandias* for her English class—misplaced doubt in that instance, because Julia had always done what she was supposed to do. She'd been the perfect daughter. Susie had been the who-gives a damn daughter. Adam, who took after their mother except that he had the nose he was born with instead of a surgically sculpted one like hers, was the son, in a class by himself.

"You don't look like barf," Julia observed, "but you *are* a little pale. Are you okay?"

"Other than starving to death, yeah." To avoid Julia's questioning gaze, Susie wandered around the room, tugging on a drawer handle, pulling back the window drape to check the view—a parking lot and beyond it a small strip-mall with a fried chicken place, a pizza place, and a Chinese restaurant called Wok's Up, Doc? Susie sighed deeply. A veritable banquet awaited her, just across the parking lot. So near and yet so far.

She felt Julia's gaze on her for a moment longer. Then her sister turned back to the closet to hang up the dress she'd been holding. Susie had stuffed a few things into her suitcase, and they were probably so wrinkled, hanging them up now wouldn't make any difference. "We've got two beds," she remarked, waving at the pair of double beds with their bolted-to-the-wall headboards and their cardboard-looking green bedspreads. "I could sleep in one and you and Joffe could share the other. Or he could sleep in one and you and I could share."

"Grandma Ida would have a stroke," Julia said with a sigh.

"There are worse things in the world," Susie muttered, then shook her head, fending off a pang of guilt. "That's a terrible thing to say."

"You just spent four hours in a van with her," Julia said, her tone brimming with forgiveness. "You're allowed to say terrible things."

Susie flopped down on one of the beds. The bedspread felt as stiff as it looked. "She spent the entire drive lecturing me on how she and Grandpa Isaac built Bloom's from a sidewalk push cart into the biggest deli in the world. Her words," she added before Julia could correct her. "And her other topic was, 'Susie, what are you doing with your life?'"

Julia pulled a blouse from her suitcase and hung it next to her dress. How many outfits had she brought? This was a one-night trip, not a cruise on the QE II. "Did you tell her what you're doing with your life?" she asked Susie, sounding just a bit too interested.

"I told her was living it, more or less. I didn't go into details." Susie watched her sister closely, hoping she wasn't going to interrogate her the way Grandma Ida had. Not long after Julia had become president of Bloom's, she'd informed Susie that Grandma Ida had told her she thought Julia was a lot like her. Julia had laughed when she'd shared this tidbit with Susie, as if the idea was preposterous.

Susie hadn't even smiled. She could see in Julia more Grandma Ida than Ben Bloom: the stubbornness, the focus, the determination. The vaguely judgmental curiosity that made her want to hear Susie's answers to Grandma Ida's nosy questions. Julia was taller than Grandma Ida, and her hair was black thanks to nature, not the ministrations of Bella, the colorist from hell. But yeah, Susie could picture Julia fifty-odd years from now, dressing in cardigan sweaters and frumpy skirts and comfortable shoes, her wrists circled with gold bangles and her mouth pinched as she scolded a wayward granddaughter for having crayoned a picture of purple bananas and orange grapes.

One of Susie's earliest memories of Grandma Ida was of her criticizing Susie's drawing of a tree with blue leaves. To this day, she saw nothing wrong with that childhood picture, and everything wrong with her grandmother for having disparaged it.

"So, what's really bothering you?" Julia asked abruptly.

Susie propped herself on her elbows. "Huh?"

"Something is. I can tell." Julia zipped her suitcase shut and placed it on the chrome rack next to the TV armoire.

"My stomach," Susie said. "I want lunch."

"Besides that." Julia sat on the other bed, crossed her legs yoga-style and rested her chin in her hands. "I know you, Susie. I know when something's troubling you."

"My sister is troubling me," Susie retorted. "And my grandmother. Let's get some food. Joffe must be bored waiting for us in the lobby."

"Joffe is probably in the motel restaurant, stuffing his face," Julia said. "And you're going nowhere until you tell me what's wrong."

"Who died and made you president?"

"Dad died and Grandma Ida made me president. Come on, Susie. I'm your sister. And I'm so sick of obsessing over my damned wedding. I'd much rather obsess over you for a change."

Susie sighed. Julia might have certain Grandma Ida tendencies, but she was the only person in the world Susie wholeheartedly trusted. She wasn't prepared to discuss her Casey situation with anyone, yet—but if she had to discuss it, Julia was the one to discuss it with. "Casey asked me to move in with him," she said.

Julia's eyebrows shot up. "You're kidding!"

"Why should I be kidding?" Susie asked indignantly. "We've been seeing each other for a year."

"No—I mean, he just strikes me as kind of..." Julia seemed to grope for the right words. "I don't know. I would have expected him to ask you to marry him, not move in with him."

Susie made a face. "You think I'd spend a year with the kind of guy who'd ask me to marry him?"

"No, I guess not." Julia toyed with the lace of her canvas sneaker, but her gaze remained on Susie. "What did you tell him?"

"I said no."

"Susie!" It was Julia's turn to make a face. "You're living with two roommates in that teeny-tiny disgusting walk-up in the East Village where the stairway always smells of fried onions, and he's got a great big apartment!"

"In Queens," Susie reminded her. "In Forest Hills." Light-years removed from civilization.

Julia nodded. "Exactly. He lives in Forest Hills. A nice middle-class neighborhood. That's why he's the kind of guy who'd ask you to marry him."

"He lives there because you can get more square footage for the dollar. Plus he grew up in Queens and he has friends there, for some reason."

"And family," Julia pointed out.

"I don't think that was a deciding factor."

"I think it is."

"Yeah, like you know Casey better than I do."

Julia smiled. "I know he's got long hair and a stoner smile. He's still a family man. He refused to have sex with you until he got to know you, remember? He's a traditional sort of guy, Susie."

"More traditional than me," Susie agreed dolefully. She couldn't argue with Julia. Casey did have long hair, and his smile did have a vaguely druggy appearance, although in the year they'd been together the strongest drug she'd ever seen him take was Tylenol Plus.

And he loved Susie's tattoo, and he hadn't been inside a church since his great-uncle Mike keeled over while watching some professional wrestling show on TV last October, and even at the funeral Casey hadn't taken communion. But other than his hair and his agnosticism and his professed adoration for Susie, he harbored some pretty old-fashioned values. When they'd met, a little more than a year ago, she would have happily jumped his bones within minutes of catching his eye. She'd walked into Bloom's, made her way to the bagel counter and spotted him standing behind it, all six-foot-two inches of him, with his dirty-blond hair pulled back in a ponytail and his hazel bedroom eyes glittering as he'd handed her an egg bagel, and the saliva filling her mouth had been for him, not the bagel. He'd been the one to insist that they spend some time learning about each other before they got naked.

She'd been intrigued. She'd never before met a man who actually cared more about getting to know a woman's mind than getting her to spread her legs, but she'd admired his attitude. It had challenged and amused her, and their conversations had been great and the sex, once they'd finally gotten around to it, had been even greater and...

Damn. She wasn't ready to settle down yet. Not even with Casey.

"So...by turning him down, does that mean you've broken up with him?" Julia asked.

"I don't know," Susie admitted. "He raised the subject last night. This morning I rented a van and drove to Ithaca. It's not like we worked everything out."

"In other words, you have no idea what you're going back to."

"A pissed off boyfriend, I'm guessing." Susie sighed. She didn't want him to be pissed off. She wanted to return to New York City tomorrow evening, unload Adam's junk from the van, and then spend the night screwing Casey senseless. Somehow, she didn't think that was the way things would proceed.

"I'll be honest with you," Julia said. "I like Casey. He's done a fantastic job of running the Bloom's bagel department with Morty."

Susie snorted. "Yeah, that's always a big item on my list. I sure don't want to get involved with any guy who can't do a fantastic job of running the Bloom's bagel department."

"And he's crazy about you."

If he were really crazy about her, he wouldn't have put her on the spot with this stupid invitation. "I don't want to break up with him," she moaned. "But, I mean, cohabitation! It's so serious! You're marrying Joffe, and you're still not living with him."

"Technically," Julia muttered. "And only because my apartment has another eight months on the lease."

"And because you don't want Grandma Ida to have a stroke."

"That, too. But you're right, Suze. Moving in together is a big thing."

"I love Casey. I really do. If he breaks up with me, I swear I'll hate him." She felt a tear tremble on her eyelashes and wiped it away, hoping Julia wouldn't notice it.

No such luck. Julia climbed off her bed and onto Susie's, butted hips with her, and arched a sisterly arm around her shoulders. "I wish I could make it better," she murmured. "If he breaks your heart, do you want me to fire him?"

"If you fire him, your bagel department will go to hell. And Bloom's earnings support us all," Susie pointed out.

"All right. I won't fire him. I'll just give him lousy hours or something."

Susie managed a limp smile, even though that first tear turned out to be the drum major leading a whole parade of tears. One of the problems with warm weather was that she didn't have long sleeves to wipe her eyes with.

After giving her shoulders a squeeze, Julia climbed off the bed and crossed to the bathroom. She returned carrying a tissue. "You're right," she said as she handed the tissue to Susie. "That bathroom is ugly."

The phone on the table between the beds rang so shrilly, they both flinched. While Susie mopped her damp eyes, Julia lifted the receiver. She said, "Hello," listened for a minute, then said, "Okay," and hung up. "Mom and Grandma Ida are unpacked and they want to head over to the campus," she reported.

"Fine." Susie sniffled and rose from the bed. "Let me just wash my face. We'd better get something to eat, too, or I'll faint," she warned as she wandered into the bathroom. She splashed some water onto her cheeks, then patted them with a towel and inspected herself in the mirror. Her hair had settled down somewhat, her eyeliner had survived her little bout of weeping unsmudged, but she still looked like barf. If Casey saw her now, he sure as hell wouldn't want her moving in with him.

Or maybe he would, because that was the kind of guy he was.

Why did he have to be so damned perfect? Susie wasn't ready for perfect yet.

Chapter Four

"That's your best shot," Mose taunted, "and you ain't hit it yet."

Casey grunted. What could he say? Mose was right.

They were playing one-on-one on the asphalt outside the Edward Mandel School. At four-thirty, the elementary school kids were long gone and the adults who worked regular hours weren't done with their jobs and available to play, so they had the basketball court to themselves.

Because Casey arrived at Bloom's around six a.m. most mornings to fire up the bagel and bread ovens, no one minded when he left at three or three-thirty. Unless, of course, there was a sudden frenzy of customers desperate for bagels. This happened quite often, for reasons he couldn't fathom. The department would be gliding along for hours, never more than one or two people waiting behind those being served, and then abruptly it would be inundated by scores of crazed customers all screaming at once: "Garlic bagels! I must have garlic bagels!" and "I claim that last poppy-seed!" and "I'll take one pesto and one dill-pickle and one cranberry and two blueberry—no, two cranberry and one blueberry—and three dill-pickle, and skip the pesto, and slice them all, wouldja?" and "Back off, *chazzer*,

I was here first!" When things got crazy, he ignored the clock and stayed behind the bagel counter, counting, slicing and keeping the *chazzers* from trampling one another.

Casey had been working at Bloom's long enough to know that *chazzer* meant pig. He'd picked up a few Yiddish words from Morty Sugarman, his partner in the bagel department, and a few other words from Susie. She didn't lapse into Yiddish the way some of her relatives did. She was too many generations removed from steerage, he figured.

Susie. What the hell was he going to do?

One thing he wasn't going to do, apparently, was make his best shot—a three-pointer from the left side of the hoop. Usually the ball swooshed right through, all net, but today he'd bounced it off the rim twice and off the backboard once. Bad enough to keep missing like that. Worse to keep missing in front of a witness.

Especially when that witness was Mose, who knew Casey's moves on the court better than Casey himself did. They'd met as undergrads at St. John's, when both of them had had the ludicrous idea of joining the university's basketball team as walk-ons. They'd both spent an afternoon strutting their stuff for an assistant coach, who had bluntly directed them to the intramural program. "No try-outs necessary," he'd barked. "I think you'll make a team."

"He *thinks*?" Mose had whispered to Casey as they toweled off their sweat and headed for the gym door.

Eight years later they were still playing, just because they loved the game. Every Tuesday evening during the months of Daylight Savings Time, they played with a group of friends. And Friday afternoons, if Mose could leave work early, they tried to catch a couple of hours on the court, just the two of them, playing one-on-one. Basketball was one of those things, like ice-cold ale, or a warm, chewy "everything" bagel with a thick *schmear*—another Yiddish word Casey had picked up from working at Bloom's—or Jackie Chan movies or good sex, that a person could love without being able to pinpoint specifically what made it so lovable.

Susie had once suggested that basketball was like ballet, and he'd nearly choked on the ice-cold ale he'd been enjoying. Basketball was like ballet the way a shell sirloin was like soy curd. Casey knew a thing or two about food; if pressed, he could incorporate soy curd into a recipe. And if his life depended on it, he could probably sit through a ballet. A short one.

"The jumping," Susie had tried to explain. "The way you move your arms. The grace. It's very balletic."

If that was what she thought, maybe their breaking up wouldn't be such a bad thing.

Mose slipped past him for a lay-up, not terribly difficult since Casey's feet were planted on the asphalt and his mind was lost in Susie-land. Not until Mose threw the ball at him, hard, did he drag his attention back to the court. "Wake up, Woody," Mose snapped.

"Shut up, Wesley," Casey shot back. The nicknames came from the stars of *White Men Can't Jump*, since Casey was white like Woody Harrelson and Mose was black like Wesley Snipes. That movie was right up there with ale and the best of Jackie Chan, as far as Casey was concerned. Maybe it was even right up there with sex.

"Where's your focus, man? Where's your concentration?"

"It's focusing and concentrating on something other than b-ball," Casey admitted, dribbling to his favorite spot, on the left curve of the three-point line, and lofting the ball toward the basket. It circled the rim, then rolled off.

"You suck," Mose said amiably.

"No shit." He crossed to the bench beside the court and dug in his pack for his water bottle.

Mose joined him. A sheen of perspiration coated his skin and he pulled a bottle of turquoise Gatorade from his bag. Hideous color, Casey thought, but Mose undoubtedly needed the electrolytes and minerals. He'd actually been playing hard enough to work up a sweat.

They gulped their beverages, lowered their bottles and snapped the lids shut. Then Mose stared at him. "So, what's up?"

"I'm thinking of starting my own catering business."

Mose threw back his head and laughed. When Casey didn't join him, he stopped laughing and stared harder at him. "What are you, crazy?"

"No. I've been thinking about it. I need your help."

"My help? No way."

"You're a business consultant. You've got an MBA. You get paid to give advice to people like me."

"You gonna pay me?"

At that, Casey cracked a smile. "What do you think?"

Mose took another sip of Gatorade, then shook his head. "Okay, Blondie, I'll give you some advice and I won't charge you a nickel for it. Don't start your own catering business."

"Why not? I moonlight for that catering outfit on Queens Boulevard—"

"The one run by that gorilla guy?"

"Vinnie Carasculo. He's not a gorilla."

"He's got hairy arms. I wouldn't wanna eat his catered food."

"Okay, so I should open my own catering business. Then you could eat my catered food."

Mose searched Casey's face, amusement and disbelief warring in his expression. He had to look up slightly; even sitting, Casey had two inches on Mose. When they played basketball, the height differential never bothered Mose because, as he loved to point out, white men couldn't jump. But when they sat, Casey's height seemed to vex him. "You've got a sweet deal going at Bloom's," he reminded Casey. "They love you there. You're in tight with the boss's daughter—"

"The boss's sister," Casey corrected him.

"Whatever. You got a good deal, man. They pay you well, you can leave at three in the afternoon and you get to invent weird bagels."

"What's weird about them?"

"Oh, come on. What was that new flavor you were telling me about last week? Scallion bagels?"

"Chive."

"Same thing. What do you wanna leave that place for? They give you a nice, fat salary to make chive bagels."

"I'm bored there," Casey said. He hated lying to his friend, but he wasn't ready to tell him his other reason—that if things were as bad between him and Susie as he suspected they were, he didn't think he could continue to work for the Bloom family.

Maybe things weren't that bad. Maybe he'd misunderstood Susie when she'd said no. He'd asked her to move in with him, and she'd said no, but maybe she'd actually meant, "No, but I love you Casey," or "No, but ask me again next week and I'll say yes," or "I know what you mean."

Sure. There were so many different ways to interpret the word no.

"Casey, my friend." Mose leaned forward and adjusted his voice into a smooth baritone—the voice he no doubt used when he was in his office on Park Avenue South, reassuring a client while explaining to him that declaring Chapter-11 bankruptcy was his best course of action. "You do not do boredom. Your brain waves move so slowly that boredom would not register on them. You don't get bored concocting new bagel flavors. I would find that boring. Most people would. Which isn't a put-down—I'm just saying, you operate on a different plane, and that's good. It's enviable. You are spared the albatross of boredom while dreaming up ways of incorporating prunes and peppermint into bagels."

"Albatross?" Casey interrupted.

Mose reverted to his familiar jive. "Something like that. Sounded good, didn't it?"

"It sounded ridiculous. So does the idea of peppermint bagels. Prunes I've got to think about. Raisin bagels are so popular, why not prunes? Or apricots."

"See?" Mose beamed a smile at Casey, his point apparently proven. "You love what you do. You love bagels. I give you a boring speech and you decide to make apricot bagels. You don't want to leave Bloom's—especially not to start your own catering company."

"I think I do," Casey said, wishing he sounded more positive. He slumped forward, resting his arms on his thighs and staring at a tag of graffiti someone had painted onto the asphalt near the bench. "Bingo," it said. Why would anyone paint "Bingo" onto a schoolyard basketball court?

"You're a bagel man. You work with dough. You really want to set up shop making stuffed mushrooms and miniature egg rolls and caviar on toast points? That's not your thing."

"There's money in it."

"There's headaches in it. Catering, you're working on everyone else's hours. Kiss your nights goodbye. That's when people have catered parties, right? At night."

Casey shrugged, not seeing this as a problem. Without Susie, he was going to have to fill his nights somehow. Might as well fill them stuffing mushrooms.

"Your specialty is bagels. You want to go into business for yourself, go into the bagel business."

He eyed Mose, feeling a sudden pop, like a camera flash bursting through muddled darkness. He'd thought of a catering business because he'd been working after hours for Vinnie Carasculo, who had his own catering business, one that didn't involve caviar or miniature egg rolls. Vinnie was usually hired for Italian weddings, and the most popular items on his menu were lasagna platters, stuffed manicotti, six-foot-long garlic breads and fried calamari. Casey knew how to cook all those things, so he'd figured he could run a catering business. But someone planning an Italian wedding wasn't going to hire an Irish guy named Keenan Christopher Gordon, Jr. to cook the food.

But bagels. Bread. Rolls and muffins and scones. He could do that. On his own hours, too. He wouldn't be at the mercy of tantrum-throwing brides and their mothers, or biddy ladies in Roslyn who hosted bridge parties and refused to pay unless every last detail, from the paper napkins to the chocolate mints, was perfect. Vinnie had dealt with customers like that. Casey had witnessed a few scenes.

A bread store. He'd need a little real estate, a few ovens, flour and yeast and his imagination. He could do what he'd been doing all along for Bloom's—something he truly enjoyed—but without doing it for Susie's sister. Or her grandmother. Or for Susie herself.

She'd said no. He didn't need a map; he could find the door himself. A door that led out of Bloom's and into a bread store... Yeah, he could see it.

Chapter Five

"She's fat," Sondra Bloom observed, her stage whisper echoing through the common room on the first floor of Adam's dorm.

"No she's not," Susie argued, shooting Julia a look. Julia shot a look back, one of her *there goes Mom, but it's not worth getting into an argument* looks. They were seated on uncomfortable vinyl-upholstered sofas in the oversized, under-decorated lounge, having just sent Joffe upstairs with Adam and his girlfriend, Natasha, to make sleeping arrangements. Sondra and Grandma Ida sat across a scuffed and stained coffee table from Susie and Julia. The couches looked as if they'd been subjected to torture by some tinhorn dictator or underground spy agency. Scuff marks on the vinyl indicated that they'd been kicked; swatches of duct tape held tears in the fabric together, and Susie could see at least three places on the arms where cigarettes had been extinguished.

She wanted food. She'd already searched the dorm's first floor for a vending machine, but couldn't find one. Adam had mentioned something about a math department reception—reception meant food, didn't it?—but first Joffe's overnight accommodations had to be secured. So Susie sat next to Julia on one of the abused sofas and listened to her mother critique Adam's girlfriend.

"She looked fat to me," Sondra insisted.

"She's sturdy," Susie argued.

"If anyone knows from fat, it's me." Unlike her thin daughters—unlike all the thin Blooms—Sondra Bloom was cursed with the inability to burn as many calories as she wished to consume. Over the past few years, she'd developed a pear shape, her body spreading beyond its natural borders just south of her waist. Susie would call her mother sturdy rather than fat, but she didn't know from fat the way her mother did. Sondra often implied that she considered herself well beyond plump and hurtling toward obese.

"If you're going to criticize Adam's girlfriend," Julia muttered, "you could start with the fact that she doesn't shave her legs."

"Tush," Grandma Ida said with a sniff. "What kind of a name is Tush?"

"Tash, Grandma," Susie said. "It's short for Natasha."

"How is Tush short for Natasha?"

"It's *Tash*," Julia corrected Grandma Ida, who became hard of hearing whenever the mood struck her.

Obviously, the mood struck her now. "Go through life being called Tush? Like someone's *toches*? It's embarrassing!"

"She's not Jewish," Sondra hissed, her words once again resonating beyond their decibels. "A Jew wouldn't name her daughter anything that sounded like Tush."

"Who cares if she's not Jewish?" Susie snapped, managing to keep her voice lower than her mother's and grandmother's.

Her mother's eyes zeroed in on her. Sondra's hair looked impeccable, every brown strand doing its part to create the perfect pageboy around her face. For a

51

fifty-four-year-old woman with a pear-shaped body, she was attractive, her cheeks smooth, her lips slicked with a peach-tinted gloss, her eyebrows gently arched when she wasn't staring hard, the way she was staring at Susie right now. The only feature that appeared out of whack was her nose, which she'd had surgically resculpted when she was sixteen. Susie had never known her mother with any other nose, but this nose looked like flesh-hued Silly Putty protruding from the center of her face, shiny and shaped to some abstract ideal, the tip too round, the nostrils too angled, the bridge too narrow.

Her glare implied that she was thinking Susie, of all people, wouldn't care if Adam's girlfriend wasn't Jewish because Susie herself was involved with the distinctly not-Jewish Casey Gordon. Or at least Sondra believed Susie was involved with Casey. Susie had no idea if that was true.

She still hadn't convinced herself that discussing her dilemma with Julia had been a wise thing. She certainly wasn't going to bring joy and satisfaction to her mother by mentioning that she and Casey were on shaky ground. Her mother probably liked Casey well enough—he made damned good bagels for the store, after all—but Susie suspected Sondra would have preferred for her to hook up with someone more affluent, more grounded, more traditional and definitely more Jewish. She never exactly came right out and said so, though, probably because she was just so relieved that her daughter was dating someone steadily. Like maybe this meant Susie was on the verge of settling down.

Settling down was the last thing Susie was on the verge of.

Adam and Joffe arrived in the common room, rescuing her from her mother's scathing frown. "Tash is going to meet up with us later," Adam announced. "She's got some stuff to do before her parents arrive. I was thinking we may as well head on over to this reception the math department is hosting."

Food. "Let's go!" Susie said brightly.

"So, it's all worked out for Ron tonight?" Sondra asked, rising from the sofa and then helping Grandma Ida to her feet.

"Yeah, everything's cool," Adam said, flashing a grin. "Joffe can have my bed, and I'll stay in Tash's room."

Standing behind Sondra and Grandma Ida, Julia shook her head violently, while Susie grimaced and slid her index finger across her throat.

Unfortunately, Grandma Ida's hearing suddenly recovered. "You're staying in that girl's room?" she asked Adam, her face contracting into a scowl.

"And that girl is staying with a friend," Julia said swiftly, taking Grandma Ida's elbow and steering her toward the door.

"What room? What room is Tush staying in?"

"She's staying with a friend," Julia assured her grandmother in soothing tones.

Lips pursed, Susie's mother directed her disapproval to Adam, which left Susie feeling both relieved and sympathetic. It would be fun having Adam home for the summer; he could share black-sheep duties with her. Before college, he'd been quiet, shy, and well behaved. God bless Cornell for having unleashed his inner rascal.

His shoulders looked a little wider than Susie had remembered them. As they all exited the dorm into the sunny afternoon, she noticed that her baby brother had added a slight swagger to his walk. Arnold Schwarzenegger was never going to run in fear from him, but her kid brother looked less like a boy than a man. He was a day away from becoming a college graduate, after all. And he was sleeping with Tash—who was not fat, just sturdy, and she'd probably weigh a couple of pounds less if she shaved her legs.

Tash didn't have to be perfect for Adam. She didn't even have to be right for him. Next fall he'd be heading off to that chicken university with the Indians. Better that he should start graduate school with a little experience. Thanks to Tash, he would.

Sondra accelerated her pace to catch up with Joffe, who had accelerated his pace to catch up with Julia, who was keeping pace with Grandma Ida, who strode across the campus in a surprisingly brisk gait for an old lady. This left Susie and Adam to bring up the rear, which was fine with Susie except that she didn't want the others to arrive at the reception ahead of her and pick the platters clean before she had a chance to grab some food. Then again, they didn't know where the reception was. Eventually, Adam would have to move to the head of their procession, and Susie would move with him.

In the meantime, they could lag and talk. "Don't discuss that you're sleeping with Tash in front of Grandma Ida," she warned.

He tilted his head slightly. He didn't exactly tower over her—Blooms were too short to tower, and even as the tallest in her family Adam was barely five-foot-ten—but he loomed. His Cornell T-shirt and khaki slacks bagged on him. Unlike his sweetheart, he didn't quite qualify as sturdy. "Why?" he asked. "Did Grandma Ida turn into a Republican or something?"

"I don't know if she's even registered in a party," Susie told him. "And she doesn't care what anyone does behind her back. But in front of her, you have to be tactful. The reason Joffe's sleeping in your bed to-night is because Grandma Ida was so scandalized by the thought of him sharing a hotel room with Julia."

"They're getting married."

"And I'm sure they're porking each other every chance they get. Behind Grandma Ida's back, though. That's the thing."

"She's such a busybody," Adam muttered. "How can you stand working for her?"

"I'm working for Julia, not her. She hardly ever comes to the store, and when she does, she's usually hanging off Lyndon's arm."

"Hey, she lives out of wedlock with Lyndon, doesn't she?"

Susie laughed. Lyndon Rollins was Grandma Ida's caretaker, cook and companion. He was also young, black and gay. They were not porking each other. Grandma Ida didn't even seem to mind that Lyndon porked other men without benefit of marriage. They weren't doing it in front of her, after all. And Lyndon wasn't her grandson.

"Does she hassle Rick and Neil about their love lives?" Adam asked, referring to the sons of their father's brother Jay. Neil lived in southern Florida, where he ran a charter yacht business, sailing tourists around the Keys for an exorbitant fee. Rick lived in New York and was one of Susie's closest friends, which meant she knew more de-tails than she wanted about his love life, and those details weren't particularly exciting. Rick was a great guy, but the majority of his love life occurred in his imagination. He'd prefer it to occur in the company of her roommate Anna. He'd probably settle for a love life with her other roommate, Caitlin, but Caitlin was so lusty she seemed to scare Rick a little, and Anna was Chinese-American, which Rick found exotic.

"Or you," Adam pressed her. "Does she give you a hard time about Casey?"

"You're not listening to me, Adam. She doesn't care if her grandchildren are attending orgies every night, as long as they don't do it in front of her. In front of her, she gets upset. You don't want her to have a stroke, do you?"

"Is there a real risk of that?"

She glanced up at Adam and saw that he was smirking, his brown eyes churning with laughter. "When did you get to be so snotty?" she teased.

"I'm not snotty. I'm going to go nuts this summer. She lives right above Mom. I won't be able to do anything."

Their mother occupied a lavish apartment on the twenty-fourth floor of the Bloom Building, above Bloom's. Their grandmother occupied the apartment directly above their mother's. The likelihood was far greater that Sondra would hear activity in Grandma Ida's apartment than that Grandma Ida, whose auditory ability ebbed and flowed, would hear activity in Sondra's. But if Adam chose to host an orgy in their mother's apartment... The hell with Grandma Ida. Their mother would probably have a stroke.

"Didn't they teach you anything about discretion at this fine institution?" she asked, waving a hand at the ivy-covered gothic halls surrounding the broad lawn across which they were ambling.

"Nothing at all." Adam sighed. "I don't know how I'm going to stand living in New York this summer. I should have found a job in West Lafayette."

Susie wrinkled her nose. When she thought of Purdue, she didn't think of chickens or Indians like Grandma Ida, but she pictured wide open spaces, flat geography, a university surrounded by nothing.

Did they have poetry slams in West Lafayette? Did they have really bad plays staged in warehouse lofts, midnight showings of cheesy martial arts flicks, transvestites strolling through busy intersections and not being gawked at? Did they have genuine bagels and bialys and smoked nova, delicacies you could buy at Bloom's?

How could anyone want to spend a summer there?

"You'll have fun in New York," she consoled Adam. Even though he was bigger than her, he was still her baby brother, in need of comfort. "If things get wonky at Mom's, you can probably live in Julia's apartment. She's always over at Joffe's place, anyway. You could even stay at my apartment, if you don't mind sleeping on the living room couch."

Adam's expression was a mixture of gratitude and revulsion, as if sleeping on the couch of Susie's overcrowded East Village walk-up was no better than taking up residence in a cardboard box in an alley. True, she shared the place with two roommates. But on the other hand, they were female roommates.

"And Julia will hire you at Bloom's. She'll find you something interesting that pays good money."

"A little nepotism, eh?"

"Don't knock it. Anyway, I don't think it counts as nepotism when it's a family business."

"I'm not going into the family business," Adam said firmly. "I'm going to get a Ph.D. in mathematics and then I'm going to teach. And do research. And not sell knishes."

"Big talker," Susie teased. "So how will you spend the summer, then? Hanging out in Mom's apartment and not doing anything?"

"It looks that way."

"Working at Bloom's would be better than that." Susie hooked her hand through his elbow. "You'd get to be surrounded by good food all day. Speaking of which, if there isn't any food at this math department reception, I'm going to come back outside and start eating the grass. I'm famished."

"There'll be food," Adam promised, letting her march him more rapidly down the path. "The department has to feed us. We math majors don't know how to feed ourselves. We're all nerds."

"You're not a nerd." Maybe he had a few nerdish tendencies, but she wasn't going to let him put himself down, especially not the day before graduation.

"Anyway," he said, "the math profs keep an eye out for us. There's always food."

"I should have majored in math," Susie said, smiling because she'd be eating soon.

Chapter Six

Rick would rather go to his father's than his mother's for dinner, any day. For one thing, his mother served weird food—sun-dried mushroom casseroles, turnip fritters, warm sauerkraut with raisins in it. It was a cuisine that matched her personality, just as his father's cuisine—expensive and not too healthy, heavy on the red meat and rich sauces—matched his.

For another thing, while they ate, Rick's mother would always interrogate him on what he was doing to make the world a better place, which, he had to admit, wasn't much. Whereas his father would talk about frivolous things like golf and his beloved BMW Z3.

For yet another, Rick's mother was a devout feminist, whereas Rick's stepmother, Wendy, was a Barbie doll.

Most important, though, Rick was more likely to get money from his father than his mother.

He actually wasn't totally broke at the moment. He'd managed to land a temporary job as Camera 3 at a sudsy drama that filmed at a studio on West 52nd Street. The usual Camera 3 had taken a maternity leave, and a friend of a friend of a guy he knew had hired him to fill in. During the two months he'd been working at the studio, Cameras 1 and 2 got most of the action; as

Camera 3, he was usually scripted to focus on some secondary character, and the director would use Camera 3 shots only when the secondary character was reacting to something the main characters were doing. Earlier that day, for instance, they'd filmed a scene in which an actress had to tell an actor that he was the father of her son. The Camera 3 script had Rick aiming at the nanny the whole time. At the end of a three-minute scene, Camera 3 was activated for a two-second shot of the nanny hugging a heavily swaddled doll to her bulbous chest and looking shocked.

But it paid, so Rick wasn't complaining.

Tonight was going to be a much bigger payday, though. Rick had a plan, one that was going to get his father seriously jazzed.

He arrived at the ritzy Upper East Side building where his father and Wendy lived. Rick and his brother Neil had grown up across town, in the apartment building above Bloom's, just down the hall from Uncle Ben and Aunt Sondra and the cousins. When Rick's parents divorced, his mother had refused to give up the spacious apartment where she'd raised her sons, so his father had moved across town and bought an apartment just as big in a sleek new building.

This was why having money was good, Rick thought as he pawed his unkempt hair and smiled at the doorman in the glittery marble lobby of his father's building. Have enough money, and when you get a divorce you can afford a nice apartment. Have enough money and divorce doesn't even have to enter the picture—you can afford a nice apartment, period. The one-room apartment where Rick currently lived, in a tenement around the corner from Houston Street, wasn't much bigger than a walk-in closet. The kitchen was a three-foot-wide stretch of linoleum, with a mini-fridge underneath it and a two-burner hot plate on top it. The bathroom was so small, Rick could pee into the toilet while standing in the shower. He knew this because he'd done it many times. City housing regulations required all domiciles to have a window, and Rick's was gray with soot and offered a view of a dirty brick wall.

It was not a nice apartment, and he could barely afford it.

The doorman glowered at him from beneath the brim of his snappy militaristic cap, then buzzed upstairs to see if Jay and Wendy Bloom could possibly want this scruffy, disheveled young man to darken their doorstep. Rick imagined Wendy's sunny voice chirping into the intercom that of course Rick was welcome, she couldn't wait to see him and feed him red meat. One of Wendy's most charming traits was her enthusiasm. Give her pompoms and a short skirt and she'd be ready for anything.

The doorman lowered his intercom phone and sent Rick a reluctant nod. Grinning, Rick shuffled through the lobby to the elevators. The Velcro on one of the straps of his Teva sandals was losing its grip. That was what he got for wearing them all year long. Now, at least, the weather matched his footwear. He also had on olive-green cargo shorts and a baggy T-shirt reading, "Yes, I'm Warm Enough," which he'd worn a lot that past winter, to much better effect. He was always warm. It drove his mother crazy, except for the period a few years ago when she'd been going through menopause and sweating constantly.

The elevator swept him up to the fourteenth floor, which was actually the thirteenth floor, except that the building had no thirteenth floor. Most buildings in New York didn't. Thirteenth floors were considered bad luck, so most buildings went directly from the twelfth to the fourteenth floor, as if the fates didn't know how to count and wouldn't notice that the thirteenth floor had been mislabeled to deceive them.

He rang the bell and Wendy opened the door. As usual, she looked perky and chipper, her blond hair bouncing with waves and her boobs just plain bouncing. She had on a summery outfit, flowery pastels that matched the turquoise color scheme of the living room. Rick had often thought that if he had to make a movie in his father's living room, the vividness of the turquoise walls, the striped turquoise-and-white upholstery of the couches and chairs, the turquoise, white, green and yellow pattern of the drapes and the dark turquoise wall-to-wall carpet would burn holes through the camera lens. It was so frickin' bright.

But that was Wendy, too. She glowed like a fluorescent bulb—a little hummy, a little flickery but emitting a whole lot of lumens.

"Rick!" she exclaimed, sounding surprised to see him, even though she'd been the one to invite him for dinner and he'd been announced just minutes ago by the doorman. "Come on in! Look at you! You shaved, didn't you?"

The beard had refused to fill in. He'd cultivated it for over a year, but it looked so scraggly he'd finally given up on it. "Yeah, I shaved," he said.

"Jay!" Wendy hollered, waltzing barefoot across the sea-hued carpet. The living room had had a beautiful inlaid parquet floor, but she'd insisted on covering it with carpet because she liked to walk barefoot. "Jay, guess what? Rick shaved!"

He heard the sound of a toilet flushing, and then his father lumbered down the hall and into the living room. His father was a good twenty years older

than Wendy, which was undoubtedly one of the reasons he'd married her. Still, for a guy inching past his
mid-fifties, Jay Bloom didn't look bad. He still had a
thick head of dark hair with only a few strands of silver
threading through it—Rick wondered whether he was
using one of those hair-color products with the man-
ly names, as if hair dye for men had to be an entirely
different product from hair dye for women—and he
was trim and fit, thanks to his regular squash and golf
games. His father had always been a natural athlete.
So had Neil. Rick could put a spiral on a football if he
had to, but fortunately he didn't have to very often,
because it was a bit of a challenge for him. He hadn't
inherited his father's jock genes, but he hadn't inherited his mother's dour intensity, either. Sometimes he
wondered whether he was really theirs. Maybe they'd
found him in a basket outside their door.

His father pumped his hand and slapped his back
hard enough to dislodge a rib. "How's it going, Ricky?
You enjoying that new job of yours?"

It was only a short-term gig, but if his father wanted to think of him in conjunction with a job, Rick
couldn't blame him. "Yeah, it's good."

"Get the boy something to drink," his father urged
Wendy, then thought to ask Rick, "You want something to drink?"

"Sure."

"Get him something to drink," he repeated.

Wendy sent Rick another high-wattage smile.
"What do you want to drink?"

"I don't know. What are you offering?"

"What are we offering?" Wendy asked Jay.

"Come on," Jay said to Rick. "I'll get you a drink."

The kitchen was a little less turquoise than the
living room, which soothed Rick's eyes. His father

produced a beer from the fridge and Rick accepted it gratefully. His father preferred harder stuff, expensive stuff. Rick had simpler tastes than his father, which was fortunate because, given his perpetual lack of funds, he couldn't afford complicated tastes.

He took a swig of beer straight from the bottle while his father clinked ice cubes into a crystal highball glass, then poured in something expensive and complicated. It was only after the beer slid cold and sour down his throat that Rick realized no red meat was sizzling in the broiler or sitting on a plate on one of the polished granite counters, marinating in its own juices.

Panic seized him. He had been invited for dinner, hadn't he? They were planning to feed him, weren't they?

"We thought we'd do take-out," his father said.

Rick sighed with relief that he wouldn't have to feed himself—and spend his own scarce funds to do so. "Bloom's food?" he asked. According to Susie, Julia was always encouraging people—not just Bloom's employees but Bloom family members—to eat the store's food. She had this novel theory about how they should take pride in what they sold and should familiarize their taste buds with the store's products. In years past, when Uncle Ben ran the place, Blooms rarely if ever ate Bloom's food. His mother considered it an unjustifiable extravagance in a world where children on distant continents had to eat twigs and grubs to keep from starving. His father considered much of Bloom's inventory too oppressively Jewish. His Aunt Sondra, Uncle Ben and Grandma Ida had maintained that eating Bloom's food equated to eating the store's profits. Julia was trying to change the culture of the business. A mighty ambitious task, considering that it required changing the culture of the family.

The fact was, Bloom's food was delicious. Rick had probably eaten more of the stuff in the year since his cousin took over the store than he had in his entire life up to then. Not that he could afford Bloom's food on a regular basis—and since he lived downtown, Bloom's wasn't exactly his neighborhood deli—but Susie frequently brought Bloom's food home with her after she'd spent a day doing whatever she was doing for Julia at the store, and if he timed things right, he could show up at her apartment right around when she and her roommate Anna did. Her roommate Caitlin wasn't bad, but Anna really spiked his pulse rate. She had that whole Asian thing going for her, the stick-straight black hair, the eyes, the cheekbones, the tight little ass. If he timed his arrival just right, he could wind up sharing with Susie and Anna a feast of pot roast and stuffed derma, or bagels with smoked-whitefish pâté spread on them, or two-inch-thick corned beef sandwiches on seeded rye, with dill pickle spears so sour they made his tongue curl. And sometimes during one of those meals, Anna would look at him and smile, leaving him with the distinct impression that all was not hopeless.

"Chinese," his father said, startling Rick. Had he spoken Anna's name aloud? Mentioned her ethnicity to his father? He relaxed when his father explained, "There's a new Szechuan place around the block that Wendy wanted to try. How does that sound?"

Free food was free food. "Great," Rick said.

They returned to the living room to give Wendy the word about dinner. She was so excited about trying this new Szechuan place that she actually clapped her hands and gave a little skip. "I'll call in an order. You boys leave the choices to me. I promise, you won't be disappointed."

Jay watched her prance down the hall, then shook his head and smiled. "She never disappoints me," he murmured.

Rick decided that wasn't a topic he wanted to pursue with his father. He cleared his throat, took a sip of beer, cleared his throat again and waited until his father stopped ogling Wendy. Rick was real happy his father had found bliss with his blond trophy wife, but they had more important things to talk about.

"Listen, Dad, I've got this idea," Rick said.

The last vestiges of Jay's smile vanished. "I'd better sit down."

Rick labored not to look hurt or indignant. He knew his father thought he was a fuck-up. Just because he hadn't managed to become the next Spike Jonze or Todd Solondz yet, just because after earning a degree in cinematography from NYU's film school he'd managed to produce a grand total of one commercial—for a cheese grater, the manufacturer of which was trying to get Bloom's to carry his product—and he was now Camera 3 on "Passion and Power," and he still hadn't found anyone to produce his masterpiece, a script which could change the face of cinema if only he could get a fifty-million dollar budget and a few A-list actors to star in it...none of this meant he was a failure. But his father often acted as if he was.

He took another sip of beer, flopped onto the fluffy turquoise-and-white armchair across from the couch where his father sat, apparently braced for bad news. "I've got this idea for a TV show," he said.

"If you're looking for financial backing—"

"Hear me out, Dad, okay?" Sure, he was usually looking for financial backing when he approached his father with an idea, but wasn't that what fathers were for? "It's a show about Bloom's. I was thinking, like, a cooking show. An infomercial-type thing. Maybe a half-hour long. We could have people demonstrating how some of the Bloom's specialties are prepared, or a video essay about the history of chopped liver or something. We could have someone doing recipes. You know, preparing the batter for latkes, then spooning them into sizzling oil and shouting '*L'chaim!*' It would be an extension of what you're doing with the website and mail-order businesses. It would increase sales. Cooking shows are popular. And it would be fun."

His father looked puzzled. He stared into his glass, took a sip, frowned, shook his head. "A Bloom's TV show?"

"We could get it started on local access, or You-Tube. Or late night TV. Insomniacs could watch it and race to their computers and order stuff. There are a lot of channels looking for filler. If they can run infomercials about exercise balls, they can show infomercials about Bloom's."

"Do they show infomercials about exercise balls? What the hell's an exercise ball, anyway?"

"It's this ball that you roll around on for exercise, I think," Rick answered, honestly not sure. "The thing is, I bet there'd be a market for a Bloom's infomercial. Or a series of infomercials. I mean, we're talking about Bloom's. The most famous delicatessen in America."

His father's frown deepened. "I don't know, Rick."

"What don't you know?" It was such a brilliant concept! And he'd get paid to do it. Real money. And his father would look good, too, because he was supposedly in charge of non-print marketing for the store, and an infomercial would qualify as non-print marketing.

"I don't know how you came up with such an idea."

"I'm a filmmaker, Dad. It's my career." *Career* might be a stretch, but if his father was going to sneer at him anyway, what difference did it make if he puffed himself up a little?

"What about your film? The one with the car chase and the guy disconnected from life?"

"The infomercial would be a credit. It'll open doors for me. I'd do it dramatically, artistically."

His father's eyes narrowed. "How dramatically and artistically?"

"How dramatic is a bagel? I'm trained in this stuff, Dad. I could pull it off."

His father shook his head. "What I can't get past, Rick, is that it seems like such a good idea. I know there's got to be something wrong with it."

Rick laughed. "It's a good idea. Give me a green light. I'll win Bloom's an Oscar."

His father shook his head again, regarding Rick with an expression that could imply either astonishment or pride. "I've got to think about it. I probably have to run it past Julia, too."

Julia would say yes. Rick would get Susie to get Julia to say yes. If she said yes, his father would say yes. He'd be so proud one of his sons was doing something important for the store.

Rick was going to make his Bloom's show. He was going to direct it. Produce it. Cast it. Film it. Rack up credits left and right. Build his name. Prepare his Oscar speech.

"Ten minutes!" Wendy sang out from the other end of the hall. "They said dinner'll be here in ten minutes. I hope you're in the mood for hot-and-sour soup, because I ordered a lot!"

"I hate hot-and-sour soup," Rick's father muttered, then smiled. "But for Wendy, I'll eat it."

"So will I," Rick promised. He'd eat just about anything, as long as someone else was paying.

Chapter Seven

"I need a rhyme for pastrami," Susie announced She already had one rhyme, *salami*, but she needed another. Limericks made such demands on a poet.

She sat at the desk Julia had set up for her on the third floor of the Bloom Building, directly above the store. All the Bloom's offices were there, accessible by both the store's back stairway and the apartment building's elevators. To avoid entering the store, Susie had ridden up on the elevator. If she'd gone through the store, she might have run into Casey, and she wasn't ready to see him yet.

Monday mornings were awful under the best of circumstances, and today's circumstances most assuredly didn't qualify as best. The weekend had been hectic enough: watching Adam graduate, snapping so many photos that if she ever downloaded them all her computer would crash from the overload, soothing her mother when she began blubbering about her little birds flying the nest, explaining the ceremony to Grandma Ida when she decided she couldn't hear the speakers—which Susie would have considered a blessing, given that their speeches were about as stimulating as a cup of warm milk—and making nice with Adam's girlfriend's flaky parents. Tash's father kept ranting about the puny wages Cornell paid its maintenance staff, and her mother—whose legs were as hairy as Tash's, and probably Tash's father's, too—seemed to believe chlamydia was the biggest problem on college campuses today.

Maybe it was. Susie hadn't spent serious time on a college campus in four years, and when she'd been at Bennington, the biggest problem on campus had probably been a three-way tie: discovering that the library had only one edition of the book you absolutely needed for a research paper, and it had been checked out by someone who'd taken it home over winter break and neglected to bring it back; discovering that the guy you were madly in love with was boinking your roommate; and discovering that the food service had run out of brownies before you'd arrived at the dining hall, and you were stuck eating oatmeal-raisin cookies for dessert. Chlamydia wouldn't have even made the Top Ten.

"No, it's true," Tash's mother had insisted. "Chlamydia has flooded the nation's college campuses." Grandma Ida's sporadic deafness had vanished in time for her to hear this comment. Fortunately, she seemed to think chlamydia was some sort of seafood chowder.

Susie had survived the commencement festivities. She'd helped Adam pack his crap—and most of it truly was crap—into the van, and she'd won him as her companion for the drive home, leaving Grandma Ida to ride home in Joffe's brother's Toyota. She'd helped Adam unload his crap at their mother's apartment, and then she'd driven downtown and dropped the van off at Truck-A-Buck. The clerk insisted that there were more dark red splatters on the driver side door than there had been when Susie and Julia had picked up the van Friday morning. Susie had argued that she hadn't added any new splatters while the van had been in her possession, and in any case, what difference did it make? The clerk agreed with her that another splatter more or less made no difference at all, and he'd accepted the van without tacking on any extra charges.

From Truck-A-Buck, Susie had taken the subway to her apartment. Both Caitlin and Anna had been home, devouring take-out Thai and bickering over whether Lester Holt was sexy. Anna thought he looked like someone's uncle, and uncles by definition weren't sexy. Caitlin thought he was worth sleeping with, although she pretty much felt that way about anyone with a penis.

There had been enough leftover pad see ew for Susie to turn into a meal for herself. Ignoring the Lester Holt debate, she'd checked her emails. Nothing from Casey.

Well, she hadn't really expected an email from him, had she? He never sent her emails. When he wanted to contact her he phoned, and she'd had her phone with her the entire time she'd been in Ithaca, so if he'd punched in her number he would have reached her.

And said what? "Susie, I love you so much I don't want you moving in with me," or "My question Thursday night was merely one small step in a long journey, so if we don't take that step, no big deal," or "Ha, ha, just kidding!"

"Tommy!" Sondra shouted through her open office door, snapping Susie back into the present. Yes, *Tommy* rhymed with *pastrami*, for what that was worth.

Simultaneously, from the open door next to Sondra's office, Deirdre Morrissey called out, "Balmy." Deirdre had been Susie's father's right-hand woman when he'd been alive. She still worked at Bloom's, only now she'd expanded her duties to serve as everybody's right-hand woman.

"Swami," Julia called through her open door.

"Economy," Myron the accountant called through his.

A normal person might have wondered at the communication system of the Bloom's third-floor offices. All the doors remained open and people bellowed back and forth. No one ever used phones to talk to colleagues. They just hollered.

Susie didn't have an office. Julia had wanted to give her one, but having an office would be too official. She wrote the *Bloom's Bulletin* and oversaw the store's window and shelf displays, but if she had an office it would imply that her fancy title, creative director, actually signified something meaningful. She'd insisted that Julia give her a desk, a chair and a computer, period. The desk Julia had found for her stood nestled within a wall niche that had been created by protruding ventilation ducts. From her station, she could hear everything the executive staff shouted through their open doors.

"Economy doesn't rhyme with salami," her mother objected.

"Sure it does," Myron countered from the safety of his office. "If you accent it like economics, you can make it rhyme. *Eh*-cah-*nah*-mee."

"No, Myron," Deirdre vetoed him.

Susie sighed and leaned back in her chair, after looking both ways to make sure she wouldn't knock into anyone walking behind her. Did other business offices operate this way? She didn't have vast experience working in offices—to be sure, she'd never worked in one in her life, unless she counted doing her homework in her mother's office when she'd been a kid, and even then, she hadn't really *worked*. She'd just blown through her assignments and raced downstairs so she could play in the store. Other children might not have considered a bustling, aromatic food emporium the greatest playground in the world, but Susie had always loved skipping up and down the aisles, rearranging products on the shelves so the boxes and jars would look more symmetrical or colorful, contriving to bump into rude customers, and hanging around the bagel counter hoping for one of the countermen to recognize her and slip her a bagel.

Now, of course, she intended to stay as far from the bagel counter as she could. Casey worked there, just two floors down, distributing bagels, twisting ties around plastic bags, replenishing the bins, thanking the customers who praised his more outrageous bagel flavors and listening solemnly to those who had to tell him they honestly believed that adding a Dijon-mustard tang to bagel dough was sacrilegious.

If she went downstairs, she might see him. God knew, he was more likely to slip her the finger than to slip her a bagel.

"If you were from Jamaica," Myron was yelling, "you'd say it *eh*-cah-*nah*-mee. Calypso style."

"And if you were from Weehawken, New Jersey, you'd say, 'Up yours, buddy,'" Uncle Jay growled.

Susie sighed again. Not only weren't other business offices like this, but other families weren't like this. Uncle Jay's supply of patience was usually about as big as a spider's turd, but he generally targeted blood relatives for his petulance. Maybe Myron had been with Bloom's long enough to be considered family. A slight, balding fellow partial to bowties, he might well have been sitting exactly where he was now when the

Bloom's Building was constructed, forcing the architects to build his office around him. Julia had confided to Susie that Myron's bookkeeping methods were so archaic she was surprised he didn't do his calculations on an abacus, but he was a sweet man and eventually he'd retire. In the meantime, Julia said, he wasn't doing any harm.

"Never mind," Susie shouted. "I'll come up with my own rhyme." And she'd take as long as she could to do that, too. Eventually, she would have to go down to the store to interview Rita Martinez for an employee profile. A cashier, Rita had been with Bloom's for eight years, which made her the doyenne of Bloom's checkout staff. But Susie was in no hurry to interview Rita. The longer she could put off running into Casey...

She was being ridiculous, of course. She couldn't spend her life hiding from him—and why would she want to? She'd been away all weekend. He hadn't tried to contact her. This was the way relationships fell apart: one weekend, one panic attack, one swear word at a time.

At least, she assumed that was the case. She'd known a lot of guys in her life, but she'd never really been in a relationship before, anything serious enough that its conclusion required breaking up.

And she hadn't broken up with Casey, anyway. All she'd done was tell him she didn't want to move in with him. If he couldn't accept that, it was his problem.

She scrolled through everything she'd written for the new edition of the *Bloom's Bulletin*. The left side of her monitor held a list of sales prices and specials she'd included in the flyer—writing wittily about discounts on marinated artichokes and marble halvah wasn't as difficult as coming up with limericks including words like pastrami in them, but it wasn't easy, either—and the right side contained the artwork for the newsletter, photos of deli trays and line drawings of braided loaves. Uncle Jay did the scanning for her, but she had to plan the layout.

She could stare at the monitor for the next hour, trying to will into being a poem about a balmy swami named Tommy eating pastrami, or she could suck it up and march downstairs to interview Rita Martinez. Susie might be a lot of things—stupid, frivolous, and reckless among them—but she wasn't a coward. Drawing in a deep breath, she pushed away from her desk and stood.

She probably should have worn something more enticing. She gazed down at the outfit she'd thrown on that morning: a black denim skirt and a black crocheted shell over a forest green tank top. If Casey saw her, he'd think she was glum and morbid—or else he'd think she was dressed the way she always dressed, as if she'd bought her wardrobe after having her colors done by Morticia Addams. She really should stop wearing black all the time. She should probably get a personality transplant, too.

Taking another deep breath, she pushed her chair into the well of her desk and sauntered down the wide hall that doubled as a reception area for the offices, all of which opened onto it. A few cheaply framed Chagall prints featuring smiling, upside-down cows floating through pastel skies adorned the walls, and some ugly chairs that appeared to have been rejects from a dentist's waiting room stood randomly around the carpeted floor, as if there might be such a long wait to see one of the third-floor employees that a person would need to rest his feet. Once through the door, she crossed the elevator vestibule and shoved open the stairwell door. She clomped down a flight, used her employee key to open the door into the store's housewares department, and moved past aisles lined with pots, pans, woks and fans, pepper mills and knife sharpeners, jar openers and nutcrackers, to the broad stairway that led down to the first floor. The stairway was lined with clocks, and their multitude of faces, all displaying different times, always unnerved her. Despite her reluctance to get to the first floor, she scampered down the stairs so she wouldn't have to pay attention to all that tick-tock-ing time.

A row of cashier counters was located about twenty feet to her right at the foot of the stairs. But Rita and the other cashiers could have been on Uranus for all Susie noticed them. The instant the sole of her sandal touched the hardwood planks of the first floor, she spotted Casey. Damn the guy for not being behind the bagel counter, which was around the bend and not visible from the stairway. No, he had to be at large in the store, carrying a wrapped party platter of bagels to a well-dressed woman in a motorized wheelchair which was idling near Rita Martinez's checkout post.

Casey saw Susie, too. He froze in midstep, eyed her up and down, then proceeded to the woman in the wheelchair. He thoughtfully hunkered down to be eye-level with her before speaking. No doubt he was saying all kinds of charming things. He was probably praising her taste in bagels, or her spiffy wheels. With him, it wasn't sweet talk. It was just the way he was, attentive and kind.

Why couldn't he be a schmuck?

Susie watched him straighten up and felt she had to do something. Standing immobile at the base of the stairway like some new Bloom's display for black apparel struck her as stupid, frivolous, reckless, *and* cowardly. She forced herself to take a step—by which time his lanky legs had carried him the distance from the cashiers to her side. "Hey," he said.

"Hey." She gazed up into his pale, shimmering eyes and clamped her lips shut to keep from babbling. Those eyes had always done wild things to her. So had his height, his lean build, his softly waving blond hair and the intriguing hollows of his cheeks. When it came to Casey, her vision qualified as an erogenous zone.

If she opened her mouth, all her feelings would come tumbling out: that she missed him, that she adored him, that she wanted to lock lips and other body parts with him right this very instant—but no, she would not move to Queens. She was more than willing to give him her heart; he had no right to expect her to give him her life, too.

She swallowed repeatedly to keep the words down. He stared at her for a few long seconds, then asked, "How was your brother's graduation?"

"Fine," she managed, then pressed her lips tight again to keep any extraneous words from leaking out. Damn it, she wanted to tell him about the weekend, about how self-righteous Adam's girlfriend was and how goofy he'd looked in his mortarboard. Susie was used to sharing things with Casey. He was so much fun to talk to.

The hell with it. Cowards might remain silent to prevent the wrong words from emerging, but she wasn't a coward. "Adam's girlfriend was like a relic from 1969—except I don't think they had vegans then, did they? She was so not like what I would have expected Adam to fall for. To call her a tree hugger would be euphemistic. This girl is a tree tonguer. A tree *schtupper*. You remember what *schtup* means, don't you?"

"I remember." His dimpled smile was sexy enough to put Susie in mind of *schtupping*. Specifically, *schtup-*

ping him. Her thighs tensed and the back of her neck grew so hot she expected steam to seep through her hair.

"Come on," he said, taking her hand and leading her through the store, past the coffee corner, past the pastries, past the bagel counter where Morty Sugarman, the department's senior manager, was counting bagels into a bag for a skinny orange-haired woman with a large nose and a voice like chalk scraping across a blackboard who felt it her duty to critique each bagel he lifted from the bin. Casey held up his hand, five-fingers splayed, and Morty nodded.

Good. Wherever he was taking her, they'd be there only five minutes. Not too much could happen in five minutes.

Well, yes, a lot could happen. She could burst into tears. He could call her a bitch. He could ask her to move in with him and she could say yes. The planet could get hit by a meteor and wind up knocked out of its orbit. Five minutes was an eternity.

He ushered her into the building stairwell and let the door shut behind them. The stairwell was brightly it, echoing and private; few people ever used the stairs. The first time Casey had kissed Susie, a little more than a year ago, they'd been standing in this stairwell.

And now, a little more than a year later, he kissed her again. Damn his soul to a hell populated with skinny, screechy, orange-haired ladies who were excessively particular about their bagels. That was the only punishment suitable for someone who could kiss like Casey Gordon.

The first time he'd kissed her, she'd fallen in love with him. And every time he kissed her since then, she fell deeper. She plunged like Alice down the rabbit hole, only unlike Alice, she didn't glimpse books and other household objects on the wall's shelves. She glimpsed pieces of her life—the fun, single, care-free pieces—and splinters of her resolve. How was she supposed to resist a man who smelled like fresh dough and was fluent in lingua lust and knew how to slide his hands over a woman's tush so it felt as if he were hold-ing her entire soul in his gently cupped palms?

Oh, God, she'd missed him. Two days in Ithaca and she'd missed him the way a chocoholic on a hun-ger strike missed fudge. Maybe there was a twelve-step program for people like her. Caseyholics Anonymous. *Hello, my name is Susie, and I've just tumbled off the wagon in a very big way.*

The kiss seemed to last forever, but when he fi-nally slid his mouth from hers she realized it couldn't have taken as long as five minutes. Casey was a man of his word. He wouldn't strand Morty Sugarman at the bagel counter longer than he'd promised.

"So, other than Adam's girlfriend, how was Cor-nell?" he asked.

How could he talk about Adam and Cornell? Su-sie's mouth felt as if he'd shot it full of Novocain—com-pletely detached from her and beyond her control. The only word she seemed able to utter was, "No."

"No?"

Sensation returned in stinging twinges. "No, I don't want to talk about Cornell."

"You want to talk about the other thing?"

"Don't ask me to move in with you, Casey. Please."

If you ask, I might say yes, and I'm not ready for that.

He shrugged. "You want to get married?"

"What?"

"All right, look." He slouched against the wall and raked a hand through his hair. His fingers got trapped at the elastic band which held it into a health-code mandated ponytail, and he let his arm fall. "I wasn't going to ask you that. I wasn't going to make this harder than it has to be."

"How hard does it have to be?"

"Either we move forward or we let it drop. I don't like treading water. It's tiring."

"We're not treading water," Susie protested.

"What do you want, Susie? What exactly do you want?"

"What we have right now," she answered honestly. Kisses hot enough to ignite the sky. Sex so explosive the Homeland Security Department might want to issue a warning whenever Casey and Susie were alone together. Long, meandering conversations about everything and nothing. The realization that she couldn't glimpse Casey without smiling, a reflex that had been fully operational until last Thursday night.

That was what she wanted.

"I want more," he told her, then turned, edged open the door and left the stairwell without a backward glance, leaving her alone, surrounded by cinder-block walls and stainless-steel railings sloping up and down alongside the stairs.

"You asshole!" she shouted after him, although the door was swinging shut and he couldn't possibly hear her. "I hate you!"

Her voice resounded throughout the stairwell, a pathetic lament. There she was, dressed as if in mourning, howling over the prospect of losing a guy who was obviously wrong for her. He was greedy. He was selfish. He was demanding, manipulative, and pushy. Why the hell should she grieve over him?

She really needed to start wearing bright colors. She needed to accept that Casey's prowess in bed—or in the stairwell, or wherever they happened to be when the kissing started—was not a good enough reason to forget about everything that mattered to her, every dream she'd ever had, every concept of herself she'd ever entertained. She was a visionary, an explorer, an adventurer. She wrote poems and drove a rental van nearly big enough to qualify as a truck. She counted among her friends unemployed musicians, unemployed actors, unemployed gallery owners, and unemployed filmmakers—and even unemployed food preparation professionals. She needed to remind herself that Casey Gordon wasn't the only tall, gorgeous, charismatic bagel maker in the world.

Chapter Eight

Sleeping till noon got old pretty fast.

Adam rolled out of bed, blinked his eyes until his surroundings came into focus, and groaned. Ten past twelve was a decadent time to be getting up, especially since Tash wasn't in bed beside him so he couldn't blame sleeping all morning on having not slept all night. He felt as if his skull was crammed with damp cotton, and his back felt weird. Uncricked. Pain-free. After four years of sleeping on spongy, sagging dorm beds, he wasn't used to sleeping on a high-quality mattress.

Noon light filtered through the shades. He stared at the piles of cartons stacked against the wall across from the bed and flashed on a memory from many years ago, when he was a toddler. That wall, where the detritus of four long, busy years of Ivy League living currently stood in cardboard boxes, used to hold a colorful fabric hanging covered with zippers, buttons, pockets, flaps, and, at the bottom, two yellow strips of cloth with a blue shoelace crisscrossing them together. He recalled having nightmares about the shoelace. Maybe he'd thought it was a snake. Or else his dread had come from a legitimate fear of flunking childhood because he'd taken so long to learn how to tie his shoes.

The wall hanging was long gone. So were any other objects that marked the room as Adam's. His shelves were cleared of books—he'd brought his favorites up to college, and his mother must have disposed of the rest. His magnetic dartboard was gone. His collection of soccer trophies, meaningless because every kid on every team received one at the end of every season, regardless of his skill level or his team's win-loss record, no longer stood like a chrome and fake-marble army along the back edge of his dresser. His speakers were still packed up; he ought to unpack them so he could add a musical soundtrack to this dismal summer.

He didn't feel like unpacking. He didn't feel much like doing anything, other than getting out of bed before the rest of the day disappeared on him.

He tossed on a pair of shorts and one of his many Cornell T-shirts, then staggered out of his room and into the bathroom. From there, he headed to the kitchen. His mother was always on a diet, which meant he'd have to look in unexpected places to find the good food: frozen waffles hidden behind a package of frozen spinach, a box of Frosted Flakes tucked discreetly at the back of a cabinet filled with virtuous Special K and fat-free crackers. No whole milk, only skim, which had an unfortunately blue cast to it. He added a splash of it to a heaping bowl of Frosted Flakes, figuring the sugar would disguise the faintly sour taste of the diluted milk.

He needed to find something to do. In school, when his days had been crammed with studying, research, and exams and his nights with concerts, parties and midnight pizzas, he used to spend his rare free moments fantasizing about having infinite free moments, endless stretches of time uncluttered by obligations. But he'd been home for a day now, long enough to be bored. He wanted—well, not obligations but *stuff*. Concerts, parties, and midnight pizzas.

As if that would ever happen. His mother would freak if he brought a pizza into the house. She'd see his having introduced such empty-calorie temptation into her home as a personal affront, a mean-spirited attempt to undermine what little willpower she had when it came to food.

He wolfed down the cereal without tasting it, then returned to his bedroom for his wallet and keys. A walk would clear his mind and give him some ideas about how to fill the abundance of free moments he was suddenly saddled with.

He donned his sunglasses, stopped back in the bathroom to brush his teeth and glanced at his reflection. His hair was a mess, but it was a punkish, rakish mess and he liked it. His chin was dark with a stubble, but he liked that, too. With the sunglasses, he looked kind of cool. Well, maybe cool was stretching it. At least he didn't look like a math geek.

Fortunately, the apartment building had its own lobby and front door, so he didn't have to go through Bloom's to get outside. He didn't want to set foot inside the store. A year ago, after school had let out for the summer, he'd wandered into the place to see how it was faring under Julia's management, and the next thing he knew, she'd talked him into a summer job. It hadn't been the worst summer job, either—stock clerk sounded menial, but the people he'd worked with had been pleasant and he could think of worse fates than to be surrounded by excellent food for eight hours a day. But he was a college graduate now, his sights set on a doctorate and a career in academia. That a university might someday pay him to hang out on campus, listening to good tunes and schmoozing with colleagues and playing with numbers all day astounded him. Working at Bloom's couldn't begin to compete with that.

The sun was bright overhead as he walked to the corner of Broadway. The store loomed to his left, occupying a city block. Pedestrians flocked to its showcase windows, and its doors repeatedly opened as shoppers came and went. The place seemed to be bustling. People needed their bialys and blintzes.

He deliberately crossed the street and strolled downtown, away from the store. Broadway had changed a lot during his lifetime; twenty-two years was several evolutionary cycles in terms of the neighborhood. When he was a kid, even a teenager, the avenue hadn't included so many outlets of national chains. Nowadays, Upper Broadway could pass as an outdoor, noisy, Muzak-less version of a mall—expensive restaurants and chic boutiques mixed with big-name brands, lining block after block, beckoning shoppers. Thank God for places like Bloom's, independent old stalwarts that would never rent space in a climate-controlled mall in Dubuque or Scottsdale or West Lafayette, Indiana.

He hastily erased that thought. One reason he wanted to go to graduate school in West Lafayette, Indiana was because Bloom's would never open a franchise there.

He wondered if West Lafayette had seedy vendors selling questionable merchandise from folding card tables along its sidewalks. Used and remaindered books, cheesy paintings in cheap frames, knock-off watches, sun visors, New Age knickknacks, and brass paperweights shaped like the World Trade Center towers with the words "God Bless America" etched across their red-white-and-blue bases—were all these folks licensed to sell such crap? Did anyone care?

Of course not. This was New York.

A few blocks south of Bloom's, he purchased a hot pretzel from a guy with a pushcart. The dough was chewy, the salt crystals crunchy. He hadn't bought a sidewalk pretzel in years, and he'd forgotten how good they tasted. Much better than Frosted Flakes with skim milk.

By the time he'd finished the pretzel he'd reached Lincoln Center. He tried to recall the last time he'd seen a production at the performing arts mecca. When he and his sisters were younger, his mother used to take them to matinees there all the time. His dad rarely joined them; he was always working. But in the evening, over dinner, Adam and Julia and Susie would describe what they'd seen: "This lady played a harp, Daddy, and she sounded just like heaven!" or "A bunch of fat people sang very loudly and their voices wobbled," or "The dancers wore tutus, Daddy! That's what those funny skirts that look like petticoats are called. Tutus. Like a tutu train."

His sisters had been enthralled by the ballets their mother had taken them to. Adam had found them excruciating, all those skinny ladies in their tutus, kicking and flicking their feet and doing swoopy things with their arms, and guys in tights jumping around a lot and fluttering their fingers. And his mother would have to whisper the story the dance was supposed to be telling them. "He's an outlaw, Billy the Kid," she'd murmur.

"He looks like a cowboy—except he's wearing tights."

"He's a cowboy outlaw. Look, he's shooting people."

Adam preferred movies, where he didn't need his mother to explain to him when someone was shooting someone else. In the ballet, the Billy guy might have been shooting someone, but it just looked like jumping and fluttering fingers to Adam.

All right. His mother deserved points for trying to imbue him with high culture. Adam deserved points for having escaped her influence.

He climbed the stairs to the sun-filled plaza at the heart of the Lincoln Center complex. The fountain was churning low, perhaps to save water. Many of the umbrella-shaded café tables were occupied by people eating lunch, reading, and talking. Folks streamed in and out of the Performing Arts library. A pigeon bobbed over to a toddler, no doubt looking for breadcrumbs or some other culinary freebie, and the toddler screamed, raced to his mother and hid his face against her knees. Pigeons—the stuff of nightmares to a three-year-old. Just as scary as a blue shoelace on a wall hanging.

Near the café tables stood a food cart. Adam wasn't hungry, but the pretzel had whetted his thirst. He took his place behind a girl who appeared barely out of her teens. While she ordered a latté, he surveyed the beverages listed on a placard behind the cart. Iced mocha. That sounded good.

The girl in front of him reminded him of a drinking straw, for some reason. Her body seemed stretched out, her neck, bare arms, and denim-clad legs too long, her toes pointing outward like a penguin's. Her dark blond hair was combed back from her face so smoothly it could have been painted onto her scalp, except for where it bulged in a tidy bun the size of a ping-pong ball at her nape. As she bent over to poke through her purse for money to pay for her latté, Adam found himself staring at that nape, a few loose wisps of hair curling against her skin. He vaguely recollected a college lecture on the eroticization of the woman's nape in ancient Japan, or something like that. It wasn't math, so he hadn't bothered to remember it.

Had he ever noticed Tash's nape? Had he ever even seen it? Her hair was so thick and curly, and she never bound it into such a severe bun.

"I'm sure I've got another quarter in here," the girl said, digging deeper into the purse. It was really more a quilted cloth pouch, not much bigger than a paperback novel. Adam didn't think a quarter could get lost inside it.

He pulled his wallet from his pocket. "Here," he said, handing a ten-dollar bill to the guy behind the counter. "For her latté and an iced mocha for me."

The girl spun around to look at him. Her face was as delicate as the rest of her, skin pale, eyes round, nose as sharp as a paring knife. "You don't have to do that," she said. Her front two teeth overlapped slightly.

"I don't have to vote, either. But I do it."

"Voting is an obligation," she said solemnly.

"No it's not. It's a privilege. Although, given some of the candidates, I'm not sure how much of a privilege it is."

She smiled. "I'm not sure how much of a privilege it is to buy a stranger a cup of latté, either."

"It's more fun than voting," he told her, then dropped some change into the tip jar and lifted his mocha.

"I've only voted twice, so far," she told him, taking her latté, "and I enjoyed it."

Maybe she had a low threshold for enjoyment. Or maybe...maybe she was flirting with him.

Oh.

Nobody had flirted with him since he and Tash became a recognized couple more than a year ago. Tash herself never flirted. She probably considered flirting politically suspect. He'd forgotten how much fun it could be. A hell of a lot more fun than voting.

"My name is Adam," he said, angling his head toward the café tables. "Wanna sit?"

She smiled again, flashing him those crooked front teeth. "My name's Elyse, and I guess I can spare a few minutes."

Flirting. Why not? He had nothing better to do.

The Bloom's Bulletin
Written and edited by
Susie Bloom

A woman in town from Miami
Came to Bloom's to stock up on salami..
"Since I'm here," she said, "first
Slice me some liverwurst
And why not? A nice pound of pastra-
mi."

Welcome to the May 28th edition of the *Bloom's Bulletin*. Spring has sprung, and the shelves of Bloom's have sprung full of delicious spring fare—fresh salads, chilled soups like gazpacho and zucchini soup and hot and cold sandwiches perfect for picnics in Central Park. To wash down your al fresco feasts, Bloom's sells bottled water, both sparkling and still, from spas around the world, as well as fruit juices, gourmet sodas and iced tea. Don't hold me to it, but I've heard green tea cures everything.

Cooking the Books? No—Bloom's is booking the cooks! On June 1st, Bloom's will begin a new lecture series featuring well-known chefs and cookbook authors. Every month a different cook will teach some simple recipes and answer your questions. All sessions will begin at seven p.m. Our first guest will be potato maestro Tina Klopewitz, author of *Tina's Taters, More Tina's Taters*, and *Mashed, Hashed and Crashed—Potatoes for the New Century*. She will be demonstrating creative ideas for stuffing potatoes and solving the age-old dilemma of what to do with the skins. Come meet the queen of spectacular spuds, who promises to make you think about potatoes in an entirely new way.

Feeling your oats?

Imported Scottish steel-cut oats are on sale all this week. Denying yourself the pleasure of delicious porridge made from steamed Scottish oats would be downright gruel!

Did you know...

The Yiddish word "tsimmis" is used to describe an imbroglio or a complicated, out of control problem, as in, "Don't make such a tsimmis out of the fact that your sister spilled purple grape juice on your favorite white cashmere sweater." But *tsimmis* is actually the name of a stewed carrot dish. Bloom's founder Ida Bloom never made *tsimmis* herself, but she remembers her mother's *tsimmis*: "She would slice the carrots into thin sticks and stew them with spices and maybe onions, I don't remember. Caraway seeds, maybe. Then she'd put the *tsimmis* in jars and refrigerate it. Of course, she didn't have a refrigerator. In those days, it was an icebox. Sometimes the *tsimmis* got ice particles in it. Not that it mattered. I hated the way it tasted."

Employee Profile:

Cashiers come and cashiers go, but Rita Martinez came and never went. For eight years, Rita has been scanning merchandise, counting change, and double-bagging frozen food items for satisfied Bloom's customers. Why does she stay? "Bloom's is great," she says. "Being here is like being with family."

Rita moved to New York City from Arecibo, on Puerto Rico's northern coast, when she was five years old. "At first I was scared of the big city," Rita admits. "All those tall buildings, and everyone talked a foreign language! But I started school and learned English and New York became my home. One thing I loved about living here, right from the start, was all the different kinds of food. Italian, Thai, Cuban—which is similar to Puerto Rican, but different, too—and of course kosher-style food like we sell at Bloom's. The first time I ate a knish, I thought, *ay*, what is this? So good! Better than fried plantains, even! And bagels. My whole family loves bagels. Last year at Christmas, we hung bagels on our tree." According to Rita, cranberry bagels, with their red tint, looked especially festive in contrast with the pine needles.

Rita is married and has two *bebés*, Joey and Viviana. "They love rice and beans," Rita says, "but they also love kugel." Rita says her pet cat, Carmella, also likes Bloom's Heat-'N'-Eat kugel, but only if it's cut into tiny pieces.

Wise Words from Bloom's founder Ida Bloom: "You want to make a fool of yourself? Who's stopping you?"

On sale this week: marble halvah, imported Jarlsburg, Heat-'N'-Eat *flanken*, marinated artichokes, and more. Details inside!

Chapter Nine

"**R**on. Stop," Julia said in the firmest voice she could muster—which wasn't very firm, because she wasn't entirely convinced she wanted him to stop. Lying naked and sated in the afterglow of some spectacular sex, their legs still entangled and the bed sheets twisted around them, Ron traced an invisible line on her right breast with the tip of his index finger. Everywhere he touched he left a tingle, and whenever his finger strayed particularly close to her nipple it twitched and grew pointier, as if to alert him to its presence: *Here, Ron! Touch me here!*

Her nipple might want his touch, but her mind didn't. She had too many things to worry about.

"Stop what?" he murmured, sounding both sleepy and sexy.

"Stop distracting me."

"Is that what I was doing?" He lifted his head from the pillow and smiled down at her. She took in his dark, disheveled hair, his angular face, his intense brown eyes, and his wicked so-sue-me grin. His expression should have warned her that he was up to no good, but his kiss still took her by surprise. If he'd kissed her lips she could have handled it, but no, he had to kiss her yearning, burning nipple.

"Ron, come on!" She nudged him away. "We've already made love."

"Oh—did we use up our quota?" he asked, faking a look of shock and innocence.

She shoved him a little harder. "Don't tease me. I'm trying to be worried and you're not letting me."

"Well, shame on me," he said, settling back into the pillow beside her. "Better call the police and have me charged with abuse. Denying you the right to worry? What kind of bastard am I?"

"Can you get serious for just two minutes?" She pushed herself to sit and pivoted to face him. She crossed her legs, noticed where his gaze was focused, drew her knees together, pulled her legs up against her chest and wrapped her arms around her shins, folding herself into a neat little bundle with all her X-rated parts concealed. "The dinner party on Friday is going to be a disaster."

Ron could have sworn to her that the dinner party would be fine, but theirs was a relationship grounded in honesty. So he only shrugged and said, "Big deal. It'll be a disaster. If we're lucky, it won't end with someone lying on the floor with a butter knife stuck between his ribs."

"*His?* You think the murder victim is going to be a man? Who? You?"

"I don't think there'll be a murder victim. Especially not from a butter knife."

Julia sighed. Ron had a habit of making light of things. She found his attitude exasperating. She also loved him for it. She envied his ability not to take things too seriously, not to feel responsible for the whole damned world. Perhaps this attitude was due to his refusal to allow his family to become so involved in his life.

Well, they were going to be involved in his life Friday night. His life and Julia's. And it was going to be a disaster.

"First of all," she said, trying not to respond to his lazy smile, his sleek chest, his magician hands, and his enticingly flat abdominal muscles—thank God the sheet draped the way it did, or the rest of his body would be visible and he wouldn't even have to touch her to distract her. "We're going to have both your parents in the same room. At the same table. Maybe you're onto something. Maybe we should just set the table with butter knives. Steak knives could be too dangerous."

"My parents aren't going to kill each other," Ron promised. "They've had ample opportunity to do that over the past several decades, and they haven't yet."

"But they hate each other."

"They're divorced. They're supposed to hate each other."

"They thrive on that hatred. It feeds them. It nullifies all their positive energy. Haven't you ever wondered why neither one has remarried?"

Ron rolled his eyes. "Sounds like it's time for some cheap psychology. Let me guess. You think they're still in love, right?"

Julia didn't consider the possibility deserving of ridicule. "Do you? You know them better than I do."

"My parents got divorced twenty-two years ago. If they still loved each other, they probably would have figured it out somewhere along the way."

"But they never remarried."

"Maybe they decided they just weren't cut out for marriage."

Which led to one of Julia's biggest worries. What if Ron, their firstborn, the result of their genetic merger, the product of their rancorous household, was inherently not cut out for marriage? He'd asked Julia to marry him and she'd said yes, and he'd given her the most beautiful engagement ring in the world, nothing ostentatious, one single, perfectly set carat in a band of white gold. And he doted on her—when he wasn't teasing her—and phoned her when he got held up at work, and freely mingled his dirty laundry with hers. And when he made love to her, he made love to all of her, not just certain specific anatomical regions. He whispered to her and stroked her hair and peered into her eyes, and when they came he groaned with such sweet relief and gratitude and triumph, obviously as thrilled for her as for himself.

He loved her. She was convinced of that. But what if growing up in a broken home had taught him damaging lessons about marriage?

And what about her? Her parents had been married for thirty years and would still be married today if her father hadn't eaten contaminated sturgeon and succumbed to salmonella poisoning two years ago. But her father had also been sleeping with Deirdre Morrissey at the office—tall, gawky Deirdre, the executive who knew the store better than any Bloom family member. Julia hadn't learned about the affair until a year after her father's death, and by then it had seemed quite beside the point. Deirdre was essential to the smooth running of the store, and if Julia's mother didn't mind having an office right next to Deirdre's, why should Julia make drastic changes?

Still, like Ron, she was the offspring of a dysfunctional marriage, even if no one had ever bothered to acknowledge how dysfunctional it was. Maybe she carried a betrayal gene within her cells. Maybe someday she'd turn to a skinny, buck-toothed assistant for comfort.

Oh, Sure. With a guy like Ron Joffe at home in her bed, she was going to look at anyone else?

So maybe her marriage was congenitally doomed, and maybe it wasn't. She still had plenty of other things to worry about. "My mother doesn't cook very well, so I asked Lyndon to do the cooking."

"Then you have nothing to worry about," Ron reassured her. "Lyndon's a great cook."

"But Grandma Ida isn't invited. She's going to be pissed that Lyndon is taking off the evening and leaving her all alone in her apartment so he can go downstairs to my mother's apartment and whip up a feast for us."

"So invite Grandma Ida," Ron said calmly, as if it were the most reasonable idea in the world.

"Are you kidding? She'd dominate the entire evening. She'd issue edicts. She'd insist on controlling the whole wedding."

"She'd probably come down on your side," Ron pointed out. He toyed with her feet, running that mischievous index finger between her toes, over her polished nails, up and down her instep. She considered slapping his hand away, but his touch felt too good. She would simply have to keep her mind focused and not let him detour her.

"What do you mean, my side?"

"She'll want the wedding catered by Bloom's, won't she?"

"Who knows? With Grandma Ida—" her toes wiggled when he located a ticklish spot along her arch "—you never can predict what she'll do. She'll go deaf for a moment, then snap out of it and decide we should have the reception at Elaine's, because the same outfit that supplies Bloom's with salt and pepper also supplies Elaine's."

"Really?" Ron seemed to find this possibility fascinating.

"It's probably the same outfit that supplies every food service company in the city with salt and pepper. The thing is, who cares? Grandma Ida gets hung up on *mishegas* like that." Julia sighed, half from frustration and half from pleasure as Ron wrapped his hand around the back of her ankle, along her Achilles tendon, and rubbed. God, that felt good.

"So don't invite Grandma Ida."

"She'll be pissed. And hurt."

"Big fucking deal." Ron let his hand drop and rolled onto his back. "You worry too much."

She knew he was exasperated with her—but, as he himself would put it, big fucking deal. He might not care where their wedding was held or who catered it, but he wasn't the president of a major food emporium with its own catering department. He was the business columnist at *Gotham Magazine*, where unless you were a local celebrity of some sort, no one cared where you got married or what your guests ate at the reception.

"And my brother. What are we going to do about him?"

"Adam?" Ron shrugged. "Why do we have to do anything about him?"

"Mom says he wanders around the apartment in a daze. She said he keeps saying he's got to call Tash but she's overheard him on the phone talking to someone named Elyse."

"Your mother is eavesdropping on his phone calls? Jesus." Ron rolled his eyes again.

"So who's Elyse?"

"Am I supposed to know?"

"Adam's going to want to join us for dinner because Lyndon will be making real food. My mother always makes low-calorie stuff, salads with fat-free dressing, fish fried in Pam."

"Tell Lyndon to fix a plate for Adam to eat in the kitchen. This is not a crisis, Julia."

It was a crisis. She figured her wedding to Ron would be the only one she ever had, and she wanted it to be perfect. She wanted everyone to get along and no one to be petty or selfish or overly demanding. She wanted to look beautiful, and she wanted Susie, her maid of honor, to be happy, and she wanted a pretty gown that didn't cost as much as a Lear jet, and she wanted Bloom's to cater the reception. Right now many of the key members of the wedding were not getting along, most of them were innately petty, selfish, and demanding, she had an incipient pimple in the crease next to her left nostril—although she suspected that by the time she and Ron booked a place for their wedding they'd be lucky to get a date a year from now, and the pimple would probably be gone by then. She had a brooding, melancholy sister and the few gowns she'd looked at so far, while not as expensive as a Lear jet, carried price tags that made her think of all the starving children in the world and left her paralyzed with guilt. And her mother was still whining about having a reception at the Plaza because her brother hosted his son's bar mitzvah there.

"Maybe we should elope," she said dolefully.

"Fine with me."

"Just take the subway down to City Hall, sign some papers and be done with it." She closed her eyes for a moment, savoring the fantasy.

"We could even bring some bagels from the store with us and eat them afterward. That way you could say Bloom's catered the reception."

She scowled. "You're making fun of me."

"You won't let me make love with you. This is the best alternative I can come up with."

"I will let you make love with me," she retorted. "Just not now, while I'm busy worrying."

He clamped a hand onto her shoulder and pulled her down against him. As worried as she was, she couldn't help nestling into him, resting her head on his chest and extending her legs along his. "Listen to me, Julia," he said, his voice vibrating in his chest, against her ear. "We're not going to elope, because you want a nice wedding. And that's what we're going to have."

"How are we going to have a nice wedding when I can't even agree with my mother about the food?" she mumbled into the curve of his neck. "And your parents are going to kill each other with butter knives, and—"

"Julia. All these problems you're worrying about aren't *your* problems. If your brother doesn't like your mother's fat-free cooking, he can get his ass in gear, find a job and buy his own food. If your grandmother doesn't like it that Lyndon is preparing the dinner Friday night, explain to her that slavery was abolished a hundred fifty years ago and she doesn't own the guy. He's free to cook for whomever he wants. And if my mother and father get into it, that's their shit. Butter knives aren't going to draw blood."

She sighed. Ron was right. Even if he wasn't, pretending he was soothed her. "In other words, you're saying Friday night is going to go fine."

"No. It's going to be a disaster." He chuckled. "But who cares?"

Chapter Ten

Three-thirty-ish was a good time for Rick to visit Susie at Nico's. Earlier, she'd be cleaning up from the lunch rush; later, she'd be prepping for the dinner rush. But at the afternoon's midpoint, the downtown pizzeria experienced a lull, and Susie was usually available to talk then.

He paused outside the eatery to admire her latest window arrangement for the restaurant. A poster displayed the image of a young graduate robed in solemn black, clutching a diploma rolled into a tube and tied with a red ribbon. In place of the standard mortarboard hat, the graduate wore a pizza, with stretchy strands of melted mozzarella dangling over the crust to resemble a tassel. A whiteboard propped next to the poster bore a poem in Susie's even print, adorned with drawings of small red tomatoes:

> *To all who've had recent graduations,*
> *Nico's offers congratulations!*
> *As you travel along life's many stations,*
> *May we be a part of your celebrations.*
> *Now's the time for some taste sensations,*
> *Some shrimp or crab or other crustaceans.*
> *We prepare our dishes with care and patience.*
> *So come and try our tasty creations!*

Shielding his eyes with his hand, he peered through the window into the café. An elderly man was ensconced at a corner table, reading a newspaper. On the table in front of him sat one of those thimble-size cups restaurants served espresso in. What a scam—put a few chintzy drops of bitter coffee in a doll-house cup and charge twice as much as for an eight-ounce mug of regular joe.

He spotted Susie at another table, near the counter. She was busy doing something; he couldn't tell what, but whatever it was, it couldn't be that important. He pushed open the door and she looked toward him and smiled. The old geezer with the espresso didn't even glance up from his newspaper.

Rick crossed the dining room to Susie's table. As he got closer he could see she was refilling table dispensers of grated Parmesan cheese. The dispensers stood in a row like large glass onions, their chrome lids unscrewed while Susie spooned the powdered cheese into them from a large plastic vat. The cheese was the same dingy color as Susie's complexion. Her eyes were outlined in black, her lips tinted a ruby hue, but her cheeks were awfully pale. Give her a striped shirt, white gloves and a top hat, and she could pass as a street mime.

"Hey, Cuz," he said.

She forced a vague smile. "What's up? You hungry?"

"Always, Susie. Hunger is my middle name."

"Richard Hunger Bloom. Yeah, I could see your mother saddling you with a name like that." She screwed the cap onto one of the table shakers and pulled another closer to her for filling. "We might have an old slice of pizza destined for the trash. You want it?"

Jeez. She didn't have to make it sound as if he was picking food out of a Dumpster. The old slices were perfectly edible leftovers from lunch, a slice here and there that didn't get bought. "If you've got one of those extra slices, I'll take it," he said, refusing to let her undermine his pride. "No need to heat it up. I'll eat it cold." He said that to spare her from reminding him that she couldn't stick it in the oven without attracting Nico's attention. Her boss was in the kitchen, doing set-ups for the dinner stretch. It wasn't as if he'd fire her for feeding the leftovers to her perpetually starving cousin, but why get him involved in the transaction? Life was simpler if Nico remained in blissful ignorance.

Susie stood and walked around the counter. She had on khaki shorts and a black T-shirt under her apron. He had never seen her in khaki before. Maybe that was why she looked so wan; her face reflected the gray-tan of her shorts.

He watched her slide a limp slice of pizza onto a paper plate and carry it back to the table. Her movements were sluggish. Maybe the lunch hour had been more hectic than usual, or maybe juggling this job and her responsibilities at Bloom's demanded too much of her. Or maybe that drive all the way up to the hinterlands of Ithaca last weekend had wiped her out.

And here he was, ready to ask her to drive to the hinterlands with him. Different hinterlands, though— and Grandma Ida wouldn't be part of the deal.

He accepted the pizza from her and tried not to wince at the congealed cheese and glistening oil coating the wedge. As she resumed her seat, he took a bite, chewed and smiled. Not great, but edible. "Thanks."

"I live to serve."

"So...how's it going?"

She eyed him sharply. "Why are you asking?"

Because you look like shit, he almost said, but he didn't think she'd appreciate his honesty. "I've got this gig and I need your help."

She pursed her lips and screwed a lid onto the jar she'd just filled. "Why is it that I only see you when you want my help? Or food," she added, cutting him off before he could defend himself.

He tried to muster some indignation, but there was too much truth in what she'd said. "Food is always helpful," he said, hoping to finagle a smile out of her. She glowered and started in on another empty Parmesan dispenser. He consumed a little more of the cold, rubbery pizza, giving her a chance to forget how often he came to her looking for aid. "So listen," he said. "The help I need from you is going to be fun. I've been hired to make a documentary."

"Really?" Her face brightened at that. "Who hired you?"

"Bloom's. And it's not exactly a documentary," he continued when her expression changed from excited to skeptical. "It's kind of an infomercial."

"An infomercial for Bloom's?"

"Yeah—but calling it a documentary sounds so much cooler, don't you think?"

"Well, which is it?" she pressed him. "An infomercial or a documentary?"

He used his thumbnail to pick a twiggy-looking piece of oregano out of a hardened bulge of cheese. After scraping the oregano onto the pleated edge of the plate, he took another bite. "Okay, here's the deal. My dad convinced your sister to cough up twenty-five thousand dollars to make a video promoting Bloom's. He's thinking infomercial. That's the way I pitched it to him. But I'm thinking, why aim low? Why do something boring when I could do something with vision? Something artistic?"

"Maybe because something with vision and artistic isn't going to promote Bloom's," she pointed out.

"But it is!" His enthusiasm bubbled over. He hoped some of it would splash onto her. She had always been the only Bloom who understood him, who thought like him, who didn't consider him a complete loser—although maybe she was just good at pretending she didn't consider him one. Maybe she truly believed he was interested only in getting her to give him help and food.

No, she knew he was interested in other things. Film, for instance. And her poetic window displays. And her roommate Anna.

"I had this idea," he explained. "I wanted to bounce it off you. Tell me honestly what you think." *Not too honestly,* he wanted to add. *Just be honest if you absolutely love the idea.*

She lowered the spoon she was using to scoop Parmesan with and stared expectantly at him.

"Bloom's Soup," he said.

"Bloom's soup? What, like the chicken soup with matzo balls?"

"No. Like Stone Soup. Remember that old children's folk tale?"

She frowned. "Some guy makes a pot of soup with a stone or something?"

"That's the one." He waited until she resumed her chore, then continued. "The guy is a soldier. He and his men are starving, and they come to this village hoping to mooch some food from the local citizenry."

"I can see why you relate to this story," Susie teased. "Starving men mooching."

He accepted the ribbing with a grin. "The townspeople don't want to give him their food. So he tells them he's got this magic stone, and if they'll supply him

105

with a cauldron of boiling water, he'll put his stone in the water and it will create soup for the entire village."

"This rings a bell," Susie said with a nod.

"So the stone is boiling in the water in the cauldron, and the soldier says, 'Man, this smells good, it's gonna be great soup. But you know, it would be even better if I could add an onion to it.' So one of the townspeople goes and gets him an onion and he cuts it up and tosses it in. And he says, 'Wow, this is going to be one outstanding pot of soup! But you know, it would be even better if I could add a few potatoes.' So someone else goes and gets him some potatoes, and he slices them and sticks them in the pot. And it goes on like that—he says the stone soup is going to be exquisite, but it would be even better with a carrot or two, and a couple of meat bones, and some peas and some leeks or whatever, and the villagers bring him their supplies and he adds them to the pot...and then finally he says, 'That's it! The soup is done. And of course it's delicious, and he and his men and all the villagers have some."

"And then he winds up running for office, because he's such a con artist," Susie said, screwing the last lid onto the last jar.

"I don't think that's part of the original story."

She shrugged. "Okay. Explain to me what that has to do with Bloom's."

"It's just a jumping-off point. I'm thinking we'll make this film about interesting ingredients, and how food relates to family and memory, how Bloom's is about all kinds of food coming together in this amazing metaphorical broth."

"A metaphorical broth," she echoed, clearly dubious.

"We'll mention the store over and over. And talk about some of the ingredients Bloom's cooks use and how they use them, and what they signify."

She contemplated his vision, then said, "There's one word in all this that I'm not so sure about."

"What's that?"

"*We.* You said *we'll* mention Bloom's name over and over. What do you mean, *we*?"

"Come on, Susie! I need your help on this. I've got an amazing vision for this thing. Sure, it can be shown on local-access cable, or on YouTube. But I'm thinking big, Suze. I'm thinking Sundance."

"Film festivals?"

"I'm thinking Cannes. I'm thinking credits. Better credits than being Camera 3 at 'Power and Passion' while someone's on maternity leave. I'm thinking Oscars."

"I'm thinking you're nuts."

He ignored her. "My dad's wrangled the funding. This is a huge opportunity, Suze. It could launch me. How do you think Spielberg started?"

"By making infomercials for a deli?" Susie guessed.

He gave her his most winsome smile. "You've got to help me with this. You're so creative."

Susie sighed. "What do you want me to do?"

"Be the star."

"What?"

"I can't afford to pay a real actor. But that's beside the point. You're a Bloom. I want a Bloom at the center of the story of Bloom's Soup."

"I'm still not clear what the story is. I'm supposed to make soup in this documentary?"

"You're supposed to take direction." He could tell she was wavering, and he tried to recall what his brother had taught him about fishing. A lot of Neil's clients in the Florida Keys liked to fish, so the Jewish kid from New York had learned a thing or two about deep-sea fishing. What Rick recalled Neil telling him was that once you hooked a fish you had to reel it in slowly. He was pretty sure he had Susie hooked; he only had to reel her in. "You'll be great. You won't have to act—you'll just be yourself. And you'll look great. The camera will love you."

"I still don't understand the story. If I'm not making soup—"

"I haven't written the whole script yet, but don't worry. I'll take care of it."

Her eyebrows twitched. "That's what I'm afraid of. If this is going to be like that script you wrote about car chases and ennui—"

"It's not. It's about Bloom's."

"It's about soup."

"Soup as a metaphor." He gave her what he hoped was an earnest gaze. He really, really wanted her to be a part of this. The only person he'd rather have be a part of it was her roommate Anna, but that was for entirely different reasons. "Here's the deal. For twenty-five thou, I can't rent studio space in New York City. So I was figuring we'd take the show on the road, do some filming outdoors to save money and travel around a bit. We could film food stuff on the road, adding local ingredients to the story and talking about Bloom's, what Grandma Ida and Grandpa Isaac might have put in their soup, stuff like that. Grandpa Isaac was the soup maven, wasn't he?"

"I don't know the family lore," Susie said, then shook her head. "Of course, Grandma Ida recited the family lore all the way to Ithaca, so I should know it. But I tried to tune her out."

"I tune her out whenever she starts doing the family-lore thing, too. But so what? We can invent our own family lore." He popped the last of the soggy crust into his mouth, hoping his casual attitude would equate to reeling her in slowly. "Could you get away from the city for a week or so?"

"To travel around making this movie?"

"Yeah. If you could work things out with Nico—"

"I can always work things out with him," she said, gesturing vaguely toward the kitchen. "Leave the city for a while, huh..."

"Would it be a problem?"

Her face brightened again, genuine pink shading her cheeks. "I'd love to get out of the city."

"You would?" That surprised him. Susie adored New York. She thrived in the place. The noise, the hustle, the funk, the poetry slams—and of course Casey, the love of her life. New York was her world, her home.

"Some time away from the city? Absolutely." She nodded and her eyes shifted, as if she were viewing something far off, somewhere outside the city. She seemed to like what she saw. "Perfect." Then her eyes came back into focus on him. "But I've also got the newsletter to do, you know, the *Bloom's Bulletin*..."

"Bring your laptop along. You can work on the newsletter when we aren't filming."

"Right. Okay. Fine. I'll be your star," she said so abruptly, he wondered why he'd been so cautious about reeling her in. Hell, if he'd known she was going to leap out of the ocean and fling her scaly body into his boat, he'd have asked for a free Coke to go along with his pizza.

Chapter Eleven

Casey's mother collected statuettes of people with birth defects. Casey didn't know how else to view the row upon row of porcelain dwarfs and trolls and bandy-legged gremlins that filled the towering mahogany hutch that consumed one wall of the living room. Susie would call his mother's collection *tchochkes*. He called them creepy.

But they made his mother happy. She proudly insisted that they were leprechauns, as if being a hunched, bow-legged fellow with a pituitary disorder and a pathetic fashion sense wasn't really a problem as long as the little guy was Irish.

The hutch dominated one end of the living room and the TV the other. In between stretched a beige and brown desert—brown rug, beige sofa and chairs, brown tables, brown lamps with beige lampshades, beige window shades flanked by brown drapes. Above the brown sideboard hung two sepia-toned prints of unidentifiable landscapes in brown wood frames. If it weren't for the broadcast on the TV screen and the gaudy attire of the dwarf statuettes, the room would have no color in it at all.

What would Susie think of the place? What would she think of his parents? It no longer mattered. Bringing her around to meet the folks wasn't on the agenda.

If Casey wanted to obsess about her, he might wonder why he hadn't bothered to introduce her to his parents in the year they'd been together. Perhaps because he'd known she would burst into hysterical laughter at the sight of his mother's tacky figurines, all lined up on the hutch's shelves like soldiers. Or more like army rejects, 4-F's on parade.

From the kitchen came the smell of food boiling, offering another good reason for him never to have brought Susie to his parents' house. What if they'd invited her for dinner? She would have discovered the appalling secret of Gordon cuisine: boiling. When he'd decided to apply to the Culinary Institute, his parents had been shocked; hadn't they raised him to understand that the only way to cook food was in hot water? In the cases of poached eggs or corned beef and cabbage, such a preparation worked. In the case of chicken...well, his mother called it stewed chicken, but it was basically chicken she boiled in water, along with onions and carrots and whatever else she had cluttering her refrigerator.

He wasn't sure what was boiling right now, although the scent of onions clued him in to the likelihood that chicken would be a part of it. He had to get out of the house before his parents strong-armed him into a chair at the kitchen table and forced him to eat. And not just because boiled chicken and onions excited his taste buds about as much as light beer served at room temperature. He was supposed to meet Mose at a neighborhood eatery in twenty minutes. They had business to discuss, and the establishment served *real* food. Baked, roasted, broiled, fried, flavorful food.

"I really can't stay," he told his father, who sat in his oversized armchair across the living room.

The chair was angled toward the TV set, but his father twisted to face him where he was perched on the end of the sofa nearest the entry foyer. "You'll break your mother's heart," his father pointed out.

"I'll come for dinner another time, Dad. It's just that I've got plans for tonight."

"With the boss's daughter?"

Casey sighed. "It's the boss's sister, and no. Not with her."

His father glanced at the TV screen, where a local news anchor breathlessly reported on a scandal involving subway fare cards, a third grade teacher from Staten Island, and a missing ferret. "You've got a problem with that girl? She's causing you problems?"

"He should find a nice Catholic girl," his mother hollered from the kitchen.

His father waved his hand toward the hall down to the kitchen, as if he could sweep her words out of the living room with his fingers. "Don't worry about that. So she's not Catholic. You can always get her to convert."

Casey wisely kept his mouth shut.

"Thing is..." His father hunched forward, six feet and two inches of beefy middle-aged body mass crowned by a silvering mop of hair. "You've got a sweet deal, am I right? You stay with the boss's daughter, you're on your way. Your foot is in the door—maybe more than your foot, if you catch my drift." He winked, and Casey shifted uncomfortably at the thought of a certain part of him getting caught in a door. "Play your cards right and you've got yourself a nice little management position, a fancy title, a corner office. They can call the store Bloom's and Gordon's."

"I'm not looking for a corner office," Casey argued. "That has nothing to do with the women I date." As if he and Susie were dating. As if a term as archaic as "dating" had ever described what he and Susie had shared—and what they no longer shared.

112

"The point is, so what if she's not Catholic? Catholic, Jewish, it doesn't matter. All roads lead to God, anyway, am I right?"

"You aren't talking anti-Church, are you?" his mother yelled from the kitchen.

"Margaret, love of my life," his father yelled back. "I'm simply having a chat with my son. No crime in that, is there?"

"He's staying for dinner, right? Casey, you're staying for dinner."

"I really can't," Casey insisted, though not loudly enough for his mother to hear him over the din of boiling pots in the kitchen. He aimed his words at his father: "I stopped by to return your socket wrench. But Mose is expecting me in—" he checked his watch "—fifteen minutes."

"So, you're not seeing that girl?"

"No, I'm not." The stark truth, he thought grimly. Days had passed since he'd last seen Susie—and kissed her. He could still taste her kiss, the kiss that had convinced him they ought to get married, because when two people kissed and it felt that good, that right, that perfect, why mess with fate? If he were religious, he'd say that kisses as spectacular as what he and Susie experienced when they kissed were God's way of telling them that they belonged together. But he wasn't religious and God obviously wasn't talking to Susie, because she'd said no. She had no compunction about messing with fate. Hell, she probably saw messing with fate as an exciting new challenge, like getting a tattoo or flunking trigonometry, both of which she'd done before she'd met Casey.

Her no was finally beginning to sink in. He wasn't seeing her. Apparently they were supposed to screw fate and go their separate ways.

113

Meeting with Mose tonight represented the first step of Casey's separate way. If only he could figure out a strategy for leaving his parents' house that wouldn't launch a dinner crisis. His first big mistake had been to sit. If he'd remained standing, he could have handed his father the socket wrench and vanished before his mother started slicing onions into her pot.

"I really have to go," he said, gripping the arm of the sofa with one hand and the seat cushion with the other, preparing to heave himself out of the too-soft upholstery.

His father's gaze sharpened, as if he knew what Casey was up to. If the old man had a gun, he would have reached for it. He wouldn't have drawn, but he'd have let his hand rest menacingly on the butt, a warning that he was prepared to do whatever was necessary to keep Casey from bolting without eating dinner first.

Casey relaxed the muscles in his shoulders, as if his only intention all along had been to shift his weight on the sofa. His father kept a wary watch, but he no longer had that ready-to-draw glint in his eyes. "So, there's a problem with the girl?" he asked.

"No problem," Casey lied.

"I have nothing against Jews," his mother bellowed from the kitchen. "All I'm saying, it's better if you're the same faith, for the sake of the children."

"What children?" he asked his father. He felt no need to shout to include his mother in the conversation. She had uncanny hearing, or else she'd wired the house with eavesdropping bugs. As a child, he'd often suspected the latter. He and his grade-school buddy Brian would be whispering in his bedroom and suddenly his mother would whip the door open and say, "Just for the record, you are not going to start a frog farm in the basement," and Casey and Brian would stare at each other in astonishment, wondering, *how did she know?*

"Your mother wants grandchildren," his father explained. "God knows why. She drives that school bus five days a week, morning and afternoon, and then she spends the whole evening crabbing about how noisy children are."

"Maybe she thinks I'd raise my children better," Casey opined, then cringed inwardly. How did they trap him this way? Not only hadn't he made his escape, but now they had him talking about the children he was going to raise.

"Kids are noisy. No two ways about it. Your sister was noisy. Then you were born and you were noisier. Girls shriek. Boys shriek and belch. It's a noisy business. You and that girl want to give me grandchildren? Fine. But they're going to be noisy, I can guarantee you that. Noisy and gassy. It's the way children are."

"You want romaine or iceberg?" his mother shouted.

So far she hadn't figured out a way to boil salad. But the prospect of fresh, crisp greens wasn't enough of an incentive for Casey to stick around. "Neither," he called toward the doorway. "I'm not staying for dinner." There. The gauntlet had been thrown down.

His father's fingers twitched, as if searching the air around his hip for a holstered gun. His mother materialized in the doorway, just the way she had the time she'd declared her ban on frog farms in the house. Tall, thin and armed with a cooking spoon, she gave Casey a fierce stare. "You have to stay for dinner. I made too much for Dad and me."

"So you'll have leftovers," Casey said. "I've already got a dinner plan." Now that he'd stated his intention and the words couldn't be retracted, he went ahead and stood.

His father sprang to his feet and sidled toward the foyer, as if he planned to block the front door. The socket wrench lay on the coffee table next to the three remote controls it took to operate the TV and a stack of round cardboard coasters with "Czerny's—Home of the Mile-Long Kielbasa" printed across them. For a brief, crazy moment Casey contemplated grabbing the wrench and brandishing it like a fencing sword, using it to hold his parents at bay. His mother's spoon was longer, but the wrench had more heft.

"You having dinner with that girl? The boss's daughter?" his mother asked.

Correcting her about Susie's twig of the family tree wasn't worth the effort. "No."

"So what am I supposed to do with all these left-overs?"

"I'll call you tomorrow and give you a recipe for them," he promised, edging toward the door, his eyes never leaving his father. It was like playing one-on-one in slow motion, feinting slightly toward the coat closet to get his father to veer in that direction, then spinning the other way and reaching the door. He could do it—he was younger and much quicker than the old man—but he didn't want to risk committing a foul. Fouling one's own father would be disrespectful.

"When are you going to bring her here so we can meet her?" his mother pressed him.

"I don't know." *Never, Mom. She turned me down. She said no.* "I've got to go."

"He's got to go," his mother grumbled to his father, who had fallen for Casey's fake and was moving toward the closet door. "Such a busy man, never has time to eat dinner with his parents."

"I had dinner with you last week," Casey protest-ed, then winced. Getting snared in an argument over how often he had dinner with his parents would ruin his timing and trip him up. "I'll see you soon," he said swiftly. "Thanks for letting me borrow the wrench."

"You should buy your own tools," his father chided.

"You're right. I should. I'll call you with a recipe, Mom," he said, gracefully swerving to his right and yanking open the front door. "'Bye." He practically leaped across the threshold, slamming the door behind him.

He drew a breath deep into his lungs. Mild late-spring air, it smelled like grass and his mother's roses, evening and freedom. Before his parents could charge out the door, waving spoons and wrenches and screaming for him to get his butt back inside and eat some of their overabundance of boiled chicken, he descended the steps and sprinted to the corner, around onto the cross street, away.

He'd been outrunning his parents since he'd matured beyond the crawling stage. He'd always been fast, and now that they were on the far end of their fifties, they didn't even try to catch him. They probably just tucked themselves back into their color-free house and complained about what an ingrate he'd turned out to be.

He loved his parents, really. He just didn't fit with them. If he hadn't looked like them both—he had his father's thick, wavy hair and hazel eyes, his mother's sharp chin and angled cheekbones, his father's height and his mother's wiry build—he'd have assumed they'd adopted him. They were both impatient yet docile, intelligent yet uncreative. They seemed incapable of perceiving anything outside the tight little sphere of their own experience. It would never occur to his mother to fry the onions in a little olive oil, rub some herbs onto the chicken and broil the whole thing.

Susie complained about her family all the time, and Casey only shook his head. Her mother could be pushy and whiny, but hell, the woman had lost her husband only two years ago, and lots of women had trouble dealing with growing older, especially growing older alone. Susie's grandmother was crusty, but a person knew where he stood with her, and beneath her gruffness Casey sensed a generosity that Susie refused to acknowledge. Susie's sister Julia was great—the best boss he'd ever had—and the only reason he would choose not to work for her was that he'd rather work for himself. He also thought it best to remove himself from Susie's world, now that she'd said no. Casey barely knew Susie's younger brother, but he seemed okay.

Casey's sister was a dog groomer. Every conversation he had with her wound up being about the difference between a Continental Clip and an English Saddle clip on a poodle, or about flea baths. Celia was a font of wisdom on the subject of fleas.

So Susie felt like the oddball in her family? She had no idea.

And he wasn't going to think about her anymore. She'd said no.

Nearing the neighborhood eatery where he'd arranged to meet Mose, he checked his watch and discovered he was five minutes late. Not too bad, considering that if he weren't quite so deft he'd be staring down a plate of his mother's boiled chicken rather than entering this cacophonous restaurant, with its laminated menus, its neon wall decorations and its hamburger aroma.

He gave a quick nod to the hostess who tried to stop him inside the door, then strode past her station and scanned the room. The after-work crowd was dense, lots of guys in inexpensive blazers and loosened polyester ties hoisting tankard-size mugs of beer. Mose had managed to score the booth closest to the restroom. Not the greatest location, but it was better than standing.

Compared to his parents, the hostess was a mere amateur at trying to keep Casey from his destination. Dismissing her with a smile, he forged through the crowd, weaving and nudging his way to the booth. He sank onto the hard wood bench across from Mose and groaned. "Waiting long?"

"No, but I had to fight tooth and nail to defend this table."

"Sorry. I was being held hostage by my parents." A waitress showed up and Casey asked for a Killian draft.

Mose ordered a bourbon. "I ain't drinking that Irish piss," he declared.

"It's too subtle for you," Casey teased.

"Don't forget who's got the MBA at this table." Mose settled against the high back of the booth seat. Like the majority of the restaurant's patrons, he had on a blazer and his tie hung loose below his unbuttoned shirt collar. But his tie was silk and his jacket was well tailored. As he explained it, he counted on his apparel to convince prospective clients that he knew what he was talking about. "They aren't gonna take business advice from a black guy unless he's wearing a Christian Dior tie," he'd told Casey on more than one occasion.

Casey would take business advice from Mose even if he were wearing a grass skirt and pink earmuffs. But he had to admit the Christian Dior tie Mose had on was reassuring.

"Okay," Mose said, pulling a folder from the leather briefcase propped on the bench next to him. "I still think you'd do a whole lot better to forget this scheme and find yourself a new lady. Spare yourself a whole lot of shit that way."

"Are you kidding?" Casey laughed bitterly. "Work is easy. Ladies are where the shit comes from."

"I could ask LaShonna to set you up with a friend," Mose offered.

Casey's laugh was more relaxed this time. His parents were having enough trouble trying to act like liberals about their son dating a Jewish woman. Imagine if he started dating a black woman. His father would have a heart attack; his mother would drown herself in a pot of boiling water. Both of them, with their dying breaths, would swear that they had nothing against black people but they were only concerned about how he'd raise his children.

In any case, LaShonna was a social climber, devoted to Mose primarily because Mose earned a nice salary, had that MBA and knew the difference between polyester and silk. Her friends would probably share her values, which meant they'd have no use for a bagel baker. "If I wanted blind dates, I'd go to LaShonna," he said. "I want business advice, so I came to you."

"Yeah. Okay." Mose accepted Casey's words with a reluctant shrug and a look of vague disapproval. "I crunched you some numbers, and I really think that if you want to open this specialty bread store, you ought to think again."

"Thanks for the optimism," Casey muttered.

"You're talking big bucks, buddy. If you really want to go through with this—"

It wasn't necessarily that he wanted to, although he did. The real issue was that he had to. He had to get out of Bloom's, away from the Blooms. Away from one Bloom in particular.

"—then you ought to consider locating in the outer boroughs."

"No. It's got to be Manhattan," Casey insisted.

The waitress returned to their table, carrying their drinks on a tray. Mose smiled and nodded at her. Casey kept his eye on his glass, gauging with some displeasure the amount of foam the bartender had left. When she was gone, Mose grinned at Casey. "She was hitting on you," he said.

"Who?" Casey frowned and searched the crowd. "The waitress?"

"Didn't you see the way she leaned over to put down your glass? Nobody needs to bend that low to put a glass on the table. I thought she was going to pull your head down into her cleavage."

"Really?" All Casey had seen was the foam. Jesus. He'd been with Susie so long, he didn't notice other women, not even when they were coming on to him with their cleavage.

All right. Three days ago he was proposing marriage and getting turned down. He couldn't be expected to notice buxom waitresses so soon after getting his heart stomped on.

He touched his rib cage gingerly, as if to make sure his heart was still there. The weird thing was that in the past three days—the past week, if he counted back to when Susie had rejected his invitation to move in with him—he had no pain in his heart. Some severe discomfort in his groin, sure. He was horny, though not for waitresses who leaned over. He missed Susie in a deeply physical way. And an intellectual way. Every evening, he reached for his phone and touched his thumb to her name on his contact list. He didn't press it hard enough for the call to go through, but he wanted to. He wanted to talk to her the way they used to talk, about their days, their thoughts, their dreams. About everything.

But his heart didn't ache. He didn't even feel in-flamed with anger. Not once had he thrown a dish against a wall and called her a fucking bitch.

Did that mean he didn't really love her? Or just that reality was only just beginning to sink in? Was it kind of like dental work, where it took a while for the Novocain to wear off, and once it did he was going to be gasping from the excruciating agony?

He'd survived a root canal. He supposed he could survive Susie, too.

He could survive her a lot better if he wasn't mak-ing bagels for her sister, though.

He opened the folder Mose had pushed across the table. It contained pages filled with numbers. "Initial expenses: cash layouts, loans—basically what it'll cost you to start your little carbohydrate boutique," Mose told him, jabbing at various columns of figures with his index finger. "Way expensive in the outer boroughs. Break-the-bank time in Manhattan."

"I want it in Manhattan," Casey said.

"Look at the numbers I crunched for you, Woody. Manhattan, you're gonna have to win the lottery first."

Casey flipped through the pages until he found a sheet of storefront rentals in Manhattan. Damn. The Novocain must have worn off, because those gigantic numbers sparked a genuine pain in his heart. "I want Manhattan," he repeated, ignoring the ache.

"Do it in Queens, it's almost affordable for you. Plus you've got a better commute."

"Manhattan is where the customers are," Casey explained. "They're used to paying high prices to cover the cost of the real estate."

"Look at me, man." Reaching across the table, Mose snapped the folder shut to get Casey's attention. "Are you doing this to settle a score? To win points or something? Because if you are, I got nothin' to say to you. I'm not gonna waste my time. You want to think like a businessman? Think Queens. Better yet, think the Bronx. Real cheap rents there."

Casey grimaced. "I'm not going to sell bread in the Bronx."

"Okay, well, I don't blame you. I mean...the Bronx." Mose sipped his bourbon and sighed. "So explain Manhattan to me. What's in Manhattan, besides people willing to pay high prices?"

"Bloom's is in Manhattan," Casey said.

"And...what? You want to set up shop across the street from them? Compete directly with the world's most famous bagel retailer?"

Actually, that would suit Casey just fine. Maybe he did want to settle a score. Maybe his heart wasn't hurting because the pain was somewhere else: In his gut. In his gray matter. In his ego.

"Yeah," he said. "Across the street would be great. Are there any empty storefronts for rent on that block?"

Mose shook his head. "You want my advice? Be reasonable. Use your head. Add up the numbers, Casey. You'd kill yourself doing it in that neighborhood. Bankrupt your future. As a professional, I'm telling you, don't do it."

"How about as my friend?" Casey asked. "What's your advice then?"

"As your friend?" Mose regarded him thoughtfully. From the far side of the room, where a group of happy-hour patrons clustered at the bar, an off-key, booze-juiced chorus of the "Happy Birthday" song arose. Mose glanced toward the revelers, shook his head and turned back to Casey. "As your friend," he said, "I understand where you're coming from. I get it.

Manhattan would be the place. Now forget I ever said that."

Casey smiled. Sometimes it was better to get advice from a friend than from a professional. Especially a friend in a Christian Dior tie, which made even his bad advice sound absolutely right.

Chapter Twelve

The glorious aromas filling her mother's kitchen should have soothed Julia. She hovered just inside the doorway, breathing in a blend of mouth-watering fragrances—roasting fowl, herbs, mushrooms, wine—and watching Lyndon and his boyfriend Howard waltz around the room in a graceful duet.

Julia's kitchen was barely big enough for two people to stand in, let alone perform a choreographed ballet. Her mother's kitchen was so large Julia could stand in it without getting into either Lyndon's or Howard's way as they glided from the stove to the counter, from the refrigerator to the oven. Clad in a cream-colored sweater that would have been splattered with sauce and grease if Julia had worn it while she cooked, Lyndon seemed to be doing most of the work, stirring something in a pot, peeking at something in the oven, lifting a sheet of aluminum foil from a bowl and peering inside. Howard's chief tasks seemed to be rinsing things at the sink and stepping out of Lyndon's path two beats before Lyndon swept by.

Howard was Lyndon's kitchen-mate as well as his life-mate. The past two *Pesachs*, he'd come to Grandma Ida's apartment to help Lyndon prepare the Seder. Julia wasn't sure exactly what he'd done those times, other than hang around the kitchen being Jewish, a responsibility Lyndon couldn't fulfill since he was raised in the AME Baptist church. Howard's presence added authenticity to Lyndon's matzo-ball soup and *charoseth* at Passover, and he might say prayers over the food before Lyndon served it. Whatever Howard's culinary contributions, the Seder meals were always delicious, so Julia had no objection to his being present for this dinner party.

Besides, as tall and thin as he was, with a beak nose and frizzy, slightly receding red hair, Howard looked a lot like Art Garfunkel. Julia wondered if his voice resembled Art Garfunkel's. She had the feeling someone might need to sing "Bridge Over Troubled Water" before the evening was through.

"Is there anything I can do to help?" she asked. "You both look so busy."

"So you don't have to be," Lyndon assured her. "We're doing the kitchen work, Julia. You can save your energy for doing the hostess work."

"Why can't my mother be the hostess?" Julia asked, then sighed. The task of waiting for impending disaster tired her out.

"Because she's your mother," Lyndon answered, even though the question had been rhetorical. His answer didn't clarify much, anyway.

"Do you think we should have made red meat instead?" Julia fretted. "A roast beef, or a prime rib or something."

Both men looked at her as if she was crazy. She didn't think she'd said anything that outrageous, except for the fact that it was five-thirty and a little late to be tinkering with the menu. "Cornish game hens are perfect," Lyndon told her.

"I'm sorry. I should just keep my mouth shut." She sighed again, and gave Lyndon her most contrite smile. "Joffe hasn't phoned, has he?"

"No, he hasn't. And if he did, he'd call you on your cell, so you'd know it before we did," Lyndon pointed out. "He'll get here."

"His parents might get here first."

"Then you'll be a proper almost-daughter-in-law and entertain them until he arrives. Howard will have a nice tray of hors d'oeuvres you can serve them. Right, Howard?"

Howard glanced up from the sprigs of parsley he was patting dry. "This is going to look wonderful," he assured her, carrying the bright green garnish to a cut-crystal platter and arranging it with the precision of a landscape architect. "Trust me, Julia. I know my parsley."

She trusted him and Lyndon a lot more than she trusted Ron to arrive on time, her mother to remain open-minded, Ron's parents to avoid bickering, and herself to stay calm and stop expecting the worst. She didn't know why she was so jittery. She'd survived law school, hadn't she? Passed the bar, worked for a big white-shoe firm, taken the helm at Bloom's without any preparation other than having been born a Bloom, and returned the store to profitability. She was an executive. A hotshot. A certified success.

Yet the thought of staging this dinner and convincing everyone present that she was capable of deciding how her wedding should be catered made her want to find herself a dark corner, curl into a ball, and suck on her thumb.

"Was Grandma Ida upset about your coming down here tonight?" she asked Lyndon.

Lyndon shrugged. His halo of short braids trembled like springs as he rubbed the salad bowl's surface with a clove of garlic. "Your grandmother is upset about lots of things. You know her."

"She wanted to be invited to this dinner, didn't she."

Lyndon smiled cryptically. "She made some comments."

"Oh, God." Julia sank against the granite counter. She meant to fold her arms across her chest, but her hands wound up near her shoulders so she was in effect clinging to herself in a desperate hug. "What comments?"

"Just that she was free this evening, and if there was nothing good on TV she might drop by."

Grandma Ida lived directly above her mother, on the twenty-fifth floor of the Bloom Building. Dropping by could either mean riding the elevator down to the twenty-fourth floor or cutting a hole in the ceiling and falling through it. Julia wouldn't discount either option. "Is there anything good on TV? Any old Alfred Hitchcock movies?" Her grandmother was a fan of scary films, as long as they were in black and white. Color, she said, made them too real.

"One of the cable channels is having a Ferris Bueller fest," Howard noted. "They're going to play *Ferris Bueller's Day Off* over and over for twelve straight hours."

Somehow, Julia didn't think that would keep Grandma Ida glued to her TV. Before she could calculate the shifting odds of Grandma Ida's making an uninvited appearance at the party, her cell phone chirped. *Ron,* she thought as a fresh wave of panic surged through her. *He's calling to say he's running late and will have to miss dinner, and would I please give his love to his parents, and if one of them goes after the other with a butter knife, would I please throw myself between them so they won't kill each other.*

She hauled the cell phone out of her purse, which sat on the counter next to her mother's set of empty art deco canisters—"Why should I fill them with flour and sugar?" her mother often said. "It's not like I'm going to be baking any time soon, all that work, all those calories"—and hit the connect button.

"Julia? It's Susie," her sister said.

Julia let out a long breath. At least it wasn't Ron calling with bad news. "Susie," she said, forcing brightness into her voice. "I can't talk right now."

"Oh." Susie's sigh sounded moist. Damn it, she was crying.

"What's the matter?"

"Nothing. You can't talk."

Julia closed her eyes, trying to collect herself. The sound of bare feet squeaking against marble flooring forced her to open them again, in time to watch Adam lumber into the kitchen. "Hey, it smells good in here. Like real food."

"You're not invited," Julia reminded him, then quickly said into the phone, "I was talking to Adam, not you."

"Am I invited?"

"No."

"Great. Thanks a lot." Susie was clearly trying to come across as flippant, but a wail edged her voice.

"Oh, Susie," Julia said sympathetically. "I really wish I could talk right now, but—Adam, don't touch that," she snapped as he helped himself to one of the cute little canapés Howard was nesting amid the parsley hedges. Back into the phone, she said, "I'm at Mom's. Joffe's parents are coming to dinner. It's going to be a disaster."

"Both his parents? At the same time?"

"Yes," Julia said grimly.

"That should be fun." Susie sounded notably cheerier. "Can I come? I love to watch disasters, as long as they aren't mine."

"You can come and baby-sit for Adam. He's a disaster," Julia said, deliberately loud enough for her brother to hear.

He sent her a bright smile, then plucked from the tray a Melba round topped with a dab of cream cheese and a sliver of smoked salmon. "Mm, delicious," he said, still chewing. He wore a pair of bright red Cornell athletic shorts and a T-shirt that featured a tear along one shoulder seam, frayed ribbing at the neckline and a silkscreen of a sequoia along with the words "All we are saying is give trees a chance" printed up one side of the trunk and down the other. His hair was uncombed, his cheeks unshaven, his unshod feet clean but ugly. Had he always had such knobby toes? Maybe he hadn't consumed enough vitamin C as a child.

"Do you want me to come?" Susie asked.

Julia closed her eyes to block out her view of her brother's feet. "No, I don't want you to come. I love you too much to subject you to this. But this is the worst possible time in the world for us to talk—"

Her mother abruptly swept into the kitchen, clad in black slacks and a beaded green sweater, an ensemble that downplayed her middle-aged droops and bulges in a flattering way. She'd brushed her brown pageboy back behind her ears and made up her face with a light touch. "How do I look?" she asked breathlessly.

"Fabulous," Julia, Howard and Lyndon all said at once.

"I think I'll wear a different top," Sondra said, darting out of the kitchen.

"What's fabulous?" Susie asked into the phone.

"The way Mom looks. Looked. She's changing into another top, so who knows how she'll look in five minutes? Listen to me, Susie. Whatever you do, don't get married. It's not worth having to go through a night like this."

"I'm not getting married," Susie said firmly.

"Good."

"I'm leaving town."

Lyndon chose that moment to turn on the food processor. It issued a deafening buzz, drowning out Susie's words. Julia stepped out into the hall, pressed her free hand against her unoccupied ear and shouted, "What?"

"It's not important. You can't talk now," Susie said, her voice wavering around a sob.

"You're leaving town?"

"I'm going to make a movie with Rick. We'll be gone awhile."

"What movie? Rick's making a movie?" Her heart thumped. Why did her cousin have to choose tonight of all nights to make a movie?

"It's about Bloom's," Susie said. "I'm helping him. I'll do the *Bloom's Bulletin* long-distance."

"A movie?" Her heartbeat accelerated. She felt as if she had a hyperactive gerbil trapped inside her ribcage. "Rick's supposed to be making an infomercial for the store."

"Yeah, whatever. Same thing. I've just got to get out of town for a while, Julia. I can't stay here."

"What about Casey?"

"That's why I can't stay. But you don't want to talk right now."

"I *do* want to talk," Julia assured her, even if it wasn't entirely true. Susie sounded dreadful. She needed her sister. And Julia felt like shit for not being able to drop everything and hop on a downtown train to Susie's apartment this very instant. But with the estranged Joffes about to invade her mother's apartment, and her wedding at stake, she couldn't. "I'm stuck with this ghastly dinner party—"

"It's all right. Anna and I are going to check out a Jet Li flick that's playing a couple of blocks away. Unless you want me to baby-sit Adam..."

The doorbell rang. *Please, let it be Ron,* Julia prayed, moving down the hall to the entry. "Someone's here," she told Susie. "Don't leave town. I'll call you back later." She disconnected before Susie could say anything, and wondered how much later "later" would be. What if she couldn't get back to her sister until tomorrow? Susie might be gone by then.

Gone where? Making what kind of Bloom's movie? She'd given Rick the go-ahead for a low-budget thirty-minute sales pitch disguised as a television show, appropriate for YouTube. The way he and Uncle Jay had described the project, it would feature a cook talking about all the wonderful foods Bloom's sold. No one had to leave town to produce a video like that.

The doorbell rang again. She jammed her cell phone into the pocket of her slacks and opened the door. Her smile was intended for Ron, and it melted at the sight of his mother.

Julia had met Esther Joffe twice before. Neither meeting had gone well. At the first, Julia had splashed a droplet of coffee on Esther's tablecloth, which Ron assured Julia was a K-mart blue-light special, but Esther had fussed over the small stain as if Julia had destroyed a priceless family heirloom. Esther had spent most of the hour they'd sat around the table blotting at the spot with a wad of paper towels, muttering, "Don't worry about it," through gritted teeth.

The second meeting had been at Julia's apartment, when she'd invited Esther for dinner. She'd served Heat-'N'-Eat pot roast from Bloom's—transferred onto her own plates, of course—and Esther had gotten a strand of beef caught between her teeth. "It's very stringy, this meat," she'd complained. "You should talk to your butcher. Meat this stringy, it's not right." Ron had laughed off the incident, but Julia had been humiliated. At least she'd had the foresight not to tell Esther the meat had come from Bloom's. If Esther believed the store sold stringy meat—which it didn't; Julia had found the pot roast tender and tasty, and she had no idea why Esther had made such a big deal about borrowing a few inches of dental floss and clearing the shred of beef from between her molars—she would never agree to let Bloom's cater the wedding reception.

This evening, Esther had on a yellow sweater set and a flowered skirt. It was a pretty ensemble, except that yellow wasn't her color. The top clashed with her copper-colored hair, and it gave her skin a jaundiced hue which emphasized her sunken cheeks. Esther's face was all sharp angles. Ron took after her, only on him those angles looked wonderfully masculine. On his mother, they looked not so wonderfully masculine.

"Esther," Julia said, infusing her voice with as much cheer as she could manage. "Come on in! The doorman didn't signal that you were on your way up."

"He was all tangled with a woman who had four... what are they called? Those little bratwurst-shaped dogs."

"Dachshunds?" Julia guessed.

"Yes, that's it. This woman had four of them, and she was like a spider web with all those leashes. So I just came up without being announced. You gave me the apartment number. Very smart of you." She kissed Julia's cheek, and Julia made a mental note to find a mirror and check for a lipstick smear. "You're a very smart girl, Julia. I'm glad my boy is marrying a smart girl."

Gazing past Julia, she fell silent. Julia spun around in time to see her ragamuffin brother entering the hallway, chomping on a cracker topped with pâté. "Hey," he said cheerfully, padding down the marble floor in his bare feet. "You must be Joffe's mom."

"And you must be...I'm afraid to ask," she returned, inching behind Julia as if seeking protection.

"That's my brother, Adam," Julia said, aiming a fierce frown at him. "You have things to do, don't you?"

"Actually, I don't," he said, his smile gently mocking. Wonderful. Just what she needed: Adam teasing her. "This is great chopped liver," he added, lifting the uneaten half-cracker toward Julia in a toast before he popped it into his mouth. "Nice finish of garlic."

"Go away," Julia said, figuring tact would be pointless. She turned to Esther and forced another smile. "Please come into the living room. I'll get you a drink."

"Is Ronny here?"

"Not yet."

"He's always late," Esther complained, following Julia into her mother's living room, a chilly expanse of leather, chrome and glass, the décor chosen because her parents had always believed that furniture with clean, simple lines required less dusting. "You'd think a get-together like this, he'd consider it important enough to arrive on time. Evidently, no."

"Actually, you're a little early," Julia said, more to defend Ron's honor than because it was true. "And he can't help being late sometimes. He gets held up at work."

"I work and I didn't get held up," Esther pointed out. "You work, too."

"I work downstairs in this building. It's easy for me to get here." Julia didn't add that she'd left her office an hour early so she could come upstairs and fret. But as the boss of Bloom's, she could leave her office whenever she wanted. Ron didn't have that freedom. He was a magazine journalist, which meant he had to deal with a demanding editor, elusive data, and writer's block. Such obstacles didn't automatically disappear at five p.m. "Now, what can I get you to drink?"

"You got sherry? A little sherry," Esther answered. "Not too much, just a little. Say an inch." She held her fingers up in illustration; they were easily more than two inches apart.

Julia's forced smile caused an ache in her cheeks. "I'll get you some," she said, turning to find her mother sweeping into the room. The top she'd changed into was a simple knit shell in an aqua shade, which she accessorized with a silk scarf in a floral pattern, tied like a Boy Scout neckerchief. The outfit looked no better than what she'd had on earlier, but it looked no worse, either.

If she'd been wearing striped pajamas Julia still would have considered her a welcome sight. She didn't want to deal with Esther alone. "Mom! I'd like you to meet Ron's mother, Esther Joffe. Esther, this is my mother, Sondra Bloom."

Sondra crossed the room to the couch where Esther sat. Her smile looked much more natural than Julia's felt. She clasped Esther's hands, then plopped onto the sofa next to her. "What a pleasure! Isn't it wonderful, our two children getting married? I never thought I'd have such *nachus.*"

"Why didn't you think you'd have such *nachus*?" Esther asked. "You thought your daughter wouldn't get married? You thought she wouldn't find a suitable husband?"

Sondra handled Esther's negativity more deftly than Julia could have. "I always knew she was worthy of a fine man, but your Ronny is obviously the crème de la crème." That seemed to mollify Esther.

"Mom, I'm getting Esther a drink. Can I get you something?"

"Tell Lyndon and Howard to serve the drinks, sweetie. You should sit and visit with us."

"No, I don't mind." Julia wanted to get the drinks. She wanted to go back to the kitchen, where the cooking food smelled so good and no mothers were present.

"I'll have a Manhattan. Have Lyndon fix it, Julia. He makes the best Manhattans. Esther, do you want a Manhattan?"

"I'm having just a little bit of sherry. Not much," Esther leaned past Sondra to remind Julia, "Just an inch." Again she held her fingers up several inches apart.

"Get a drink for yourself, too, Julia," Sondra said.

Julia wasn't much of a drinker, especially when it came to hard liquor. Tonight, however, the idea of drinking herself into oblivion held a certain appeal.

No. She was made of sterner stuff. She had a mission to accomplish—to convince her mother and her future in-laws that Bloom's was the perfect caterer for her wedding reception. A second mission might be to facilitate a friendship between her mother and Ron's parents. A third mission might be to keep Ron's parents from plunging butter knives into each other.

Squaring her shoulders, she marched into the kitchen. "Lyndon, can you fix my mother a Manhattan? She says you make the best."

"She's right," Lyndon said without a hint of boasting. "Howard, keep an eye on the wild rice."

"What do I have to keep an eye on?" Howard shot back. "It's steaming. The pot's just sitting there."

"Keep an eye on the pot." Lyndon glanced at the assortment of liquor bottles arrayed on one of the counters, then checked the contents of the silver ice bucket. "Where does your mother keep glasses?" he asked.

Julia provided him with one stemware glass and poured two and a half inches of sherry into another.

"You want a drink?" Lyndon asked her.

"Water. I'm on a mission," she said with grim determination. "Three missions, actually."

"Uh-oh." He grinned. "Look out, Howard. She's on three missions."

"Maybe she should keep an eye on the pot," Howard suggested. "If she can handle three missions with such panache, she can certainly handle a fourth."

The doorbell rang. "What's with the doorman?" Julia muttered, wondering whether the poor guy was trapped in a web of dachshund leashes. She put down the glass of sherry and exited into the hall.

She needn't have rushed. Adam was at the door, swinging it wide. *Please, please, please, let it be Ron,* she whispered.

"I'm overdressed," Norman Joffe said.

Julia had met Ron's father only once. She and Ron had traveled to New Jersey to visit his brother, and his father had been there. Tall and thin, with a mix of silver and slate-gray hair as wavy as his son's, he'd said little, explaining that he'd had dental work done that day. He'd exerted himself to move his jaw only when the conversation settled on one of three topics: the Yankees, tax loopholes and the risk of bee stings causing anaphylactic shock. He was an accountant, so she could understand his interest in tax loopholes, and as a native New Yorker he'd probably been born afflicted by Yankee fever. But his obsession with bad reactions to bee stings had mystified her. According to Ron, he didn't suffer from allergies.

"Norman!" Julia smiled and hurried down the hall to nudge Adam out of the way. Ron's father stood in the doorway, holding a massive bouquet of flowers wrapped in green tissue paper. He wore a sport coat and khakis, and his complexion was the sort of tan she expected to see in mid-August, not the last week of May. She wondered if he'd gone to a tanning salon. She'd advise Ron to discuss skin cancer with him. "Come on in," she welcomed him. "This bum is my brother. He doesn't know how to dress properly."

"They didn't teach that at college," Adam confessed with a sheepish smile.

"Why don't you go call Tash or something?" Julia suggested. Turning back to Norman, she saw that he still hadn't entered the apartment. She cupped her hand around his elbow and pulled him inside. "These flowers are lovely."

"They're for your mother," Norman said.

"How sweet. Come, you can give them to her yourself." Her hand still at his elbow, she swiveled him away from Adam and into the living room.

"Oh, my!" Sondra gasped when she saw the flowers. "What's this?"

"For you," Norman said, extending the bouquet. His gaze collided with Esther's and his courtly smile vanished.

"You never brought me flowers," Esther complained.

"You told me you didn't like flowers."

"I had to save face." She addressed Sondra as if they were old friends. "A husband never brings his wife flowers, she has to save face, right?"

Julia's mother was too busy inhaling the delicate perfume of the blossoms to respond. "Would you like me to put them in a vase?" Julia asked her.

"Yes, and then bring them in here so we can all enjoy them."

Julia glimpsed Esther's scowl. She would definitely not enjoy them.

She carried the flowers into the kitchen. "Wow," Howard said. He'd abandoned his vigil over the rice pot to complete arranging the platter of canapés.

"Did Joffe bring you those?" Lyndon asked, a drink in each hand. "He's a good man. Marry him."

"He's a late man," Julia muttered as she rummaged in her mother's cabinets for a vase large enough to hold the bouquet. "His father brought these."

"Maybe you should marry him instead."

The doorbell rang. Julia refrained from dropping the flowers and racing down the hall to answer the door. Ron could damned well wait—or else he could deal with Adam.

Adam's voice drifted down the hall, and then he appeared in the doorway. "Grandma Ida's here," he announced.

"I knew she wouldn't like *Ferris Bueller*." Lyndon issued a grim sigh.

Julia clutched the flowers so tightly she snapped the stem of a lily. "What am I going to do?" she whispered to Lyndon.

"Set another place at the table. There's enough food."

"I don't want her here!"

"She's your grandmother," Lyndon reminded her.

"I'm bringing the hors d'oeuvres into the living room," Howard announced, lifting the magnificently arranged platter and leaving Julia and Lyndon alone to strategize.

"If the dinner is cooked and just needs to be served, I can take care of it," she whispered. "Howard can help me. You can take Grandma Ida back upstairs to her apartment, and—"

"Julia." Lyndon clamped his warm brown hands onto her shoulders and stared directly into her eyes. "Be gracious. You're the first of her grandchildren to get married."

"I've already got my mother driving me nuts. And Joffe's parents."

"So what's one more nut? Go be a blushing bride. Give your grandma a kiss and stop worrying."

Julia managed a sickly smile. "Thanks for the pep talk. But I'm never going to be a blushing bride."

"Of course not." With pats on both her shoulders, he released her and nudged her toward the living room. Once again she reminded herself that she was tough, strong, a former attorney, a company president. A Wellesley graduate. A big sister—whose little sister was apparently having some kind of breakdown and whose little brother looked like a poster child for the National Slob Foundation.

She could handle this. She handled everything. Handling things was her *raison d'être*.

Walking into the living room, she shaped another false smile—she'd had so much practice faking smiles, she was getting good at them—absently rubbed her cheek in case Esther had left a lip print on it, and headed directly for Grandma Ida, who sat at the edge of an oversize leather chair, apparently afraid the thing would swallow her if she settled too deeply into it. "Grandma," Julia greeted her. "What a lovely surprise! You'll stay for dinner, won't you?"

o

Adam couldn't remember the last time anyone had hosted a party in this apartment. Not that this gathering exactly qualified as a party. They were playing no tunes, inhaling no illegal substances, chugging no beer. No one was flirting. No one was even smiling. That phony smile of Julia's didn't count.

The food sure smelled good, though. Trying to eat like a normal person in his mother's home was more challenging than getting his honors thesis on imaginary numbers finished before the due date. Adam had grown up learning about the four food groups, but his mother had only two food groups in her kitchen: diet food and off-her-diet food. Celery sticks and Cheez Nips. Cherry tomatoes and Cherry Garcia ice cream. Fat-free yogurt and fudge.

He wanted some of that good food Lyndon and his friend had whipped up. But he didn't want to have to tolerate the company the food was intended for. If Joffe were around, it wouldn't be so bad. He was cool, and Adam was both pleased and a little surprised that Julia had found him. Before him, she'd always dated yuppie guys suffering from ego-erectus. Joffe had a healthy ego, but it seemed proportional to the rest of him.

Of course, Adam wouldn't be tolerating the company because Julia had made it very clear he wasn't welcome to join them. Maybe Lyndon could fix him up a plate to bring back to his room, where he could watch *Saturday Night Live* reruns on his laptop while he ate.

Shit. He was so bored. In the past two weeks he'd seen dozens, maybe hundreds of *Saturday Night Live* reruns featuring every cast from Chevy Chase onward. He needed something more. He needed things to do. He needed his friends.

Julia had told him to call Tash. Not a bad idea, except that it was only the middle of the afternoon in Seattle and she was probably busy liberating a dolphin or something. His ex-roommate Buddy was down in D.C., same time zone, but he'd landed an internship at the Department of Agriculture and Adam couldn't bear the thought of whining to him about how he had nothing to do.

He should get a job, but doing what? Selling shoes? Delivering restaurant take-out orders on a bicycle? Even working at Bloom's would be better than that.

He needed a job, and he needed some local friends.

Closing his eyes, he pictured a skinny, duck-toed woman with a toothy grin. He'd gotten her phone number that day at Lincoln Center. What the hell? They could have some laughs, if she wasn't busy doing whatever dance students at Juilliard did to give them those graceful hands and flexible hips.

When he opened his eyes he was smiling. Elyse, he thought. Why the hell not?

o

Ron arrived at six-forty, weary and apologetic. His editor had gotten an angry call from a Fortune-500 company whose questionable hiring practices had been the subject of Ron's business column in last week's *Gotham Magazine*. Ron had had to spend the next two hours reviewing his notes with his editor, playing the tapes of his interviews and proving to her that he could substantiate every single word he'd written, every accusation, every fucking punctuation mark.

"Don't use that language," Julia whispered. "Everyone's here, including my grandmother."

"Have my parents killed each other yet?"

"No. Your mother is drinking sherry and critiquing the quality of the living room couch's upholstery. Your father has barely said a word. He brought flowers, though."

"Why is your grandmother here?"

"She didn't want to watch *Ferris Bueller's Day Off*. Don't ask."

Ron gathered her into a hug. She could tell he was tired by the weight of his arms and the faded glow in his eyes. His kiss was slow, more warm than hot, but it reassured her. He made a sound that was half a sigh, half a groan, then pulled back. "This is going to be fun," he said, and she caught a glint of a smile teasing his lips.

His kiss had been fun. Leaving her mother's apartment after this doomed dinner party, returning to Ron's apartment and kissing him some more—even if he was so tired the kisses led nowhere further—would be fun. The hours between now and their departure were going to be excruciating.

"I liked the eloping idea we discussed," she murmured.

"We can still do that. It's not too late."

"Ronny?" Esther bellowed from the living room. "Is that you? Finally?"

"It's too late," Julia said, slipping her hand into his and leading him into the living room.

"Hi, everyone," he said, then made the rounds of the room, hugging his father, kissing his mother's cheek, kissing Julia's mother's cheek, and smiling and nodding at Grandma Ida, who shrank from him as if afraid he might try to kiss her cheek, too.

"You should have gotten here earlier," his mother carped. "This is an important occasion. We have to make wedding plans."

"Nobody's made any plans yet," Sondra said, giving Ron a warm smile. "We're just getting acquainted. Look at these beautiful flowers your father brought. Aren't they lovely?"

"It was lovely of you to invite us," Norman said. "Lovely flowers for a lovely hostess."

Julia didn't think now was the right time to mention that she'd made all the arrangements, issued all the invitations, and twisted all the arms to make this dinner party happen. If Norman wanted to think her mother was the lovely hostess, Julia wouldn't interfere.

Lyndon appeared in the doorway to announce that dinner was ready. "I don't have any help," Esther told Julia's mother as she rose from the couch. "You're very lucky, having help. I understand your husband died a couple of years ago?"

Sondra's smile dissolved into an appropriate expression of sorrow. "From food poisoning, may he rest."

"Not that it's my business, but it's nice you don't have to be all alone. You have help."

"He's my help," Grandma Ida announced. Esther looked bewildered, but she let the subject drop.

The group filed into the dining room. Julia realized that Grandma Ida's presence made the table more symmetrical. Her mother sat at one end, Grandma Ida at the other, and Lyndon deftly guided Esther to one side of the table and Norman to the other, steering them to seats that weren't directly opposite each other. "What fancy plates," Esther commented, lifting her dinner plate and tilting it to scrutinize its gleaming surface. "What is this, Wedgwood?" She flipped the plate over to look. "Royal Doulton. Very nice."

"It was our wedding pattern," Sondra said, slightly misty-eyed. "All these years, and I still love it. Julia, you and Ron haven't registered yet. Add it to your to-do list."

Julia didn't want to register for china. She had attractive ceramic dishes; she didn't need a set of expensive bone china that would take up precious cabinet space and never get used.

"What are we supposed to register for?" Ron asked.

"I'll explain it later," Julia told him.

"Your daughter has excellent taste," Norman commented, his cheeks creasing with dimples as he smiled at Sondra.

"You mean, for when she registers her patterns?"

"I mean, she has excellent taste in men."

"She takes after me," Sondra boasted. "I have excellent taste in men, too."

Julia swallowed to keep from gagging. Besides the discomfort of being referred to in the third person while she was in the room, she knew her father had been a difficult man and a less than wholly devoted husband. Her mother's taste in men was debatable.

She noticed her mother's smile was not quite so misty as she gazed at Norman. Sondra touched her hair lightly, tucked a strand behind one ear and tilted her head toward him when she made that remark about her taste in men. Was she flirting with Ron's father? The possibility was too horrible to contemplate.

Howard circled the table, filling the crystal goblets with chardonnay. "A toast to our wonderful children," Norman proposed, raising his glass.

"Can I toast with my sherry?" Esther asked, ignoring the wine and lifting her glass of sherry.

"Do you really think it matters?" Norman asked acerbically. "We're drinking a toast to the children."

"I don't like white wine," Grandma Ida said. "I'll toast without." She held up her empty hand, her fingers curled around an imaginary glass.

"To our wonderful children," Sondra said quickly, and everyone drank—or, in Grandma Ida's case, mimed drinking—before tempers could flare out of control.

Julia steered her mind back to the subject of registering. While Lyndon carried serving dishes out to the table, she pondered what she should register for. Not china, not silver flatware, but maybe some kitchen appliances. A new microwave would have features her old one lacked. A matching set of utensils would be nice, and perhaps one of those wooden blocks with the different-size knives protruding from stab-sized slits. And neither she nor Ron owned an electric eggbeater. If they ever wanted to make meringue, they'd be in big trouble.

All those items were sold at Bloom's. Would it be terribly tacky to register at her own store? Did they even have a bridal registry? If they didn't, they should. She'd have to talk to Deirdre about setting one up. Susie could do a nice article about it in the *Bloom's Bulletin*.

Assuming Susie didn't leave the city for good. Why was she running away? What was going on with her? Why couldn't she and Casey resolve things between them, one way or another? People broke up and made up all the time without leaving town. And why did Susie have to leave town to work on Rick's movie? Why did she call it a movie, anyway? It was supposed to be an infomercial. Cheap and informative and utterly lacking in cinematic artistry.

She realized Norman was holding the platter of poultry for her to help herself, and she dragged her focus back to the table. "You never told me your mother was so charming," he murmured.

She almost retorted that she'd met him only once and during that meeting, the subject of tax loopholes had dominated the conversation. She might have added that after twenty eight long years of knowing her mother, she had a better comprehension of her mother's charm quotient than he did. But she only smiled and used the two serving forks to lift the smallest hen onto her plate.

"The Plaza is very expensive," Esther was saying. "Not that I want to count pennies at a time like this, but I'm a court stenographer—a *divorced* court stenographer," she added, shooting Norman a hostile look "—and money doesn't grow on trees."

"The bride's family pays for the wedding," Grandma Ida announced.

"But the groom's family has certain obligations," Esther argued. "The liquor, for instance. Liquor at the Plaza—"

"I'll take care of it, Esther," Norman muttered.

"The way I see it," Sondra declared, "Julia and Ron will have one wedding in their lives, am I right? You don't scrimp at such a time."

"Wait a minute!" Julia held up her hands like a traffic cop trying to halt vehicles in all directions. "We're not getting married at the Plaza Hotel, so—"

"Now, Julia. We've already talked about this."

"*You've* talked about it. I've looked into some other options." She gazed around the table to find everyone watching her. Norman looked curious, Sondra impatient, Esther apoplectic, Grandma Ida surly, and Ron highly amused. Nothing about the discussion was amusing, and she resented him for finding anything to smile about at a time like this. "As you say, Mom, we'll have only one wedding in our lives. It should be what *we* want."

"*Oy, gevalt.*" Grandma Ida pressed a hand to her chest. "You're not going to have one of those weddings on Coney Island, with everyone barefoot and the rabbi rowing a boat onto the beach, are you?"

The concept had never occurred to Julia. She exchanged a glance with Ron, who shrugged as if to say, *What a great idea!*

"There are some lovely venues we can rent," Julia said. "The Explorer's Club, the Player's Club, some other townhouses. The Cloisters is available for catered parties, too, although—"

"The Cloisters? The medieval museum?" her mother asked.

"Yes. They're pretty restrictive, so—"

"That's a beautiful spot," Norman commented.

"But all those crosses and stuff." Esther shook her head. "The artwork there is very Christian. Paintings of Jesus, paintings of saints—as artwork, yes, it's very impressive. But at a Jewish wedding?"

"Still, they have lovely gardens," Norman insisted.

"A lovely garden with a big wooden crucifix? This is where you want Ronny getting married?"

"All right—forget the Cloisters," Julia said, intervening before a major war erupted between Ron's parents. "The sculpture garden at the Museum of Modern Art is another possibility. What I'm saying is, we can find a nice venue and have Bloom's do the catering."

"Bloom's! What, you're going to serve bagels and lox at your wedding?" Esther shrieked.

"What's wrong with bagels and lox?" Grandma Ida retorted. "It's better than rowboats at Coney Island."

Julia rolled her eyes—and hallucinated the oddest sight: Adam walking down the hall past the arched dining room doorway, carrying the platter of leftover canapés, and behind him a sylphlike young woman with exquisite posture, her blond hair twisted into a bun at her nape and a neck as long as Alice's after she'd eaten the cake that said "Eat Me." Who was that? Where was Adam taking her and the hors d'oeuvres?

As if it mattered. As if any of this mattered.

Elopement was sounding better all the time.

Chapter Thirteen

Susie took the elevator up to the third floor of the Bloom Building. Amazing to think that a few weeks ago she would have gone out of her way to walk through the store, just to catch a glimpse of Casey, to exchange a wink and a smile with him. Now here she was, sneaking up the back way like a coward.

She wasn't a coward. She was a mess, but cowardice had nothing to do with that.

She'd survived a long, dreary weekend, taking in two Jet Li movies, one Jackie Chan movie and a festival that her roommate Caitlin had dragged her to at a scuzzy little theater on Saturday night, featuring semi-pornographic videos of Japanese transvestite rock stars licking each other's faces, crotches and guitars. Susie wasn't sure what the videos were supposed to be about, especially since she didn't understand Japanese. Caitlin said they were called Fan Service, but as far as Susie could tell, it was the rock stars, not the fans, being serviced.

Not that she'd count herself as a fan. The videos made her painfully aware that these days, the kind of men who attracted her tended to be tall and blond, with hazel eyes.

Casey would have found Fan Service fascinating. If he'd gone with her to the festival, he would have sat up half the night with her, picking apart the videos, laughing over the sillier stunts and dissecting the music. He would have spent the other half of the night licking her in all sorts of interesting places.

Julia had phoned her on Saturday while she was out. They'd played phone tag for the rest of the weekend, until Susie realized that she could talk to Julia on Monday when she went to the third floor to work on the *Bloom's Bulletin*. She felt totally uninspired about putting together the newsletter this week; the odds of her coming up with a clever limerick were about as good as the odds of her father returning from the dead with a new recipe for gefilte fish in his pocket. But she could write up the pages of the bulletin pertaining to sales and specials at the store, interview Myron for an employee profile and spend enough time sitting at her hallway desk to make people think she took her job as Bloom's creative director seriously.

And she could talk to Julia.

Julia's door was open, and Susie entered without knocking. The office had changed since their father had occupied it. Although Julia hadn't lavished a lot of money upgrading the carpet, painting the walls a brighter shade, replacing the worn leather sofa, or removing the scratched and scuffed desk, now tucked into a corner of the small room, that their grandfather had used when the office had been his, she'd perched a few potted plants along the window sills and hung some framed prints of the Manhattan skyline on the walls. She had picked up the prints from a sidewalk vendor, and they reeked of cheap sentiment. One of them featured the World Trade Center against a violet sunset sky, obviously a play for melancholy nostalgia. Susie wished Julia would find something better to decorate her walls with. A Rocky Horror Picture Show poster, maybe. Or a mirror. Staring at herself would be less depressing than staring at the Twin Towers.

At her entrance, Julia glanced up from her desk, leaped to her feet when she saw who her visitor was, and raced over to the door to close it. This placed her within three feet of Susie—close enough to indulge in a deeply analytical inspection of her face. "You look like shit," Julia said.

Okay, so maybe staring at the Twin Towers was the happier choice.

The word shit could not be used to describe Julia. Her glossy black hair was clipped neatly back from her face, her tweedy gray pants suit looked comfortable and her eyes had the glow of a woman who'd been licked in all the right places in the not too distant past.

Julia grabbed Susie's hand and dragged her over to the battered sofa. Unlike the smooth, elegant leather furniture in their mother's living room, the surface of this couch was webbed with lines and cracks, more weathered than Grandma Ida's face. But the cushions were comfortable, and Susie was happy to sink into them.

"Tell me what's going on," Julia demanded, dropping down onto the couch next to her. "Why are you running away?"

"It's either that or get married," Susie explained, wondering if her answer sounded as ridiculous to Julia as it did to her.

"Married? To whom?

Leave it to Julia to use impeccable grammar at a time like this. "Casey," Susie said, then leaned forward and rested her chin in her hands, feeling terribly sorry for herself.

"Casey wants to marry you?"

Susie nodded.

"And you said no?"

"I just can't see it, Julia. I'm only twenty-six. When you were twenty-six you were working as a lawyer and dating that creepy Wasp guy who ate sushi all the time. I'm twenty-six and I don't know where my life is going, either."

"Don't compare yourself to me," Julia advised her. "We're very different."

"Yeah. You've got your act together. I don't even know what act I'm in." Susie dug her chin into her palms and issued a sigh deep enough to empty her lungs. Self-pity could be fun in its own perverse way. If she was going to indulge in it, she might as well enjoy it. "Ever since Casey popped the question, I've been having nightmares about picket fences and preschools and routines. *Routines*, Julia. You know what I mean?"

"I know what a routine is."

"I dream that an alarm clock wakes me up at the same time every morning, and I'm always where I'm supposed to be, and Mom talks me into getting laser surgery to remove my tattoo."

"Mom would be so thrilled if you got married, she'd probably never mention your tattoo again," Julia pointed out.

Susie didn't believe that. Until the day she died, Sondra Bloom would hate Susie's tattoo—which was one reason she'd had it done. "I have nightmares of waking up one morning and realizing I have absolutely nothing to say to Casey, because we've said everything we could possibly say to each other already," she lamented. "I have nightmares about..." She hesitated, then forced out the words. "*Doing laundry.* Once a week. The same day every week. And using bleach in the white load."

Julia grimaced.

"You have laundry nightmares, too, don't you," Susie guessed. "You dream about dryer sheets and wake up in a cold sweat."

Julia shook her head. "Actually, no."

"You don't have laundry nightmares?"

"I don't have any nightmares at all."

Susie cursed. Why couldn't her sister have nightmares? Why did she have to be so freaking perfect? "I bet your dinner party was a nightmare," Susie grumbled.

"I was awake for that," Julia argued. "It doesn't count."

"How did it go?" Susie asked. Even if it didn't count, the dinner Julia had hosted at their mother's apartment might have been calamitous enough to undermine Julia's perfect life, at least a little. Not that Susie wished her sister ill—of course not—but it was awfully hard having a sister who was perfect all the time. A bad dinner party would go a long way toward restoring Susie's ego.

Julia slouched back in the sofa and sighed. "The food was excellent. Lyndon and his friend Howard prepared a feast. Adam invited this girl over."

"He invited a girl to your dinner party?"

"They weren't at the party," Julia explained. "He just invited her over, and they ate leftovers in his bedroom."

"In his bedroom?" Susie smiled for the first time in days. "Adam had a girl in his bedroom? In Mom's apartment?"

"The door was open. They watched TV."

"Even so... What about Tash?"

"Tash is in Seattle. Adam's in New York." Julia gazed toward the window, as if a vision of Adam's dinner companion had appeared on the other side of the glass. "I don't know who this girl was, whether he knew her at Cornell, what. She was really thin and her feet pointed out. What's that called? Duck-footed? She had great posture. She held her chin up, like this." She demonstrated, pointing her chin toward the philodendron sprouting from a plastic pot on the sill.

"She sounds like a freak," Susie said. "Does she shave her legs, at least?"

"I don't know. She was wearing jeans, and I wasn't about to ask. I had my hands full as it was."

"Full of what?"

"Grandma Ida decided to join us for dinner. She was a grouch. I thought she'd back me up when I said Bloom's should cater our wedding, but she didn't. She said she didn't want to eat bagels and lox at the wedding, as if that was what we were planning to serve. Then she spent the rest of the evening being critical. She told Ron he chewed too slowly. She told his mother that yellow wasn't her color—she was right about that, but still. She told Ron's father he shouldn't have brought flowers because they might attract bugs into the house. She told Lyndon he should have made *flanken.*"

"She sounds like quite the belle of the ball," Susie muttered.

Julia wasn't done. "Joffe's mother's a kvetch. She had nothing nice to say. Joffe's father said nothing at all."

"How about Mom?"

"She's not talking to me."

"Julia?" their mother's bellowing reached them through the closed door.

"She's talking to you now," Susie whispered.

Julia groaned, shoved herself to her feet and crossed the office to the door. She opened it and Sondra Bloom swept in, her hair flying about her face and her eyes a touch too bright. "You'll never guess who just phoned me."

"Eleanor Roosevelt," Susie called from the couch.

Her mother leaned sideways to peer around Julia. "Susie! I didn't know you were here."

"I'm always here on Mondays. I have to write the *Bloom's Bulletin.* I'm the creative director, remember?"

Sondra planted herself across the coffee table from Susie and scrutinized her. "You look terrible," she said.

"Thanks." *Terrible* was an improvement over *like shit.*

"Is something wrong?"

"No," Julia and Susie said together. Just one reason why Susie loved her sister so much: she protected Susie from their mother's nosiness. "Who phoned you?" Julia asked. "It wasn't Eleanor Roosevelt, was it?"

"Of course not. Eleanor Roosevelt's dead," Sondra said, as if anyone in the room didn't already know that. Then her cheeks flushed and she smiled almost bashfully. "Norman Joffe."

"Ron's father? Why? Is there a problem?"

"No problem." Sondra's gaze widened to encompass both daughters. She touched her disheveled hair absently. "He asked me if I'd like to go out for coffee with him."

"Coffee?" Susie blurted out. Either Joffe Senior was cheap or he was out of practice. A man interested in a woman would ask her out for a real drink, not coffee.

A man interested in a woman? Wait a minute. This was their mother they were talking about. Their mother and Ron's father.

"You're kidding," Julia said, going very pale.

"Why would I kid about something like this?" Sondra sounded almost giddy. She touched her hair again, then clasped her hands together in front of her. "What should I wear?"

"What do you usually wear when you drink coffee?" Susie asked.

"Did he ask you out on a *date*?" Julia's face was rapidly losing its last traces of color.

"He asked me for a cup of coffee. It's not a date." But the way Sondra preened and fluttered, she clearly thought a cup of coffee was more than a cup of coffee.

"When?"

"Saturday morning at ten."

"That sounds like a date," Susie said.

"It's not a date," Sondra insisted, her voice rising into coloratura range.

"It's a date," Julia said glumly.

"It's coffee. We'll drink coffee and discuss the wedding. That's all." She turned to Susie. "Norman was so generous about wanting to contribute to the cost of the wedding. Of course there are things the groom's side is supposed to pay for—the liquor, the flowers, the rehearsal dinner..." She ticked items off on her fingers and stared at the ceiling, trying to conjure a list. "What else, Julia? The band? I don't remember. And presents for the ushers, of course."

"How many ushers is he going to have?" Susie asked.

Julia looked exasperated. "Who the hell knows? His brother will be the best man. Other than that, he doesn't tell me anything."

"Well, just as long as the ushers like bagels and lox," Susie said, her spirits more buoyant than they'd been in days. She was a rotten human being, allowing her sister's obvious angst to cheer her up. But there it was.

"The menu hasn't been settled yet," Sondra said firmly. "Well, I've got a few days to figure out what to wear. Nothing fancy, of course. It's just coffee."

"You might order a croissant," Susie pointed out. "Then it would be more than just coffee."

"No croissants," her mother responded. "They're too fattening. Do you think I could lose five pounds by Saturday?"

"No," Susie and her sister chorused. "Don't even think about it," Julia added. "You look fine. And as you said, it's just coffee."

"Right. Black coffee. No cream, no sugar, no calories. Susie, I'm worried about you. You really look lousy. Who's cutting your hair these days?"

"The same guy at Racine who cut it when you said it looked fabulous," Susie told her. "I've got my period, that's all." She didn't, and even if she did it wouldn't make her look lousy. But she wanted to end her mother's interrogation before it gained momentum.

"Mom, Susie and I have to go over the material for this week's bulletin," Julia said. "I'm thrilled beyond words that Norman wants to discuss the wedding with you over coffee. But I've got to get these details worked out with Susie."

"Fine." Sondra seemed too elated to mind that Julia was blowing her off. She leaned over the couch and gave Susie a bruising hug, then hugged Julia, then pranced out of the office.

Julia followed her as far as the door, shut it and leaned against it, her eyes closed and her cheeks the color of library paste. "Oh, God. I can't believe this."

"What?"

Julia's eyes snapped open. She stared at Susie, evidently appalled that Susie wasn't as appalled as she was. "Mom and Ron's father? I'm going to be sick."

Instead of vomiting, however, she stalked to her desk, lifted the phone receiver and punched in a number. Susie figured that if Julia had wanted privacy for the call she'd have asked for it, so she kicked her feet up on the coffee table and settled in to eavesdrop.

"Ron? It's me," Julia barked into the phone. "We have a disaster.... I know you're working. I'm working, too. Do you think I'd call you if it wasn't a disaster?... Okay, in this particular instance, I'm calling because we have a disaster. Your father asked my mother out for coffee." She held the receiver away from her ear; Susie heard Joffe's muffled voice through the plastic. She couldn't make out the words, but she could guess they were pungent.

"Well, she's a widow and he's divorced," Julia said into the phone. "And neither of them is in possession of a single cell of functional gray matter.... So talk to him. Tell him coming on to your future mother-in-law is not a wise idea.... No, *you* talk to him. He's your father.... Why? Who the hell knows why? She hasn't been on a date since my father died. That's two years. And your father showed up with that damned bouquet of flowers. The woman is obviously having a midlife crisis."

Julia listened a bit more, then exhaled wearily. "Okay. We'll strategize tonight. I've got to go now. My sister is here. I've got to solve her crisis, too.... Right. 'Bye." She hung up.

"You don't have to solve my crisis," Susie said indignantly, although deep down she'd be overjoyed if Julia would do that.

"I don't even know what your crisis is," Julia said, collapsing into her desk chair. It had been bought for their father, who, while not a huge man, had been nearly half a foot taller than Julia. The chair dwarfed her. Her feet didn't quite touch the floor.

"I don't have a crisis," Susie fibbed.

"You called me Friday and said you're leaving town."

"That's not a crisis. That's an opportunity."

"And you're having nightmares about picket fences and alarm clocks. I think you should go into therapy."

Susie couldn't tell if Julia was joking. She decided she didn't care. "I like Casey. I probably even love him. I just don't want to marry him. Is that a crime?"

"So don't marry him."

"He gave me an ultimatum. Either we go forward or we quit."

"So quit."

"But I like him."

"And you probably even love him." Julia shook her head. "Days like today, I miss working at the law firm. I only had sixty-hour work weeks then, doing tons of tedious doc reviews. It was a piece of cake compared to this." She moved her arm in an arc that encompassed her office. Her hand landed on a folder on her desk. "Here are the sale items for this week's bulletin. Are you planning to quit that, too?"

"The *Bloom's Bulletin*? And give up my fancy title, all that power, all the perks? No. I can do the bulletin while I'm away and email it to you."

"How long are you going to be gone?"

"I don't know. It depends on Rick's production schedule."

"Rick." Julia mouthed a curse and pinched the bridge of her nose. "Another disaster. What kind of movie is he making? It's supposed to be a glorified advertisement."

"It'll promote Bloom's."

"He's planning something elaborate, isn't he." Julia scowled. "Something with explosions and simulated sex."

"It's about food," Susie promised. "I don't think there's any sex in it."

"Does he have a script?"

"He has...a concept."

"Shit." Julia shook her head. "I never used to curse this much. Running Bloom's has given me a bad case of potty-mouth."

"Maybe Joffe did that," Susie said.

"Ron gives me many things, but potty-mouth isn't among them." She slumped against the high back of the chair and eyed Susie wearily. "The only good thing about your running away to work on Rick's movie is that you'll be able to keep an eye on him. Will you do that? Will you keep the movie on track?"

"I don't know," Susie said cagily. "That kind of responsibility...maybe you should give me a raise."

"Maybe I should give you a kick in the ass. You want your fancy title and your perks, you'll make sure he makes a movie we can get some mileage out of. Uncle Jay talked me into giving him a twenty-five thousand dollar budget. I want my money's worth—and it better not be artsy-fartsy dreck."

"I'll do my best," Susie promised.

"Okay. Now, what about Casey?"

What little pleasure Susie had experienced from witnessing Julia's torment over their mother's hot date with Joffe's father vanished. What about Casey? She liked him. She loved him. They'd broken up because she wouldn't marry him. Julia's *tsurris* with the wedding plans and their mother's hot date were nothing compared to the sharp, stabbing pain Susie felt whenever she thought about Casey.

"Will you solve my crisis?" she asked plaintively.

"There's only one way to solve your crisis," Julia told her. "Figure out what you want, and then go for it."

Susie snorted at the simplistic advice. "Thanks. Everything's clear now."

"What do you want me to say?" Despite her stern tone, Julia rose from her chair and crossed to the sofa. She looped her arms around Susie. "There's no easy answer. If you were ready to get married, you'd get married. You're not, so you won't."

"Even if it means losing Casey?"

"Figure out what you want, Susie," Julia repeated. "If you don't want to lose Casey, figure out a way not to lose him."

"This is getting a little too Zen for me," Susie protested. "I already know a way not to lose him—marry him. If I do that, I lose myself."

"*Om*," Julia chanted.

Susie laughed, which was almost as good as having her crisis solved. "Okay, I'll write your stupid newsletter," she grunted, shoving to her feet and moving to the door. She swung it open in time to see Casey entering the reception area.

Chapter Fourteen

He'd come upstairs to check with someone named Helen on the status of his Bloom's pension. Helen was some sort of administrator. He'd never met her—she'd been hired a few months ago, when Susie's sister had decided that the company needed to be run a bit more like a company—but he'd received a few chirpy, impersonal memos from her: "Hi! I'm Helen, the new office administrator. If you have any questions, let me know!" She never promised to answer those questions, but her memos had made an impression on him, all those happy exclamation points.

Mose had suggested that he find out just how much money was stashed in his pension account, and how much he could get his hands on. He'd also suggested that if Casey chose to be so unrealistic that he wouldn't at least consider opening his bread boutique in Queens, he could find himself another advisor. Also another best friend.

Because best friends were hard to come by, Casey had spent most of the weekend convincing himself that setting up shop in Queens made a lot of sense. It would mean a shorter commute, for one thing. And a shorter commute meant more time to practice his shots on the court. His three-pointer still hadn't come back to him.

The downside of opening a business in Queens was that his parents would stop by all the time. They wouldn't buy anything—they'd complain that his breads were too expensive, not a surprising observation from people used to buying two-day-old loaves of white bread from the half-price rack at the supermarket. But they'd come in to see how he was doing. His father would lecture him on the opportunity he'd let slip through his fingers when he'd failed to capture the boss's daughter, and Casey would remind him that Susie was the boss's sister and his father would forget and refer to Susie as the boss's daughter again before the conversation was over. His mother would pass him the phone numbers of unmarried lay teachers at the local parish school and assure him he was better off finding himself a good Catholic girl. His sister might mosey in, too, between dog grooming appointments. She'd tell him the very concept of a bread store was pretentious, and then she'd pass him the phone numbers of unmarried lay teachers at the local parish school.

But the upside was that he could afford Queens. Depending on how much money was in his pension account.

Susie worked on the third floor most Monday mornings. That fact had slipped his mind today, though, because she hadn't pranced through the store to say hi to him, something she always used to do on Mondays except for those days that began in Queens because she'd slept over at his place Sunday night, which she could have been doing every night if she'd moved in with him.

When he hadn't seen her in the store that morning, he hadn't given her absence any extra thought, because she was absent from his entire life. That particular truth occupied a large chunk of his brain at all times, like a chronic sinus infection, achy and impossible to ignore.

He saw her standing in the doorway of her sister's office. She appeared pallid to him, her hair lacking its usual shine, her eyes circled in shadow, her maroon T-shirt and short black skirt hanging on her like laundry left on a clothes line too long. Hell. It didn't matter how drab she appeared. Ever since the first time he'd seen her a year ago, when she'd stepped up to the bagel counter and he'd had no idea who she was, he'd loved looking at her.

If he opened his store in Queens, he might never see her again. That might be a plus.

"Casey," Julia said, giving him a warm smile. If Susie had been smiling, her smile would have been as warm as a glacier on the darkest day of winter. Fortunately, she wasn't smiling, so the only frostbite he felt came from her eyes and the tension in her mouth.

"I was just leaving," Susie said abruptly.

"I've got to see Helen," Casey said, not sure which Bloom sister he was telling this to.

"You two have to talk," Julia announced, overruling them both.

"Julia..." Susie glared at her.

"You want me to solve your crisis? Fine, I'll solve it. You two have to go somewhere and talk."

"Where should we go? My office?" Susie snorted. Her "office" was a desk that jutted out of a wall in the broad hallway that doubled as a reception area. No way would Casey hang out in the hallway with her while they had this talk Julia was demanding.

"You can use my office," Julia said magnanimously, stepping through the door and beckoning Casey with a wave.

He didn't want to use her office. He didn't want to talk to Susie. He wanted to jump her bones, he wanted to hear her say he was right and she was wrong and she was sorry for being such a stubborn bitch because she loved him with all her heart and wanted to spend the rest of her life with him. But other than that, he didn't want to talk to her.

Julia stood beside her open door, arms folded, smile growing smug. "Come on, Casey. She won't bite."

"How do you know?" he shot back. In the heat of passion, Susie could get a little carried away.

"In you go. Into the office." Julia addressed him as if he were a three-year-old afraid to climb into the bathtub. He eyed Susie, who had backed deep into the office, leaving him a wide berth. Resigned, he crossed the threshold. Julia shut the door behind him.

He'd been in this office before, but never with the door closed and never alone with Susie. His gaze circled the room in search of a safe place to sit. The sofa didn't look too promising. Julia's desk chair—well, that would be overstepping. Maybe he should just remain standing.

Susie moved to the sofa and sat. "Julia can be so bossy sometimes," she said.

"She's the boss. It comes with the territory."

"You're pissed, aren't you."

"Who, me?" he said sarcastically. "Why should I be pissed?"

"I can't marry you, Casey." Her eyes sparked with energy. "I just can't. I can't live in a house with a picket fence."

"Who said anything about a picket fence? I've got an apartment on the fourth floor of a mock-Tudor building. Not a picket fence in sight."

"You know what I mean."

Actually, he didn't. About a third of the time, he had no idea what Susie meant. That had always been part of her appeal.

She looked small and vulnerable seated on the sofa by herself. If he joined her there, he'd probably regret it. But he couldn't bear the sight of her hunched over, her hands cupping her cheeks and her eyes so big and wistful.

He'd done stupid things before. What was one more stupid thing? He walked over to the sofa and sat down beside her, leaving a couple of feet of space between them. "I don't know what we're supposed to talk about," he said. "We're at an impasse."

"This is what's so great about you," Susie said, tilting her head to peer at him. "You're a bagel designer, but you use words like 'impasse' in casual conversation."

"Is this a casual conversation?"

"Caitlin took me to this movie Saturday night. It was really a series of videos, of androgynous Japanese rock stars licking each other."

Her non-sequitur threw him momentarily. "Androgynous is a bigger word than impasse," he finally said.

She cracked a smile. A small one, but enough to remind him of how much he wanted her in his life. "What did you do Saturday night?"

"Nothing worth mentioning." At her questioning look, he elaborated. "Nothing at all."

"Can't we just go back to the way things were before?" she asked plaintively.

He thought about it, thought hard. Thought about the way things were before. Long, tiring subway rides between her place and his. Sleeping with her in the living room of her apartment while her roommates slept

167

in the bedroom, and rushing through sex in case one of them wandered out to get a glass of water. Or Susie at his place, whining about how Queens was too quiet and boring. Endless phone conversations, trying to figure out where to meet, where to go, where to end the night. Too many nights ending alone.

When he was eighteen or twenty or twenty-four, he wouldn't have minded. He was twenty-seven, though, about to start his own business and ready to stop being a kid. He'd asked Susie to join him as he ventured into this new stage of his life, and she'd said no. How could they go back?

He shook his head. A large tear rolled down her cheek, big enough to dissolve everything inside him. He'd never seen her cry before. "Come on, Susie. Don't."

"I want to be with you, Casey. I just don't want to marry you. Why is that so hard for you to understand?"

Because it made no sense, that was why. Because when people wanted to be together, the easiest, most efficient way to go about it was marriage. Or at least living together, creating a home, making a commitment.

But she was crying, and he had to do something. Aware that it was a huge mistake, but unable to stop himself, he arched his arm around her. The space he'd carefully left between them disappeared as she slid toward him and leaned against his shoulder.

She didn't erupt into full-fledged sobs. It didn't matter; the damage had been done. He had Susie in the curve of his arm, pressed up against him, and the possibility of his ever letting go of her seemed absurdly remote.

She nestled into him, apparently as content to be held as he was to be holding her. And damn it, her head was too close, her hair brushing his chin. All he had to do was tip his face down to kiss the crown of her head.

"Casey," she whispered, angling her face up so he could kiss her mouth instead. He did. Joy blew through him like a hot wind. Too many miserable days had passed since he'd last kissed her—and that time, they'd been standing on the stairway landing, and the kiss had gone nowhere because she'd said no.

She was going to say no again, but for just this one minute he could pretend things were different. He kissed her as if his existence depended upon it, as if his life was riding on the pressure of her lips and the jabs of her tongue. He kissed her as if they were in an inflatable lifeboat on a stormy sea and their kiss was necessary to keep the boat from deflating. He kissed her as if she'd said yes.

She sank back until she was lying on the couch, and pulled him down with her. At another time, he might have had second thoughts about sprawling out on top of her on an old sofa in his boss's office. But right now he was still sailing along in that little inflatable dinghy, the yes boat, and he didn't care.

He felt her hands between their bodies, working the knot holding the waist tie of his apron shut. His own hands roamed her body, petite but strong, every curve and surface as familiar to him as the house he'd grown up in. When he reached her skirt he kept going, groping for the hem and shoving it up her legs. She abandoned the waist tie of his apron and pushed the front flap up. It bunched between their bellies, but that wrinkle of fabric didn't feel anywhere near as uncomfortable as the hard-on pressing painfully against his fly.

Her fingers reached for his zipper. "Susie," he warned.

"I know," she mumbled, then kissed him again and slid the zipper down.

Once again, he had no idea what her words meant. But he had a pretty clear idea what she was doing with her hands, and he couldn't find it in him to resist. He wedged a finger inside her panties and she was so wet he nearly came just from the feel of her.

"I know," she said again, wiggling her hips to help him strip off her panties. Once they were down to her knees, she contorted one leg until it slid free of the leg hole, then shoved Casey's jeans down past his butt and pulled her to him.

One of the greatest moments in his relationship with her had occurred on New Year's Eve, after they'd left some weird nightclub in Alphabet City and returned to her apartment to discover neither of her roommates was back from Times Square yet. They'd appropriated the bedroom, locking the door so Anna and Caitlin couldn't barge in on them, and stripped naked, and when he'd reached for a rubber she'd said, "Casey, we've been together for so long. I'm on the pill, and I'm not screwing around, and I don't think you are, either. I trust you." And he'd made love to her, skin to skin, human to human instead of penis to plastic.

They were human to human today, Casey to Susie, two lovers who'd been apart for too long. It was hot, it was fast, his damned apron and her skirt were in the way, he hadn't even touched her breasts, and she was already coming before he found his rhythm, her amazing body pulsing around him, every spasm daring him to let go.

He did. No sense going for style points. This was a desperation fuck, and that realization smacked him as fiercely as his own climax—and as suddenly as a vision of babies. For the first time since she'd told him to stop using condoms, he imagined making a baby with her. He imagined that baby being born—his blond hair, her dark eyes, tiny but with big feet, indicating the potential for basketball-star proportions by the time the kid had passed through adolescence. He imagined Susie nursing their baby. and he imagined himself playing with it, and changing its diapers, and pushing a stroller on long walks with his wife through Flushing Meadows Park...and going home to a house surrounded by a picket fence.

He got it now. He understood what Susie meant. What she feared was exactly what he wanted. The whole thing, the constancy, the security, the knowledge that everything that mattered most to him could be found safely inside that picket fence.

She was breathing heavily and running her hands aimlessly through his hair. He lifted himself slightly so he wouldn't crush her, and gazed down into her face. She looked wary, perhaps even a little scared.

"You really want to give this up?" he asked her.

"No. You do." Her voice wavered, but she remained dry-eyed.

"I don't want to give this up," he argued. "I want this all the time."

"You want sex in my sister's office all the time?" She propped herself on her elbows and he pushed back onto his knees. His jeans and briefs were clumped around his thighs, making his legs feel stiff and clumsy.

Susie swung her feet around, plucked her panties from her ankle and put them on correctly. Casey pulled himself together, too. He'd never before had sex in an apron. He wondered if it qualified as kinky, then thought about some of the other times he and Susie had had sex, the situations, the positions. Sex in his apron wouldn't even make the top ten.

He smoothed his shirt into his jeans, then smoothed the apron down over it. His prick was damp, his balls twingeing. He couldn't bring himself to look at her.

"Julia said we had to talk," Susie reminded him.

"So talk."

"I'm leaving town for a while," she said. Her voice sounded wobbly again, hesitant, almost teary.

She was leaving town. He didn't bother to ask how long "a while" was. *Good-bye* was all he had to know.

"I'm going to help my cousin make a movie."

Her cousin was flakier than phyllo pastry. Running off to make a movie with him was the exact opposite of a picket fence.

"I don't want to go," she admitted. "I mean, I do want to go, I think it'll be an interesting adventure. Maybe we'll rent a truck."

He couldn't think of anything to say. *Bon voyage? Have a good life? Take another little piece of my heart?*

"But I don't want to leave you. I just feel..." She sighed shakily. "I feel like I don't have a choice."

"You do have a choice," he disputed her.

"Not the choice I want."

"Okay." He felt his emotions leaking out of him like hydraulic fluid out of an old car engine, leaving behind a collection of dry, rusting metal. "Go and make a movie." He stood, gave himself a minute to make sure his legs were steady and strode to the door. He wanted to look back at her, one last glimpse. But it would only hurt.

So he opened the door and walked away without turning.

Chapter Fifteen

Susie wound up renting the same Truck-a-Buck van—the one with the blood stains on the door—that she and Julia had rented for Adam's graduation weekend. She saw this as some sort of sign; she wasn't sure of what. Maybe a sign that Truck-a-Buck had a very small fleet of vans available for rent.

She and Rick had loaded up the back with video equipment, two suitcases, and—rather ominously—sleeping bags and a tent. Susie had inherited Rick's brother Neil's sleeping bag when she'd left for college, but she'd never used it for camping as her Aunt Martha had thought she would. Mostly she'd used it for sleeping on other people's floors. Camping seemed awfully quaint in a world where roofs, electricity, wall-to-wall carpeting and indoor plumbing were relatively easy to come by. But Rick had suggested that they bring camping gear with them, just in case, and Susie had been too chicken to ask just in case *what*.

She'd driven the first leg of the trip, through New York and Connecticut and across the Massachusetts border, where she and Rick had pulled off at a Mass Pike rest stop in a little building that looked like a Walt Disney World set for *The Crucible*. After using the facilities and stocking up on maps and vending machine snacks—pretzels and corn chips for Rick, M&M's and a chocolate-covered granola bar for her—they traded positions. Rick took the wheel and Susie settled into the seat that Grandma Ida had occupied on the drive to Cornell.

Sunglasses perched on her nose, legal pad propped on her knees, Susie tore open the wrapper of her granola bar, took a lusty bite and assured herself that it was a healthful snack, despite its chocolate coating. All those oats and nuts and fiber inside...surely that had to count for something.

She didn't like the limerick she'd come up with for the next *Bloom's Bulletin*. Rhyming "sweet" with "treat" was such a cliché. But the theme of the limerick was desserts, and "meat" just wouldn't work. The store didn't sell anything with feet still attached, and anything with feet would probably qualify as meat. She could use "Heat-'N'-Eat," but the "Heat-'N'-Eat" products were all entrees, not desserts.

But it was too late to worry about the limerick anymore. She'd sent the text of the upcoming bulletin to Julia's work computer last night, and while she could probably squeeze under the printer's deadline if she emailed Julia a new limerick tonight, she lacked the inspiration. The rhymes she came up with for sweet sucked: discreet, deplete, beat. Why torture herself? Why torture Julia?

She decided to work on the film script, instead. Rick had diagramed a bunch of scenes and shots, but when Susie had skimmed his working script yesterday, she'd discovered it alarmingly lacking in words—specifically, the words she was supposed to say on camera. "You can write that part," Rick had told her. "You know what you want to say."

She couldn't begin to guess what she wanted to say. "Tell me again why we're going to Maine," she asked.

Rick rolled his shoulders in a lackadaisical shrug. "Food," he said.

She wished he sounded a bit more definitive. She wished he knew what the hell he was doing. While she was glad to be out of the city, riding in a truck, cruising along the Mass Pike, whizzing past fir trees and speed limit signs and SUV's with "Live Free Or Die" New Hampshire license plates on them, or Red Sox bumper stickers, or Harvard decals, she couldn't shake her apprehension about this trip.

At least one positive thing would come out of it: having more distance between Casey and herself. She couldn't believe they'd banged each other on the couch in her sister's office. More than that, she couldn't believe it had been so easy to have sex with him. She couldn't believe it had felt so natural. She couldn't believe it had satisfied such a deep hunger, one she'd refused to acknowledge until that encounter on the old leather couch.

Sex wasn't everything. It was a hell of a lot, of course, but there had to be more for a relationship to matter. With Casey, of course, there was more, a lot more: laughter and ideas and empathy, trust and shared tastes, companionship and comfort. She and Casey were out of sync, though. Their dreams didn't mesh—and dreams were much more important than sex.

She took another bite of her granola bar and let the chocolate melt on her tongue, gooey and sweet, with just a hint of bitter. Thank God for chocolate. When a woman had to go without sex, chocolate was like methadone—the next best thing.

"So what kind of food is in Maine?" she asked, perusing the camera shots Rick had outlined as if they were supposed to make sense to her.

"Lobster," Rick said.

"We can't use lobster in this movie!"

He glanced over at her, his eyes obscured by his Ray-Bans, his hair clamped down beneath a baseball cap with a Daffy Duck appliqué stitched onto it. He wore fraying cargo shorts, and a T-shirt depicting a heap of empty Budweiser cans and the caption "Cans Film Festival." Around his neck a camera lens hung on a lanyard. He'd started wearing the lens necklace right after he finished college. Susie wasn't sure what purpose it served, other than to announce to the world that he was a pretentious cinéaste.

"Why can't we use lobster?" he asked, turning back to the road.

"Lobster is *trayf.*"

"Oh, like anyone cares about that," he said with a snort. "Like Bloom's is *glatt* kosher."

"It's not *glatt* kosher," Susie said. "They sell meats that aren't kosher. They sell cheeses just one aisle over from the meats, so yes, Ricky, it's possible for a person to enter Bloom's empty-handed and emerge with a salami and cheese sandwich. But you can't put lobster in this film. Lobster isn't just something you can't eat with cheese. It's something you aren't supposed to eat at all."

"You eat lobster."

"Yeah, if someone else is buying." Susie loved lobster, but who could afford it? "I'm not kosher."

"Bloom's customers aren't kosher, either."

"But the store is kosher-*style*. Have you ever seen them sell a lobster in there? Or even a lobster salad? Even a teeny tiny little shrimp? Has clam chowder ever been the soup du jour?"

"Shit," Rick muttered, then shot her another look. "I was figuring on filming down on Cape Cod, doing something with clams."

"You can't," Susie said firmly. If nothing else, she would protect Julia's investment in this film. Protecting it meant not letting Rick depict Bloom's as a store that sold non-kosher delicacies. "People have this image of Bloom's as the kind of place Jews go to," she explained. "Wizened old Jews named Hymie and Rivka. Feisty, loud-mouthed Jews who run unions and vote straight Democratic, no matter what. Yuppie Jews who haven't been inside a temple since their bar mitzvah, but now they've got a baby and they want to return to their roots."

"Lots of non-Jews shop at Bloom's," Rick argued.

"Of course they do—because they want that Jewish-ish experience."

"Jewish-*ish*?"

"You know what I mean. They don't want to go to some orthodox shul and watch men in prayer shawls *daven* for four hours on a Saturday morning. They just want some bagels. They consider it exotic."

"What does this have to do with lobsters?" Rick asked.

Susie had to think a minute, to remember where the discussion had started. "If you put lobsters into the Bloom's Stone Soup, it's going to make the place seem less Jewish-ish. It's going to undermine the store's identity."

"Okay. Fine." Rick brooded for a minute. "Can we use potatoes?"

"Potatoes are kosher."

"Great. Maine is full of potatoes."

Susie wrote *potatoes* on the top yellow sheet of the pad. He was going to use potatoes. Did he have even the slightest clue of what he was going to use them for?

This road trip was a mistake. Susie's entire life was a mistake. She should have been Julia, the mature and sensible Bloom daughter, the sort of woman who, faced with the option of attending law school or getting a tattoo, would never choose the tattoo. If Susie were more like Julia, she could be planning her wedding right now, instead of fleeing to Maine with her crackpot cousin to make a movie about potatoes.

Of course, Julia was halfway to meltdown planning her wedding, so that was no bargain.

Crackpot, Susie thought. *Crockpot.* "Instead of soup, I think we should make Bloom's stew."

"What's the difference?"

"Stew is thicker," Susie told him. "Beyond that, the word resonates as a metaphor."

"A metaphor for what?"

"I don't know, but it resonates." She wrote *stew* on the pad. Potato stew? It sounded so bland. She took another bite of her granola bar, just to remind herself what flavor was all about.

"Okay, so stew." Rick pondered the word. "So we'll start in a potato field. I thought a seaside shot would have been great—real picturesque, you know? Waves rolling in, a breeze, marsh grass, and you'd be saying something like, 'Lobster. It's great, with or without drawn butter.'"

"I'd never say anything like that. I don't even know why they call it 'drawn' butter. What's it drawn from?" She shook her head. "I'd probably say something along the lines of how ugly lobsters are. I mean, what could have possessed the first person who ate a lobster? He pulled this ugly green beast out of the ocean. The normal reaction would be to throw the thing away, and he'd probably still have nightmares about it for a few days. Instead, this mook tosses the thing into a pot of boiling water, and when it turns red he pulls it out, cracks the shell open and discovers it's pretty tasty."

"Yeah, and thinks to dip it in drawn butter, too," Rick added.

"It's just weird. If you didn't know what a lobster was, would you eat it?"

"If you didn't know what a potato was, would you eat it?" Rick countered. "They grow in the ground. They're dirty and lumpy and gray. How did they figure out baked potatoes were the way to go?"

"Yeah, or latkes," Susie said, jotting notes. This was a promising concept. "Imagine the first person who made a latke. Grating the potato, adding egg and onion and what else?"

"How should I know? I've never made latkes."

"Neither have I."

"You're a girl." Rick grinned. "I thought girls were supposed to know how to make latkes."

She decided not to let him provoke her. "Flour, I think. Or matzo meal. I could phone Lyndon and ask him to ask his friend Howard. Lyndon and Howard aren't girls, and they know how to cook things."

"Speaking of girls, how's Anna doing?" Rick asked, his tone so casual Susie knew he was intensely interested.

Susie sighed. She truly hoped this expedition wouldn't turn into a how-can-I-get-Anna-to-like-me marathon. "You've had a crush on her for, what, two years? Get over it, Rick."

"Why? What does she have against me?"

"Nothing. She likes you. But there's no chemistry."

"She hasn't seen my lab," he said. "Is she dating anyone else?"

Susie weighed whether to be honest or helpful. Helpful would entail nudging Rick in a new direction, helping to wean him from his Anna obsession. But she couldn't lie to her cousin. "She goes out sometimes, but nothing serious."

He relaxed visibly in his seat. "I love her hair. It's so long."

Susie ran her fingers through her cropped chin-length hair. That was such a guy thing, loving long hair. Susie had worn hers long for a while, and it had been a pain, always getting snarled, catching in the hinges of her sunglasses, taking forever to dry after a shampoo. She'd also tried a punkish cut, very short, around the time she'd gotten her tattoo. But dykes had kept coming onto her, so she'd grown it in a bit. She liked the length it was now. She'd had one of the stylists at Racine give it a trim yesterday so it would look fresh for the film. She'd even contemplated having the film's budget pay for the haircut, but twenty-five thousand dollars wasn't much. They had to make it last.

Casey liked her hair the way she wore it. He'd probably like it long, too. Or buzz-cut short. That was the problem with him—he cared more about the woman than her hair. Why couldn't he be a shallow jerk like Rick? Then Susie wouldn't be missing him so much.

Damn. They'd barely reached the New Hampshire border, and she was already missing him, languishing like a Gothic heroine with consumption. Thinking about the way his hands felt in her hair caused a sharp twinge in her chest, and a softer twinge lower down. She missed him. He was the greatest single straight guy on earth, or at least in New York, and she'd walked away from him. Run away. What was wrong with her?

Potato stew. The words stared up at her from the pad. That was her life—starchy, soggy, and of indeterminate taste. Casey was the finest chocolate, not this stale granola bar, not a bag of M&M's but sinfully rich Godiva. And Susie was a lobster—ugly, wrapped in a shell and distinctly unkosher. Potato stew had to be easier to digest than a lobster-and-chocolate combination plate.

Chapter Sixteen

"So what are we going to do about our parents?" Julia asked Ron.

He bent over to peek through the window in the microwave, which was wedged into the few square inches of counter space between the fridge and the coffee maker in his cramped kitchen. "Heat-'N'-Eat something?" he asked, straightening up and sliding off his old tweed blazer. He wore T-shirts or work shirts and jeans to work, but usually with a jacket. He'd once explained to Julia that the jacket was his nod to professionalism.

She happened to know that his real nod to professionalism was the brilliant weekly business column, his blog, and the occasional feature articles he wrote for *Gotham Magazine*. But jackets flattered him. They flattered him even more when he removed them. "Heat-'N'-Eat stuffed cabbage," she told him, trying not to ogle him as he closed in on her by the sink, where she was transferring the mixed-green salad she'd brought home from Bloom's onto two salad plates. "Your favorite."

"Who needs a wife who can cook when you've got one who runs Bloom's?" he teased, wrapping his arms around her from behind when she turned from him.

"Well, lucky you. You're going to wind up with a wife who runs Bloom's and can't cook. Don't evade my question. Your father is taking my mother out tomorrow. What are we going to do?"

"He's taking her out for coffee. And we aren't going to do anything."

"The whole thing just seems...icky."

"It's not icky. They're two unattached adults. What, do you think we should chaperone them?"

Actually, that wasn't a bad idea. But if Julia said so, Ron would laugh at her. He had a habit of not taking things as seriously as they ought to be taken. Like the catering for their wedding, or this potential romance between their parents.

They couldn't chaperone their parents' coffee date. They would be spending tomorrow checking out three different wedding venues. Finding nice sites that would allow her to provide her own catering had proven a challenge, but she'd scheduled visits at a private mansion in Greenwich Village, a loft in Chelsea and another mansion on the Upper East Side. She also wanted to check out some locations in Central Park, even though liquor was prohibited from wedding receptions there.

If only she'd knuckled under to her mother, she could have reserved a banquet hall at the Plaza and left the catering and liquor to their in-house service. It would have been easier. But damn it, she was the president of Bloom's. If only she could fit a hundred fifty people into her apartment or Ron's, she'd host the party herself.

They could probably fit a hundred fifty people in her mother's apartment, if they set up some tables in the bedrooms. But her mother would never allow that. Her brother's son Travis had had his bar mitzvah at the Plaza, after all. Sondra Bloom couldn't be shown up by her own brother.

Grandma Ida, though... Her apartment was just as big as Julia's mother's, clean and cheerful in a Depression-era sort of way. If they trimmed their guest list down to a hundred, they could fit the wedding there. But with Grandma Ida, one never knew what she'd say or do. She might agree to have the wedding at her place and then change her mind after the invitations had been sent. Or she might insist that the doorman be invited, since she'd known him for decades and made several donations to the Puerto Rico Statehood and Freedom Brigade at his request.

The microwave dinged. She concluded that Ron loved Bloom's stuffed cabbage more than he loved her, based on his speed in releasing her and racing to the microwave to remove the food. She smiled, admiring his tight butt in his snug-fitting jeans and thinking, for not the first time, how amazing it was that fate had brought them together.

How did love triumph, anyway? She'd dated such a variety of losers—rich losers, struggling losers, handsome losers, selfish losers. With another woman, some of those losers might actually be winners, but with her they'd been duds. She'd never felt comfortable with them, never felt completely like herself. She'd never looked at their butts and fantasized about skipping dinner and dragging them to the bedroom.

She entertained that little fantasy now, but didn't act on it. If the dinner menu had been hamburgers or peanut butter sandwiches, Ron would have gladly allowed himself to be dragged. But...she just didn't want to test her hypothesis and hear Ron say, "Not tonight, dear. I've got stuffed cabbage."

Ron pulled a couple of beers from the fridge, popped the caps off the bottles and set them down on the tiny table crammed into a corner of the room. He and Julia had to sit at right angles from each other, because there wasn't enough room to pull the table out of the corner, but the mere presence of that table qualified the room as an eat-in kitchen. Julia's kitchen was so small, she'd had to situate her dining table at one end of her living room. If they had their wedding in her apartment, they could accommodate Susie, Ron's brother, and maybe Adam, period. "Sorry," they'd have to tell their parents, Grandma Ida, and all the aunts and uncles. "We'd love to invite you to our wedding, but there's no room." They could exchange vows, serve a brunch of bagels and nova, bialys and creamed herring, mimosas made with fresh-squeezed orange juice and coffee made with fresh-ground beans, and not have to worry about her mother flirting with his father, Uncle Jay bragging about how wonderful he and his sons were, his wife Wendy being prettier than the bride, and Aunt Martha and Esther Joffe forming a first-wives club and trying to stab people with butter knives. No *sturm und drang* at the wedding. Just siblings.

Actually, that sounded like a lovely idea.

"So, did Susie get off all right today?" Ron asked.

Maybe it wasn't such a lovely idea. Susie was in the middle of some *mishegas*. "Yeah," Julia said, then took a sip of her beer. "She and Rick are on their way to fame and glory." She sighed.

"You don't want them to find fame and glory?"

"I want them to make a commercial video for the store. Maybe a pilot for a Bloom's cooking show. Something that'll hype Bloom's. Why they have to schlep all the way to Maine to do this is beyond me."

"Maybe studio rentals are cheaper in Maine."

"Maybe." Julia didn't know much about studio rentals, or movie-making in general. She'd lopped fifteen thousand dollars off the cost estimate Uncle Jay had provided for her, partly because Uncle Jay wasn't always the most reliable person when it came to spending money and partly because his estimate was based on what Rick had told him and Rick was even less reliable. Even so, she'd handed over a nice chunk of change from the company's promotion budget, and she wanted something to show for it once the money was spent. Susie had promised to keep an eye on Rick and his expenditures, but how close an eye could she keep on them when she was in the midst of her *mishegas*?

"You know what?" Julia said. "My family is driving me crazy."

Ron laughed. "There's a news flash."

She took a bite of her stuffed cabbage and instantly felt better. The sweet tang of the sauce, the crumbly texture of the chopped-beef-and-rice stuffing, the slippery, sour jacket of cooked cabbage leaves—it was tasty enough to soothe her. Doctors ought to prescribe it for their stressed-out patients.

Swallowing, she gazed up at Ron. He was still laughing. Not quite benignly—he didn't do benign—but more gently than she would have expected. "It's not your job to fix everything," he reminded her. "If your mother and my father screw up, that's their business. If your sister and your cousin screw up, Bloom's is out some money, so chalk it up to a bad investment and move on."

"My sister's not just screwing up," Julia explained, acknowledging her a-number-one worry on a long list of worries. "She's broken up with Casey, and she's miserable about it."

"It's not your problem," Ron insisted.

"Of course it's my problem! Casey works for me, and Susie is my sister. I love her and she's in pain."

"Who caused that pain?"

"Casey? Or maybe she caused it herself. I don't know," Julia reluctantly admitted.

"Then let her deal with it." He forked a hefty chunk of stuffed cabbage into his mouth, chewed, swallowed, and sighed contentedly. "You're the president of Bloom's, not the president of the Blooms. Relax. Let them clean up their own messes. Find something more important to worry about."

"Okay," she said, returning his smile. "I'll worry about where we should have our wedding."

o

Adam ought to have felt miserable, or at least something other than pleased. For one thing, he faced the dreaded prospect of sitting through a ballet. For another, he was supposed to be in love with Tash. For yet another, thanks to Elyse, he'd wound up with a summer job he didn't want.

But in spite of it all, he was pleased.

He'd called Elyse that morning to see if she wanted to grab a movie with him. "I've got a class," she'd said.

"What class? It's summer. Doesn't Juilliard close in the summer?"

"Dancers don't get summer vacations. It's like a sport. If you don't work out every day, you lose everything."

He'd wondered what exactly she would lose if she took a day off. Her flexibility? That delicate way she had of holding her hands, her slender fingers slightly arched and her knuckles arranged at precise angles? If she went a week without a workout, would her head hang, her chin sag, her neck shrink?

If she wouldn't go to the movies with him, he'd have no one to go with. Everyone in the world had something to do during the day, except for him.

"If you'd like," Elyse had added, "I've got tickets to a free dress rehearsal at the New York State Theater this evening. It's a ballet troop from Brazil. They're really good."

A really good ballet troop equated to a really sweet lemon in Adam's mind—intriguing, if you happened to like sucking on lemons. But he'd agreed to meet her outside the theater at Lincoln Center at six-thirty so they could catch the dress rehearsal. She could watch the dancers prancing and mincing. He'd watch her.

Which brought him to the second thing that should have made him miserable: Tash. They'd emailed back and forth, but as soon as he turned off his laptop, she vanished along with the icons on his monitor. According to her emails, she'd participated in three protests since arriving in Seattle, one against the World Trade Organization, one against loggers and one against manufacturers of stuffed animals, which, according to Tash, objectified and anthropomorphized animals, enabling people to forget that animals were in fact feral and not adorable beings who existed solely to amuse and comfort humans. Adam had spent the first six years of his life intensely attached to a stuffed koala named Koko, and he considered this new cause of Tash's less than compelling.

He'd thought he would be spending the summer pining for Tash. Sure, he was horny, but when he thought about sex, he thought about a sylph-like woman with blond hair that he'd never even seen loose—she always wore it twisted into a little blob at the back of her head—and limbs like willow branches, and her toes always pointing outward. Maybe he was unfaithful, maybe he was disloyal, maybe he was just a shallow piece of shit, but Tash wasn't front-and-center in his fantasies anymore.

He climbed the steps to the plaza at the heart of Lincoln Center, thinking he ought to be pissed as all get out not only because he was going to have to sit through this ballet dress rehearsal but because Elyse's inability to go to a movie with him, combined with his abject boredom, had convinced him to ride the elevator from his mother's apartment down to the third floor of the Bloom Building to talk to his sister Julia that morning. "I really don't want to work at Bloom's," he'd said, not the best way to begin an employment interview.

"So get a job somewhere else," Julia had advised him. "I'm sure other places are hiring."

"What's the point of working other places? It would be the same kind of work—stocking shelves, running a register, whatever. No one's going to give me a real job knowing I'll be leaving for Purdue at the end of August."

"Well, summer jobs are what they are," Julia had said. "You don't get to run Goldman Sachs for ten weeks and then skip off to grad school."

He still couldn't quite get past seeing his sister sitting at their father's desk, doing their father's job. She was Julia. He'd grown up with her. He'd showered in a bathroom filled with her fancy soaps and scented lotions. He'd heard her ear-shattering shrieks when some boy did or didn't call her in high school. He'd shared whispered jokes with her during Passover Seders, and he'd once caused her to choke on matzo from laughing too hard. She'd tattled on him for getting green ink on the living room rug and for stealing and eating all the Hanukkah gelt, three mesh bags filled with gold foil-wrapped chocolate coins that their parents had given, one apiece, to each child. She'd also covered for him when he was sixteen and had gotten shit-face drunk at a classmate's Christmas party while she was on her winter break from law school. She'd kept him from waking their parents—he'd been blitzed enough to see nothing wrong with bellowing "Joy to the World" at two in the morning, but Julia had muzzled him, gotten him washed and out of his clothes, cleaned up the kitchen sink when he'd barfed into it, helped him brush his teeth, and tucked him into bed, all without their parents ever finding out.

So it had been unsettling to see her, dressed neatly if not too formally, enthroned in their father's big leather swivel chair, running Bloom's. Even more unsettling to ask her for a job after he'd adamantly insisted he would not be working at Bloom's this summer.

"Do you need money?" she'd asked.

"Money's nice," he'd conceded, then shrugged. "I'm bored. I need to do something." *While Elyse is in her ballet classes,* he'd almost added, but he hadn't been quite ready to admit to that.

"I can find something for you," Julia had promised. "You could restock shelves. Work inventory. You'll get to use the price gun."

Oh, joy. The price gun. "Sure," he'd said.

"Okay. You can start Monday. Go see Helen."

"Who's Helen?"

"Our new administrator."

"I didn't know we had a new administrator."

"I've made some changes," Julia had said.

Making some changes wasn't always a bad thing, he reminded himself. If Julia could hire a new administrator for Bloom's, surely Adam could renege on his pledge not to work there this summer. And surely he could spend an evening watching people in leotards tripping around a stage on tiptoe and fluttering their hands. It wasn't as if there were any movies he was dying to see, anyway.

He spotted Elyse standing near the doors to the State Theater, on the southern edge of the plaza. The horizon still held a few traces of waning light, and the fountain spewed arcs of silver water into the air. If he were a romantic type, he'd consider the setting very romantic—the fountain, the first few evening stars poking through the sky, and a graceful babe with outstanding posture and pretty blue eyes watching for him. He quickened his pace; she spotted him and smiled.

He smiled back.

The Bloom's Bulletin
Written and edited by
Susie Bloom

A fellow in need of a treat
Came to Bloom's to pick up something
sweet.
He ate like a slob, 'cause
He loved those Bloom's babkas
And the rugelach couldn't be beat!

Welcome to the June 3rd edition of the *Bloom's Bulletin*. Mother Nature is turning up the heat—and Bloom's is ready! Browse through our frozen-foods departments. You'll find delicious, nutritious fruit pops (made of 100% fruit juice, no sugar added), frozen yogurt, and yes—rich, creamy ice-cream with a high enough butterfat content to send your cardiologist screaming into the night. Go ahead—eat, *bubbela*! Enjoy! Also make sure to check out our delicious summery salads, prepared fresh every day: fruit salads, mixed-greens salads, potato salads, pasta salads, all guaranteed to bring your cardiologist back home again.

Fill your belly and feed your head! Thanks to the success of our first "Booking the Cooks" program, Bloom's will be instituting a variety of lectures and classes. Coming up over the next two months: Glynnis Montebello will speak on "Napkin Origami" and teach attendees how to fold napkins into boats, flowers, swans, and crowns, the perfect way to dress up a table for a festive dinner party. Nutritionist Larry Glick will present "What Color Is Your Brunch?" He will explain what the colors of foods indicate about their nutritional value. Sami Gorshan will repeat his fascinating talk on Middle Eastern cuisine and politics, "Couscous and Kiss-Kiss—Breaking Bread as a Path to Peace." Child psychologist Jana Popowitz will give a talk called "Eat Your Peas—Healthful and Hug-full Strategies For Feeding Your Child." Check page four for times and dates.

In the spring, a woman's fancy... turns to chocolate. Specials on imported chocolates this week. Perugina, Lindt, Toblerone, all at prices guaranteed to start your cardiologist screaming again. Indulge!

Did you know...
We often use the word "lox" in reference to smoked salmon. However, lox isn't smoked salmon at all. It's salmon that has been cured in salt brine. In the 19th century, curing salmon from the Pacific Northwest in salt helped to preserve it for the long cross-country railroad trip to New York. In the early years of the 20th century, immigrant Jews loved lox because it was inexpensive and kosher whether served with dairy or meat. Smoked salmon offered a less salty alternative to lox. Smoking techniques developed in Europe for Atlantic salmon were imported to New York, also in the early 20th century, and the milder smoked salmon eventually eclipsed the heavily salty lox in popularity. No one knows who invented the combination of a bagel,

cream cheese, and lox or smoked salmon—but whoever it was should have won the Nobel Prize.

Employee Profile:

You may never have seen Myron Finkel, but he's as much a Bloom's fixture as the cash registers, the cold-cuts counter and the showcase windows. Myron has served three generations of the Bloom family as the store's in-house accountant. He started his career here as a fresh-scrubbed graduate of City College when founders Ida and Isaac Bloom ran the place, and remained when Isaac and Ida handed over the reins to their son Ben. After Ben's death two years ago, Myron was on hand to help the store transition to new leadership under Ben's daughter, Julia.

Known for his bowties and his passion for Bloom's cranberry bagels with strawberry-flavored cream cheese—"All that pink, it's so *pink!*" he enthuses—Myron is a native New Yorker who currently makes his home with his wife Muriel in Co-op City. "It's a long subway ride," he says, "but not so long that a Heat-'N'-Eat dinner goes *kaput* on the ride home."

Myron knew nothing about the food industry when he first started working at Bloom's. He considers himself a modest expert now. He's learned why some cheddar cheeses are more expensive than others—"It has to do with the age of the cheese, mostly. Plus the kind of milk used, and where it was made," he explains. To be sure, he knows more about cheddar cheese than computers. "I got my start on adding machines and that's what I like," he says. "I feel comfortable with them. Computers? They freeze on you. I never once had an adding machine freeze on me. I did have one that the multiplication key sometimes got sticky, but wiggle the key a little and it always came unstuck."

Besides eating cranberry bagels, Myron's greatest joys are playing with his grandchildren, balancing his checkbook, and working at Bloom's. "We're all family," he says. "I'll never retire."

Wise Words from Bloom's founder Ida Bloom: "Horseradish is God's way of telling you he's stronger than you are."

On sale this week: cracked-wheat crackers, pimento-stuffed olives, acidophilus milk and more! See inside for details.

Chapter Seventeen

Eva had a kind of Halle Berry thing going. Her hair was short, with tufts pointing in all directions like a shag rug after someone ran a vacuum cleaner over it. She had more curves than Halle Berry, which Casey didn't mind, and round eyes, and her skin was the color of lightly-done toast. Mose had told Casey that LaShonna had told Mose that she thought Eva would be perfect for his newly unattached buddy.

She wore a simple dress with a scoop neck. A gold cross dangled on a slender chain just above her bosom. For that alone, Casey's mother would consider Eva an improvement over Susie. His mother seemed to think that if Casey fell for a Catholic girl, his lust would lead him back to church. Fat chance.

In any case, he doubted he would fall for Eva. Her assets notwithstanding, her voice contained an unpleasant whinnying quality, and she loved telling knock-knock jokes and laughing uproariously over them, and she was drinking one of those weird, chic cocktails that bore a distant relationship to a martini but glowed a neon green that strained his eyes and was served in an odd-shaped glass, and she'd never seen a Jackie Chan movie in her life and couldn't imagine why she should. Like LaShonna, she seemed to have set her sights on snagging a businessman on his way up. Apparently LaShonna had told her Casey was an entrepreneur. Eva hadn't been able to hide her disappointment when Casey had explained that he was a bagel specialist hoping to open his own gourmet bread shop.

Still, she was being a good sport about this blind date, and Casey supposed he could be a good sport, too, even though a large chunk of his brain had been hijacked by Susie. He had no idea where the hell she'd gone—but wherever it was, she'd taken a significant piece of him with her, leaving him incomplete and off-balance.

LaShonna had dragged Mose out to the dance floor, abandoning Casey and Eva at their dark little table against the wall. A retro spinning-mirror ball strafed them with floating dots of light, and the club smelled vaguely of beer and peppermint and assorted perfumes. Casey nursed his Killian's Red while Eva nursed her neon-green whatever, and he scrambled for something to talk about while she bounced her shoulders in time with the music.

"I'm sorry," he said, acknowledging what those shoulders were telling him. "I'd ask you to dance, but I'm really a lousy dancer."

"Nobody's a lousy dancer," she argued with a smile. "Some people are good dancers with lousy attitudes, that's all."

"My attitude has two left feet." He smiled apologetically.

She stopped twitching her shoulders, apparently resigned that he wasn't going to take her out on the dance floor. "So tell me, Casey—is that some kind of a nickname?"

"Is what some kind of a nickname?"

"Casey. Is that a nickname or something?"

He took a deep breath and prayed for patience. He'd never had to suffer through small talk with Susie. From the first, their talk had been—well, not necessarily big, but interesting. Never this getting-to-know-you crap, this poking and probing on issues that were ultimately irrelevant.

His name, for example. "My name is Keenan Christopher," he told Eva, then added, "Junior."

"Wow, that's a mouthful. Keenan Christopher Junior? Imagine if you were in big trouble at home and your mama had to call you on it. 'Keenan Christopher Junior, I've got a mind to thrash your butt!' Yeah, that would sure scare a naughty little boy. How'd you get from Keenan Christopher to Casey?"

"The initials," he said. At her perplexed stare, he broke it down for her. "Keenan starts with K. Christopher starts with C. KC. Casey."

"Oh. Okay. Wow. Yeah."

One of his molars began to ache—purely psychosomatic. Really, there was nothing wrong with Eva. She seemed like a nice person, and she was attractive, and...

God, he missed Susie.

"So how come Mose calls you Woody?"

"From the movie," Casey explained, willing his fingers not to drum out their tension against the table top.

"What movie?"

"*White Men Can't Jump.*"

"Never saw it," Eva said.

Great. She didn't watch Asian martial arts films and she didn't watch *White Men Can't Jump*. "The two main characters are this white guy and a black guy who hustle folks playing basketball. Mose calls me Woody because the white guy is played by Woody Harrelson, and I call him Wesley because the black guy is played by Wesley Snipes."

"Wesley Snipes," Eva purred. "Now that's one fine looking man. Well, I guess I'm relieved. When Mose called you Woody, I thought maybe he was referring to your anatomy or something."

Casey swallowed, but a laugh escaped him anyway. Were all blind dates this bizarre? Was the bizarreness due to Eva or him, or the two of them together, combining in a particularly strange way?

"Knock, knock," Eva said.

Casey tried not to cringe. "Who's there?"

"Woody."

"Woody who?"

"Woody-who like to bite my ass?" Eva laughed so hard she snorted, sounding like Mr. Ed suffering an asthma attack.

Casey laughed, too, partly out of politeness and partly because Eva's laughter was so awful. "That was pretty good."

"I just made it up," she boasted. "Right on the spot. Now tell me more about this store you're opening," she demanded. "I just can't believe it's all gonna be nothing but bread."

"Well, bread, bagels, rolls—gourmet carbs," he explained. She stared blankly at him. "I think there's a market for it."

"People eat bread, I guess," she said dubiously. "A classy place, though—you should open it in Manhattan."

"I know." At last, something they agreed about. He took a slug of beer and leaned forward. The deejay was playing loud hip-hop, and Casey had to narrow the distance between Eva and himself if he had any hope of her hearing him. "I'd love to open it in Manhattan, but the rents there are way out of my price range."

"Manhattan is the cool borough. People in Manhattan would spend money on boutique bread. In Queens, people spend money on Catholic school tuition and Mets tickets."

True. "But people are more homebodies in Queens," he argued, trying to convince himself as much as her. "They're more likely to eat at home, and to eat well-rounded, well-prepared meals."

"That's what you want? Homebodies?" Eva sniffed contemptuously. "If I was opening a store, I wouldn't want homebodies shopping in it. Did Mose tell you I'm working toward a real estate license?"

Casey felt his eyebrows climb toward his scalp. "No, he didn't mention that." He'd told Casey that Eva had attended Queens College with LaShonna and currently worked in a cubicle at an insurance company, and that she did flamboyant things to her fingernails— they were polished a glittery purple hue but otherwise pretty tame, Casey thought; his sister put teeny dog decals on her nails, so it took a lot to impress Casey, manicure-wise—and that the odds of scoring with her on the first date were about thirty/seventy, maybe thirty-five/sixty-five. Mose valued precision.

Casey had no intention of scoring with Eva on the first date. For one thing, he preferred to know a woman well before he slept with her, and for another, he wasn't too thrilled about having to go back to donning the old form-fitting latex sleeve. Which was actually just another way of admitting that he wasn't ready to sleep with another woman so soon after Susie had walked out on him.

Scoring, schmoring, as Susie would say. Mose had neglected to tell Casey the most important stuff about

Eva: she liked to dance, she didn't know who Jackie Chan was, and she was studying to be a Realtor.

He sipped some beer, then leaned forward again. "Does that mean you have access to rental information for stores?"

"I've got MLS," she told him. He must have looked the way she'd looked when he mentioned Jackie Chan, because she elaborated. "Multiple Listing Service. It lists all the properties in an area for sale or rent. You can access the MLS and find out what's on the market. Now, what you need, not that it's my business or anything, is a chic place for this bread store, an address that would make people willing to spend lots of money on bread. If it was my store, I'd want it to be the chic-est bread store in the city. I'd want movie stars who just happened to be in town, you know—doing a talk show or maybe filming some scenes from their next big movie—to drop by and pick up a few rolls. Of course, movie stars can't eat rolls. Too many calories." She shrugged. "I'd want it to be the kind of place where the Knicks would do their carbo-load before a game, or the mayor would grab some biscuits, or some famous fashion designer would want to be seen. I'd want Jay-Z buying his pumpernickel from me."

"Is there a store in your MLS that would guarantee me that kind of business?"

"No guarantees, Casey-Woody Junior. But I bet I could find you some storefronts to look at in Manhattan. Downtown in a funky neighborhood, you might get a decent rent."

"How far downtown?" he asked. Jay-Z wouldn't buy his pumpernickel in City Hall Plaza, would he?

"I'm thinking Lower East Side, Alphabet City, down around there."

Susie's neighborhood. Christ. He'd be selling pumpernickel to Jay-Z and Susie Bloom.

He couldn't let her determine where he would set up his store. She didn't want to be in his life, so fine— she could buy her damned pumpernickel somewhere else. She could pick up bread at Bloom's when she was doing her third-floor stints there. For all he cared, she could suck on stale pizza crusts at Nico's.

"So, how do you access MLS?" he asked.

She smiled seductively. "You want to come on up and see my iPad?"

If he went on up, her iPad was all he'd want to see, especially after she snorted another equine laugh. He would have to play the scene carefully to keep her from being insulted over his refusal to see anything else. He would have to convince her he was a gentleman who wanted to know her better before he shifted his attention from her laptop to her lap.

He wouldn't be lying if he said that, either. Who knew what might happen if he and Eva got to know each other better? He might give her some laughter coaching. She might lose the gold cross. They might catch a Jet Li flick and she might like it. Never say never.

And in the meantime... "Yeah," he said, "I'd love to see your iPad."

Chapter Eighteen

"I'm feeling really stupid," Susie complained.

Rick adjusted the tripod slightly higher, then checked the videocam's screen. He wished he could be working with a real camera and film stock. But given the puny budget Julia had provided for his project, that wasn't going to happen.

To save money, he and Susie were sharing a motel room. The motel they'd found had resembled an Infidelity Inn, each room opening directly onto the parking lot. Their room was walled in pink plastic vinyl textured to resemble paneling. The window overlooked the parking lot, and the sill resembled a scene from a housefly version of *The Killing Fields*. Susie had screamed when she'd opened the blinds and discovered the carnage, at least a dozen dead flies lying feet up along the ledge. Rick had given them a quick burial in the toilet.

They'd eaten dinner last night at a restaurant across the parking lot from the motel because they'd been given discount coupons for the place when they'd checked in. He wasn't sure what he'd been expecting—lobsters, maybe; they were in Maine, after all—but the cuisine had seemed more suited to Arkansas. Chicken-fried steak? Hush puppies? In *Maine*?

The waitress had called all her customers "Hon" and the background music had included a lot of songs with lyrics about loyal dogs, dirty lowdown cheats and what a great country America was.

Okay, so he didn't have a gazillion-dollar budget. He wasn't doing this film the Stephen Spielberg way. He couldn't afford to give his star her own trailer and stylist. He couldn't dawdle on this shot because the only lighting he had to work with was what Mother Nature was kind enough to provide, which that morning was a lemon-white watered-down sun that made Susie look as if she was suffering from hepatitis.

But damn it, he was going to make his movie. And she was going to make it with him, because she'd said she would. Everything would be great if she'd only stop whining.

Even though she didn't have a trailer and a stylist, Susie evidently intended to behave like a prima donna. As her director, he'd have to humor her. "What's the matter?" he asked gently, when what he really wanted to ask was, "Are you on the rag or what?"

"Well, I'm standing in the middle of a potato field," she said.

He hoped it was a potato field. This early in the summer, before the crops began ripening, every field looked like every other field to him. For all he knew, she could be standing in a corn field or a pumpkin field or a zucchini field. He was a New Yorker. What did he know about agriculture?

"That's a great opening line," he remarked, hoping to encourage her. She'd scribbled, read to him, and crossed out a lengthy list of opening lines last night, her voice arching from her bed to his. All her opening lines had sounded better to him than anything he could have come up with. He was a director, not a scriptwriter. Susie was the writer in the family, so he deferred to her.

"I'm standing in the middle of a potato field in Maine," Susie repeated, apparently unaware that Rick had hit the record button. "And I'm holding a potato—" she lifted her hand to display the potato they'd purchased at a supermarket across the street from the motel "—and, I mean, what am *I*, Susie Bloom of Bloom's in New York City, doing in the middle of a potato field in Maine?"

"What are you doing?" Rick asked.

"I'm thinking..." She stared at the oblong spud in her hand. "I'm thinking I know more about latkes than I do about raw potatoes."

"Tell me about latkes," Rick urged her.

Her eyes sharpened on him. She must have realized that he was taping her. A sly smile caught her lips. "Latkes are what potatoes were born to become," she said. "Latkes are high in calories, high in salt, high in fat—and a life without latkes is not worth living."

He didn't know if she was ad-libbing, and he didn't care. "What about knishes?" he called to her.

"Knishes are fine. Knishes are delicious." She shoved absently at the droopy sleeves of her black mesh sweater. She also had on slim black jeans. The black looked striking against the soft, new green of the plants sprouting around her, even if it accentuated the yellow undertones of her skin in the faded morning light. "The thing about a knish is you can eat it on the move. It's like a hot dog only with less protein and a greater chance of causing heartburn—depending on the hot dog, of course. Latkes, though... You sit down and eat them off a plate, with a fork. They're part of a meal. You need sour cream or apple sauce to dip them in. You're with family. Maybe it's Hanukkah or some other holiday. Latkes represent a lot more than knishes."

"How about potato salad?" he cued her.

"How about it? Bloom's has the classic kind, with mayo and celery and hard-boiled eggs cut into it, and an herbed red bliss potato salad with a wine-vinegar dressing. You like potato salad, you'll like what Bloom's has." She sighed, tossed her potato into the air, caught it one-handed, and glared at him. "Jesus. I sound like some over-the-hill actress doing commercial spots because I need the money."

"You're not doing it for the money," Rick said. "I'm not paying you."

Her glare intensified. "No kidding."

"Remember that poem you wrote last night?"

"The potato poem?"

She'd penned it during the eleven o'clock news. She'd emerged from the bathroom, clad in a baggy T-shirt and moaning over the lack of a hotel-supplied hair dryer, then plopped herself onto the center of her bed, grabbed the legal pad and scribbled furiously. When he'd asked her what she was writing, she'd said, "A poem about potatoes." He hadn't been sure whether she'd been joking; her tone had been drenched in sarcasm.

Apparently, she *had* written a poem about potatoes. "You want me to read the poem in the film?" she asked. "Now?"

"Yeah. I'll edit it into the right place later."

She shrugged, then dug into a pocket of her jeans and pulled out a sheet of yellow legal paper folded multiple times. She flattened it out, squinted at it, and read:

*"Potato. Hard word, T's and P's, un-
yielding vowels.*
*Hard food, hard skin, long buried, soil
clinging.*
Who was the first person
To cook a potato? Who thought
*To toss this rock, this gray rock into the
fire,*
*To break through that skin, to eat the
molten heart?*
*Heat releases the potato from its hard-
ness,*
Smooths it, soothes it,
Melts raw starch into comfort.
Potatoes hug us from the inside. They
Live within us. Sustain us. Assure us.
Fill us, fuel us, sometimes fool us.
They are the root of all."

Rick didn't quite get poetry, but Susie's poem sounded terribly profound to him. It would make a great voice-over. *The root of all.* Pretty cool.

He recorded some long, panning shots of the field, a concrete shed in the distance, rolling hills in the greater distance. When he was done, Susie, her crinkled paper, and her potato joined him back at the van. "That was good," he told her.

"What does it have to do with Bloom's?"

"Trust me," he said, because he lacked a better answer. For him, movies always came together in the end, in the editing. Sure, he wrote out a shooting script. He usually designed a story board. He had vivid ideas of what he wanted to appear on film. But the meaning never rose to the surface until he could run his movie through the computer and get everything into some sort of order.

"I trust you," Susie said dubiously. "Julia doesn't. Are we going to show knishes and latkes in the film?"

"Absolutely," Rick said, making a mental note to include some shots of knishes and latkes. "Maybe even blintzes, too. Let's find another backdrop and we'll tape some stuff on blintzes."

"Potato blintzes are boring," Susie muttered, climbing into the driver's seat and tossing her potato behind her into the tangle of video equipment and camping gear. "Cheese or fruit blintzes are much better."

"We'll segue into that. We can start with potato blintzes, then move onto blueberry blintzes. What we need is a blueberry farm." He wedged his camera and tripod behind his seat, then opened a map. "I'm pretty sure they grow blueberries around here somewhere."

She leaned over the gear stick to study the map with him. It showed the Maine coast, lots of red and blue lines—interstate highways and rural routes—and counties outlined in dotted brown, and islands swimming in the ocean. Shadings indicated mountainous areas, and Baxter State Park and Acadia National Park appeared as emerald patches against the beige background.

Nowhere did the map indicate the location of blueberry farms. The GPS on his phone might duplicate this map, but it wouldn't show where the blueberry farms were, either.

Of course, nowhere did the map indicate potato farms, but they'd found this one. Rick gazed out the windshield at the tidy rows of foliage, wondering whether they might in fact be blueberry plants. He didn't think so.

"Crank her up," he said, gesturing toward the ignition key. "We'll find a blueberry patch somewhere."

Susie pursed her lips and started the engine. "Somewhere. Sure. Tell me again: I'm supposed to trust you?"

"Don't be nasty," he said as she steered down the narrow asphalt lane. "I mean, what's wrong? We did some excellent filming this morning." He fingered the fuzz on his chin, his own private proof that the movie was going to be fine. He never shaved during a project. Just as baseball players had their routines—spitting on their palms, fingering their St. Christopher medals, banging their bats against their cleats—to bring luck and improve their performance at the plate, Rick also had his rituals. While working on a film, he didn't shave, he avoided chewing gum, and he wore briefs instead of boxers. He'd established the chewing gum rule after a very early exercise in a film class had come out all jittery because he'd been chomping on a wad of bubble gum while the camera had rested against his cheekbone. The briefs had been the brainchild of a psychotic but brilliant professor of his who'd sworn that film makers had to restrict their sexual appetites so all their ardor would pour into their art. Rick didn't have such a wild sex life to begin with, but he figured briefs were more restrictive than boxers. As for not shaving, it saved time, so what the hell.

"Did Anna ever mention my beard?" he asked Susie as she steered down the ruler-straight row, passing more agricultural fields.

"Not really."

"What do you mean, not really? She sort of mentioned it?" He hoped he didn't sound too eager.

"Actually, no. She never mentioned it."

"What does she think of me, Suze? Does she absolutely hate me?" He braced himself, although he considered the odds of Susie answering yes pretty slim.

"No, she doesn't hate you."

"Then why won't she hook up with me?"

"There's a long distance between not hating someone and hooking up with him," Susie pointed out. "Where am I driving, Rick? Give me a hint."

"Keep going straight. We're going to hit a main drag in another mile or so." He gazed at the map, not really seeing it. "I mean, because I really like her."

"I know you do." Susie lifted her sunglasses from the dashboard and slid them up her nose. "She knows you do, too."

"And she doesn't want to hook up with me." He sighed. It seemed to him that the distance between not hating and hooking up was immense. In miles, that distance would take him from Maine well past Manhattan. Probably all the way to Alaska.

"She likes you, Rick. She thinks you're fun. She also thinks you're a cheapskate and a mooch."

"Me?" Indignation seized him, even though he had to admit Anna was right. "I can't help it that I'm always broke."

"Sure you can. You could get a job. Do you think I waitress at Nico's because that's my career goal? I want to write poetry. I want to explore the world. I need money to live, so I wait tables at Nico's."

"Whoa, slow down," he urged her. Just ahead, looming on the road's shoulder, was a gigantic lobster, faded red. "I've got to get a shot of that."

"You can't put lobsters in the movie," she warned.

The hell he couldn't. Somehow, some way, he was going to find a place for that lobster in his film. "Trust me," he said as she slowed the van to a halt. He unbuckled his seatbelt and reached behind him for the camera. Then he got out of the van and shot that sucker, up, down, and from every side. The lobster itself was about six feet long, perched on its tail atop a cement base that added another two feet to its height, and it was one of the ugliest pieces of fiberglass roadside art he'd ever seen, paint peeling from the claws, chips flaking from the shell and one feeler noticeably shorter than the other. He was half in love with it. He wished there was some way to bring it home with him.

He pressed gently against it. It rocked and teetered. Hunkering before it, he realized that the cement base was eroded pretty badly. He straightened, hugged his arms around it and gave a tug. It came loose.

"Oh, my god!" Susie yelled through the open door. "What are you doing?"

"We can use this lobster, Suze. It's perfect." A leitmotif, he thought, a recurring image throughout the movie.

"First of all, you can't just take it. That would be stealing. And second of all, it's a lobster. We already had this discussion, Rick. You can *not* use a lobster in the movie."

"First of all," he shot back, "I'm not stealing it, because I'm going to leave some money for it." He lugged the lobster, which was fairly light despite its bulk, around to the rear of the van, swung open the doors and set to work pushing things around to clear a space for it. "And second of all," he shouted forward to her, pausing to pull five twenties from his cash stash in a pocket of his duffel, and an envelope from another pocket, "it's a kosher lobster."

"What the hell does that mean?" Susie had climbed out of the van and marched around to the rear, so she could glower at him up-close-and-personal. "There's no such thing as a kosher lobster."

He took a moment to jot a note on the envelope—
and really, the statue had to be worth significantly less
than the hundred bucks he was leaving. He sealed the
money inside the envelope and wedged it into a crack
in the cement base. Then he returned to the van to
continue wiggling the lobster into place inside.

"Since when do you give a rat's ass about kosher?"
he asked.

"Since Julia asked me to make sure you made a
good video."

"I'm going to make the best damned video in the
history of the medium," he bragged, already tired of
Susie's negativity even though they'd spent less than
thirty hours together since they'd departed from New
York City yesterday. If she was going to be so pessimis-
tic and cranky, he was going to unleash his ego. Film
directors had enormous egos. It was a requirement. He
could out-diva her, any day of the week.

"Most videos suck," she argued. "So what are you
saying? Yours is going to suck less?"

"Mine is going to be brilliant."

"Yeah, right. A six-foot plastic lobster. Real brilliant."

"It's the root of all," he said, quoting from her
poem.

"The root of all bullshit," she grumbled, stomping
back around to the front of the van and taking her seat
behind the wheel.

He finished shoving equipment around and eased
the door shut, careful not to slam it and accidentally
damage the lobster's tail.

Kosher lobster, he thought as he circled back to
the passenger seat. Why not? This video *was* going to
be brilliant. And Susie could stuff a sock in it.

"How much money did you leave?" she asked as
he strapped himself into his seat.

"A hundred bucks."

"A hundred bucks? What are you, crazy?"

"No. And I'm not such a cheapskate, either. You can tell Anna."

"Julia told me to keep an eye on our budget. A hundred bucks for a fake lobster?"

"A hundred bucks is nothing. You know how much money James Cameron spent on the china alone for *Titanic*? And all that china did was slide off the shelves and shatter when the boat sank. Our lobster—" he glanced back to make sure the beast didn't shift as she steered around a curve "—is not going to shatter."

"Oh, well then it's definitely worth a hundred big ones."

If the lobster were just a bit smaller and lighter, he'd consider swinging it at Susie's head. "You're really being a pain in the ass. I thought you wanted to help me with this movie."

"I do." She seemed to shrink in the seat. Blooms weren't exactly huge people to begin with, and she was the smallest Bloom of their generation. He wondered if she had trouble seeing over the steering wheel.

"Then why are you acting like such a bitch? The Susie you used to be would have thought that lobster was fantastic."

She sighed. "I'm not acting like a bitch," she argued. "I can't imagine ever thinking that lobster would be fantastic, but..." She sighed again, adjusted her sunglasses and attempted a lackluster smile. "My life is a mess right now, okay? I'm sorry. It has nothing to do with you."

"Is Grandma Ida—"

"It has nothing to do with her, either."

"Is Julia giving you shit?"

"Let's not play twenty questions, okay?"

"So tell me and I'll stop guessing."

"I broke up with Casey," she said.

Oh. That was a biggie. "Why?"

"He wanted to marry me."

Rick chewed that over. The bridge of his nose developed a cramp from his frown. Didn't women want the men they loved to marry them? Didn't women usually break up with men because the men refused to marry them? Had he been given the wrong information on all this?

"You didn't want to marry him?"

"If I married him, would I be driving around Maine with you and Claws back there?"

"I don't know."

"No. I wouldn't be," she told him. "I'd be in Queens, doing wife stuff. Waiting for Casey to get home from work and having a hot meal on the table for him."

Rick snorted. "If that was what Casey wanted, why would he want to marry you? You can't cook."

"How do you know I can't?" she asked defensively.

"You're a Bloom. None of us can cook. My mother's probably the best cook in the family, and she cooks things that have lentils in them. Your mother's idea of cooking is to thaw some frozen supermarket bagels and open a tub of cream cheese. I've had enough brunches at her apartment to know."

"Our mothers aren't Blooms," Susie reminded him. "They married in."

"Anyway, doesn't Casey cook? Maybe if you married him, he'd be the one waiting in Queens with a hot meal for you."

She sent him a skeptical look. "Cooking isn't the issue. I'm not ready for marriage."

"Is Casey that much older than you?"

"A year and a half. An eternity," she added grimly.

"So—you mean, if I asked Anna to marry me, she'd never want to see me again?"

Susie grinned. "If you asked her to marry you, she'd probably laugh so hard she'd dislocate her tonsils. Don't even think about it."

He pondered Susie's situation for a minute and found himself unable to make any sense of it at all. "Well, look," he said sympathetically. "Whatever's going on, I'm sorry."

"Thanks." She reached across the console and gave his hand a squeeze. "And I'm sorry for acting like a bitch."

He gave them a moment of silence so their apologies could sink in, then pointed to a convenience store up ahead. "Let's stop there and ask where the nearest blueberry field is," he suggested.

"Okay." She slapped lightly at her cheek, and he realized a tear had leaked down from behind her sunglasses.

He was kind enough not to comment on it. "I think we ought to name the lobster," he said as she slowed the van.

"Name it what? Louie the Lobster?"

"Big Red," he said.

She wrinkled her nose. "It's got to start with an L. Libby. Lucy. Larry. Lenny. Linus—that's it! Linus."

"Linus?" He glanced behind him as she steered into the dirt lot in front of the store. A wiry red plastic lobster antenna stared back. "Yeah," he agreed. "He looks like a Linus." Maybe he did, maybe he didn't. But if letting Susie name the lobster Linus boosted her spirits, who was he to argue?

Chapter Nineteen

"**Y**our Aunt Martha is here," Lyndon said.

Wonderful. Just what Julia needed. She'd phoned Grandma Ida from her office downstairs and asked to come up, and Grandma Ida had said of course, come, and so she'd come. If Aunt Martha had been on the schedule, Grandma Ida would have said so, but since Aunt Martha lived just downstairs from Grandma Ida, she must have dropped by uninvited.

When Uncle Jay and Aunt Martha had divorced, they'd engaged in a fierce custody battle over their apartment, a spacious, rambling residence on the twenty-fourth floor of the Bloom Building, down the hall from the apartment where Julia had grown up and her mother still lived. Uncle Jay had finally ceded the apartment to Aunt Martha, since the divorce was his idea and his new wife, Wendy, was more of an East Side type, anyway. They'd found an elegant apartment on East 63rd, and Aunt Martha had remained in the Bloom Building.

Julia wouldn't have wanted to evict Aunt Martha from the family—she was Julia's cousins' mother, after all, and a part of Julia's life. But Aunt Martha was a little hard to take. She had all the optimism of Eeyore, and none of his charm. She took classes at the New School on gynocentric evolutionary theory and literary deconstruction as an economic fallacy, and she attended lectures on repression in Tibet and depression in menopause. She was the most earnest woman Julia had ever met. Like a cloud, she darkened every room she entered.

So now she was darkening Grandma Ida's apartment. Julia could spare only a half hour to make her plea, which she didn't want to make in front of Aunt Martha, because Aunt Martha was full of opinions and had no qualms about sharing them. She was certain to have plenty of opinions about Julia's wedding.

"Will she be leaving soon?" Julia asked Lyndon as she stepped into the foyer.

Lyndon shrugged and grinned. "Who knows? It's Martha," he said, then kissed Julia's cheek and nudged her down the hall to the arched living room doorway.

Not a single aspect of Grandma Ida's apartment had changed throughout Julia's entire lifetime, other than the fact that Grandpa Isaac no longer lived there. Even when he was alive, he didn't leave much of a mark on the place. His cheery personality had warmed the rooms, but he hadn't been like, for instance, Ron, leaving masculine detritus throughout the residence. Entering Ron's apartment, no one would doubt for a moment that a man resided within it. Countless water stains the exact circumference of a beer bottle marked the coffee table. Subscription renewal cards from *Sports Illustrated* served as bookmarks in trade paperbacks about Wall Street scandals and novels about spies who could bring down megalomaniacs, hack into top-secret computers and give women multiple orgasms without breaking a sweat. The power button on the TV set had not a single fingerprint on it, because it had never been used, but a pile of spare AAA batteries sat in an old ashtray, ready to power any of the several remote controls scattered across the coffee table amid the beer-bottle stains. Throw pillows on the sofa and chairs were askew because they were actually used as pillows and not just decoration. The kitchen trashcan contained a suspicious number of disposable plastic containers from take-out restaurants.

Of course, the same could be said of Julia's kitchen trash can. Thanks to Ron, she'd become a devotee of Bloom's Heat-'N'-Eat entrees.

Her grandmother's living room, which was utterly devoid of guy clutter, looked like a stage set from a World War II drama about the home front. The furniture was old and massive, dark mahogany and burgundy velvet. The Persian rugs covering the hardwood floors featured patterns Julia had memorized as a child; she could still find the vaguely teddy-bear-shaped blobs in the borders, and the swirls that used to remind her of the Grinch's cheeks, and the patch near the window where Susie had splashed watercolors while painting. The stain had come out easily enough, but Julia still remembered the day it had happened, the tension in Grandma Ida's voice as she'd scolded Susie, Susie's lower lip protruding as she'd stubbornly refused to cry, and Grandpa Isaac sneaking both girls into the kitchen and slipping them pieces of toffee once Grandma Ida had run out of steam and stomped off down the hall.

Grandma Ida's apartment was a place where Julia could never escape from her memories. The mirror above the fireplace mantel—she recalled with pride the day she was finally tall enough to see the top of her head in it. The wide windows overlooking Broadway, where she and Susie would press their noses to the glass and count how many yellow taxis zoomed below them. The pink Depression-glass candy dish that Susie used to perch upside down on her head and say, "Look! A yarmulke!" The meandering route that Adam used to steer his Tonka dump trucks around the legs of chairs and tables until Grandma Ida would snap, "*Nu*, does this look like a highway to you? Go play in the hall."

No Tonka dump trucks littered the floor today; no young children played here. Julia hesitated in the doorway as an image flashed before her of her own baby, hers and Ron's, crawling across the rug, seeing teddy bears and Grinches in its fading patterns. The vision brought tears to her eyes—whether of joy or panic she couldn't say—and she hastily blinked them away and marched into the room, beaming a smile at her grandmother and her aunt. Grandma Ida was ensconced in her favorite armchair, dressed in her usual dowdy but comfortable apparel—A-line skirt, cotton blouse, leather oxfords and gold bangle bracelets circling her wrists. Her hair was a cloud even darker than Aunt Martha, so black it sucked light out of the room.

Aunt Martha looked like a superannuated girl scout in browns and khakis, white socks and Birkenstock sandals, a braided cord of leather around her neck and her long, lumpy salt-and-pepper hair held back in a clip. She returned Julia's smile, although her smile was clearly ambivalent. It always was. She didn't do happy very well.

"Hello, Julia," she said in her glum, gravelly voice. "How are things at the store?"

"Fine," Julia answered, latching onto an idea. "Actually, Aunt Martha, I came upstairs to discuss the store with Grandma. I've got only a few minutes, and we need to talk shop."

Aunt Martha was gloomy, but she wasn't dense. "Oh, of course. I wouldn't dream of interfering. I came by just to drop off this book I think your grandmother will enjoy." She gestured toward a hardcover tome lying on the coffee table. Julia lifted it and read the title: *Broads of the Bible: A Feminist Trades Jabs With God.* "A friend of mine from the Women's Center recommended it. I found it absorbing."

"I don't know why you think I'd like it," Grandma Ida barked, refusing to join the smile-fest Julia and Aunt Martha were caught up in. "I don't like that word, broads. It's like what truck drivers say."

"The book is supposed to be humorous," Aunt Martha explained dolefully. Her idea of humorous was probably anything that didn't make a person want to drink Drano.

"It's full of jokes? A book that big, I'm supposed to laugh? I can hardly pick it up. My arthritis." Grandma Ida lifted her hands and her bangles clinked.

"Just have a look at it, Ida," Aunt Martha urged her as she rose from the sofa. "I think you'll be surprised."

"I'm too old to be surprised," Grandma Ida muttered.

Aunt Martha didn't seem to hear her. She started toward the door, pausing to give Julia a hug en route. "How's your mother?"

Julia wasn't about to discuss her mother's current insanity with anyone. "She's fine," she lied. "I'll give her your regards."

"Please do. I've got to have her over for tea. I've discovered these wonderful cakes made out of red bean curd. They're Chinese. I bet she'll love them."

"I'm sure she will," Julia agreed, realizing she'd have to steer her mother clear of Aunt Martha at least until she stopped acting like an infatuated schoolgirl and babbling about the magnificent time she'd spent having coffee with Norman Joffe. Actually, it had been magnificent in only some of the tellings. In others it had been glorious, delightful, and so much fun. Norman was such a gentleman. He was so soft-spoken. He was so generous—he'd insisted that she order the double latté, and he'd practically forced a boysenberry scone upon her, which implied that he didn't think she was too fat—and he was very smart, he knew so much about tax preparation, and he hadn't said a single negative thing about his ex-wife, which Julia's mother considered fabulously discreet. She could see where Ron had come from, such a wonderful young man. He'd obviously inherited a lot of genes from his father.

If Julia remembered her high school biology better, she could determine exactly how many genes Ron had inherited from his father. The number wasn't important now, though. What was important was to keep her mother from doing something seriously inconvenient, like falling in love with Ron's father.

In the meantime, until she was positive her mother was immune to anything as stupid as love, Julia had to keep her from running into anyone she might babble to. Norman Joffe might be the epitome of discretion, but Sondra Bloom was not.

Aunt Martha lumbered out of the living room. Julia waved at her back, then settled onto the couch, deliberately sitting one cushion over from where Aunt Martha had sat. She heard Aunt Martha and Lyndon chatting in the entry, and then the front door swinging open and shut.

"That woman is an idiot," Grandma Ida announced.

"She's not so bad," Julia argued, lifting the book. The weight strained her wrist. Were there really so many jabs to be traded between a feminist and God? Julia wasn't overly religious, but she suspected that

God could win such a bout in well under a hundred pages. Under fifty, if he put his all into it.

"So? What do you want?" Grandma Ida asked, clasping her gnarled fingers together and staring at Julia with piercingly clear eyes.

Julia inhaled. A year ago she would have been intimidated by her grandmother's relentless gaze and crotchety attitude, but she'd spent that year running Bloom's and discovering that she was blessed with great intelligence, competence, and resources. Grandma Ida had named her, rather than her mother or Uncle Jay or any of the cousins, the president of Bloom's because Grandma Ida trusted her and had faith in her. Having Grandma Ida's trust and faith had done wonders for Julia's self-confidence.

Even so, what she was about to ask wasn't simple, nor was Grandma Ida's reaction predictable. "Here's what I was thinking," she said. "I want my wedding catered by Bloom's. I want it to have a homey feel to it, a Bloom's feel. And I'm having a hell of a time finding a venue that will let me bring in my own caterer. I guess they all make their biggest profits on the catering."

"What's a venue?" Grandma Ida asked. "I don't know that word, venue."

"A location," Julia defined the term. "A place to have something."

"It sounds like a street. Park a-Venue. Fifth a-Venue."

"Well." Julia paused, then launched back into her pitch. "I kept thinking, if only I had a home big enough, I'd host the wedding there. I don't, though."

"That apartment you have, it's the size of a toilet," Grandma Ida remarked.

"It is not! It's much bigger than a toilet," Julia protested.

"It's a little place. You put two people in it, one has to breathe out while the other one's breathing in or you'll run out of air."

If Grandma Ida thought Julia's apartment was small, she ought to have a look at the dive Susie was sharing with two other women. Cousin Rick's apartment was even tinier. But Grandma Ida never visited their places. Anything south of 34th Street didn't exist for her. "On 34th Street you've got Macy's and Penn Station," Grandma Ida pointed out on occasion. "What's south of there? Wall Street? *Feh*. City Hall? Who needs it? Greenwich Village? Hippies. *Feh*."

But in her contempt for Julia's apartment, Grandma Ida was providing ammunition for Julia's argument. "You've got a big enough apartment, Grandma," she said, trying not to sound too eager. "We could fit eighty people in here."

"Eighty people? In my apartment? *Oy!*"

"We could do it. Or maybe we could cut the guest list down to seventy-five. We could have a buffet of Bloom's food in the dining room, set up some tables in the living room, cocktails in the den and musicians in the foyer. We could do it."

"Where would people dance?"

Julia stifled a laugh. That her elderly grandmother cared about dancing amused her. Of course, Grandma Ida herself wouldn't dance. She'd just sit—in the very chair she was sitting in now, no doubt—and make snide comments about the guests who did want to dance.

"In the living room," Julia answered. "The tables we'd set up would be little end tables, places for people to put down their plates. We could roll up the rug, or lay a temporary parquet over it."

"What are you talking, a temporary floor?"

"Just a smooth surface over the rug to make dancing easier. I could work with a rental company on that. We'd rent dishes, silverware, stemware—everything. No one would touch your plates."

"And you want Lyndon to do all that work?"

"Of course not. I'll hire servers. They'll do all the set-up and clean-up. Lyndon will be a guest at the wedding."

"He'll want to bring that friend of his, Howard," Grandma Ida warned in a whisper. "They're *faygelas*, the two of them."

"They're a lovely couple," Julia said.

"Howard, at least he's Jewish. A Jew and a black man, I don't know..."

"Don't worry about Lyndon," Julia said, guiding her grandmother back to the subject at hand. "What do you think about having the wedding here? We'd have professional cleaners come in before and after. They'd do all the work. The day after the wedding, you'd never know it had been here."

"I wouldn't know? You think I'd forget my first grandchild's wedding?"

"What I mean is, everything would be left the way it is right now. All the furniture would be in place, the kitchen scrubbed down, everything back to normal."

"It's a *farkakte* idea," Grandma Ida declared. "It's *meshuggeneh*."

Grandma Ida's words stung, bringing fresh tears to Julia's eyes. She'd always associated Yiddish words with warmth and affection and family ties—but they could also be weapons. She'd thought her grandmother might object to turning over her residence to such a big party, having strangers taking over her kitchen and arranging guest towels in her bathrooms. She might have complained about the inconvenience, the risk to her furniture, the noise. But *farkakte*? Me-

shuggeneh? Those words weren't aimed at the idea. They were aimed at Julia.

"I think it's a good idea," she argued, struggling to keep her tears out of her voice. "Where did you get married? In your parents' home?"

"In the *shul*, of course. The rabbi was there, we had a *chuppa*, Isaac, may he rest, smashed a glass and we broke bread and drank wine. And the next day we were back at the pushcart, selling knishes. No honeymoon. No caterer. None of that stuff."

"Well, Ron and I are going to have a honeymoon. And a caterer."

"So have your wedding in your mother's apartment. It's as big as mine."

"She would never let me," Julia explained. "She wants to have the wedding at the Plaza Hotel, because her brother's son had his bar mitzvah there."

Grandma Ida clicked her tongue and shook her head. "Your mother," she muttered. "And Martha is an idiot, so you can't have your wedding at her apartment. Uncle Jay's apartment—"

"—Isn't as big as yours," Julia completed the sentence. "The Plaza won't let me use Bloom's to cater. Central Park won't let me serve liquor."

"What? No wine at a wedding?"

"Obviously Central Park is out." Julia sighed. "There are venues—places," she corrected herself, "that rent out for weddings, but they aren't necessarily bigger than your apartment."

"And, what, you want to set up a *chuppa* here?"

"We can have the actual ceremony in a synagogue. This would just be for the reception."

"What synagogue? You belong to a synagogue?"

"There are eleven synagogues within ten blocks of here," Julia assured her. A person couldn't walk more than a few steps on Manhattan's Upper West Side without stumbling upon a synagogue. Ron had promised he'd call the neighborhood temples and find out what they'd require of him and Julia in order to hold their wedding there. If they had to join a congregation, they would. But that was his headache. They'd divvied up the headaches: he'd won the service and she'd won the reception.

"So, the synagogue doesn't have a basement room?"

"I don't want to have my reception in a basement room," Julia protested. "Basement rooms have no windows."

"And I've got windows, so you want to have the reception here."

"I want to have it here because you're my grandmother." Julia hated her plaintive undertone, but she couldn't swallow it down. Her wistfulness was unjustified; she couldn't have hoped for Grandma Ida to magically turn into one of those plump, doting grandmothers eager to spoil her grandchildren with home-baked cookies and lavish indulgences. Grandma Ida had never once opened her arms to Julia and said, "Bubbela, whatever you want." She'd never said, "You are gorgeous," or a genius, or perfect, the way grandmothers were supposed to gush over their grandchildren, the way Grandma Ethel, on Julia's mother's side, did. Grandma Ethel would have been the ideal exemplar of grandmotherliness—plump and overflowing with indiscriminate compliments—except that she'd moved down to Boca Raton three years ago and now spent more of her time playing golf and bleaching her hair platinum blond than spoiling her grandchildren. But when she'd lived in Riverdale, she'd always lavished unwarranted praise on Susie, Adam and Julia, as well as Travis and his sister Corinne.

The greatest praise Grandma Ida had ever given Julia was when she'd said, "You remind me of me." Which could have been interpreted as an insult.

So Julia shouldn't have expected her to say, "Of course you can have your reception in my apartment! I would consider it an honor!"

"All right, never mind," Julia said briskly, refusing to let that whimpery undertone filter into her voice again. "I've got to get back downstairs. I have to iron out a problem with one of our yogurt suppliers."

"*Gonefs*, all of them," Grandma Ida grunted. "So I'll think about this idea of yours. It's *tsadreit*, but I'll think about it."

Should Julia be grateful? Was Grandma Ida really going to think about the idea, or was she simply stringing Julia along, coming as close as she'd ever come to "Bubbela, whatever you want"? It almost didn't matter. Julia felt drained and glum, as if Aunt Martha had left her cloud behind when she'd departed and it had settled just inches above Julia's head, poised to spit rain on her.

Suppressing a sigh, she stood and bent over to kiss her grandmother's cheek. "Don't let those yogurt people steal you blind," Grandma Ida warned, as if Julia needed such counsel. She was tempted to retort, in a sweet voice, that she hoped Grandma Ida would enjoy the book about broads versus God. But she held her sarcasm and faked yet another smile. Grandma Ida did say she'd consider Julia's *farkakte* plan, after all.

Lyndon had disappeared into the nether reaches of the apartment, so Julia let herself out without saying goodbye to him. She was so edgy, she actually contemplated climbing down the twenty-two flights of stairs to her office rather than taking the elevator, but she was wearing shoes with clunky heels, and if she took the stairs she'd be *farschvitzed* by the time she got downstairs.

Twenty minutes in Grandma Ida's company and she was thinking in Yiddish.

She pressed the elevator button and commanded her brain to clarify itself. No matter that Grandma Ida had said she'd think about it—Julia couldn't count on having her wedding on the twenty-fifth floor of the Bloom Building. She had to find another location.

She'd telephoned a couple of boating outfits. A wedding party on the Hudson River would be delightful, assuming none of the guests suffered from seasickness, but the companies had all insisted on supplying their own caterers. Maybe her cousin Neil could find her a more open-minded yacht rental service. He ran a sailing charter business in southern Florida, but half of southern Florida was transplanted New Yorkers like Grandma Ethel, so she shouldn't discount the possibility that he knew some boating firms in the city.

She'd check with the Cloisters again, too. So what if the place was full of medieval Christian art? At least it was beautiful medieval Christian art. Last time she'd spoken to a representative there, he'd informed her of the museum's formidable deposit—"in case an irreplaceable artifact gets damaged," he'd explained, and she'd flashed on a vision of Adam gesticulating too broadly and smashing his hand through a priceless stained-glass window—and the museum also banned alcoholic beverages.

Which meant she was back to the loft and townhouse venues, all of them exorbitantly priced and prepared to fight to the death over who would do the catering.

If she'd realized planning a wedding would be so complicated, she would have purchased two tickets to

Las Vegas and had an Elvis impersonator marry her and Ron in a ticky-tacky chapel on the Strip.

She emerged from the elevator on the third floor and strolled through the broad hallway, past the open doors to her office. "Julia," Deirdre Morrissey shouted through her door, "Melvin Slatnik from Galicia Cured Meats called to discuss our pastrami order. He wants you to call him back immediately."

Julia rolled her eyes. Everything with Slatnik was always an emergency.

"Also, one of the cash registers is down. I called the service company. Also, our Bel Paese delivery is going to be delayed a day. Don't ask me why. The guy on the phone didn't speak English. Also, Morty Sugarman from the bagel department wants a minute with you sometime before the end of the week."

So many crises, so little time. "Thanks," Julia shouted through Deirdre's open door. Through her mother's open door, adjacent to Deirdre's, Julia heard the phone ring. She prayed that whoever was on the other end of the line had a crisis her mother could handle without her help.

She clomped into her office, sank into the oversize chair and punched the speed-dial button for Ron's office. Whatever Melvin Slatnik's problems with pastrami might be, they couldn't be more important than Julia's impending nuptials.

"Joffe here," Ron answered his phone.

"It's me," Julia said, cringing when she heard the whine creep back into her voice. "My grandmother was extremely lukewarm about our using her apartment for the reception."

"How can someone be extremely lukewarm?" Ron asked. "Lukewarm, by definition, isn't extreme."

"Don't argue semantics with me," Julia snapped. He was a writer; he cared about the connotations of words. Julia ran a deli and she didn't give a damn about connotations. "We have to find another place to hold the wedding. Maybe we should look outside the city. Brooklyn, maybe."

"Brooklyn? You want to get married in Brooklyn?" He sounded as if she'd suggested Spokane, or maybe the dark side of the moon.

"No, I don't want to get married in Brooklyn. I don't even know what I want—except for life to be easier than it is right now."

"Here's an idea," Ron said, sounding as amiable as she felt bitter. "How about NYU?"

"NYU?"

"You got your law degree there. I got my MBA there. Your cousin graduated from the film school there. Maybe we could rent a classroom or something."

"Oh, a classroom," she grunted. "A nice chemistry lab, perhaps. All that counter space, built-in sinks, and those little Bunsen burners we can use under the chafing dishes. What a fabulous idea."

"They've got reception rooms, Julia," he said patiently.

They did. Some very nice ones, in fact. Grandma Ida would kvetch about having to schlep all the way down to Greenwich Village with the hippies, but big deal. Julia could arrange to have a car service bring her downtown. Or maybe Susie could rent a van from Truck-a-Buck and shuttle all their uptown guests to the party. In her maid of honor dress, she'd make quite a glamorous chauffeur.

But NYU... Hell, she wasn't even a lawyer anymore. She'd gone there, made law review, passed the boards, gotten a job with a major firm—and left it to run a delicatessen. The law school might not even allow her to show her face in the buildings, especially since as an alumna she'd ignored all their plaintive mailings requesting donations. "NYU won't work," she said.

"Oh, you're right." It was apparently Ron's turn to be sarcastic now. "What could I have been thinking, giving you a good idea? My mistake."

"I'm trying to be serious."

"You're trying to be fatalistic. You sound like someone died."

"Someone *is* going to die if he doesn't take this seriously. It's our wedding I'm talking about."

"Maybe we could rent a warehouse in Jersey City," Ron suggested.

Julia groaned. "You are an asshole. I'm hanging up now."

"I'll see you tonight," Ron said cheerfully. "Wear something sexy so I can tear it off you with my teeth."

She hung up. Through her open door she heard her mother shriek, "Julia! What's this about your getting married in Grandma Ida's apartment?"

Before she could respond, Uncle Jay materialized in her doorway. "You're getting married in my mother's apartment?"

"Or on Neil's boat."

"Neil's in Florida," Uncle Jay reminded her.

"If he loves me, he'll sail to New York," Julia said.

Julia!" her mother bellowed. "You can't get married in Grandma Ida's apartment!"

"Is she getting married in Ida's apartment?" Myron shouted across the hall to Sondra.

"I'm sure Neil loves you," Uncle Jay said, "but asking him to sail all the way to New York—"

Her phone rang, giving her the opportunity to swivel away from Uncle Jay, who was now lounging comfortably against the doorjamb. "Julia Bloom," she said, hoping it was Ron with a brilliant idea for their wedding.

No such luck. "Julia? It's Susie," her sister said into the phone, her voice filtering through static and what sounded like the Doppler Effect. "Listen, we're including a six-foot lobster in the movie. I just wanted to warn you. Don't worry—it's going to be fabulous."

A lobster in the video. A mother having conniptions. An uncle loitering in her office when he ought to be getting his work done. A grandmother with a will of iron and an intellect of flypaper twisted into mobius strips. An asshole fiancé who wanted to tear her clothing off with his teeth.

Given the train wreck that was her life, she was awfully grateful for the asshole fiancé.

Chapter Twenty

S usie's cell phone chirped.

She and Rick had just returned from dinner at the hillbilly restaurant across the parking lot from the motel. Susie's fried chicken had come with a side of grits, and after one bite of the gluey white mush, she resolved to persuade Julia never, ever to allow grits onto the shelves of Bloom's. Rick had ordered a rack of ribs, and he had a smear of rust-colored barbecue sauce on his T-shirt, right below the bright green "K" among the letters stretched across his chest, reading, "Take Direction."

He'd insisted on bringing Linus into the room for the night. Susie had argued that no one would steal a six-foot long plastic lobster, and Rick had pointed out that he'd stolen the six-foot long plastic lobster, so she'd relented and let him lug the creature inside. It lay on the floor between their two beds, looking more comfortable swimming in the green shag carpeting than she felt sprawled out on the spongy mattress of her bed. Rick sat cross-legged on the other bed, a map spread open in front of him as he plotted their next move.

The phone chirped again and Susie dug it out of her purse, assuring herself that her momentary breathlessness was nothing more significant than an emotional hiccup. She was not hoping Casey would phone. She did not wish to speak to the man. She did not want to hear him make pronouncements on marriage and commitment and other unpleasant topics.

Retrieving the phone, she vowed to herself that if her caller was Casey, she wouldn't be thrilled. The screen said her caller was Anna, and despite her vow, she had to fend off a major twang of disappointment. "Hey, Anna, what's up?" she asked, falsely cheery.

Rick's gaze jerked away from the map and he stared at Susie. "Is it Anna?" he whispered, his eyes unnaturally bright.

"It's Anna," Susie told him, then said into the phone, "That was Rick. He wanted to know if it was you."

"Tell him it's me," Anna said.

Susie obeyed, although she felt kind of silly relaying trivial messages back and forth between the two. "So, what's up?" she repeated into the phone.

"Not much. Caitlin says she's in love with these guys she met last night."

"Guys? How many is she in love with?"

"Two. Identical twins. You know Caitlin."

Susie sighed. She couldn't believe Anna had telephoned her all the way in Maine to tell her about Caitlin's latest infatuation—or infatuations, plural.

She was right. Anna had telephoned her all the way in Maine to tell her something else: "You'll never guess who I ran into this afternoon on the corner of Avenue A and East 4th."

"Who?"

"Casey."

"In our neighborhood?" What would he have been doing there? It was such an onerous trip for him, after all. That was why he'd initially asked Susie to move into his apartment in Queens, before he'd gotten carried away and introduced the subject of marriage.

"Can I talk to Anna?" Rick called over from his bed.

Susie glanced at him and realized he'd tossed the map aside and was blatantly eavesdropping on her phone conversation. He had a fleck of barbecue sauce at the corner of his mouth, too. If Anna saw him as he was right now, sauce-stained and tousle-haired, his feet smudged with soil from traipsing around farms in his sandals and that idiotic tuft of beard adorning his chin like a scrap of drier lint, she'd sure be turned on, Susie thought sarcastically. "No," she said to him, then cupped the phone closer to her ear and stared at her knees. "What was he doing?"

"This is so weird, Susie. He wasn't alone. He was with a woman."

Susie tried to pretend her heart wasn't contracting into a tight little wad of pain at Anna's words. So Casey was with a woman. Big deal. Susie had broken up with him, hadn't she? They'd had explosive sex on her sister's office couch and then said good-bye. She had no claim on him. He had no claim on her. She didn't, didn't, *didn't* care that he was strolling around her neighborhood with a woman. "Did he introduce you?" she asked, struggling to rid her voice of emotion.

"Yeah. I don't remember her name. I do remember that she was black."

Maybe she was a friend of Mose's. Susie and Casey had gone out with Mose and his girlfriend LaShonna a bunch of times. Maybe Casey was with LaShonna herself.

And maybe Susie was some kind of racist for assuming that just because Casey was with a black woman, it would have to be someone he'd met through Mose.

"She looked like Halle Berry," Anna continued.

Shit. The most gorgeous woman in the world.

"When I asked him how come they were downtown, he said they were looking for a place to rent."

"What!" Susie couldn't contain her emotions any longer. Casey—who less than two weeks ago had asked her to be his wife—was looking for a place to rent in her neighborhood with another woman, one who just happened to resemble Halle Berry. Susie might as well not come home. She might as well drive the Truck-a-Buck van all the way to the Pacific Coast, and then steer it over a cliff and into the ocean. She'd seen pictures of the coastal highway out there. Plunging over a cliff would be a piece of cake.

The hell with that. She wasn't going to kill herself over Casey, that dickhead bastard.

"What?" Rick called over to her.

"Nothing," she answered him, then glanced away before he could glimpse the tears filming her eyes. To Anna she said, "They were looking for an apartment?"

"He said a place to rent. I don't know. The woman he was with said they didn't have time to chat because they were supposed to meet someone. A prospective landlord, I figured."

Susie's tears filtered through her lashes. All the blinking in the world couldn't hold them back.

"You still there?" Anna asked.

"Why don't you talk to Rick for a minute?" Susie suggested, unwilling to let Anna hear her sobbing. Before Anna could respond, Susie tossed the cell phone over Linus's prostrate body to Rick's bed.

He caught it before it hit the mattress and held it to his ear delicately, as if it were a precious artifact.

235

"Hello?" he murmured, his mouth shaping a dopey grin. "Anna?"

Susie swung off her bed and stormed into the puny bathroom. Once she'd shut herself inside, she unrolled a strip of toilet paper and used it to blot her cheeks and blow her nose. She had to get control of herself, and quickly. Anna could probably tolerate only about five minutes of Rick's lovesick blathering before she demanded that he give the phone back to Susie.

Casey and a gorgeous black woman, moving into her cozy little Manhattan neighborhood. If he'd wanted to move to the East Village, why hadn't he ever mentioned this to Susie? Why had he stressed the idea of her moving to Queens? Why had he waxed rhapsodic about the lower rents and the bigger units in his remote borough, the open sky, the schoolyard basketball courts, the cheaper stores and relative absence of gridlock on the roads? All of a sudden, this other woman comes along and he's willing to relocate to Alphabet City? Why? Who was she?

Someone who looked like Halle Berry. That could explain a lot.

Susie sniffled a bit, blew her nose again and tossed the soggy toilet paper into the toilet. Then she emerged and checked herself in the mirror above the sink. She looked nothing like Halle Berry. If she resembled anyone from the silver screen, it was Edward Scissorhands.

"Um, yeah," Rick was saying into the cell phone. "That was Susie's idea."

What was Susie's idea? Susie didn't have ideas. All she had was a hypocritical heart, one that protected itself against commitment yet shattered into a zillion pieces the moment Casey turned his attention to someone else. Any idea that might be attributed to

Susie was bound to be truly wretched because she was stupid and stubborn and unforgivably shallow, and if Rick didn't realize that...

"Sure," he said. "So I guess I'll be seeing you." Smiling like someone who'd drunk several large shots of high-quality whiskey and was feeling its heavy sweetness in his veins, he handed the cell phone to Susie.

She sank onto her bed, feeling the soft cushions give beneath her. "He said it was your idea to name a giant lobster Linus?" Anna asked.

"Oh. Yeah. Our mascot." Susie heard no hint of tears in her voice, thank God.

"I thought you guys were making a movie."

"We are. Linus is my co-star."

"It sounds weird."

"It is weird. Life is weird. Very, very weird."

"Look, I'm sorry, maybe I shouldn't have called you. I just thought you ought to know about Casey."

"I appreciate it," Susie said. "Really." What if Anna hadn't given her a heads-up, and she'd waltzed back to New York and found Casey at the bagel counter and said, *Okay, let's see what we can do to make this thing work,* and he'd said, *Too late, Susie—Halle Berry wants to marry me, and unlike you, she's ready to settle down and have a grown-up relationship.* Susie would be mortified. It was better to know.

"Oh, one other thing," Anna added. "The woman Casey was with? She laughed like a horse."

"Like a horse?"

"Through her nose, this neighing sound. Very horsey."

"What was she laughing about?"

"I don't remember. Something Casey said, something that wasn't all that funny."

"She obviously thought it was funny."

"Or she thought he thought it was funny, and she was doing the girlie thing and pumping his ego."

"Like a horse, huh?" Susie tried to picture Halle Berry laughing through her nose. She knew she was only grasping at straws, but anything that made the woman just a little less irresistible in Susie's imagination was a balm to her tender feelings.

"Snorting like a bronco. It wasn't pretty."

"Thanks." Anna had probably made the horse laughter part up. The woman undoubtedly had a laugh like tinkling crystal. But friends did what they could to sustain other friends, and Susie would be eternally grateful to Anna for lying to make Susie feel better. "If you see them again, will you let me know?"

"Of course."

"How's everything with you?"

"Same old. Rick wants to take me out for dinner when you get back to town. He says maybe he'll even have enough money to cover the bill."

"Right," Susie muttered, recalling the few times Anna had agreed to go out for dinner with Rick, only to have to pick up the tab because he was tapped out. "And maybe the ice caps will melt in the next few days and our apartment will turn into waterfront property."

"They're already melting," Anna reminded her. "I gotta go. I'll talk to you soon. Stay mellow."

"I will." Fat chance.

"Kiss Linus good-night for me."

Susie forced a laugh and disconnected the phone. Turning, she found Rick smiling sheepishly and gazing moon-eyed at the air molecules in front of his nose. Susie wanted to smack him, or the pink vinyl paneling on the walls, or a not-quite-dead fly staggering drunkenly along the window sill. She was mad, she was hurting, and she wanted to lash out.

But she wasn't a lashing-out type of woman. So she only gave Rick a crooked grin and said, "Anna said I should give you a good-night kiss for her." She knew as well as Anna did that lying to make a person feel better wasn't such a bad thing.

Chapter Twenty-One

Adam didn't mind working in the basement, but he would never admit to anyone with the last name Bloom that he actually enjoyed the job.

The basement was where the store's inventory was stocked. It arrived in trucks that double-parked on Broadway; the drivers sent the stock directly to the storage area via a gently sloped conveyer belt accessible through metal doors in the sidewalk. Closed, they lay flush with the sidewalk and pedestrians tramped right over them. Open, one led to a staircase into the basement and the other to a long ramp of metal cylinders that food items rolled down. Stuff that couldn't slide down the ramp had to be brought in through the alley around the back and carted downstairs on the elevator.

Unloading items from the ramp was one of Adam's responsibilities, and—don't tell Julia—he found it fun. Bending, lifting, hoisting and sorting gave a solid workout to the muscles in his shoulders, arms and back. Maybe by the time he left for Purdue, he'd be too buff to look like a grad student in mathematics.

Hell, he'd never be that buff. But he'd be a bit stronger, and that had to be worth something.

As he lugged a crate filled with bags of gourmet pasta from the belt to the shelves where pasta was stored, he thought about buff bodies, which automatically led him to think about Elyse. He'd learned from her that ballet dancing, for all its twinkle-toes delicacy, was about as strenuous as running marathons with weights strapped to one's limbs. The male dancers boosted ballerinas into the air with less effort than Adam exerted lifting sixteen cellophane bags of Nonna Rossini's Fresh-Dried Rigatoni onto a shelf. Those ballet guys could jump higher than most track stars, too. When they wore their form-fitting costumes, Adam could see their muscles bulge and flex. Ballerinas didn't bulge and flex so much; they had to stay lightweight, Elyse explained, and muscle mass weighed a lot. But even though she was only a student, she had some nice definition going for her. Her calf muscles were rock-hard ovals and her abs were as taut and rippling as wind-filled sails. He knew this because last night he'd had a chance to caress those abs and calves.

He hadn't slept with her. Yet. He had an idea of how flexible her hip joints were, because she'd sneaked him into a practice room at Juilliard. It could have passed as a small gym except for the mirrors on the walls, the waist-high railing protruding from one wall, and an atmosphere that smelled more like hair gel than old sweat. She'd kicked one leg up onto the railing, said, "This is the barre," and then swooped her head down until her nose touched her knee.

Okay. Loose hips. Supple thighs. Just thinking about her pelvic elasticity turned Adam on in a major way.

They'd done some intense lip-locking last night. Her tongue muscles were in as good shape as her biceps and quads. When she'd sat on his lap, she'd felt feather-light. He wasn't a muscle-bound ballet dancer, but he could probably lift her pretty high without straining himself.

Unfortunately, they'd had to do this kissing in an empty practice room. Not the ballet studio she'd shown him, but a tiny, insulated booth for flute students. The room had contained two chairs and a music stand, and the walls and ceiling were coated in thick soundproofing foam. He'd felt a little claustrophobic, but once the kissing had gotten underway he'd lost his awareness of their surroundings.

He wished he could bring her back to his room. With his mother in the apartment, though, that wasn't feasible. And Elyse was living with her aunt's family on Riverside Drive and 112th while she was studying at Juilliard, and her aunt had two preteen sons who Elyse said were really obnoxious. "They're at the age where they think farting is hilarious." Adam didn't bother to enlighten her to the fact that most boys never outgrew that stage.

Maybe if he hadn't spent so much time foreplaying with her in the flute practice room last night, he'd be feeling a little less cheerful about unloading pasta from the chute today. But honestly, working at Bloom's wasn't so terrible. As long as he didn't let his family suck him in, he'd be okay. And he liked filling his wallet with cash. One thing about Julia—she paid decent wages.

The last load of pasta came down the ramp in another crate, and Adam lugged it over to the shelf. Nonna Rossini's was only one of the brands of gourmet pasta the store carried. The old lady's cellophane bags shared shelf space with Palazzia Negri Ziti in boxes illustrated with paintings of Tuscany landscapes suitable for framing, and Segalini Lasagna in rectangular tins, and Chechi Gnocchi in rustic paper sacks. Adam was cynical enough to assume they all came from the same factory in Jersey City.

Once he'd gotten the crates unloaded onto the shelves, he pulled from his belt his inventory gizmo—it had a fancy name, itemized scanner or something like that, but Adam found gizmo easier to remember. The gizmo scanned the UPC's of all the items in. As soon as he'd recorded the Nonna Rossini's shipment, he could bring the gizmo upstairs to the third floor and enter the data into a computer there so the store would know just how much of what they had in stock. Uncle Jay had set up the system at Julia's behest. Last year when Adam had worked as a stock clerk, they'd recorded all the deliveries by hand on a clipboard.

This new electronic system was an improvement, but it still seemed unwieldy to Adam. Why couldn't a computer be kept in the basement, networked into the third-floor computers so the stock information could be entered directly? Why trek up and down in the elevator to enter the data? Not that it was his business, not that he had any investment in how the inventory was monitored, not that he wanted to interfere with Uncle Jay's way of doing things, but if Julia was going to computerize the inventory records, why not do it right?

He could set up the software in an hour, tops, he thought as he scanned the bags of rigatoni with his gizmo. Julia must have a spare computer somewhere on the third floor that Adam could bring downstairs and set up. He would bet good money Myron never used the computer in his office. The man still took off his shoes and socks to add.

Not that Adam had the least bit of interest in streamlining things at Bloom's.

Hell, he could donate his laptop for the summer, and good riddance, too. The last time he'd checked his email, he'd had three notes from friends and five from Tash. She qualified as a friend, of course, but reading her emails infused him with guilt. She was spending her days picketing the Space Needle in downtown Seattle with a group of women who felt it was a phallic symbol and therefore insulting to the female citizens of their fair city. This coven of picketers had dubbed themselves the Needle Needlers, and they'd gotten a decent write-up in the local newspaper, which had in turn attracted a half-dozen vituperative letters to the editor.

Tash was in her glory, having the best summer of her life. And Adam was trying to score with a ballet student at Juilliard.

The truth was, he didn't give a flying fuck about the Space Needle. He'd seen pictures of it, and the only way it could be phallic was if a guy wrapped a rubber band tightly around the middle of his schlong and glued a tiny umbrella to the tip—and glued a needle to the umbrella. The tower just wasn't prick-shaped.

Another truth, while he was admitting truths to himself, was that his lap felt more comfortable with Elyse perched on it than with Tash. He had nothing against *zaftig* women. He'd dated Tash for more than a year. But Elyse was lighter than a dollop of whipped cream. When she sat in his lap, his knees didn't threaten to buckle under her weight.

Guilt had never been Adam's long suit. He figured Julia claimed the monopoly on that character trait. Susie didn't do guilt, and Adam had long ago decided not to do it, either. He could spend his summer feeling like a piece of shit because he was pursuing Elyse and ignoring Tash, or he could spend his summer feeling great because he was pursuing Elyse and ignoring Tash. The second option seemed preferable.

He finished scanning, squinted at the LCD monitor on his gizmo and shook his head. Simplifying the process would save man-hours, which meant it would save money. And despite his lowly status as a summer employee, Adam was a Bloom and the company's profits were his inheritance. If he could program a computer to transmit the data from the basement to the third floor, he might ultimately wind up with just a little more money in his wallet, which was a good thing any way you looked at it.

As a committed socialist, of course, Tash would disagree.

Right now, Adam didn't care.

o

Ron kissed Julia's breasts. She loved when he did that, loved it so much she often found herself wondering whether nursing a baby could possibly be a sexual experience, which led to fantasies of having babies with Ron, which, given that they weren't even married yet, was definitely a dangerous track for her train of thought to speed down.

A woman shouldn't think while she was having sex.

So she closed her eyes, let her head sink deep into the pillow, and ran her hands up and down his arms and across his smooth, strong shoulders while he did amazing things to her breasts with his lips and tongue. She focused on the heat of his mouth and the chill of the air, the sweet burning in her nipples, the way sensation slid between her body and his, warming her belly where his chest pressed down into it, warming her thighs as they shifted against his hips. He had such a hunky physique, and he knew just what to do with what he had, and she was the luckiest woman in the world to be engaged to him because he wasn't just sexy, he was smart and successful and even Jewish, speaking of which, she needed to find out whether he'd gotten information on the synagogues in the area, although he'd said they might be able to set up a *chuppa* in the reception room at the Torch Club at NYU, which meant they could skip joining a synagogue for now, although if they had children they'd really have to join one so their children could have bar mitzvahs and bat mitzvahs thirteen years later...

He lifted his head and peered into her eyes. "Am I losing you?"

"No, no." She sighed, raised herself enough to kiss the crown of his head and fell back against the pillow. "I was just thinking."

"Stop thinking," he ordered her, then bowed and sucked her nipple into his mouth.

Okay. She would stop thinking about anything other than the gathering tension between her legs, and the way her entire being pulled tight, wanting him, burning for him...and her cell phone beeped.

"Don't answer it," he murmured, sliding his mouth from her breasts to her midriff, licking the hollow between her ribs.

It beeped again. How could she not think when her phone was ringing? The only people who would dial her cell phone at eight p.m. were her relatives. They probably assumed she was just finishing dinner. She and Ron had in fact started dinner— Heat-'N'-Eat falafel on pita, from the store—but then he'd started playing footsie with her, and they'd decided the falafel could wait, and they'd raced into his bedroom and stripped off their clothes and...

It beeped again. "I have to answer," she said. No way was this lovemaking going to end well if her phone kept ringing.

He rolled off her and let out a ragged breath. "You should have turned it off."

"Now you tell me." She grabbed it from the night table and pressed the connect button. "Hello?"

"Julia, it's Mom," her mother said. "I'm not interrupting your dinner, am I?"

"No," Julia said, not bothering to tell her what she *was* interrupting.

"Is Ron there?"

She glanced to her left. He was lying on his back, frowning, his penis trying to decide if it should stay aroused or give up. It fluctuated at half-mast, but when she stroked her free hand down his side it shot back to attention. "Yes, he's here," she said. "You want to talk to him?"

"No. I just wanted to let you know his father called me. We're having dinner together Saturday night."

Julia yanked her hand away from Ron and sat up. "Dinner?" she said, her voice emerging in a squeak. "Why?"

Ron couldn't help noticing her anxiety. He sat up, too, touched her shoulder, and when she turned toward him, mouthed, *What's going on?*

She shook her head and turned away.

"Why?" her mother echoed. "So we can eat. That's usually why people have dinner."

"I thought you wanted to lose twenty pounds before my wedding."

"Have you set a date yet?" her mother asked. "I can still eat until you set a date. Unless you're planning to get married in the next month."

"No, of course not."

Ron poked her shoulder again, and when she turned he mouthed, *What?*

My mother and your father, she mouthed back.

He fell back against the bed and groaned. Ignoring him, Julia said, "Where is he taking you?"

"Tavern on the Green."

Oh, God. Out-of-towners believed Tavern on the Green, tucked into a cozy corner of Central Park, was the most romantic restaurant, especially on a Saturday night. "You said yes, I take it."

"I should say no? Of course I said yes."

"Your daughter is marrying his son," Julia reminded her.

"So we'll discuss the wedding. I just wanted you to know." Her mother paused, then issued a giddy laugh. "I don't know why you always used to complain about the dating scene. Dating is fun! I don't want to keep you. Go eat your dinner. I'll see you tomorrow." With a click, the connection was severed.

"Your father is taking my mother to Tavern on the Green," Julia reported, tossing her cell phone onto the night table and watching Ron's face for signs that he recognized the potential for disaster in this date.

"Big spender," Ron muttered. "Forget about it."

"How can I forget about it? It's important."

"Not that important." He snagged her with one long arm and pulled her on top of him. "Your mother and my father are grown-ups. They're allowed to have dinner together. Okay?" He dug his hands into her hair and pulled her down for a kiss.

It was a lovely kiss, almost lovely enough to keep her from thinking. But her brain refused to shut down. "What if after dinner they wind up like this?" she asked, stretching her body along his.

His eyes darkened with horror. "Yuck."

"Exactly."

"They're grown-ups," he repeated, clearly able to dismiss ghastly thoughts more easily than she.

He kissed her again, slid his thigh between her legs, cupped her bottom and came very close to empty-ing her mind. He pressed his thigh higher and she groaned, every last thought draining from her.

"Good," he whispered, arching against her. His penis was at full alert once more, pressing and poking, needing just a little assistance to line up properly...and her cell phone beeped again. "You didn't turn it off?"

"Obviously not."

He reached for the night table but she got there first, grabbing her phone and tapping it. "Hello?"

"Julia, it's me," Susie said, the words dissolving in a sob. "Casey's dating Halle Berry."

Julia rolled off Ron and sat up. Her womb ached. Her thighs clenched. Her entire body screamed at her to get off the phone and back to Ron—but her heart, her soul couldn't abandon Susie. "Halle Berry?"

Ron sat up and mouthed *What?* Julia ignored him.

"Some lady who looks like her," Susie said.

"Where are you?" Julia asked. Her sister's voice seemed strange, and not just from crying. "You sound like you're standing inside a metal barrel."

"I'm in the bathroom," Susie whimpered. "It's a very small bathroom. I don't want Ricky to see me crying."

"He can handle it," Julia assured her in a soothing tone. "He loves you."

Is it your mother again? Ron mouthed. Julia shook her head.

"I'm supposed to be the sane one on this trip, remember?" Susie sniffled. The noise echoed off the bathroom walls and through the phone. "I can't fall apart. Anyway, Ricky talked to Anna and he's all goo-goo. Anna was the one who told me. She called to say she saw Casey with this Halle Berry lady in the East Village."

"You broke up with him," Julia reminded her. "He's allowed to date other women."

"Just because I don't want to marry him doesn't mean I want him dating other women!"

"Susie, look. There's nothing you can do about it now. When you come home—"

"He'll probably be married to her by then. He wants to settle down."

"Believe me, he won't be married to her that fast. Planning a wedding takes time."

"We should elope," Ron said, responding to Julia's end of the conversation.

Susie must have heard him. "Is that Ron? Oh, Julia, I'm sorry. I'm interrupting something, right?"

"Don't worry about it. You're not the first interruption."

"Oh. Okay. I'm okay, Julia, okay?"

"Stop saying okay."

"Okay." Susie drew in a long breath. "I'll get off now. I don't think I'm crying anymore."

"I'll talk to you tomorrow," Julia promised.

"Okay. I mean—whatever."

Julia disconnected and put her phone on the night table. "Did you turn it off?"

"Yes," she said.

"Good. Maybe I won't have to kill your family." He pulled her into his arms but she didn't melt into him. "What?"

"My sister's heart is breaking." Julia ruminated for a moment. "It's her own fault because she ended things with Casey, so what can she expect? He's seeing someone else. Surprise, surprise."

"She'll get over it."

"Probably. But right now she feels like shit. She was crying on the phone."

"Not your problem." He lifted her hair off her neck and kissed her nape. A bolt of heat flashed the length of her spine.

"It is my problem," she said, although the words lacked conviction. "She's my sister. I love her."

"She's tough. She'll survive." He trailed kisses down her back. She sighed, turned to him, covered his mouth with hers...and his phone rang. "God damn fucking shit!" he howled.

She laughed. "Don't blame me. It's not mine."

Spewing curses under his breath, he reached over her and lifted his phone from the night table on his side of the bed. "What?" he snarled. He listened for a minute, closed his eyes, and handed the phone to her. "It's your brother," he said with such venom she believed he was once again plotting a hit on her family.

She pressed the receiver to her ear. "Adam?"

"Hi, Julia. I tried your phone, but it was busy, and then it was dead. Maybe the batteries need recharging."

"They don't," she said, feeling Ron's tension rolling over her in waves. "I turned the phone off."

"Oh. Well, sorry."

"What do you want?"

"I've got this cool plan to program some new software for the store. I meant to talk to you about it during the day, but I got so into theorizing, and then I wanted to try some stuff on my laptop. I think it'll work. It'd be really cool, Julia. I'm really psyched about it."

"Can we discuss it tomorrow?"

"Sure we can. Sorry. I was just psyched."

"I'm sure I'll be psyched when you tell me about it, too," she said. "Right now I've got to deal with Ron."

"Yeah. Okay."

"Don't say okay," she growled.

"Uh-huh. Tell him I'm sorry." The phone went silent.

She leaned over and placed Ron's phone on his night table, then gave him a hesitant smile. "He says he's sorry."

"Is it too late to back out of this marriage?" Ron asked.

She used her thumb to twirl her engagement ring around her finger. The diamond's facets winked light at her. Her smile grew. "I'm afraid so," she said, settling into the curve of his arm and resting her head against his shoulder. "You're stuck with me—and my whole family."

"Terrific," he grunted. She kissed his throat and he muttered something unintelligible. She slid her hand down his torso and he muttered something else that included the words *Bloom* and *hell*. She wrapped her fingers around his penis, which instantly revived, and he stopped muttering. In fact, she'd be willing to bet he stopped thinking altogether—which was really the best way to go about having sex.

Chapter Twenty-Two

Casey's mother had a pot of fish boiling on the stove. Cod, probably, with some carrots, black pepper and chunks of potato mixed in. Where she'd learned to cook this way he couldn't guess. It sure as hell wasn't the Culinary Institute.

He'd come to his parents' house because his father had received an audit notice from the IRS and Casey, as the only member of the family with a college degree, was expected to solve this problem. "There's nothing to solve," he told his father after reading the letter. "You and your accountant will meet with the auditor and go through your records."

"What if I don't have the right records?" his father moaned. He was seated in his usual chair in the brown and beige living room, and Casey was seated on the couch, his gaze trained to the Mets game being broadcast on the TV so he wouldn't have to look at the leprechauns leering at him from the shelves of the hutch. Fumes of boiled fish wafted in from the kitchen, reminding Casey that he hadn't eaten since breakfast—and that he'd rather fast for a full week than dine on his mother's boiled fish.

"Of course you have the right records," he told his father. "You gave the records to your accountant so he could put together your return. You haven't thrown the records out since then, have you?"

"No, I've got them in a box in the basement," his father said, his face going paler than his silvery-blond hair. "It's a box from O'Malley's Liquor, from when I bought that case of Hennessey's. Expensive stuff, but he'd had it on sale, and then there was a discount if you bought by the case, so..." He sighed. "I'd better put my records in a different box. A liquor store box wouldn't look good."

"I don't think they care, Dad."

His father lapsed into a tense silence, his lips arced downward and his eyes glassy with panic. "What if they arrest me?" he whispered.

"They're not going to arrest you," Casey said, hoping he sounded patient and reassuring. In truth, he wasn't feeling either. He had headaches of his own; he didn't want to suffer his father's headaches as well.

His life was spinning like a pinwheel in a hurricane, so swift the points dissolved into a circular blur. Barely two weeks ago he was asking Susie to marry him. Now Eva was insisting that the bakery she'd found for sale on Avenue B, two doors north of 4th Street, was perfect for him and he'd better grab it before the owner sold the business to someone else to finance his retirement in Hialeah. "Grabbing it" would entail Casey's taking over the remaining three years on the lease and buying the shop's ovens, refrigerators, display cases, and other equipment, some of which was okay and some of which was ancient enough to belong in the Smithsonian.

The place wasn't bad. He could use the archaic equipment until he had enough money to replace it— money on top of what he'd need to take over the lease. Mose had told him that between loans and investors

Casey could pull it off. Mose knew about financing new businesses. Eva knew real estate.

Casey didn't know what he knew, other than bagels and panic and the fact that his heart tightened like a fist that punched his rib cage whenever he thought of Susie. If she'd said yes to his marriage proposal, or even just to moving in with him, would he be so eager to set up his own business? If he set up his business in her neighborhood, how would he feel about her dropping by to pick up a loaf of herbed Italian bread or braided challah or a dozen bagels? If he left Bloom's, would Morty Sugarman be able to maintain the deli's bagel quality?

Morty was a terrific guy. Casey had learned a great deal from him. But he was an old-school bagel maker. It would never occur to him to create a sour-cream-and-chives bagel, or a pesto-and-sundried-tomato bagel. If the bagel department started slipping at Bloom's, would Susie blame Casey?

Would he ever stop caring? Would his fisted heart ever stop bruising itself on his ribcage?

His father broke into his ruminations. "So, if they're not going to arrest me, why are they auditing me?"

"I've heard they go after self-employed people more often than wage earners," Casey said. His father was the proprietor, president and sole employee of Gordon's Electric. He did well enough installing sockets, repairing light fixtures, bringing the wiring in old houses up to code so they could handle window-unit air conditioners, and using a simple software system to send out bills and keep track of payments. But he'd never earned such a big income that Uncle Sam could expect to fund the Pentagon on what the Gordons of Forest Hills paid in taxes. "They just want to keep you honest," Casey explained.

"I'm very honest." His father folded his hands to-gether and then shook them loose, folded them and shook them. Casey found himself momentarily mes-merized by the wedding ring on his father's left hand. Such a potent, solid symbol, such a permanent fixture. Nothing elaborate or fancy, just a plain gold band that said, *I took a vow, and I'm living by it every day.*

Casey never wore rings—working with dough could get messy, and jewelry was taboo when a per-son used certain equipment. Still, a ring like that, an-nouncing to the world that you were a grown-up, a man of your word... Wearing a wedding ring struck Casey as a profoundly honest thing to do.

"You think they'll find out about those cir-cuit-breakers I bought wholesale and then sold to Jim-my Benedetti at list price?" his father asked anxiously. "I never declared that income. He paid me in cash."

"And you made, what? Ten bucks off the deal? Forget it, Dad. That kind of thing doesn't matter to the IRS."

"So why are they auditing me?"

"You should go to confession before the audit," his mother shouted from the kitchen. "Just to be sure."

"What if the auditor isn't Catholic?" his father wondered aloud. "You think going to confession'll make a difference?"

Casey admitted, with a pang of self-awareness, that he loved his parents. They were weird, they were annoying, and he truly adored them. The possibility that worrying about this stupid audit might cause his father to go into cardiac arrest pained him almost as much as losing Susie did.

His father quit wringing his hands long enough to rake his fingers through his hair. At his left elbow the TV droned, the Cubs scoring two runs off a bases-loaded single and increasing their lead over the Mets. "I'll tell you, Casey, I haven't slept since that letter arrived." His father gestured toward the coffee table, where the vile missive from the IRS lay. "All I can say is, thank God you and your sister work for other people, your sister at Poodle-Do and you at Bloom's. Let them do all the bookkeeping. No one's gonna come after you with an audit."

Now was not a good time to tell his father how serious his thoughts about leaving Bloom's had become. Nor would he mention that he, too, had been having trouble sleeping. His insomnia was only partly attributable to his career decision; mostly it had to do with Susie. He lay awake wondering where she and her cousin were and why they were making some stupid home movie when she could be in New York, educating him about her neighborhood's shopping habits and the foot traffic on Avenue B. Could people who lived in brownstone walk-ups afford six-ninety-nine for a loaf of gourmet bread? If he charged less than six-ninety-nine, would he go bankrupt? Would the IRS audit him? Why wasn't Susie by his side, helping him make this momentous decision? Why wasn't she in his bed? What the hell was she so afraid of, anyway?

The same things he was afraid of, he supposed: committing to a course, making a change, redefining his life.

"So, they giving you a raise at Bloom's any time soon?"

"They pay me well," Casey said noncommittally.

"They ought to pay you more. You're dating the boss's daughter."

"Sister," Casey automatically corrected him, as if it mattered anymore. He wasn't dating any relative of the boss. And his boss—a woman he liked, a woman he'd imagined might one day become his sister-in-law—was going to hate him once he announced that he was leaving Bloom's, if that was what he decided to do.

"Play your cards right, your name could be up there above the door. Bloom's and Gordon's," his father said. "Of course, then they might audit you."

"He should find a nice Catholic girl," Casey's mother hollered from the kitchen. "Casey, are you staying for supper?"

He pictured the vat of boiling cod on her stove and his stomach lurched. "Can't," he said, leaping to his feet, figuring escape would be easier with his mother in the kitchen and his father demoralized over his tax situation.

"I made too much for Dad and me. You'd like it. It's like a chowder," his mother yelled.

"Sorry, Mom. I'm sure it's delicious, but I can't. Dad," he added, leaning over and squeezing his father's shoulder, "this audit thing is nothing. You'll go, your accountant will do all the talking, and the IRS will figure out that either you owe them fifty bucks or they owe you fifty bucks. A waste of an afternoon, that's all this is."

"I could wind up in jail," his father said, his hands once again fidgeting.

"Why? Did you break any laws?"

"No. Except maybe for those circuit-breakers I sold Jimmy Benedetti."

"Then you won't wind up in jail. I promise you. After it's done, I'll take you out for a beer, okay?"

"Okay," his father said so faintly Casey almost didn't hear the words. He gave his old man's shoulder another squeeze, then sauntered across the living room, past the leprechaun-infested hutch and out the door. The air was gray and muggy, evening hovering in a warm, thick mass above his parents' block. Still,

258

being outdoors was better than being in a house that smelled of boiling fish.

He strolled to the corner, moving at a gait that would almost qualify as a slow jog. He wasn't racing to get away from his parents, but was simply burning off energy. As exhausted as his sleepless nights left him, he was nearly as jittery as his father.

Starting his own business. Jesus. He wanted it, he had the culinary talent, he understood the mechanics of it, the numbers, the strategies—but did he have the passion for it? Was he really concerned about having people like Julia Bloom hate him?

What he absolutely had to do was separate his career plans from the tar pit of his love life. Susie was gone, she'd said no, and that was that. His father had the right idea: a store with Gordon's written above the door—although "Gordon's" seemed like a pretty lame name for a gourmet bread shop. Gordon's Gourmet? Casey's Casa? What was the Hispanic population of the East Village?

Bread. Staff of Life. Gordon's Gourmet Grains. Gordon's Grains and Bagels. Beautiful Bagels. If this dream were genuine, wouldn't he have thought of a name for the store by now?

He'd reached the basketball court outside the Edward Mandel School. A half-dozen guys were playing three-on-three, shirts versus skins. He recognized one of them, a six-foot-eight inch black dude who'd played with the Cleveland Cavaliers for two years before blowing out his knee. He was in his thirties now, and he still boasted quite a few slick moves for someone past his prime with a bum knee. Casey and Mose had played in some pick-up games with him. The guy was fierce. Casey loved going up against him, just for the adrenalin rush.

He spotted Casey leaning against the chain link fence and shot him a toothy grin. Casey smiled back. If he weren't wearing the cargo pants and cotton button-down shirt he'd donned for work that morning, he might have swung around the end of the fence and planted his butt on the bench, where he could wait until someone collapsed in exhaustion and he could take the guy's place.

Simply watching wasn't a bad alternative. It gave his mind a chance to run though options. His eyes recorded the ex-Cavalier's feints and spins and his brain calculated how many loaves of bread and dozens of bagels he'd have to sell to break even. If he could be guaranteed a regular, loyal clientele, even if only a small one, he could count on a steady income, and that would see him half the way home.

Susie could see him the other half of the way home, but he didn't want to think about that. God, he was such an ass, mooning over her when the world teemed with available women who weren't so determined to say no. Three-quarters of what Eva said to him qualified as come-ons, yet he was keeping his fly zipped and yearning for a woman who didn't want him. How had he turned into such a putz?

One of the skins staggered over to the bench and reached for a towel. The ex-Cav glanced Casey's way again. "Hey, wanna fill in?"

"He's gotta go home to his *lady*," one of the other players sing-songed, obviously considering the guy on the bench irredeemably pussy-whipped.

Casey smiled. He wasn't pussy-whipped. He might be inappropriately dressed, but he did have on sneakers. He started unbuttoning his shirt before he'd even walked around the fence.

He tossed his shirt onto the bench alongside backpacks, duffel bags and bottles of water and Gatorade, then rummaged in his trouser pocket for a rubber band, which he used to fasten his hair off his face in a pony-tail. The ex-Cav tossed him the ball, and he felt himself come to life. The ball felt like an extension of his hand, connected by an invisible elastic strand to his arm. He slammed it against the blacktop and it popped right back up at him. The ex-Cav came at him and he bounce-passed the ball under the guy's arm to set up one of the other skins.

The hell with love. The hell with business, bread, and IRS audits. This was what life was all about—throwing, passing, setting up a teammate, aiming for the hoop.

The ball came back to him where he stood, way outside. The shirts hovered, waiting for him to charge toward the basket. Instead, he dribbled into position just to the left of the key and sent the ball in a high arc, his favorite three-point shot. It dropped cleanly through the hoop.

"Damn! Where'd that come from?" the ex-Cav said, flashing Casey another ivory-white smile.

Casey shrugged. He'd gotten his shot back. He was going to be okay. The store would work out, he'd find the money, he'd make a go of it. He'd make a living. He'd make a life.

Fuck Susie. He had his shot back.

Chapter Twenty-Three

Susie would kill for a rhyme for stroganoff. Actually, she'd kill for a good night's sleep and a little convincing proof that she wasn't completely insane. Of course, if she killed for that, it would probably prove that she *was* completely insane.

She had to get a *Bloom's Bulletin* written and emailed to Julia by tomorrow morning, and she was hurting for inspiration. Right now, the only thing she felt inspired to do was toss her laptop out the window. And maybe toss Linus out after it. The motel where they'd taken a room, just outside Boston in the seaside town of Revere, was a giant step better than the place they'd stayed at in Maine—and a giant step more expensive, too—but judging by the conversations she'd eavesdropped on in the lobby, she concluded that the majority of the motel's guests were far more interested in assorted vices—gambling, drinking, sex—than hiking the Freedom Trail through downtown Boston. If they saw a six-foot-tall plastic lobster in the parking lot, they probably wouldn't think anything of it.

Linus wasn't the cause of her woes, and she shouldn't scapegoat him. She glanced away from her laptop monitor to find the lobster propped up in a corner of the tiny room, staring at her. Actually, she didn't think lobsters had eyes, so maybe he wasn't staring. His crooked antennae were angled toward her, though, and one claw pointed accusingly at her.

She and Rick had checked into the motel after filming a scene with her and Linus on the beach. She'd stood barefoot in the sand, trying to ignore all the strangers gawking at her and Rick as if they were hot-shot Hollywood celebrities, and she talked about food. Linus had lain at her feet in the hot sand. Despite Rick's pleas, she'd refused to hold him upright next to her as if he were her personal escort.

Once they'd finished filming and settled into their room, Rick had left to scout sites in Boston—or so he claimed. He'd promised to return with a take-out dinner. It was now nearly seven o'clock and her stomach was rumbling like a rock slide. She hoped he'd get back soon—not only because she wanted to eat but because she wanted an excuse to procrastinate writing the bulletin.

She couldn't procrastinate. She had to get it done. She'd promised Julia she'd supply the bulletins on time. It was her job.

Responsibility sucked.

Julia had emailed her all the data she needed for the newsletter: what would be on sale, what guest speakers would be making presentations, what special events the store would be hosting over the next week. Susie kept a file of Grandma Ida's sayings on her computer's hard drive, and the motel offered free WiFi if she had to do any research.

But instead of putting the damned bulletin together, she stared at the blank screen and struggled to come up with a rhyme for stroganoff. As if she really gave a shit.

She leaned back into the pillows and stretched her legs. The laptop rocked on her thighs and she set it aside. Closing her eyes against the yellow glare of the bedside lamp and the paint-by-numbers rendering of a race horse at full gallop on the wall opposite her, she let her mind drift.

To her great exasperation, it drifted to Casey.

Lying down was a mistake, especially on a bed. Her legs shifted again, her hips flexing as her body tensed with a memory of how fantastic sex with Casey had been. Good girls weren't supposed to admit that sex was everything—they were supposed to act as if a man's kindness and sense of humor were far more important than what he could do with his penis. But Susie had never considered herself a good girl, and while she certainly appreciated Casey's kindness and his sense of humor and all his other fine attributes, right now she was sprawled out on a motel bed, all alone, and sex rose to the top of her priorities list.

Was sex worth tying herself down? Of course not. How about really, really good sex? Still no, but without the of course. How about really, really, *really* good sex with a guy who also happened to be kind and have a sense of humor?

Don't even think about it.

Her purse rested on the floor by the bed, and she reached over the side and dug around in it until she located her cell phone. "Don't do this," she warned herself, her voice echoing against the ugly sea-green wallpaper, but she ignored her own wise counsel and punched the speed-dial for Casey's number.

He answered, out of breath, on the third ring. "Yeah?"

"Casey?"

A long silence, then, "Susie?"

He was panting. She closed her eyes again and pictured him, naked and sweaty, in the arms of Halle Berry. "Sorry," she said. "Forget it."

"Forget what?" His voice sounded a little stronger as he regained control of his respiration. Had he and Halle Berry just been getting started, or were they winding down? Susie's stomach lurched again, not from hunger but from anguish. If Rick walked into the room at that moment carrying a bag of Chinese takeout, she might just vomit.

"Anna told me she ran into you on Avenue A the other day."

"Yeah."

He clearly wasn't going to volunteer information about the woman he'd been with when Anna had encountered him. And Susie was a wuss, because she couldn't find the courage to ask him about his gorgeous female companion, let alone what he was doing with said companion in Susie's neighborhood. "I shouldn't have called," she muttered. "It's obvious I interrupted something—"

"I was playing pick-up," he told her. "It's getting dark so we were kind of winding down, anyway."

Then she hadn't caught him in the act. Good. Maybe he was as horny as she was, and was taking the edge off by shooting hoops. Maybe she ought to take up basketball, too.

Just because she hadn't interrupted something X-rated didn't mean his life without her was a Disney family flick, though. He still could be porking Halle Berry. He might shoot hoops not to take the edge off but to build stamina and get his blood pumping.

Don't even think about it.

"Look, Susie—did you phone me for a reason?"

I was lonely, she almost said. *I'm all alone in a motel room near Boston, and I'm homesick for New York, and this movie Rick's making is stupid, and Linus is up-*

staging me in all his scenes, and I don't want to miss you but I do. "I need a rhyme for stroganoff," she told him.

"What?"

"I've got to write a limerick for the next *Bloom's Bulletin.* I need a rhyme for stroganoff."

He said nothing for a minute, then: "Jog enough."

"What?"

"Jog enough. 'If I eat beef stroganoff, I'll be able to jog enough.' Something like that."

God help her, she was in love. How could she not love a man who created a rhyme like that?

Tears filled her eyes—an all too frequent occurrence these days. She batted them, and the painting of the race horse across the room seemed to waver through the layer of moisture. She loved Casey truly, madly and deeply. Why couldn't she love him on her own terms? Why wasn't her love enough to satisfy him?

Those were questions she couldn't ask him. They were questions she wasn't sure she could ask herself. "Thanks," she said, hoping he wouldn't hear the muffled sob in her voice. "Jog enough. It's perfect, Casey."

"Yeah," he said, not a trace of emotion in his tone. She was falling apart, and he was undoubtedly thinking she was a selfish bitch, phoning him from New England to get a rhyme out of him. Or maybe he was thinking about his play during the pick-up game, rehashing a block or a rebound in his mind. He didn't care whether Susie missed him. He'd be spending the evening with Halle, after all.

"Well, thanks," Susie said again. Saying good-bye would hurt too much, so she signed off with, "I'd better get back to work."

"Okay," Casey said, then disconnected the call. Maybe he couldn't bear to say good-bye either. Maybe he was hurting as badly as she was, hurting so much that when she came home he'd ease up on the pressure and tell her he'd be happy just to get back to where they'd been before he started this whole moving-in-together crap.

Not likely, but one thing Susie was always pretty good at was dreaming.

The Bloom's Bulletin
Written and edited by
Susie Bloom

A dieter looking for dinner
Found in Bloom's a delectable winner.
"If I work out and jog enough,
I can eat the beef stroganoff,
And the fruit salad might make me
thinner!"

Welcome to the June 17 edition of the *Bloom's Bulletin*. Summer is just around the corner, and hot weather means bare legs, bare arms, and frequently bare mid-sections. It also means Bloom's! Although Bloom's is known as a paradise for food lovers, folks counting calories need not stay away. Bloom's offers many low-fat, low-calorie delights. Fresh, delicious salads are available, including two amazing new fruit salads (citrus, and berries-and-melon) guaranteed to satisfy your taste without expanding your waist. Bloom's also has a full array of low-fat cheeses, low-fat yogurts, extra-lean meats, and sugar-free cookies. Bloom's doesn't sell low-fat bagels—but that's because our bagels are NO-fat! So show off your svelte summer bodies and indulge your palates.

Food for thought:

As always, Bloom's wants to nourish your mind as well as your body. In addition to the workshops and presentations we've already announced (a complete schedule appears on page four), we'll be exploring the mind-body connection with Noreen Kastigian, a dietician and meditation coach, who will discuss "Sanity Strategy," her philosophy of food as a form of mental sustenance and thought as a dietary supplement. You won't want to miss this special talk, which Noreen will repeat on three consecutive Thursday evenings. Another edifying lecture we've added to the schedule is Barry Sullivan-Goldberg's "Nosh or Nap," in which he will explain what foods give the most effective energy boosts during those low-energy times of the day. Mark your calendars!

Summertime, and the livin' is easy...

Bloom's wants to make your summertime easier. Check out our specials in the Heat-'N'-Eat department. Poached salmon, marinated asparagus tips, and stuffed tomatoes are all on sale. Even though they're sold as Heat-'N'-Eat dishes, you don't have to heat them to eat them! All Heat-'N'-Eat dishes are fully cooked. A chilled poached salmon entrée, with a side of cold asparagus and stuffed tomatoes, would make a delicious light meal on a hot day. And it would be so low in calories, you could top it off with a slice of Bloom's melt-in-your-mouth amaretto cheesecake. Explore the tempting contents of our dairy pastry case for more (literally) cool desserts.

Did you know...

The word *amaretto* is often confused with *amoretto*. *Amoretto* is a diminutive of the Italian *amore* or the

Latin *amor*), which means "love." *Amaretto* derives from the Italian *amaro* (or the Latin *amarus*), which means bitter. *Amaretto* is the almond liqueur—a vital ingredient in Bloom's *amaretto* cheesecake. *Amoretto* is the name of a pale pink-orange breed of rose, a gourmet chocolate-truffle candy, and a flavored cigar. A filly named Ambro Amoretto won the Breeder's Cup some years ago. Bloom's does not use horses in any of its recipes.

Employee Profile:

How to describe Deirdre Morrissey? Her official title at Bloom's is Vice-President and General Manager, and in a way that sums up what she means to the company. As the executive assistant to Bloom's president, Deirdre manages everything like a five-star general.

Deirdre originally came to Bloom's as a secretary for the late Ben Bloom. Before long, she proved herself indispensable in so many areas of the business that she rose to her current position, with her office right next door to the president's. Need a rabbi to bless the cheese delivery? Deirdre will find one for you. Problems with a coffee importer? Deirdre has the numbers of a dozen other coffee importers in her precious files. Plumbing disaster in the staff bathroom? If Deirdre can't find a plumber in five minutes, she'll do the repair herself. She monitors the inventory, double-checks the billings, and oversees all correspondence. Around Bloom's third-floor offices, the word is that Deirdre can do anything.

A tall redhead with legs like a fashion model's and a passion for stiletto-heeled shoes, Deirdre is single. "Once I started working at Bloom's," she says, "the store became my passion. I grew up Irish. I never tasted a matzo ball before I came to Bloom's. But this place stole my heart." What are her favorite Bloom's foods? "I like everything," she says diplomatically. However, she is partial to the many herbal teas that Bloom's sells, and nearly always has a steaming cup of tea at her elbow. She's also been known to nibble on the mandelbrot or sneak a chunk of halvah into her office between meals.

"Deirdre's pretty quiet," one of her co-workers recently said of her. "But I'll tell you this—Bloom's couldn't survive without her."

Wise words from Bloom's founder, Ida Bloom:
"If you can't stand the heat, don't move to Miami."

On sale this week:
Salads salads, salads! Also low-fat Muenster, low-fat Jarlsburg, and low-fat sliced turkey breast, plain, smoked, or Cajun-style. Look for on-the-spot specials in the store—they change daily! Turn the page for details.

Chapter Twenty-Four

Julia wasn't crazy about the horse joke. And rhyming Stroganoff with jog enough seemed like a stretch. But at least Susie had gotten the damned newsletter done on time.

She gave the copy Susie had emailed her a final perusal, then highlighted the horse joke and deleted it. She had never changed a word in one of Susie's newsletters before, but if the line stayed in, Julia imagined that half the city's animal rights activists would be picketing Bloom's within minutes of reading the *Bloom's Bulletin*. The block of Broadway outside the store would be jammed with protesters throwing water balloons filled with fake blood at the showcase windows, and carrying signs declaring, "Bloom's says it doesn't use horses in its recipes. Do you believe that?" Julia had a law school degree. She knew how people could imply a slander without actually coming right out and committing one.

Susie would probably never notice that Julia had removed a few of her precious words. If she did, screw it. Julia was an executive, which every now and then required her to make an executive decision. Besides, Susie was already vying for a place on Julia's shit list, having spent a week roaming the less exclusive neighborhoods of New England with Rick and a camera, supposedly making an artsy video about Bloom's. Julia was suffering severe misgivings about having funded their adventure. Bloom's was a New York City institution. Why did Rick and Susie have to go to New England to make a movie? Why couldn't they make it here in the city? Were they budgeting wisely? Would they produce something she could actually use to promote the store? Was Susie recovering from the emotional upheaval of ending her relationship with Casey Gordon? Was Rick really the person she ought to have at her side during such a recovery?

Why did being the president of Bloom's mean most of Julia's thoughts ended in question marks?

Deirdre sauntered through the open office door, carrying a stack of papers that were no doubt extremely important and boring. Along with making executive decisions, Julia had learned that being an executive involved reading reams of important, boring papers. Granted, they weren't as tedious as the legal documents she used to have to review when she'd been working at the law firm, and they were by and large written in English instead of jargon. No parties of the first part suing parties of the second part over court-reduced alimony payments. No "hereinafter" and "aforementioned." The papers Deirdre brought Julia each morning usually included whiny letters from pickle vendors announcing that a cucumber blight in South Carolina had necessitated an increase in price for the half-sours, and kvetchy missives from people claiming that their son stuck a pit from an olive purchased at Bloom's up the nostril of his sister and therefore the store should reimburse them for the bill of the pediatrician who'd had to use a special tweezers to extract the pit from little Emma's nostril, plus the cost of the olives. After receiving a note that made that very demand, Julia had contemplated banning unpitted olives from Bloom's inventory, but she'd come to her senses and instead written back to the woman that rather than blame the store, she might consider blaming her son for his nasal assault on little Emma. So what if Julia's letter cost Bloom's a customer? She wasn't going to let some woman who didn't know how to discipline her children dictate what went on the shelves of the store.

Deirdre was such a genial woman that Julia smiled and pretended she was thrilled to be receiving today's stack of kvetches and whines. "Susie did a great write-up on you for the *Bulletin*," she said.

Deirdre shrugged diffidently. "I didn't give her much to work with."

"Whatever you gave her, she made the most of it. She's very creative."

Deirdre nodded and set the stack of papers on Julia's desk. She loomed above Julia, the three-inch heels of her mules augmenting her already towering height. "I hear your mother is dating again," she said.

Julia blinked up at her. Deirdre generally avoided personal discussions of the Bloom's family. A year ago, Julia had learned that Deirdre and her father had been lovers—or, as Susie had so tactfully phrased it in her employee profile, the "store" had become Deirdre's passion. Julia had never confronted Deirdre with her discovery, nor had she mentioned it to her mother. Why stir up trouble and open old wounds? Her father was dead. Whatever might have existed between him and his right-hand woman had been buried with him.

But still, Julia wasn't sure she wanted to discuss her mother's love life with her late father's mistress. She wasn't that modern.

Deirdre was waiting for her to say something, though. "Where did you hear that?" she asked, her smile growing numb and stiff, as if her mouth had been shot full of Novocain.

"From your mother."

"Really?" The imaginary Novocain began to wear off, weaving threads of pain through her jaw and lips. She was definitely not modern enough for this conversation.

"I think it's good for your mother," Deirdre added. "Dating, I mean."

Julia peered up at the tall, thin woman. Deirdre's hair was a dull red with strands of gray mixed in, and she had a profound overbite. When Julia had figured out that her father's relationship with Deirdre had extended beyond the purely professional, she'd acknowledged that his attraction to his assistant hadn't been based on her alluring beauty. Sondra Bloom was prettier.

What Ben Bloom had fallen for was Deirdre's competence and dedication, and her downright sensibility. Now here she was, sensibly discussing Julia's mother's love life. "You think dating is good for her?" Julia asked.

"He's been dead two years," Deirdre said, not having to identify whom she was referring to. "Your mother needs a life." Deirdre had lost her man just as Sondra had, but apparently she didn't need a life. Her life was Bloom's. Julia's mother tried to pretend her life was Bloom's, but her life really was her children. Julia and Susie were all in favor of their mother getting a life, just so they wouldn't have to be her life anymore. Julia was sure that if she raised the subject with Adam, he'd feel the same way.

So it was good for Sondra to be dating. The only problem was the person she was dating. "What exactly did my mother tell you?"

"He took her to Tavern on the Green last Saturday, and when she said she didn't want any dessert he forced her to order the peanut butter chocolate lava cake."

"He forced her?" That didn't sound good to Julia. No man should force anything on a woman, even if it was peanut butter chocolate lava cake.

"Her words. I suspect he didn't have to push too hard." Deirdre sounded just the slightest bit catty. "He told her she looked terrific and women shouldn't be so hung up about the size of their rear ends. So she ordered the cake."

"She told you all this?" Julia wasn't sure what shocked her more, Ron's father lavishing cake on her mother and commenting on her rear end or her mother confiding in Deirdre. And to think that just minutes ago, her greatest concern was ridding the *Bloom's Bulletin* of Susie's joke about horse meat.

"We're friends, your mother and I," Deirdre said with a toothy smile before she pivoted on one stilt-like heel and sauntered out of the office.

Julia's jaw continued to ache, and she realized her mouth was hanging open. She snapped it shut and stared at the empty doorway through which Deirdre had vanished. *Friends?*

She frowned. Did their friendship include gossip about her father? Or only gossip about her future father-in-law?

She reached for her phone and punched the speed-dial for Ron's office. After two rings, he answered: "Joffe."

"It's me. Your father discussed my mother's rear end with her."

"What?"

"During their date last Saturday. She told Deirdre and Deirdre told me."

Ron hesitated before responding. "Don't you have a deli to run?"

"How can I run it when your father has been intimate with my mother?"

"Intimate?" At last, he seemed to understand the gravity of the situation. "How do you know they've been intimate? Did Deirdre tell you that, too?"

"I don't mean *intimate* intimate. But discussing my mother's rear end—"

"Forgive me, but your mother's rear end is hard to overlook." Before Julia could chew him out for insulting her mother, he continued. "Listen, sweetheart. Unlike you, I am not my own boss. I've got a dragon-lady editor and for some reason she wants me to get my column written and submitted by deadline. So can you maybe throw a fit about your mother's rear end later?"

Asshole. "Sorry to bother you," Julia snapped, then slammed down the phone in time to see Uncle Jay lurking in her open doorway. Clad in crisp khaki slacks and a polo shirt in a shade of green that existed only in the wardrobes of golfers, he gave her an unnervingly charming smile. He was probably on his way out to the private club on Long Island where he golfed. The morning was bright and sunny, and Uncle Jay would never let something as trivial as his job come between him and a perfect day for golf. "Just wanted to let you know I got a call from Rick last night," he informed her. "He says this movie is going to be a masterpiece."

"It's supposed to be an infomercial," Julia pointed out.

"Think big, Julia. Expect the unexpected. That boy's got more talent in his whole body than you've got in your little pinkie."

That didn't sound right, but Julia let it go because her uncle was already swaggering down the hall, whistling some tune that was probably a secret jingle for golfers.

She swiveled away from the open door, and her gaze settled on the stack of papers Deirdre had left for her. Squaring her shoulders, she lifted the top whine from the pile. Before she could read past the letter-head, her brother Adam materialized in her door. "Hey, you got a minute?" he asked.

She watched him stride into the office. He didn't look like a math geek these days. His complexion was summer tan, his floppy hair brushed back from his face, and the veins and muscles in his forearms bulged slightly, presumably a result of all the lifting and carrying his job entailed. He had on a standard-issue Bloom's apron over his T-shirt and jeans, and the steel-toed shoes she'd made him buy when she'd hired him so he wouldn't break his toes if he dropped a crate of canned sardines on his foot. His hesitant smile was the only feature that reminded her of the old Adam, her tentative kid brother, who liked to escape from the world by spinning some funky music, firing up a joint and fantasizing about numbers theory.

He was a welcome sight, at least compared to Deirdre and her pile of important, boring papers or Uncle Jay and his golf togs. He was definitely more welcome than her peanut-butter-chocolate-lava-cake-devouring mother or her nomadic sister would have been. "What's up?" she asked.

He lowered himself onto the old leather couch. A lock of dark hair slid forward onto his brow and he pushed it back. He'd turned out pretty damned hand-some, she realized, experiencing a burst of pride that was almost maternal. Slight in build—all the Blooms were slim and compact—but definitely handsome, with eyes the color of black coffee, nicely contoured cheeks and a distinguished nose, the nose their mother might have wound up with if a plastic surgeon hadn't intervened. On a woman, Julia supposed, that nose might overpower her face. But on Adam it looked terrific.

"I was wondering if I could ask a favor." His smile, still shy, grew ingratiating.

"You can ask," she said. "I can say no if I don't like it."

"Can I use your apartment?"

That was a pretty big favor. "I'm not married yet," she noted. "I still consider that apartment my home."

"I didn't mean to use it forever, like to take over your lease or anything." Adam shifted on the soft leather cushion. Julia realized he was nervous. "I just want to borrow it. Like for a couple of hours, some evening when you're at Joffe's or something. You know, like the Grateful Dead song, only I don't need a chateau."

She had no idea which Grateful Dead song he was referring to, and decided that was just as well, especially since her apartment resembled a chateau the way a bruised grape resembled a case of vintage Bordeaux. "What do you want to borrow it for?" she asked.

"Well..." He shifted again, his nerves seeming to bubble over. "See, there's this ballet dancer."

"Elyse," Julia recalled. Adam had dragged the girl through Julia's godawful dinner party a few weeks ago.

"Right. Elyse."

That was all he said. His gaze darted around the office. He jiggled one foot, his knee bouncing. In the silence, Julia was able to fill in the blanks. "You want to have sex with her?"

Avoiding her gaze, Adam nodded.

Okay. That didn't seem particularly nefarious. It was actually rather healthy. And although she couldn't say she actually knew Elyse, Julia was willing to bet the woman was an improvement over Tash.

"So, can I borrow your apartment?" he asked.

Julia couldn't think of a good reason to turn him down. But that weird maternalism made her pause before saying yes. This was Adam, after all. Her baby brother. The kid who'd humiliated her in front of her friends when they'd been building a volcano out of *papier mâché* for a school science project and he'd come into the kitchen, where they were constructing Krakatoa on the counter, and used a drinking straw to spit chocolate milk at them. This was the kid who, a few years later, had brought a group of his friends home and they'd spent the entire afternoon experimenting with a whoopee cushion, testing its entire repertory of fart noises and critiquing each variation. This was the kid who had just graduated from Cornell University with honors.

Julia supposed he wasn't a kid anymore. "Will you be careful?" she asked.

"I won't break anything."

"That's not what I'm asking." Her maternalism was in overdrive now. "I mean, you have to use birth control."

"Oh. Duh." He no longer had a problem looking at her. His smile took on a brash quality.

"Well, that's my rule," she said primly, his change in attitude annoying her. She preferred him humble and supplicating. "I don't want anything conceived in my apartment. Or caught, or spread. I don't even know this girl. You hardly know her yourself."

"I know her just fine."

"She's a ballet dancer?"

"She's studying at Juilliard."

"You hate ballet," Julia reminded him.

"We aren't going to be dancing at your apartment."

"Like hell you aren't." She sighed. "When do you want to borrow it?"

His smile transformed again, this time brimming with gratitude, lacking even a hint of swagger. "I have to talk to her. I didn't want to raise the subject with her until I talked to you first. Thanks a lot, Julia. I mean it."

"I'm sure you do," she said, pursing her lips and wishing she felt a little less squeamish about the whole thing. Adam was old enough, after all. And it wasn't as if Julia had anything against premarital sex, in theory. Or even in practice. If it weren't for premarital sex... well, she and Ron would surely have eloped by now, so their sex wouldn't be premarital.

But her baby brother, trysting with that skinny blond girl with the ramrod posture in Julia's bed... She'd have to make sure he changed the sheets afterward.

"Oh, by the way," he said, pushing himself to his feet, "how do you like the new computer network I set up to track inventory?"

"It's excellent," she said tightly. She considered him brilliant for having set it up, but she was too distracted by thoughts of him engaging in sex to talk about it.

"I've got some other ideas," he added. "I think the stock could be organized more efficiently downstairs. Not in the store—Susie's got her design ideas going, and I don't want to mess with that. I don't know anything about retail. I'm just thinking..." He measured her with a glance, as if to make sure she was paying attention. She determinedly emptied all thoughts of carnality from her mind and nodded at him to continue. "Like, you've got lighter-weight goods like crackers, cereals, pastas and stuff closer to the chute and the canned and bottled items further away. They're heavier. Shouldn't the heavier stuff be closer to the chute, so it doesn't have to be carried so far?"

"I never thought about it," she admitted. To be sure, she rarely even went into the basement. She assumed the stock managers knew what they were doing.

They probably did. But Adam knew what he was doing, too. He wasn't a fool. Purdue had accepted him as a graduate student in mathematics, and he hadn't been accepted for his discernment in whoopee-cushion sounds. He'd been accepted because he was a math genius.

"Talk it over with Larry Glickman," she said. Larry was the stock manager she knew best. "See what he says."

"Can I talk it over with Berkowitz, instead?" Adam asked, naming another manager. "Glickman always sprays saliva when he talks."

"Then talk it over with Berkowitz. Or else put on a raincoat and talk it over with Glickman. I don't micromanage how things are done downstairs."

"Okay." Adam moved toward the door, his heavy shoes leaving tread marks in the worn carpet. "Cool."

She watched him leave, then sank deeper into her chair. Her head was swimming with shark-like thoughts. They circled menacingly, as if eager to devour her. The theme from *Jaws* drummed in her ears.

Her mother and Norman Joffe. Adam and the ballet dancer. Adam and the ballet dancer in her bed, moaning into her pillows.

She lifted her phone and speed-dialed Ron's office. "Joffe," he answered after one ring.

"My brother wants to use my apartment for sex."

Ron sighed audibly. "Are you having a bad day?"

"Yes. And it's not even ten-thirty."

"I haven't finished my column yet. In fact, I haven't finished the first paragraph. What do you want me to do?"

It was her turn to sigh. "Finish the first paragraph. I'll talk to you later. I love you," she said before hanging up, to atone for the rude way she'd hung up on him last time.

She lifted the top sheet from the pile Deirdre had left on her desk, but before the print came into focus she heard a light rap on her door. Thank God, she thought, drawing in a deep breath to collect herself. Her family would never knock on her door before barging in. Nor would Deirdre or Myron. Whoever wished to see her was someone a few steps removed from the Bloom inner circle. Relief washed through her.

She rotated her chair to discover Casey Gordon filling her doorway. Like Adam, he wore a Bloom's apron over his civilian clothes, and his hair was pulled back into a ponytail in keeping with health code restrictions for food workers. Always lean, he looked almost gaunt today. Had he not been eating? Was he that heartsick over Susie?

Were all her thoughts ending in question marks again?

The hell with that. She couldn't bear the thought of Casey not eating. He was such a nice guy, and he spent his life surrounded by gourmet bagels. Susie might be weepier than usual these days, but Julia was sure she was eating. Nothing, not even a broken heart, could keep Susie from consuming great quantities of food.

"Have you got a minute?" Casey asked, smiling diffidently.

To discuss Susie? No, she didn't have a minute for that. She didn't have even a second to devote to any of her family's *mishegas*. She had a pile of important, boring papers to go through, and an eleven-thirty meeting with some people from the Fulton Fish Market, and they were going to smell fishy, and she wouldn't dare to phone Ron again, because if he didn't finish his first paragraph he would be a grouch all night, which would mean she'd be better off staying at her own place, which in turn would mean Adam couldn't have sex with his ballet dancer.

Her day was *kaput*. It couldn't go any further downhill because it was already at the bottom of the slope. She beckoned Casey inside with a wave of her hand.

He closed the door behind him, alarming her slightly, and dragged a chair over to her desk so he could sit facing her.

"How are you?" she asked carefully.

"I'm fine."

Not gaunt, but haunted, she decided. His eyes had the glassy look of someone who hadn't slept well since the Vernal Equinox. He gave off an interesting fragrance, some faintly spicy aftershave overlaid with a yeasty baking scent. His hands were clean, no residue of flour on them. She loved thinking of such a solid, grounded man creating the bagels her store sold—and she hated thinking Susie might have done anything that would cause him suffering. Of course her loyalties lay with Susie, and all she knew about her break-up with Casey was that he'd taken the unforgivable step of asking her to move in with him, but Julia was certain there had to be more to it.

"Susie's in Boston now," she said when he remained silent. "Outside Boston, actually, in a town named Revere. I think it was named after Paul Revere, but I'm not positive. She and Rick are filming in Boston, but I guess it's cheaper for them to stay outside the city. She sent me an email with the latest *Bloom's Bulletin* and she said they were going to film in Haymarket Square, which is a produce market in downtown Boston." Casey said nothing, so Julia added, "I don't know why they're filming there. I don't know what Haymarket Square has to do with Bloom's. I don't know anything at all." She realized she was babbling, so she shut up.

Casey stared at her. Haunted—and sad. He looked so sad.

"Susie misses you," she said, then wondered whether telling him such a thing was disloyal. No, it wasn't. He and Susie were being idiots, refusing to acknowledge what they were throwing away. Someone had to speak the truth. "I think she misses you a lot."

"I didn't come here to talk about Susie," he said in a low, controlled voice.

Oh. She'd just yammered for five minutes about Susie, her darling sister, who was grieving over this man, and he hadn't come here to talk about her. Wonderful.

"I have a business proposition," he said. He sat so calmly, his gaze so direct. He was the exact opposite of Adam—but then, he hadn't invaded her office to request her assistance in seducing a ballet dancer.

"A business proposition?"

"I'm planning to open my own store," he told her. "A specialty bread bakery. Gourmet breads, rolls, and bagels."

"Your own store?" How would he find time to do that? He worked long hours at Bloom's. He usually left by mid-afternoon, but that was because he arrived early, putting the first batches of bagels through their final baking so they'd be fresh for sale when Bloom's opened for business.

"What I'd like to do is be a contract supplier of bagels," he told her. "Your baking facilities can barely accommodate the number of bagels we're selling. If you contracted out to me, I could keep Bloom's supplied in bagels—the same variety of flavors I'm making for you here, same quality, same everything—and I could do it more efficiently, because I wouldn't have to work down in that crowded basement kitchen where the Heat-'N'-Eat entrees and the salads are being prepared."

Julia didn't immediately understand what he was saying. Gradually his words settled into place inside her brain. As they did, her bad day got infinitely worse, as if an army of storm clouds had marched in, ready to carpet-bomb her with hail. "You're leaving Bloom's?" she guessed, her voice cracking over the word "leaving."

"I want to open my own place," he said. "What I'm proposing is a deal where I can continue to be your bagel maker."

"But from your own place."

"Right. I'd work with Morty, figure out the orders, bake them and deliver them."

"From your own place."

"Right."

Her impulse was to grab her phone, call Ron and scream, "Rescue me!" But he had to finish his goddamn column, didn't he?

She inhaled, exhaled, flexed her fingers in her lap and prayed for serenity. "Is this because of Susie?" she asked.

"Is what because of Susie?"

"Is that why you want to leave?"

"I want my own place," he repeated.

Not exactly an answer. If Susie's breaking up with Casey meant Julia was going to lose the most creative, talented bagel maker in New York City, someone would have to die. Julia wasn't sure who, but she had no doubt that a few minutes of reflection would produce a nice, long list of prospects.

"Is there anything I can do to keep you from leaving?" she asked, loathing the querulous undertone in her voice.

"I don't think so. But if we could work out a contract, you'd still have my bagels."

"Right." She could work out a contract. Not right now, though. Right now she needed to figure out whom to kill. "I'm sure we can negotiate something, Casey. Let me think about it, okay? I'd need to talk to Morty, and Deirdre." Deirdre would know what to do. According to Susie's article in the bulletin, Deirdre was a five-star general. She might even know how to kill someone. She probably had the names of a few efficient hit men in her contacts list.

"Okay." Casey stood and extended his right hand across the desk. Julia belatedly realized she was supposed to shake it. She did, feeling as sad as the shadows that darkened his eyes. He was a good man. Her sister was an idiot. The world was imploding.

She was having a very, very bad day.

She watched him walk out of her office. Her hand instinctively draped around the receiver of her phone. Did she dare to call Ron? Given the way things were going, he might just break off their engagement if she did.

Her phone rang, vibrating against her palm. Maybe Ron had called her! He would tell her he'd felt a strange impulse to hear her voice, an e.s.p. signal whispering to him that she needed him. He'd assure her that he'd finished his damned column and found a rabbi willing to perform their wedding at N.Y.U., and he'd booked a reception room at the campus where Bloom's could do the catering. He'd tell her he had booked their honeymoon, as well—two weeks somewhere exotic, somewhere romantic, somewhere a million miles from her family and inaccessible by phone, fax or email. He'd tell her he forgave her for calling him every time she was having a bad day and didn't know how to cope.

Lifting the receiver, she said, "Hello?"

"Julia?" Grandma Ida's voice squawked through the line. "So, how come you never call me?"

Help, Julia muttered under her breath, needing rescue more than ever. "I've been busy, Grandma. How are you?"

"I'm eighty-nine years old. How should I be?"

"You sound good," Julia said, knowing she had to keep up her end of the conversation until Grandma Ida revealed the purpose of her call.

Fortunately, it didn't take her long. "So, you never explained to me how you're going to fit all those musicians in my foyer. How many musicians is it going to be? It's not such a big foyer."

Julia's eyebrows pinched into a frown as she struggled to translate Grandma Ida's words into something meaningful, something she could believe. Why should Grandma Ida be grilling her about the number of musicians? Was she willing to host Julia's wedding in her apartment, after all?

The clouds lifted, taking their hail and gloom with them. Rick's movie no longer mattered. Nor did Casey's resignation. Nor did Adam's sex life, or her mother's and Ron's father's, or Susie's anguish, or Ron's column. Nothing mattered but the size of Grandma Ida's foyer.

"Three musicians," Julia told her. "They'll fit."

Chapter Twenty-Five

"There it is." Rick nudged Susie so hard she winced. He couldn't contain his excitement, though. He wanted to scream, but the cabin looked so dilapidated a sudden loud noise might cause it to collapse. Instead, he whispered the words and did his shouting with his fingers, jabbing them into Susie's arm with enough force to make her slap his hand away.

Apparently, she wasn't quite as excited as he was. She'd driven the final three hours of their six-hour journey today, and she'd spent the last of those hours steering in circles over the hilly, densely forested back roads of the Catskills. Each circle had led them back to Broadway in downtown Monticello, where they'd stop to ask for directions and then cruise another looping route back to the center of Monticello. Rick didn't have the address, and he wasn't exactly sure of the name—Something Pines, he thought—so his phone's GPS was no help.

After their fourth orbit, they'd at last located the collection of cabins a few miles west of Monticello proper, where their families had once vacationed. Pine Haven, not Something Pines. He'd been close.

Their fathers had stayed back in the city that summer, but his mother and Aunt Sondra and all the kids had occupied the two-bedroom cabin for an entire glorious month. Surely they could have afforded a larger unit, or even two neighboring cabins. Or they could have booked rooms in one of the glitzy Borscht Belt resort hotels, with their day camps for the children and their Olympic-size pools, their tennis courts and horseback riding trails, their nightclubs starring acts no one under the age of thirty had ever heard of, and their abundant, multi-course meals.

Being Blooms, even if only by marriage, his mother and Aunt Sondra had rejected the idea of consuming someone else's pot roast and stuffed derma, cheese blintzes and potato kugel. His mother and Aunt Sondra were frugal sorts, and those hotels had been expensive. So they'd rented the lakeside shack that stood before him and Susie right now, with its sloped roof and log walls and its windows with screens that had been torn the summer the Blooms had stayed there and evidently still hadn't been replaced. The trees surrounding the cabin had seemed bigger to Rick then. Of course, he was a hell of a lot bigger now. He'd been nine that summer, and to a nine-year-old city kid, even a small tree was gigantic.

As he recalled, his mother and Aunt Sondra had occupied one bedroom of the cabin, Susie and her sister Julia the other, and the male contingent had camped out in sleeping bags on the hard planks of the living room floor. They'd loved it, especially Adam, who'd been about five years old and thrilled to hang out with older boys like his cousins Rick and Neil. Rick and Neil had spent much of the month trying to elude Adam. They'd managed to lose him in the woods one morning, but somehow he'd found his way back to the cabin. He'd probably used vectors and angles and elaborate mathematical formulas to trace a path to safety. Even as a kid, he'd been nerdy.

Susie turned off the van's engine and peered through the windshield at the cabin. "Explain to me why we're here again," she said.

"The movie is about Bloom's. This cabin is part of our family's heritage."

"The movie is about Bloom's the store, not Blooms the family."

"You can't separate the two. Trust me, Suze—this is going to be great. What do you think, Linus?" he asked, angling his head over his shoulder toward the humongous plastic lobster in the back.

"Linus thinks your brain needs rewiring," Susie muttered, yanking the key out of the ignition and shoving open her door.

Rick joined her at the front bumper. A packed dirt road led past their cabin to other, similarly decrepit cabins that teetered along the shoreline of a murky puddle. He'd recalled Pine Haven Lake as being much larger—so large he and Susie hadn't been allowed to take the rowboat out on it without an adult along, even though they were both good swimmers. Julia and Neil had been permitted to go out alone, a fact that had made Rick seethe with envy. Who knew—maybe Neil developed his first notions of opening a sailboat charter business that summer while rowing around Pine Haven Lake with Julia, both of them clad in bulbous orange life vests and smelling like coconuts from the sunscreen their mothers had rubbed onto their skin.

He was sure the lake had been bigger. Some of the water must have evaporated.

"Are we allowed to film here?" Susie asked as he tore his attention from the lake and walked to the back of the van to get out his camera and tripod.

"I don't see a problem. I mean, nobody's even going to know. The sign said 'Closed For The Season.'"

"This looks like it's been closed for the last ten seasons." Despite her negative words, she wandered closer to the cabin. She studied the building, probably debating with herself whether to climb onto the ramshackle porch. Wisely, she refrained. The whole cabin might have toppled down around her if she'd put any weight on the splintering porch steps.

Rick dragged his camera and tripod out of the van, along with Linus, although he wasn't exactly sure how a lobster would fit into the scene. He and Susie had discussed the gist of this scene during their long, meandering drive today. Now, with their hours of light limited, he didn't want her wasting precious time throwing a hissy fit.

He wasn't sure why she was in such a foul mood. She'd told him about breaking up with her bagel boy, but as far as Rick was concerned, she didn't have anything to bitch about. At least she'd had enough of a relationship with Casey to be able to break up with him. Even if Rick wanted to break up with Anna he couldn't, because not enough existed between them to break up.

But Susie had been in a particularly grumpy state ever since their first night in Revere. He'd ridden the T into downtown Boston to scrutinize the layout of Haymarket Square, where greengrocers plied their wares early in the morning and left the street littered with shreds of lettuce and carrot greens and the occasional squashed tomato for hours afterward. The area was heavily trafficked, by both pedestrians and cars, but he'd immediately realized that he could get some good shots amid the rotting vegetable trash, even if the noise of cars and trucks made it necessary to add a voice-over later. He'd strolled around Quincy Market, inventorying the chi-chi restaurants and snack stands and generating some ideas for more filming, and he'd wound up in an amusing conversation with two flirty teenage girls with stick-straight blond hair and navel rings while waiting on line to buy some calzones for his and Susie's dinner. If Susie hadn't been waiting back at the motel for him—and if the girls had been a couple of years older—he might have brought them back to his room and had himself an interesting evening.

Actually, he wasn't sure he had the guts for something like that. But it had been nice to pretend Susie was the only reason he hadn't invited Ashley and Kaylie to spend the evening with him in Revere.

Back at the hotel, he'd found Susie so sulky he couldn't explain it away as one of those hormonal-cycle things. Despite her funk, however, she'd been a trooper the next day, ad-libbing some great stuff at the various locations he'd scouted in Boston and not even curling her lip when he'd included Linus in one of the downtown shots. Nor had she nagged him about their budget when he'd been forced to pay thirty-something dollars for the privilege of parking the van in a downtown garage, and when he'd insisted that they splurge on a real dinner at a real restaurant since they were already stuck forking over thirty-something for parking.

So she was in a mood. So her mood was in fact entering Day Three. He'd brought her with him because she was a great writer and even better company, but the longer this mood lasted, the lousier her company became.

At least she was still a great writer. Off the top of her head she could recite soliloquies that made his trigger finger—the index finger that pressed the record button on the camera—tingle with joy in the knowledge that he was capturing all her words on tape. Some of her monologues would get edited out, of course, and more would be added in voice-overs, but even as she ran her marathon of misery, she was doing a terrific job in the film.

She stared grimly at the old cabin, then at the stagnant brown water of the pond, then at a maple seedling that looked more like a stringy weed than a potential tree. Lacy ferns floated around her bare ankles, and she leaned over to slap a mosquito from her leg. She was still dressed all in black—black shorts, black T-shirt. He didn't mind; it set off the lush, varied greens of all the trees and shrubs and Mother Nature surrounding the cabin.

"Doesn't it smell great here?" he asked, trying to cheer her up as he balanced the legs of his tripod on the uneven ground and locked the camera into place.

"It smells like Pine-Sol."

"Pine-Sol is supposed to smell like pines," he pointed out. "Which smell like this." He waved his arm toward the trees towering above the cabin.

"What do I know? The last time I smelled this smell was in the public ladies' room at the Central Park Zoo." She turned to examine the cabin some more, then nudged the bottom porch step gingerly with her toe. The building didn't disintegrate. "I'm going to try to sit on the bottom step," she said. "If the cabin caves in on top of me and I die, Julia can have my computer. Adam gets my CD's, except for the Indigo Girls because he only pretends to like them. Anna and Caitlin can have whatever I left in the fridge."

"I'll let Anna know the minute you kick," Rick promised, squinting at the camera's monitor and sharpening the focus. "Why does Adam pretend to like the Indigo Girls?"

"Because his girlfriend likes them. Tash, the tree-hugger."

Rick nodded, then held his breath while she cautiously lowered herself onto the step. The cabin remained upright and he exhaled in relief. "You remember what you're going to say?" he asked.

She sent him a withering scowl, then shoved her hair back, giving it a nicely tousled look, and stared into the camera. "This was our cabin," she said, all traces of her moodiness gone. She looked solemn but at peace, her gaze remaining on the camera and avoiding Linus, who lay no more than a couple of feet in front of her, his faded red shell clashing with the rust-orange carpet of pine needles that covered the ground.

"Seven Blooms in one tiny cabin for a month," she continued. "My mother, my Aunt Martha, my cousins, my sister, my brother, and me. And not a single crumb of Bloom's food. It didn't occur to my mother and Aunt Martha to bring a few bags of bagels up to the Catskills, freezing them and then thawing as needed. It didn't occur to them to stock up on macaroons and mandelbrot for snacking on. When you're staying in a cabin in the Catskills, I learned that you eat lots of peanut-butter sandwiches on white bread." She shuddered and grimaced. "One night, Aunt Martha and my mother took us to one of the big Borscht Belt hotels for dinner. There were, like, fifty courses. Fruit juice. Salads. Chicken soup with *knedlach* and too much salt in the broth. Wine for the grown-ups and Kool-Aid for the kids." She grimaced again. "Chicken with gravy. Mashed potatoes with gravy. Overcooked broccoli with gravy. Corn with gravy. Rolls with gravy. What else did they serve us? Lots of desserts, but they refused to give us ice cream because it had been a meat meal. I seem to remember date-nut bread. They didn't serve lobster, of course."

Rick took his cue and panned to a shot of Linus sprawled out on the ground.

"Other city kids might have dreamed of spending a month in the mountains," Susie went on. "I dreamed of spending a month eating Bloom's food. I wanted pastrami on fresh, sour rye. I got Jif on white bread. *White bread*," she emphasized, her nose wrinkling in distaste.

She made it sound as if she'd lived a deprived life—which, of course, she hadn't. Being a member of their generation of Blooms had meant spacious apartments, private schools and never a moment's panic about where your next meal was coming from, even if it rarely came from Bloom's. But Rick didn't mind her self-pitying tone. He was in awe of her ability to spin out a narration without even holding a stack of written note cards in front of her. She was such a natural. She ought to consider making a career of appearing before the camera, he thought. She already worked as a waitress at Nico's. Didn't being a waitress qualify her to call herself an actress?

"I dream of food," Susie continued. Rick didn't recall her emphasizing her dreams when she'd discussed the scene with him earlier that day. "I dream of food and love. Some people believe food and love are the same thing. Both bring you pleasure. Both can make you sick. You need both to live. They both nourish you.

"I especially dream of chocolate," she said, then fell silent.

Well, that was weird.

He released the record button and smiled hesitantly. Maybe she had PMS, after all. He'd read in a magazine somewhere that when women had PMS they craved chocolate. In his experience, most women craved chocolate all the time. Then again, most women acted as if they had PMS all the time.

Susie said nothing. She just sat on the rickety porch step, her elbows propped on her knees, her chin resting in her palms and her butterfly tattoo barely visible on her ankle. He pulled the camera off the tripod and wandered around the cabin, adding hand-held footage to his shots of Susie, and then recorded some video of the lake. Susie remained on the porch, as motionless as a frozen computer screen.

The camera in one hand, he used the other to drag Linus down to the water's edge. The lobster was light; it would float. Rick wasn't sure what he'd do with the scene, but he'd learned the wisdom of filming more than he needed, including scenes he was positive he'd never use. He always wound up surprising himself, discovering an excerpt in his archive of unused shots that was perfect for some other project. A filmmaker had to be a packrat, because he just never knew.

Linus floated. His antennae snagged in the sand just below the scummy surface of the pond, and he bobbed up and down in the water, looking dead. Maybe Rick would direct a mystery someday, some nasty little noir thing, and he'd be able to blur this bit of video enough to look make Linus resemble a murder victim.

"What are you doing?" Susie called to him. Glancing over his shoulder, he saw her rising from the porch step and marching down the slope to the pond's edge. "He's going to get all wet."

"He's a lobster. He's supposed to be wet."

"Right. And then you're going to put him back in the van, where he'll get everything else wet."

"I'll dry him off," Rick assured her.

"With what?"

"I've got a towel." He was pretty sure he did, anyway.

"Well, don't expect me to help you dry him off." She jammed her fisted hands against her hips, turned and started back up the slope.

"What the hell is wrong with you, anyway?" Rick yelled at her. He'd had it. Sure, movie stars were allowed to be temperamental, but she wasn't a movie star. She was his cousin.

"I want to go home," she yelled back.

He glanced at the cabin to make sure their shouting hadn't caused it to crumble. "You want to go home? This minute?"

"The sooner the better." Some of her testiness seemed to leave her. She rotated to face him and dug into the thick floor of pine needles with her toe. "I want to grow up."

"Grow up?" His trigger finger twitched and he did something he would probably feel terrible about afterward: he angled the camera toward her and kept filming. "What do you mean, you want to grow up?"

"I don't know. Maybe I don't want to. Maybe I just have to. Maybe I already have." She sighed, and panic nibbled through his flesh at the possibility that she'd burst into tears. But she remained dry-eyed as she said, "I used to think I wanted to drive an eighteen-wheeler across the country to California. I thought that would be cool. Now just imagining it tires me out."

He wasn't sure where she was going with this rant, but he humored her. "Yeah, well, California. That's a lot of driving. What, three thousand miles?"

She ignored him. "Sometimes you just have to stop and think about what matters. I mean, white picket fences? I hate them. But when you think about it..." She almost seemed to be talking to herself, and he didn't interrupt. He just kept filming. "What if what matters is waiting for you on the other side of the fence?"

It occurred to him that she might be having a psychotic episode of some sort. If she was, was he supposed to bring her to a mental institution and check her in? He'd had his share of interesting experiences with lunatics in his life—you couldn't live in New York City and not encounter plenty of nut cases. Plus, he'd known a guy in college who used to ignite his farts with a butane lighter, and a chick in his dorm who used to speak in tongues after downing a couple of beers. She'd sworn she was the reincarnation of Buster Keaton, who, Rick was pretty sure, had never spoken in tongues.

This was Susie, his beloved cousin. He'd always assumed she was extremely sane.

"So can we go home?" she asked.

"I guess. I mean, sure, why not? I still have to do some filming around the city, but we've probably got enough on-the-road material to work with."

"Can we go home tonight?"

"If we return to the city tonight," he said, walking toward her, still recording, "what'll we do with the van? The rental place won't be open until morning."

"So we'll park it. I'll find a spot."

"On the street? Are you kidding?"

"I'll drive in circles until I find a spot. I'm used to driving in circles."

"What if something happens to it on the street? What if someone vandalizes it?"

She twisted her head to glance at the vehicle, which looked almost as battered and worn as the cabin. "It obviously wouldn't be the first time."

"I've been wondering—" he drew a little closer, shifting the camera to get the van into the frame "—is that blood on the door?"

Susie shrugged. "It wouldn't surprise me."

"Why do you really want to go home?" he pressed her.

She sighed deeply. "Because when you think about it, there's really no place else to go."

That sounded so profound, he wasn't sure how to respond. Susie was a poet. He ought to expect weighty, meaningful stuff from her.

She wanted to go home because there was no place else to go. She hated picket fences, but she wanted what was on the other side of them. She dreamed of chocolate.

Okay. Chocolate he could get a handle on. "How about," he suggested, "I buy you some M&M's?"

She smiled, a shy, surprisingly pretty smile. "Peanut?"

"Sure."

"And then we'll go home?"

He caught her smile on tape. "Sure," he said.

Chapter Twenty-Six

I have been very patient, Adam, the email read, *but I just don't understand what's going on with you anymore. Where is your commitment to values and causes? Where is your embrace of the planet? How can you be spending a whole summer stocking shelves in a store like Bloom's, a monument to corpulence, when children in Africa are starving?*

Corpulence, he thought as he stared at the neat blue print on his computer screen. Cool word.

I know, I know—our grandparents used to tell us to clean our plates because children in Africa were starving...

Grandma Ida and Grandpa Isaac had never nagged him about children starving in Africa. On the other hand, his grandparents on the Feldman side of the family had had a thing about starving children in Asia, trotting out guilt-inducing reminders to persuade him to finish some food they'd served him that he didn't like—lima beans, or that lunch-loaf stuff, pink meat with pimento-stuffed green olives imbedded in it like chunks in vomit. "Children are starving in Asia," his Grandma Ethel would scold, and he'd retort, "Yeah? Name two," and Susie would say: "Cheng and Fijimatsu." She used to make him laugh so hard he snorted milk, and Grandma Ethel would be horrified and make both him and Susie leave the table, which of course meant they no longer had to eat that crud with the green olives in it.

Smiling at the memory, he turned his attention back to Tash's email. *...Children really *are* starving in Africa, Adam. I can direct you to some on-line sites that discuss the malnutrition problems and drought conditions in sub-Sahara Africa if you don't believe me. But I know you *do* believe me. You're a man of principle. You understand that we're *all* citizens of the world, sharing this ever-shrinking planet. I'm spending my summer trying to make downtown Seattle a little less gynophobic, and what are you doing? Helping overweight New Yorkers fill their pantries with kosher roast beef, which in case you forgot is a meat. Remember those statistics I sent you about how much more plant protein can be produced compared to meat protein, using the same resources?*

So maybe he wasn't a man of principle, he thought as he leaned back in his desk chair and closed his eyes. The back of the chair tilted, cradling his spine comfortably. His body was feeling better than it had since graduation weekend—and he didn't even need any weed to make him mellow.

He truly had the best sisters in the world. One had come up with the names "Cheng" and "Fijimatsu" just when he'd needed to hear them, and the other had let him use her apartment. "Thank you, God," he murmured as his mouth curved into a satisfied smile. "Thank you, God, for Susie's wit and Julia's key." He pondered for a minute and decided to thank God for Elyse, too.

Frankly, Tash's email continued, *I am astonished that you can take such pride in having come up with* a reorganization plan for how the shelves are stocked in the basement of your family's store. You're an Ivy League graduate, for God's sake, on your way to Purdue for a Ph.D., and you take *pride* in reorganizing shelves? What is wrong with this picture?

Nothing, he almost answered aloud. Nothing was wrong with the picture, or with him. Reorganizing the stock shelves had been brilliant. The stock staff in the basement would be singing his praises long after he left for Purdue.

That understanding tempered his smile. A month ago, he'd been counting the seconds until he could leave for Indiana. Now his impending departure, while still more than a month off, dampened his spirits. And that was not just because of Elyse. He wasn't the sentimental type. He didn't fall in love at the drop of a tutu. Spending a few hours with her at Julia's apartment had been pretty damned nice, but love wasn't part of the equation at this point.

It was Indiana that dampened his spirits. Grandma Ida thought Purdue was where non-kosher chickens came from. Adam knew chickens had nothing to do with the place, but plains did. Prairies. Midwestern folks who probably smiled when they walked down the street, and waved at strangers. Maybe they even said, "Howdy." And they didn't walk; they moseyed, moving at a relaxed pace, admiring the scenery around them, pausing to catch up on the local gossip with Mabel or to admire Hank's shiny new pickup truck.

Jesus. How on earth was Adam going to fit in there?

He wasn't crazy about New York. It was noisy and crowded, dirty and pushy. Auto alarms blared at three a.m. Heat rose through the subway grates as if Dante's Inferno actually burned below the sidewalks. Bike couriers would rather run a pedestrian down than veer around him. Cabbies would jump the curb if it meant beating a rival to a fare.

New York shoppers were too demanding. Whenever he ventured into Bloom's, he heard them bickering with the clerks—"How fresh is this bread? You baked it yesterday, right? I can tell it wasn't baked today—my thumb can't push through the crust. If it was fresh, my thumb would go right through," and "I told you to slice the Nova tissue thin! You call that tissue thin? I would never blow my nose with a tissue that thick!"—and arguing over who was next in line. If Bloom's was out of a certain brand of minced garlic, the world might just end.

New York was where his family lived: his mother, always asking where Adam was going, with whom and why but prefacing every question with, "It's none of my business," as if that made her prying acceptable. His sisters, who still seemed to view him as the little snot-nosed dweeb he'd been ten or fifteen years ago. His Uncle Jay, always with one foot out the door, racing off to play golf or racquetball or anything that would take him away from his responsibilities. His grandmother one floor above him, armed with a criticism for every occasion. His Aunt Martha, living right down the hall, eager to pontificate on the subjugation of women. Maybe she'd like to join Tash's Space Needle protest.

He stared at the print on his laptop screen, wondering whether to write a response to Tash's email. He could tell her about Cheng and Fijimatsu, but she wouldn't get it.

Instead, he logged onto the Internet and called up Columbia University's website. Three clicks got him to their math department. Scrolling through the faculty, he grinned. A nice smattering of unpronounceable names mixed in with the familiar ones—Asian, Scandinavian, Slavic, Greek, more men than women, but not by much. He recognized some of the names from journal articles he'd read and conference workshops he'd attended. He'd feel right at home at Columbia.

That was why he'd never applied to the graduate school there: he'd been afraid that attending graduate school in New York City would make him feel right at home.

Adam Bloom would never, not even if the earth reversed its rotational direction and the stars fell out of the sky, feel at home in West Lafayette, Indiana. The truth slapped him in the face like a wet sponge, cold and shocking. With or without Tash, notwithstanding the couple of professors at Purdue with whom he'd been corresponding about his research plans, regardless of the fact that rents were actually affordable in West Lafayette... Adam was never going to be the kind of guy who smiled and said "Howdy" to strangers and admired shiny new pickup trucks as he moseyed down the street.

Stunned, he snapped his laptop shut and leaned back in his chair again, so far back he could view the ceiling. It was a New York City ceiling, smooth and white, with molding around the corners. His room smelled like New York City. Beyond his windows the sounds of New York City bubbled and churned.

Damn it, he was a Bloom. How could he possibly survive life with all those chickens at Purdue?

Chapter Twenty-Seven

By eleven-thirty, Susie had cruised every block in Alphabet City at least three times without finding a parking space big enough for the van. Eleven-thirty was a lively hour in her part of the East Village; people swarmed the sidewalks, hooking up, panhandling, squabbling, and exiting from cafés, bars, used book stores, and all-night groceries brandishing beer bottles, lottery tickets, collector's-item comic books, and key rings. Surely one of those key rings contained a key to a car that could be driven out of a parking space, but Susie's only open curb sightings were stretches adjacent to fire hydrants and bus stops.

Although she rarely had to worry about parking a car in the city, she knew that when no spot was available, the best strategy was to stake out a promising block, double-park at one end of the street, and watch, and wait. Sooner or later, someone would get into a car and drive away. Whereas, if she kept driving through the neighborhood, she might be on another block when a spot on this block opened, and some other lucky driver would snag it.

She didn't mind watching and waiting. She needed solitude to sort through her thoughts, and for the first time since she and Rick had left the city—actually, for the first time in a lot longer than that, given that she had two roommates, worked at Bloom's and at Nico's, and lived in a city with a population of more than eight million—she was alone. Well, almost alone. Linus sprawled languidly in the back of the van. Rick had cleared out all his other gear when Susie had dropped him off at his place, but she'd wound up with custody of Linus.

What the hell was she supposed to do with a six foot tall plastic lobster who still glistened in his nooks and crannies from a residue of scummy Pine Haven Lake water? Her apartment barely had room for her and Anna and Caitlin. Keeping Linus in the apartment would sacrifice valuable square footage, and dragging him up the two flights of stairs to her floor wouldn't be much fun, either. Perhaps Nico could display Linus in the pizzeria...but then people would look at Linus and wonder why they were eating pizza instead of lobster, and they'd leave dissatisfied. And of course, Linus couldn't be displayed at Bloom's, because lobster was *trayf.*

She could give Linus to Casey. He had so much space in Queens, after all.

Assuming he was still living in Queens. For all she knew, he could have moved in with Halle Berry by now.

She gave her head a fierce shake, refusing to succumb to pessimism. Something had happened to her today. Actually, it had been happening over the past week, but today, when she'd seen the old cabin at Pine Haven, whatever was happening had reached its culmination in one of those nauseating epiphanies her Ancient Greek Drama professor at Bennington used to wax ecstatic about.

She loved Casey.

She was pissed as hell at him. She hated the corner he'd painted her into, the limb he'd led her out onto. She would resent him forever, and never, ever forgive him for putting her through this hell.

But damn it, she loved him. And if she had to grow up, settle down, beat Halle's berries to a pulp, and—she shuddered just to think of it—marry Casey, she would.

It had all come together at the cabin. She'd seen the decrepit old building and remembered that summer she and Rick and their siblings and mothers had lived there. She'd remembered the quarrels over the checkerboard, which Neil was always overturning, sometimes while Susie and Rick were in the middle of a game, so he could play backgammon on the board's flip side. She'd remembered the way Julia had dawdled in the bathroom, fussing with her hair, while the rest of them lined up in the tiny hallway, banging on the door and begging her to hurry up so they wouldn't pee in their pants. She'd remembered the way the lake had been murky even then, and its musty smell had made her sneeze. She'd remembered taking long hikes on paths that meandered through the woods, and inhaling that amazing pine fragrance—which she hadn't associated with public bathrooms in those days. She'd remembered convincing Neil to sneak away from Aunt Martha at the general store in White Lake and buy a jar of marshmallow fluff so they could make peanut-butter and fluff sandwiches. Julia would never have bought the fluff; she was too well behaved. But Neil had been willing, and Susie and Rick had donated their combined assets—a collection of linty coins dug from the deepest recesses of their pockets—and Neil had bought the fluff. When they'd gotten back to the cabin and Aunt Martha had seen the jar, she'd lectured them for what felt like an hour on the subject of nutrition and tooth decay. Once she'd run out of gas and abandoned the kitchen, Susie and her siblings and cousins had all feasted on peanut-butter and fluff sandwiches. White bread almost didn't matter if you piled enough peanut-butter and fluff onto it.

Family meant fighting for the bathroom and sitting through dreary lectures on nutrition, but it also meant sugary, sticky sandwiches and checkers and even backgammon, which Susie had gotten pretty good at once Neil had taught her the game. Family meant knowing who you were, accepting it, even embracing it. It meant being honest, because you couldn't bullshit your family. They knew you too well.

It meant understanding that sometimes love sucked, but a lack of love sucked a whole lot more.

A couple with their arms wrapped around each other's shoulders ambled down the street, holding each other so closely they looked like contestants in a three-legged race. Susie sat straighter, sending them mental vibes: *Go to a car. Get in it. Drive it away.* They walked the length of the block, then entered a brownstone.

She cursed, but she wasn't really upset. She was too wired about having acknowledged that she loved Casey to allow anger to mar the moment. Her note pad was in the back of the van with Linus and her suitcase. Maybe she ought to write a poem.

No. Writing a poem demanded intense concentration, and right now she had to concentrate on finding a parking space. Instead of writing, she poked inside her purse and pulled out her cell phone. She speed-dialed Julia's cell phone and listened to the phone ring on the other end.

"What?" Joffe growled.

"Joffe? It's Susie. Why are you answering Julia's phone?"

"It's almost midnight," he grumbled. "That's it. I'm breaking up with Julia because she refuses to turn off her fucking phone. You heard it first. The wedding is off."

"Okay," Susie said pleasantly. "Can I talk to her?"

She heard a few muffled sounds and juicy obscenities, and then her sister's voice: "The wedding isn't off. He's just being a schmuck."

"You want to marry a schmuck?"

"Sometimes he's not a schmuck," Julia said in his defense. "But it *is* late, Susie. We're in bed."

"I'm not. I'm in the Truck-a-Buck van with blood on the door," Susie told her. "I'm waiting for a parking spot to open up."

"Where are you?"

"In Manhattan. We came home."

"Really? Did you finish the infomercial? Don't do that, Ron," she said in a different voice.

"What's he doing?"

"Something X-rated. Don't ask."

"We didn't finish the movie," Susie said, "but we finished all the location shooting."

"Why is it that I keep calling it an infomercial and you keep calling it a movie?" Julia asked. Then she sighed and muttered, "Not now, Ron."

"The movie is going to be great," Susie said, choosing to duck Julia's question. "But I'm glad to be home. I missed the city. What's going on?"

"Other than what Ron is doing—which he should *not* be doing," she scolded, her voice directed away from the phone to her future husband, "Deirdre thinks it's a good thing Mom is dating Ron's father. Don't ask," she added before Susie could muddle through the questions that statement provoked. "What's going on with you? You sound better than the last time we talked."

"I am better. I think." Susie leaned forward and squinted at the middle-aged couple strolling around the corner and onto her block. They had to be suburbanites. They'd come to the East Village to slum, and now they would get into their gas-guzzling car and drive back to their fancy house in Mamaroneck. Susie scanned the cars parked along the curb in search of an oversize American sedan.

"You think what?" Julia asked.

The couple ambled past the only Cadillac on the street. Damn. "I think I've figured some things out. I've got to talk to Casey."

Julia hesitated before saying, "Do you know what's going on with him?"

"The Halle Berry thing, you mean?"

"What Halle Berry thing?"

It was Susie's turn to hesitate. Was more going on with Casey than just that he was dating a movie star look-alike? "What's going on with Casey?" she asked cautiously.

"He's leaving Bloom's."

"What?" The couple slowed as they approached a large, well waxed car. Susie could hardly focus on them, though. *Casey was leaving Bloom's?* "Where is he going?"

"He's planning to open his own store. We're negotiating a contract so he can continue to supply our bagels. He doesn't want to work for Bloom's anymore."

"That asshole! How could he not want to work at Bloom's?"

"I guess he wants to be his own boss," Julia answered. "He said you had nothing to do with it."

"Like hell, I don't. I've gotta go, Julia. Tell Joffe he can do that X-rated thing now." Susie disconnected the call and tossed her cell phone onto the passenger seat. The suburbanites were climbing into their fat-cat car, but Susie no longer wanted their space. She had wheels for the night, and she intended to use them.

o

Casey wished Mose hadn't brought the ladies along, but Mose was giving him so much help and free advice that Casey didn't think he had the right to complain. LaShonna and Eva had commandeered the living room, where they were watching some TV show they apparently found uproariously funny, given the peals of laughter and neighing that spilled into the kitchen, where Casey and Mose sat at the table beneath the unforgiving light of the ceiling fixture and crunched numbers. They were on their second round of Pete's Wicked Ale—God knew how much beer Eva and LaShonna had helped themselves to; Casey could always count the bottles later, if he cared—and they huddled over Mose's laptop, plugging numbers into an Excel spreadsheet and calculating just what Casey needed for his store to succeed.

He was beyond the "if" stage and firmly in commit mode. Whenever he thought about staying at Bloom's, visions of Susie exploded inside his head like a romantic migraine. He knew that quitting a good, solid job because of a woman was a moronic move, but he was reassured by the fact that whenever he thought about that storefront on Avenue B, whenever he pictured it filled with the rich fragrance of fresh-baked breads and rolls and imagined the sign above the door—opting for simplicity, he'd decided the store would be named

"Casey's Gourmet Breads"—his head stopped aching. So did his heart.

Opening his own store was the right thing to do, for a whole bunch of reasons. If he could think of only one reason right now—that he needed to put distance between himself and the Blooms, one Bloom in particular—it didn't mean there weren't plenty of other equally valid reasons. In time they'd come to him.

Mose frowned at the laptop screen. Casey drank some beer and dismissed the frown. Mose always frowned when he studied numbers. The expression lent him desperately needed gravitas. Dressed in a faded Knicks jersey, a pair of knit athletic shorts stretched out of shape, a pair of bad-ass red-and-silver high-tops and a bandanna tied pirate-style around his head, Mose looked more like a third-rate rapper than a rising star in the small-business consulting world.

"Okay, the way I see it, if you charge her thirty cents a bagel and she orders what she's currently selling..." Mose jabbed at a couple of digit keys and his frown deepened. "She'd basically be covering your salary plus the cost of producing the bagels. That ain't bad, Woody."

This was why Casey didn't view Mose's frown as a negative sign.

"Now, you're still talking shipping costs. Gotta run those bagels uptown for her. Bloom's has a fleet, doesn't it?"

"I don't know about a fleet," Casey said. "They've got a few trucks."

"Then you gotta negotiate that. Gotta include shipping costs in your price."

"You think she'd pay for that? It's one thing she doesn't have to pay for now."

"Yeah, but that cost'll be offset by her savings on the kitchen space she'll no longer be devoting to bagel baking. She can expand her knish production or something. Plus you'll be able to produce more for her, and more efficiently."

"Theoretically," Casey said, then took another long drink of beer.

"This whole thing is 'theoretically,' Blondie. You open a business based on theoreticals, and then a water main breaks and floods all the stores along your side of the avenue, and all your theoreticals are fucked. Or the business takes off in a way you never anticipated, and your only problem is how to increase production to meet the demand."

"I like the second scenario better."

Mose grinned. From the living room came more giggles and horse noises. Casey was unable to stifle a grimace.

"Hey, at least she's pretty," Mose pointed out in a whisper.

Yes, Eva was pretty. But Casey had spent enough time with her to realize that he considered a woman's laughter more important than her looks. "It's not going to work," he whispered back. "It's just not clicking, you know?"

"You could do worse. You have done worse."

"That's not the point," Casey argued, still keeping his voice down. "I know she's a good friend of LaShonna's, and it sure would make for a nice symmetry and all. And I'm really grateful to her for helping me on the real estate end of things. But—" A buzz interrupted him. The intercom. Someone downstairs in the vestibule wanted to see him.

He glanced at the clock built into his wall oven. Midnight. Jesus. How had it gotten so late? And who the hell was visiting him at midnight?

He pushed back his chair, crossed to the intercom panel by the kitchen door and lifted the receiver. "Yeah?"

"Casey, it's me," Susie's voice slid through the wire. Susie's voice, which did not dissolve into neighing and whinnying when she laughed. Susie's voice, which belonged to the only woman he'd proposed to. That voice had said no to him, and she'd walked out of his life. "I've got a lobster for you," she said.

"I'm not hungry," he retorted.

"It's not that kind of lobster." She paused, then asked, "Can I come up?"

Christ. She had some kind of lobster and she wanted to come up to his apartment at midnight, while Eva, among other people, was here. Not that he gave a crap what Susie thought of Eva. The moment might get awkward, but so what? He'd asked her to marry him and she'd said no. Things couldn't get more awkward than that.

"Okay," he said, then pressed the button to release the locked vestibule door that would admit her to the building.

"Who's that?" Mose asked as Casey hooked the receiver into place.

"Susie. And a lobster."

"Oh, shit," Mose said, expressing Casey's sentiments rather nicely. "Why'd you buzz her in?"

"It's midnight. She's here. What am I going to do, make her sleep on the sidewalk?"

"If you hadn't buzzed her in, maybe she would have gone away."

"What if she left the lobster behind?"

"What lobster? Are you crazy? That bitch bashed your balls. You don't need her in your life."

All right, so he didn't need her. He didn't need coffee, either, but a steaming cup of strong, freshly brewed black coffee satisfied him like nothing else. He didn't need beer, but those cold, sour bubbles sure felt good going down.

Susie sure felt good going down, too—and he'd better not let his mind wander off in that direction. They weren't a couple. They weren't even pals. He'd better keep his defenses up, high walls protecting him not just from her but from his memories of how good she'd felt going down, among other things.

"It's midnight," he repeated. "She must have come here for a reason."

"Yeah, to bash your balls again."

The doorbell rang. Casey sighed, grabbed his bottle of Pete's, and trudged from the kitchen to the living room. Eva and LaShonna smiled up at him from the couch where they lounged, their feet propped on the coffee table and surrounded by—he did a quick count—five beer bottles and the soggy white box from the pepperoni pizza he'd ordered a while ago.

"You've got company?" Eva asked, giving him her loveliest doe-eyed look. He noticed the metallic pink enamel adorning her toenails, and her casually tufted hair, and the cross glinting on its gold chain just above her cleavage. Her jeans were tight and her top was skimpy, her exposed shoulders smooth and tawny beneath the narrow straps.

Maybe having Susie see Eva in his home wasn't such a bad thing.

Sending the women a half-smile, he passed through the living room to the foyer and squinted through the peek-hole.

He saw a very large lobster.

The sight ought to have annoyed him—what kind of idiot would show up at her ex-boyfriend's apartment at midnight with a humongous lobster?—but instead, it made him laugh. Damn. His defenses obviously needed some serious fortification.

He opened the door. The lobster was nearly as tall as he was, and a whole lot uglier, its plastic surface chipped and faded to color of overcooked salmon, its feelers trembling as Susie maneuvered it through the door. She wasn't visible until both she and the lobster had crossed the threshold. The creature towered over her.

She was out of breath, but she managed a smile. "Hi."

"What the hell is this?"

"It's a lobster," she said. "I told you I had a lobster. Its name is Linus."

"I don't want it," Casey said. What Casey really didn't want was the balloon of heat Susie's nearness inflated in his gut. He didn't want his gaze to lock onto hers, and to see those big brown eyes dancing with amusement and hope and the flakiness that made Susie who she was. He didn't want to think, *There's arguably a more beautiful woman in my living room right now, but this is the woman I want to laugh with.*

Actually, the more arguably beautiful woman was no longer in his living room. She, LaShonna and Mose had all gathered in the arched entry connecting that room to the foyer. They gaped at the lobster. "What is that?" LaShonna asked. "Susie, what the hell is that shit?"

"It's not shit," Susie argued, looking more at Eva than at LaShonna. "It's a plastic roadside lobster from Maine."

"You brought that thing all the way from Maine?" LaShonna cringed and eyed Mose. "Don't you ever take me to Maine. I don't wanna go someplace where they've got things like that—" she gestured contemptuously at the lobster "—on the side of the road."

"It's a work of art," Susie asserted, her attention still on Eva. "It's also a movie star. It appeared in a lot of scenes in my cousin's movie." With a brave smile, she extended her right hand to Eva while holding the lobster upright with her left. "I don't believe we've met. I'm Susie Bloom."

"I'm Eva Robinson," Eva said, shaking her hand. "And I think that lobster is..." She stared at it, then threw back her head and emitted her trademark laugh.

Casey scowled. Susie's smile faltered slightly at the raucous sound, then grew wider. "Well," she said brightly, "where should I put this?"

"Put it where the sun don't shine," Mose muttered, pivoting and stalking away.

Apparently, Mose wasn't going to be friendly to Susie because Susie had bashed his buddy's balls. Casey appreciated Mose's loyalty. LaShonna and Eva stared at Susie for a moment longer, and then LaShonna clamped her hand over Eva's shoulder and said, "Honey, you got lipstick on your teeth."

"I do?" Eva sounded startled, but LaShonna's only answer was to steer Eva out of the foyer and down the hall to the bathroom, where LaShonna would either scrub Eva's tooth clean or else explain to Eva who Susie was.

He and Susie found themselves alone in the foyer. Or nearly alone. That creepy plastic lobster hovered over them like a chaperone.

He glared down at Susie, who looked too damned wonderful. Her eyes were rimmed with shadows and smudges of eyeliner, her hair was a mess, her clothing was black—no surprise there—and her lips were kissably free of lipstick. She looked as if she'd been through a war but had spent the last six hours doing R-and-R and popping speed to spike her energy level.

Susie didn't do speed. She was probably high on adrenaline.

"What are you doing here?" he asked, a bit more gently than he'd intended.

"I had no room for Linus. And I couldn't find a parking space. I'm sorry, Casey—I didn't know you were hosting a party." Her smile was so sad, it chiseled at his defenses, gouging the imaginary wall he'd thrown up as a shield.

"It's not a party."

"She looks like Halle Berry," Susie said, gesturing toward the hall down which Eva and LaShonna had disappeared. "Her laughter is kind of...equine."

Casey said nothing.

"Is it serious between you and her?"

He wasn't going to lie to Susie, but he wouldn't mind her reaching the wrong conclusion. It would serve her right if he was serious about Eva. "We're friends," he said, pleased that it was the truth.

"Look. Casey." Susie propped the lobster against the wall, then lowered her gaze to her polish-free toenails, visible through the straps of her sandals. "I came here because Julia told me you were leaving Bloom's."

He didn't speak. Susie was nervous, and he suspected his silence would make her even more nervous. She deserved to be uncomfortable. In truth, she deserved a romantic migraine like the ones he'd been experiencing on a regular basis lately—blinding pain, blurred vision, the sensation of someone driving spikes through his skull. She didn't seem to be suffering nearly enough, but the longer he said nothing, the more she squirmed.

"So, are you? Leaving Bloom's, I mean."

"Is it any business of yours?"

"Of course it's my business," she said, anger flaring. "I wrote you up as the employee of the week in the

Bloom's Bulletin just a few weeks ago. And now you're going to quit?"

"You can write up my replacement," he said.

"I don't want to write up your replacement. What replacement, anyway? Who could replace you? Who could come up with fig-flavored bagels, huh? Who could come up with a rhyme for stroganoff?"

"What are you doing here?" he asked again. "Besides bringing me the lobster."

"I'm here because I'm an idiot," she mumbled, still eyeing her toes. "I shouldn't have come."

He didn't think she was an idiot, of course. He thought she was one of the smartest women he'd ever known. And a part of him—the masochistic part—was far too glad she'd come, far too grateful for the chance to see her mussed black hair and her stubborn chin up close, to smell her spicy scent and hear her un-equine laughter and imagine himself reaching out cupping her cheeks in his hands.

Which made him an idiot, too, because she'd said no, and she sure as hell hadn't come here so he could cup her cheeks—either the ones shaping her face or the ones shaping her ass. She'd come here to dump a plastic lobster on him, and because she couldn't find a parking space, whatever that was about.

"Okay, so I'll leave," she finally said.

"Suit yourself." She'd hurt him, she'd left him, and he was under no obligation to make life easier for her.

She sighed, lifted her face and gazed into his eyes with such intensity he had to exert himself not to fall back a step. "Well, anyway," she said. "I'm home." With that, she spun around, yanked open the door and marched out.

Christ. She shouldn't be heading outside alone this late at night. His neighborhood was safe, but still.

He ought to accompany her back to whatever vehicle she couldn't find a parking space for, just to make sure nothing happened to her.

He swung open his door and stepped out into the hallway in time to see her disappear into the elevator. "Susie!" he shouted after her, but the door slid shut and she was gone. Two of his neighbors cracked their doors open and glowered at him for yelling in the hallway after midnight. "Sorry," he said, ducking back into his foyer and closing the door. He twisted the bolt, turned around and found himself face to face with a freaking six-foot plastic lobster.

Damn, he thought as another of those psychosomatic migraines began hammering inside his skull.

Chapter Twenty-Eight

Nico's was nearly empty—just a customer who'd come in for an eggplant parmesan hero to go, and Rick and Anna huddled at a table, sipping root beers and nibbling on single slices of Sicilian with pepperoni. Susie was glad to be stuck behind the counter, slicing and wrapping the sloppy sandwich. Eggplant was one of those vegetables she didn't get: purple until you cooked it, then green and brown, slimy in texture, with a flavor that made her think of mildew. And she had yet to figure out a way to slice a roll full of breaded and baked eggplant bleeding tomato sauce and liquefied mozzarella without the sandwich's innards oozing out along the edges.

Still, if that was what the customer wanted, that was what he'd get. The first law of retail was to satisfy the customer, and Susie Bloom, erstwhile poet and free spirit, had become quite an expert when it came to retail.

She wasn't positive, but she suspected Rick and Anna were talking about her. Not that she blamed them. She was such a hot topic, after all—Susie in meltdown, Susie in love, Susie showing up at Casey's apartment at midnight to find him entertaining his new sweetheart. Susie abandoning her lobster statue and making an ass of herself. Susie in a million pieces, every single, shattered piece seething in the knowledge that she and she alone was responsible for the debacle that was her life.

She wasn't used to being responsible. Shit happened; sometimes she was the shitter and sometimes she was the shat-upon, but she'd always wiped herself off and moved on. No big deal. Life was for living, not for worrying about your bowels.

This time, though... She was ready to sign up for a colonoscopy on her emotions. This time she'd managed to shit on herself.

She hadn't revealed to Anna or Rick every miserable detail of what had happened the night she'd driven the rental van to Queens. She'd told Rick she'd left Linus with Casey. She'd told Anna that the new sweetheart had been at Casey's apartment and had brayed a laugh that reminded her of some of the more nightmarish scenes from *Equus*, and that she'd felt like a fool and left as quickly as she could. As Anna and Rick noshed on their mid-afternoon pizza slices, they were probably comparing notes, filling each other in.

The eggplant man—thin, bearded, earringed, probably a vegetarian—handed her his credit card and she ran it through the machine. No tip for a take-out order, of course. Yet she believed she deserved some sort of bonus for creating such a neatly wrapped hero out of such disgusting ingredients. The vegetarian signed the charge slip, handed it to her and carried his take-out bag to the door. Once he was gone, she turned to discover Anna and Rick staring at her. Anna waved at her to join them.

No other customers occupied tables. Nico was in the kitchen, using the lull between the lunch and dinner surges to prepare fresh pots of sauce and fresh mounds of dough. Susie couldn't count on him to call her into the kitchen. She was stuck.

Sighing, she filled a glass of water for herself, wiped her hands on her apron and trudged across the scuffed checkerboard-tile floor to their table. She could have heated a leftover slice of pizza for herself, but what little appetite she had evaporated as she settled into a chair facing these two people who supposedly adored her and who, she knew, were about to give her a very hard time.

"You need to go to a poetry slam," Anna announced. "Rick and I decided." She tossed back her long, black hair, revealing the row of earrings that trimmed her lobe.

Susie had trouble getting around the idea of Anna and Rick collaborating on a plan for her. "You decided," she muttered.

"The only poetry you're writing these days is that crap for the *Bloom's Bulletin*," Rick said.

Self-righteous anger flared within Susie. "Those poems aren't crap. They're carefully wrought limericks. Do you know how hard it is to come up with a rhyme for stroganoff?" It had been so hard she'd telephoned Casey for help, so hard she'd been forced to acknowledge that she was in love with him when he'd provided her with the rhyme. Limericks had proven to be an emotional minefield for her.

"There's a poetry slam at that scuzzy coffee house around the corner from my apartment this weekend," Rick told her. "I think you should write something for it. Anna'll be there."

Susie gazed at Anna in surprise. Anna shrugged sheepishly. "For once in his life, Rick is paying for our food," she said, gesturing at the discarded pizza crusts resting on their plates. "How can I say no?"

"She's got a price, just like all of us," Rick said with a grin.

Susie was discouraged to think Anna's price was a whopping nine dollars plus tax. She wondered where Rick had gotten the money to splurge on this mid-afternoon snack. For him, even nine bucks was a lot. "Are you paying for this out of the film budget?" she asked, disapproval coloring her tone.

"Stop spying for your sister," Rick retorted. "She's the one who's got you writing those dumb-ass limericks. She's no friend of yours."

"The limericks were my idea," Susie said. "And besides, Julia pays me for those limericks. She pays me to write the damned bulletin."

"So? Writing a poem for the slam would pay you emotionally."

Great. Just what Susie needed: emotional compensation.

"Let it all out, Suze, that's all I'm saying." Rick patted her on the shoulder, then drained his glass, his straw making obscene noises as he slurped the dregs of root beer and crushed ice from the bottom of his glass. "Look at you. Your life sucks."

"Thanks," she snapped.

"He's right," Anna chimed in. "You need to get past this."

Get past what? Blowing off Casey and then seeing the error of her ways in time to get blown off by him? Giving her love to him when he no longer wanted it? Chasing the train down the tracks with her heart in her hands and no sight of him even waving from the window, because he was off having a drink in the club car with Halle Berry?

"Poetry would be good therapy," Anna said. "It'll get you out of the pits."

"Or at least keep you company while you're in the pits," Rick added. "I'm going to need you to do some voice-over stuff for the movie. But we can talk about that another time. You're working now."

Yeah, she was—for real money, not the emotional kind. She took the ten-dollar bill Rick extended to her and carried it to the counter. "Keep the change," he said as he and Anna rose from the table.

Big tipper, Susie thought, unable to shake her suspicion that he was tipping her with money from the film budget.

As if his minuscule tip was going to make or break anything—including her. She pocketed the change and waved limply as Anna and Rick waltzed out of the pizzeria. Given the lack of patrons filling the place, now would be a good time to sweep the floors and tidy up a bit.

Instead, she grabbed her order pad and pen and wrote, *Losing Linus.*

She stared at the title for a moment, clicking the pen open and shut a few times on her chin, then wrote:

> *Lobsters turn red when boiled.*
> *Hearts turn hard when burned.*
> *Bread blackens in the fire.*
> *Chocolate melts, messy.*
> *Love flames out or freezes, either way*
> *It is gone.*
> *Nothing to eat, and I'm hollow, needy,*
> *hungry.*

Maybe she wasn't hollow or needy, but she was hungry. She tore off the top sheet of her pad and tucked it into the hip pocket of her black jeans, then cleared off and wiped down the table where Anna and Rick had been sitting. Once it was spotless, she sauntered into the kitchen. Pots simmered on the stove, filling the room with the blended fragrance of plum tomatoes, garlic, olive oil, and basil. Susie liked to think Italy smelled exactly like Nico's kitchen.

She spotted Nico hovering just outside the back door, enjoying a cigarette with Orlando, a Puerto Rican kid fresh out of high school whom Nico was trying to turn Italian by revealing for him the mysteries of pizza and pasta preparation. They smiled and nodded at Susie, who returned the greeting before yanking open the heavy aluminum door of one of the industrial refrigerators. She grabbed a handful of pitted black olives from a tub, tossed them all into her mouth and chomped down on their flimsy flesh, letting the salty juice bathe her tongue. While she was still chewing, she tore a chunk from a large, knotted wad of mozzarella. Chocolate would have satisfied her more than cheese and olives, but Nico didn't keep desserts in that refrigerator, and she wanted to stuff her face quickly and get back to the front room.

Detouring to the sink, she held the cheese with her teeth, freeing her hands so she could rinse the olive juice from her palms. Once she'd dried them, she carried the cheese back to her post behind the counter in the front room. No one had come in, so she picked up her pen, grabbed a to-go paper plate and wrote:

> *Now the lobster is gone.*
> *Red, ugly, chipped, hard shell, cheap*
> *plastic.*
> *In the end, the lobster is gone.*
> *In the end, the end of love.*

Two tottering old men with matching duck-head canes entered the restaurant. She hid the plate on a shelf below the counter and shaped a welcoming smile for them. The men were adorable, one a few inches taller than the other, one wearing a faded Yankees cap and the other hatless, his fuzzy gray hair circling his freckled scalp like a laurel wreath. Both had age spots on their hands and wore cardigans, even though the afternoon air had reached the mid-seventies. The men bickered for a few minutes about meatballs versus sausage. "We buy only one hero and split it," the taller one explained.

"It's too much, one of those sandwiches," the shorter one said. "I can't finish it myself."

"My grandson could finish it," the taller one noted. "My Danny, he can eat everything. And does."

"He's the monster that ate Pittsburgh, your Danny."

"*Oy.* Fifteen years old and almost six feet tall, and he eats all the time."

"So we'll get the sausage?" the shorter one said.

"I hate the sausage. It makes me *fortz.*"

"Everything makes you *fortz,*" the shorter one complained. "You're an *alter fortzer.*"

"If you'd like," Susie offered, just because these men amused her and she didn't want to give the taller one gas, "I could make two half sandwiches, one with meatballs and one with sausage. How would that be?"

The men looked stunned, then ecstatic. "You would do that for us?" the shorter one asked.

"It's not a problem."

Their expressions changed from ecstatic to transported. Smitten. They were in love with her because she could make two half sandwiches with different fillings. And neither of them appeared like the sort who would force her to change her life for him, to move in and settle down and marry him.

She went into the kitchen to assemble their two-part sandwich. Slicing the roll was therapeutic; she pretended the hard crust was Casey's thick skull as she sawed the knife blade through it. She filled each half with the requested filling, slid the sandwich into the pizza oven for a minute to warm it up, then wrapped each half separately, glancing behind her to make sure Nico wasn't watching. He'd probably have a fit if he knew she was going to so much effort for a couple of old geezers.

They tipped her generously, even though they'd ordered the sandwich to go. Once they'd shuffled out of the restaurant, she grabbed her pen and a napkin and continued her poem.

It felt good to write, she realized. Rick and Anna had spoken the truth. Whether or not Susie went to the slam, she needed to write something real, something deep, something that exorcised her pain. Something that didn't entail finding a rhyme for stroganoff.

The lobster, she wrote, *is all. The lobster is gone. The lobster is red and chipped and hiding within its shell, like my heart.*

Chapter Twenty-Nine

Susie's cell phone started ringing as she climbed the stairs to her apartment, but she couldn't answer it because her hands were full. She carried a large pizza box filled with paper plates, napkins, order slips and a straw wrapper, all with bits and pieces of her poem scribbled onto them. This was a huge poem, an epic, one that required assembly. Once she got upstairs and emptied and unfolded the box—which had several fervent stanzas written inside the lid—she could put it all together and figure out if she'd created a masterpiece or dreck. She was a little worried about whether she'd be able to read her handwriting on the straw wrapper, but despite that concern, she was pretty sure what she'd created was magnificent.

She'd left Nico's early tonight—ten-thirty—because she'd worked the lunch shift. Even lugging her poem-in-a-pizza-box, she'd arrived at her building only ten minutes later, so the chirping of the phone in her purse at this hour didn't alarm her. She wasn't going to stop halfway up the stairs to her apartment to put down her box and answer it, though. Whoever was calling her would have to wait until she got inside.

Balancing the box while she unlocked the three bolts on her door was tricky enough without the damned phone nagging at her to hurry. She shoved the door open with her hip, nodded toward Caitlin and Anna, who were both seated on the sofa polishing their nails and watching a *South Park* rerun, and set her box down on the dining table near the window. The kitchen was too small to contain a table. It was practically too small to contain a refrigerator, which was one reason they had such an undersized refrigerator, the other reason being that their landlord was a cheap bastard.

"Did you bring us leftovers?" Caitlin asked, motioning toward the box with her nail polish brush.

"No," Susie said, tugging at her purse's drawstring to get to her phone. "It's a poem." She found it and tapped the screen. "Hello?"

"Susie, it's me," Julia's voice came through the phone. "I'm sorry I'm calling so late. Are you at work?"

"It's not that late and I'm not at work. What's up?" Something was, if Julia's tense voice was anything to judge by. Susie stepped inside the cramped kitchen and opened the fridge, hoping to find an open bottle of wine in it. Life was sweet; a screw-top bottle half full of Chablis stood on the top shelf. Caitlin's, probably; her palate was about as discriminating as that of the guy Susie often found sleeping it off in the alley behind Nico's. Screw-top Chablis was probably Susie's least favorite wine in the world—it tasted like water with a few mild pollutants mixed in—but wine was wine.

Tucking the phone between her ear and her shoulder, she poured some wine into a tumbler and returned to the table. "I need to kill Mom," Julia said. "Will you help?"

"Sure." Susie sat on one of the chairs and kicked her tired feet up on another. She used her toes to pry off her sandals, leaned her shoulders back and decided that the dining set she and her roommates had bought for fifty bucks from their upstairs neighbor three years ago, when he'd decided on a whim to quit his job as an auditor for the Transit Authority for work on a salmon boat in Alaska, was just barely worth what they'd paid for it. The back of the chair didn't conform to her back at all, and the seat was hard and unmolded, making her uncomfortably aware of her hip bones. "Why are we killing her?" she asked before sipping from her glass.

"I told her Ron and I were going to have our wedding reception in Grandma Ida's apartment."

"You are?" Susie nearly choked on her wine. She nudged the pizza box to one side of the table and put down her glass, then swung her legs around to a different chair so she would have her back to Caitlin and Anna. She didn't care if they overheard the conversation, but seeing them hunched over their feet, with wads of cotton protruding from between their toes, was too distracting. Susie couldn't afford to be distracted when her sister was telling her something so bizarre. "Why?"

"We weren't planning on a big reception with a huge invitation list," Julia explained. "And Grandma Ida's apartment is spacious. We can fit everyone in. We figured the musicians could set up in the foyer, and we could do a buffet in the dining room, and everyone could mill around."

"What did Grandma Ida say about this?"

"She said yes. So we decided to go for it. I want my wedding catered by Bloom's, and we were struggling to find a venue where we could bring our own caterer in. Of course Grandma Ida has no objection to letting Bloom's cater the wedding."

"Great." Grandma Ida's apartment gave Susie the creeps, but that was mostly because it was filled with so many memories of Grandma Ida criticizing her, Grandma Ida telling her to calm down, Grandma Ida complaining that she shouldn't jiggle her legs so much while she was eating because all that jiggling made her drop crumbs on the floor. She probably wouldn't be able to jiggle much in a bridesmaid's dress—God only knew what Julia had in mind for her to wear—and she'd hardly be the only guest to drop crumbs on the floor. If Grandma Ida was okay with it, Susie had no objections. "So why are we killing Mom?"

"She went ballistic when she heard the plan. She wants me to have the wedding at the Plaza."

"Big deal. It's not her wedding."

"It's her daughter's wedding, which she thinks is the same thing." Julia sighed. "I told her the wedding was going to be at Grandma Ida's, and she went whining to Norman."

"Norman?"

"Ron's father. Her boyfriend. Only he's not her boyfriend anymore, because he told her it was up to Ron and me where to have the wedding, and she should stay out of it. At which point, I gather she blew up at him and now they haven't talked to each other for days, and she thinks it's all my fault."

Their mother had a boyfriend? Where had Susie been?

Up in Maine, communing with Linus and the potatoes. In Boston, standing ankle-deep in decaying lettuce leaves at Haymarket Square. At Pine Haven, sitting on a rickety cabin porch and staring at the muddy water of Pine Haven Lake, thinking home and family were wonderful and perhaps marriage wasn't the absolute worst thing in the world.

And all that time, while she was starring in Rick's movie and rethinking her life, her mother was dating Ron's father?

Apparently, her mother wasn't dating him now, because he refused to meddle in Julia's wedding plans. He sounded like a nice guy. "Look, Julia. It's your wedding. If I've got to wear a gown, Mom can survive a party in Grandma Ida's apartment. After a few drinks, she might not even know where she is."

"I can only hope," Julia muttered. "Meanwhile, she's making me crazy. She was so happy with Norman, he was so intelligent, he was such a gentleman—by which I think she meant they weren't sleeping together, thank God—and now they're not talking because he refuses to support her in her *mishegas*."

"So they're not talking," Susie said, then took a sip of the wine and tried not to cringe. It tasted like piss-water with a finish of copper. "It's her *mishegas*, not yours."

"Right. I'm going to have a wedding where the mother of the bride isn't talking to the father of the groom."

"Well, the mother of the groom isn't talking to the father of the groom either, is she?" As Susie recalled, Joffe's parents were still fuming over their divorce, which had occurred twenty-something years ago. "It's your wedding, Julia. Have it wherever you want, and serve whatever food you want. If Mom doesn't like it, tough shit."

"You don't work two doors away from her office," Julia pointed out. "She spent most of today giving me grief. Even Uncle Jay intervened. He told her to leave me alone. Who would have guessed that Uncle Jay, of all people, would come to my aid over something like this?"

"Uncle Jay loves you." More than that, Susie thought, Uncle Jay hated their mother. However the family dynamics shook out, Julia should grab whatever allies she could find and hang onto them.

"Listen—could you come up to the store tomorrow? I know it's not your usual day to be here, but I thought maybe you could talk to Mom."

Susie sighed. Julia was the sane sister, the mature one, the one who kept the rest of the family on an even keel. She was the fixer, the peacemaker, the minister of logic in a family that embraced rational thought with all the enthusiasm of French royalty facing the guillotine. If she couldn't calm their mother down, Susie certainly wouldn't be able to.

"How about Adam?" she suggested. "Maybe he can get through to her."

"Adam is out of it," Julia muttered.

"Out of it? What, is he getting stoned? While he's living with Mom?"

"I don't know about that. I doubt it. He's just...*in love*." Julia put enough ironic spin on those two final words to cause Susie's head to buzz. Or maybe it was the bad wine creating that unpleasant hum inside her skull.

"Sure, but isn't the lady he's in love with out in Seattle eating tofu and braiding her leg hair?"

"No. He's in love with Elyse, the ballerina, and she's in New York, and she seems to shave her legs on a regular basis."

"Really? What about Tash?"

"I think he sent her a kiss-off email."

"Ouch." Susie had no great fondness for Tash, but break-ups were often painful and sometimes tragic. If anyone should know, it was Susie. "Geez. It's going to get ugly when they both settle in West Lafayette this fall. Or was Tash only planning to move there because she expected to be with Adam?"

"I don't know if he's going to Purdue, either," Julia said.

"What?" Susie felt as if she'd returned not from New England but from the far side of the moon. How could so much have happened in her absence? How could her mother have grown so close to Joffe's father that their falling out would unhinge her? How could Adam have completely overhauled his plans for next year? How could Grandma Ida have agreed to host a wedding in her apartment?

If Susie was the sanest member of her family, her family was in major big trouble.

"So, will you come uptown tomorrow?" Julia pleaded.

Susie looked at her pizza box. She thought about the words scrawled inside it, the passion, the anger and sorrow, her soulful, lyrical outpouring inked onto paper towels, paper placemats and toilet paper from the ladies' room. Much as she loved Julia and wanted to help her, she had problems of her own. One was how to piece together her poem. Another was how to piece together her heart.

"I can't," she said, ignoring the twinge of guilt at the understanding that she was abandoning her sister. It wasn't as if Julia had no one else to turn to. She had Joffe. For all his curmudgeonly pretense, he was utterly devoted to Julia. If she asked him to slay their mother, his response would be to start sharpening a carving knife.

There was a time, Susie thought sadly, when she'd been certain Casey would sharpen a carving knife for her, too. There was a time she'd believed he loved her enough to do anything she asked of him—except the one thing she'd ever asked of him, which was to relax his hold on her. She'd never asked him to kill anyone, or to change his habits for her, or to rinse the little blond flecks of beard down the drain in the bathroom sink when he was done shaving. He knew enough to rinse the sink, anyway, but she'd never asked him to do that, or to wear his hair differently, or to skip his regular basketball games to spend time with her. She'd never asked him to treat her mother with deference or change his work hours or sit through a chick-flick with her.

She'd asked him only one single thing: to respect her independence. And when she'd swallowed her pride and placed her independence on a sacrificial altar for him, what had he done? Nothing, other than to prop Linus against the wall of his entryway and stare at her as if she was the one with antennae and claws.

"Susie? Am I losing you?"

Susie could have pretended her phone's reception was fading, but she was too honest for that. "I'm here," she said. "I just can't come to Bloom's tomorrow."

"Why not?"

Because she had problems of her own. Because she was pissed and pathetic. Because she didn't give a rat's ass where Julia held her wedding.

"Because I've got to put together a poem," she said, eyeing the square white box on the table and wondering whether putting that poem together would make her feel better or worse.

"Come," Julia said. "Bring the poem with you."

Chapter Thirty

Susie strolled through Julia's open office door, carrying a large white pizza box. No aroma emanated from it, so Julia doubted it contained anything edible. That was all right with her; she'd just polished off a sesame bagel and a mug of Bloom's Kona blend, and she wasn't in the mood for pizza.

What she was in the mood for was flying to Vegas with Joffe and paying an Elvis impersonator to marry them. Yet seeing Susie imbued her with an inexplicable surge of optimism.

"I'm here," Susie announced, dropping the box onto their grandfather's old desk, which stood idle in the corner of the office. "I'll talk to Mom if you want, but you're going to have to let me spread my poem out in here so I can put it together."

"That's your poem?" Julia eyed the pizza box warily.

"Yup." Susie straightened and spun around to face Julia. She looked better than she had in weeks—more color in her cheeks, the shadows under her eyes less obvious and her hair freshly cut into a brisk, breezy style. Along with her standard black jeans she wore an orange tank top, a burst of unexpected color.

Julia smiled. If Susie was coming out of her depression, she might be able to salvage Julia's wedding. Julia wasn't used to having to depend on her kid sister to mend the family's fissures, but at least Susie looked as if she had enough energy to tackle such a challenge.

"Are you going to talk to Mom?" Julia asked.

"Actually, what I thought..." Susie surveyed the office and raked her hand through her hair. Every lock slid back into its precise place. Where was she getting her hair done? Some hip downtown salon—Julia couldn't remember what it was called, other than it was a Midwestern city with a French-sounding name. Eau Claire? Fond du Lac? Whatever—her hair looked fabulous.

"Actually, what you thought," Julia prompted her when her sentence went unfinished for a full minute.

Susie nodded. "What I thought was, you should have a meeting."

"A meeting?"

"You know, like one of your Bloom's meetings."

When Julia had become president of Bloom's last year, she'd started chairing executive meetings. Her mother, Deirdre, Myron, Uncle Jay and sometimes Grandma Ida would attend—Susie, too, if she was involved in a Bloom's project. At first, the third-floor denizens had considered the idea of gathering everyone into the same room revolutionary, if not downright incendiary. They much preferred to shout back and forth through their open office doors than sit together in the same room and talk face to face. Julia had brought everyone around by serving bagels at the meetings. Delicious Bloom's food had pacified them enough to let her manage the business in her own style.

Now, a year later, she held one meeting a week, every Monday morning. Things ran more smoothly at the store, and she'd finally established herself in her position as the head honcho. But every now and then, she brought Deirdre, Myron and various Blooms together in her office for a sit-down on a day other than Monday. She wished they had a conference room, but space on the Bloom Building's third floor was limited. If Susie had to write the *Bloom's Bulletin* from a desk tucked into an alcove in the hall, a conference room was out of the question.

"What kind of meeting?" Julia eyed the pizza box again. For some reason, she expected something to jump out of it when Susie opened it.

"A meeting of the affected parties. You, Mom, Grandma Ida—and I guess Lyndon should be included, too. And Joffe, if he can make it."

"Not his father, though," Julia warned. In truth, Julia liked the current freeze between her mother and Norman Joffe better than the previous heat they'd been generating.

"I don't think we need him. How about Joffe's mother?"

"I don't think we need her, either," Julia said, realizing that she had somehow come around to believing this meeting was a good idea. "Do you think she knows her ex-husband took Mom out on a few dates?" God, what if she did? Wouldn't that make for a pleasant atmosphere at the wedding? Vegas and an Elvis impersonator sounded better and better.

"Not your problem," Susie reminded her. "Forget about it. So, are you going to organize this meeting?"

"What meeting?" Sondra Bloom's voice resounded through the suite of offices.

"Wonderful," Julia muttered, kissing good-bye her hope of reviewing a report she'd received earlier that morning from her seafood manager, who was having problems negotiating with their long-time pickled herring supplier.

"Are we having a meeting?" Myron shouted from his office. He sounded awfully eager—probably because he lived for the free bagels Deirdre served at the meetings. Pink cranberry bagels were his favorite, especially when spread with pink strawberry-flavored cream cheese.

"It's family," Julia shouted back to him. "Go downstairs and treat yourself to a bagel if you want one."

"What meeting?" Sondra shouted again. Just seconds after her voice swept through the open door she materialized in the doorway. Clad in an A-line jumper that emphasized her broad hips, she frowned at her two daughters. Ever since her latest blow-up over the Plaza Hotel, frowning had been her expression du jour. "Are we having a meeting?" she asked.

"Let me call Grandma Ida," Julia said. "If she's available, we'll have a meeting."

"I don't want a meeting with her," Sondra retorted. "She conspired with my daughter behind my back."

"Mom." Julia swallowed a groan to refrain from saying what she was really thinking. Most of the words she'd need to articulate what she was really thinking were bad, bad words.

"Mom, come with me," Susie said, hooking her arm around their mother's elbow and steering her back to her own office. Over her shoulder, Susie added to Julia, "Call Grandma Ida. And Joffe, if you think he should be around for this."

Julia watched her sister and mother disappear, then leaned back in her oversized chair and groaned again, allowing a few of those bad, bad words to slip out. She didn't want a meeting. What she wanted was for her mother to let her have the wedding of her dreams. Was that really so much to ask for? She'd been a good daughter. She'd brought her mother such *nachus* by graduating with honors from Wellesley, then excelling in law school, then accepting a miserable job at a prestigious law firm, then quitting that job to take the reins at Bloom's. She'd met a guy who was not only smart, sexy, and employed but also Jewish, and they loved each other and wanted to get married. Why wasn't that enough to satisfy her mother? Why did the Plaza have to be a part of the deal?

All right. Susie was on the case. The least Julia could do was try to set up this meeting.

She started with Grandma Ida. Lyndon answered the phone and, after checking various schedules, announced that he and Grandma Ida would both be downstairs in fifteen minutes. She dialed Ron's office and got his voice mail, then tried his cell phone and got that voice mail. She left a message about the meeting but assured him he didn't have to attend. Actually, she'd prefer for him not to come. He'd been exposed to enough *mishegas* with her family. Any more, and he might decide he couldn't bear to marry a Bloom.

She hung up in time to see Adam hovering in her doorway. His hair had gotten long enough that she'd asked him to start wearing a cap to work. He wasn't involved in food preparation, but she tried to keep the rules uniform among all the staff. Today he'd obliged by tucking the longer front locks behind his ears and jamming on a Yankees cap. If his hair got a little longer, he'd be able to pull it into a ponytail like Casey.

Maybe she could convince him to try Susie's salon. St. Louis? French Lick? She wished she could remember the name.

"I got this great idea," Adam said, bounding into the office as soon as he saw he had her attention. "If you organized the inventory by shelf height, you could adjust the shelves to different heights and fit more inventory onto them." He grabbed a pen from her desk and started sketching diagrams of shelf heights on the back of the envelope the report about the pickled herring merchant had come in.

He was well into his explanation when Uncle Jay showed up. "I heard you were organizing one of your meetings," he said, sneering only the slightest bit. He thought her meetings were inane, and he'd made that opinion quite clear to her on more than one occasion, but he so enjoyed watching her spar with her mother that he diligently attended every meeting, apparently hoping to witness a fight.

"What meeting?" Adam asked, pen poised above an array of lines, arrows and numbers that resembled hieroglyphics to her. "I've heard about your meetings. Can I sit in?"

She didn't bother to ask what he'd heard, or from whom. "It's not a store meeting," she said. "It's just a family thing."

"I'm family," Uncle Jay said, strolling into the office and planting himself on the couch as if eager to reserve one of the more comfortable seats for himself.

"I'm family, too," Adam said, shooting Julia a hopeful smile.

What the hell. With all the open office doors on the third floor, and all the kibitzing, no meeting would be private, anyway. "If you really care that much about where Ron and I get married, be my guest," she conceded.

Adam continued drawing on the envelope for another few minutes. Then he clicked the pen shut and presented the envelope to her with a flourish. "See?" he said.

She saw an envelope covered by a lot of indecipherable jottings. "We can discuss this later," she said, thinking longingly of the report the envelope had once contained. She'd never get to it this morning, not with Adam and Uncle Jay already in her office and Grandma Ida and Lyndon heading in her direction, visible through the doorway. Grandma Ida rested her hand on Lyndon's forearm, but she was definitely moving on her own power, using him not for balance but merely as an old-fashioned escort. Not that there was much old-fashioned about Lyndon, who looked dapper in crisp olive-green trousers, a shirt with a polo-player logo embroidered onto the chest pocket, and leather moccasins, his hair neatly corn-rowed and his eyes sparkling as he ushered Grandma Ida into the office.

Julia wheeled her chair out from behind her desk for Grandma Ida to sit in. The chair was too big for her, but sometimes she complained about sitting on the couch, which she said was like sinking into a vat of cold kasha.

Susie and Sondra must have watched for them from Sondra's office, because they immediately appeared on the threshold. "Is everyone here?" Susie asked as Sondra entered, plopped herself into the kasha and glowered at Julia. "Where's Joffe?"

"I left him a message. I don't know if—" Julia trailed off when she spotted Deirdre behind Susie, towering in the doorway in her stilt-like high heels.

Why not include Deirdre? She was practically family, anyway. Julia smiled limply in welcome, and Deirdre followed Susie into the room.

People took a few minutes to arrange themselves. Adam courteously sacrificed his couch seat for Deirdre. Susie usually sat on Grandpa Isaac's old desk, but the pizza box she'd brought took up most of it, so she asked Adam to drag in some chairs from another office. Julia perched on a corner of her desk and tried to ignore the tide of hostility surging toward her from her mother.

At last, everyone was settled. Julia turned to Susie. This meeting was her idea; she could preside over it.

"Okay," Susie said, hooking her feet around the legs of her chair, then unhooking them, then crossing one leg over the other knee and jiggling her foot. "I'm no expert on love, that's for sure."

"You're going to lecture us on love?" Sondra groaned.

"*I'm* an expert on love," Uncle Jay announced. "I'm married to the most wonderful lady, and that's what love is all about. Julia, are we going to have bagels at this meeting?"

Before Julia could answer, Susie continued. "I'm not an expert, but the bottom line is, Julia and Joffe are in love and they're going to get married, and if we love Julia, the most loving thing we can do is get the hell out of her way."

Well, that was blunt. Julia would have been more diplomatic, and probably less effective. Susie had never cared if her family approved of her—the butterfly tattoo on her ankle, partly visible beneath the hem of her jeans when she bounced her foot, had caused grief and wailing among the family, but Susie wore that tattoo proudly—and she wasn't aiming to win anyone's approval now.

"Who's in her way?" Sondra erupted. "We're trying to make her wedding the best day of her life."

"The best day of *your* life," Susie argued. "Mom, it's *her* wedding."

"And her idea of a wedding is to jam a hundred fifty people into Ida's apartment? What kind of cockamamie idea is that? People will be *schvitzing*, they'll be spilling their drinks on the rugs, Lyndon'll be running around like a maniac trying to keep order—"

"I was under the impression I'd be a guest," Lyndon said, glancing at Julia.

"Of course. You and Howard." Julia turned to her mother. "I'm hiring people to serve and clean up."

"A hundred fifty people you're going to cram into my mother's apartment?" Uncle Jay blurted out. "What are you, crazy? We have a dozen people in the apartment for *Pesach* and it feels too crowded."

"That probably has to do with the identities of those people," Deirdre muttered under her breath. Julia silently agreed; when it was just the family, without non-Blooms to dilute them, their *Pesach* gathering could seem like a mob on the verge of rioting.

"Julia wants a wedding in my apartment. She should have it where she wants it," Grandma Ida said, pumping her hand up and down emphatically. Her gold bangle bracelets clattered.

"She has a wedding there, I'm not coming," Sondra said.

Silence billowed through the room.

If Julia had half Susie's guts, she'd say, "Fine. Don't come." Susie never let her loved ones blackmail her. She loved Casey, but when he'd tried to pressure her into marrying him, she'd stuck to her ideals, even at the cost of losing him. Julia should stick to her ideals, too.

But she'd always been the family conciliator, the one who knocked herself out to make everyone else happy. If sticking to her ideals meant alienating her loved ones, she wasn't sure she could do it. And the thought of her mother not attending her wedding...

"I'm not a Bloom," Deirdre said quietly, staring at Sondra with steely green eyes, "but I think you're wrong."

"You *would* think I'm wrong," Sondra shot back. "And you know what? Your judgment means nothing to me."

"Sondra," Uncle Jay intervened.

"Like *you* have anything worthwhile to add," Sondra said, twisting on the couch to face Uncle Jay. "Your son is out God knows where, burning through the store's money to make a cinematic masterpiece—"

"It's going to be good," Susie noted.

"*Feh,*" Grandma Ida interjected. "Alfred Hitchcock, now, he's good."

Lyndon cleared his throat. "Did you know," he said, "that the roof of this building is accessible? It's got an attractive safety railing and a solid flooring. I bet a tent could be set up there."

"On the roof of the Bloom Building?"

"I've been up there. Someone's set up some picnic tables and a beach umbrella."

"Who?" Sondra looked shocked. "Isn't that trespassing?"

"I've been up there, too," Susie said. "When I was a kid, I used to go up there all the time. The ground is kind of tarry, though, isn't it?"

"You went up on the roof?" Sondra shrieked. "You could have fallen! You could have killed yourself!"

"It's a really sturdy railing," Susie assured her.

"How come you never took me up there?" Adam asked. He was practically pouting. "I want to see the roof."

"You could probably lay a parquet down for dancing," Lyndon suggested. "Bring up a tent, tables, chairs and parquet, and you're all set."

347

Julia's stomach began to unclench. The roof—with a view of the Hudson River and the sky stretching overhead. Fresh air, room to move, room to dance. They might need to get a permit; even though the Bloom family owned the building, she'd want to make sure holding a party up there was safe and legal. If it was, if she could arrange it, she and Ron could exchange vows beneath the stars. Well, beneath a *chuppa*, but the *chuppa* would be beneath the stars.

"Does the elevator go up to the roof?" she asked.

"The service elevator goes up to an anteroom that opens out onto the roof," Lyndon told her. "You could cart everything up there without any trouble. Then you could reserve the service elevator for your guests. If people can reserve it to move in and out of apartments, I don't see why you couldn't claim it for an evening."

The roof. The roof of the Bloom Building, with Bloom's food and Blooms and music. "Lyndon, I love you," Julia said.

"You've mentioned that in the past," he said, grinning slyly. "But it won't work. Stay with Ron. He's a good man."

Julia returned his smile. Indeed, everyone seemed to be smiling except her mother. "The roof of this building is not the Plaza," she grumbled.

"No," Julia said happily. "It's not."

A shadow fell across the room, and she looked toward the door. Ron stood there, slightly windblown and out of breath. "I got your message," he said. "I was doing an interview with a marketing professor up at Columbia, so..." He gazed around the room. "What did I miss?"

"We're getting married on the roof," Julia told him, pushing away from her desk and striding across the room to wrap her arms around him.

He kissed her forehead with a minimum of passion, in deference to the rapt audience watching them, and gazed into her eyes. "The roof? Do I have to parachute onto it?"

"No. There's an elevator."

He smiled and kissed her again, this time on her lips and a little less timidly. "Sounds great," he said.

Chapter Thirty-One

For her first meeting, Susie hadn't done half bad.

She had Julia's office to herself. Julia and Joffe had gone upstairs to check out the building's roof—and if it met with their approval, she'd consider the meeting an unqualified success, despite the fact that her mother was still fuming. Plaza, schmaza. Sondra would get over her snit. Or if she didn't, she'd be the one to suffer because of it.

Susie was not going to suffer from her mother's snit. She wasn't going to suffer from Julia's wedding. She had her own suffering to attend to, and as she lifted the many pieces of her poem from the pizza box, she found plenty of suffering in the words she'd written. On a small paper plate she'd inscribed:

Bridge over river
Tunnel under river
Water washes through
Trying to reach each other
We drown.

She'd placed only one word, *alone*, at the center of a paper plate. She'd turned a half-used order pad into a flip book, with the word *home* printed first in tiny letters and then large ones, progressing from page to page until the word took up an entire order slip, and then, on the last few pages, the four letters that spelled *home* broke apart, so if she flipped through the pad, the word seemed to grow bigger and bigger until it burst.

On a paper towel, she'd written, *Home is not a flip-book.*

On a waxed-paper sheet, she'd written, *Home is...* and then another word which she couldn't make out because her pen hadn't worked well on the waxy surface.

Home is... what? she wondered. What had that last word been?

The ink had bled a bit on the toilet paper squares, which were filled with screeds about how a woman didn't need a man if she had a dildo and an adequate supply of chocolate. Susie considered throwing those out, but she didn't want Julia—or, more likely, the janitorial service—to find them in the trash basket. She piled them into a gauzy stack on one side of the box, figuring she could flush them down the toilet. Male-bashing rants weren't what this poem was about.

It was about love, she thought, or more accurately, the end of love, the heartbreak of love, the loss of love. Her gaze drifted back to that waxed-paper sheet. *Home is...*

What the hell was home? A peanut butter and fluff sandwich in a cabin by a scummy pond? An overcrowded walk-up in the East Village? Someplace with a white picket fence? A kosher-style food emporium on the Upper West Side? Was it a place that stayed the same, no matter how far a person traveled, or was it a place that changed every day?

Bloom's wasn't the same place it had been a year ago, or even yesterday. Casey's apartment had a six-foot-tall lobster in it, where once it had had no lobster. Everything stayed the same in Grandma Ida's apartment—yet she'd been willing to host Julia's wedding there.

Susie shifted plates, napkins and the box around on the desk, hoping to find a unifying concept in the words she'd written last night. She was convinced this was the most important poem she'd ever written, but she couldn't seem to put it together. Strange that overseeing a meeting with a bunch of Blooms had been easier than overseeing a collection of paper scraps and jottings.

Julia reentered her office alone, her hair windswept and her smile brighter than a halogen bulb. "The roof is fantastic," she said. "Even if it rains, there's plenty of room for a tent. We have to work out the details with the building's management, but if they say it's okay, it'll be a great place to have the wedding."

"Why wouldn't they say it's okay? You own the building."

"It's owned by a family trust," Julia corrected her.

"Same thing." Susie shrugged. She didn't understand the convolutions of the family's assets. She just knew that she got a small check every month that made it possible for her to afford her share of the rent on that third-floor walk-up she wasn't sure qualified as home.

"What's all that?" Julia gestured toward the papers scattered across Grandpa Isaac's desk. "Are you picking through the garbage at Nico's?"

"It's a poem," Susie said, nudging the drinking straw wrapper so it was half-hidden under the box. "I'm trying to organize it. I've got to flush some of it, though."

"Flush it?"

"Promise you won't touch it," Susie said, collecting the pile of toilet paper squares. "Promise you won't read it. It's not ready yet."

Julia pursed her lips. "I wouldn't touch it without putting on latex gloves first. I don't want to go near it."

"Good. I'll be back." Susie strode to the door, gave Julia an encouraging smile, and exited into the hall, exactly as Casey exited into the hall from the office where Helen, the Human Resources person, held court.

Amazing how simply seeing him could cause the back of Susie's neck to grow steamy. Just ten paces behind her was the couch on which she and Casey had made love for the final time. She'd been feeling kind of pumped since she'd taken Rick and Anna's advice and started work on her pizza-box magnum opus, but seeing Casey deflated her like a ten-penny nail puncturing a tire. She remembered the last time she'd seen him: her idiotic drive to his apartment in the middle of the night, her granting him custody of Linus and then running away. She was lucky he hadn't called the city's department of mental health to report that a crackpot was harassing him.

"Susie," he said, his gaze traveling from her face to the fluttering stack of toilet paper squares in her hand.

"I have to flush this," she explained—as if that would reassure him of her sanity.

"We need to talk."

"Now?"

"It's a more reasonable hour than the last time we talked."

She couldn't deny that. Stuffing the toilet paper into a pocket of her jeans, she accompanied him through the hall and out of the office suite, then into the stairwell and down two flights of stairs to the first floor landing.

This was their spot. The place where they'd first kissed. The place where they'd had some of their most important conversations. Could a stairway landing be a home? This one, with its echoing walls and too-bright lighting, was probably as close as she and Casey would ever come to sharing a home.

He turned her to face him and she stared up at him, ordering herself not to let the steamy sensation journey from her nape to other parts of her anatomy. Her body ignored that mental command and grew warm and soft for him. Her cheeks flushed with heat; she wondered if they were as red as Linus.

As if he'd read her mind, he asked, "Are you going to explain the lobster to me?"

"What were you doing on the third floor?" she shot back. "Handing in your resignation?"

He opened his mouth and then shut it, evidently weighing his answer. He must have decided that she deserved an honest response. "I'll be here through the end of the month, but I need my pension money now."

"Why?"

"For my new place." He gazed past her for a second, then refocused on her. "I guess I need to tell you this. My store is going to be in your neighborhood. It's on Avenue B at 4th Street."

"Great. I'll be sure to stop in every day," she retorted.

He ignored her sarcasm. "Bring your friends. I'll need the business."

She noticed a flicker of worry in his hazel eyes. Besides all the other emotions tangled into the world's largest string ball inside her, she still felt concern for Casey. She wanted him to be happy. She wanted things to work out for him. She despised him and wished him a lifetime of pain and suffering, but she wasn't quite done loving him yet, so she wished him good things, too. "Is your store going to succeed?"

"I sure as hell hope so." He sighed, then smiled slightly. "Mose helped me get a low-interest loan from the Small Business Administration, and I've scraped the rest of the financing together. My pension funds are part of that. Your sister..."

"My sister what?" If Julia was part of his financing, too—if she'd invested in his business—Susie would have the building's roof condemned so Julia would have to have her damned wedding at the Plaza. Or else she'd loosen a stretch of that sturdy railing and give Julia a well-timed shove.

"Your sister agreed to contract out to me as a bagel supplier. I'll still be making all the bagels for Bloom's. So there'll be a guaranteed income from that. And if you come in every day, and bring your friends... Yeah, it might succeed."

She hated that he was smiling. He was too sexy when he smiled. She also hated that a part of her longed to clap her hands and cheer at the prospect of his business thriving. She hated that his eyes were too beautiful and he had a dusty-sweet flour scent, and he was so tall, and she'd kissed him here on this landing more than once, kissed him with enough heat to detonate a nuclear device, kissed him with such joy she didn't have to question the meaning of home. Home had been kissing Casey, and now she was homeless.

"She's very pretty," she said, reminding herself of why she would never kiss him again.

His smile vanished. "Who?"

"The woman at your apartment."

He rolled his eyes, as if disgusted that she'd even mention it. Oh, right. He was sleeping with Halle Berry and Susie was supposed to pretend that didn't have anything to do with her. He dragged her back to his original question. "What the hell was the other night about? You showed up, you dumped a big synthetic lobster on me and you disappeared."

"Because you were entertaining," she explained. "I should've called first—"

"Agreed."

"But I couldn't find a parking space for the van in my neighborhood, so I figured I'd drive out to Forest Hills."

"To give me a lobster?"

"Uh-huh." She struggled to find the logic in her actions. The night she'd handed Linus over to him, it had seemed like a wise move.

"Why?"

"Because..." Because she'd wanted to tell him she loved him. Because she'd found the courage to toss aside everything she'd believed about herself, everything that mattered. And then she'd seen Halle and realized how foolish it was for her—for any woman—to sacrifice everything she believed about herself and everything that mattered for the love of a man. "Because I couldn't fit the lobster in my apartment, and Rick couldn't fit it in his," she said.

"What am I supposed to do with it?"

"Dip it in melted butter," she snapped. "You're the culinary genius. You figure it out."

She yanked open the door and stormed out into the store, passing the coffee corner, the shelves of poppy-seed cookies, the refrigerator cases of cheese and the baskets of bread. She ignored the chatter, the aromas, the browsing customers and bustling stock clerks. She ignored Morty Sugarman waving at her from the bagel counter and Rita Martinez calling out a greeting to her from behind her cash register. She didn't break stride until she was outside, standing in a summery afternoon as hot as she was.

If Bloom's was home, she thought, running away from home was a huge temptation. But she was too old to join the circus, and if she wished to drive an eigh-teen-wheeler to California she'd have to get a special license. Besides, her poem was upstairs, spread across the surface of Grandpa Isaac's desk, except for the fist-ful of toilet-paper poetry still in her hand.

So she walked around the corner to the building's side entrance, went inside and headed back upstairs.

Chapter Thirty-Two

Rick managed to borrow a screening room at the 52nd Street studio where he'd worked as Camera 3 for "Power and Passion" a couple of months ago. A vast projection-screen television consumed most of one end of the room, and the floor rose from that end in shallow steps lined with upholstered purple chairs. If Susie's life had taken a different turn, she might have been intrigued by the color.

If her life had taken a different turn, she might have been gloating about the two hundred dollars she'd pocketed last night at a poetry slam where she'd taken first prize for the poem she'd read from a pizza box. She'd edited her poem profusely over the past few weeks, juggling paper plates and her order-pad flip-book and even the skinny straw wrapper until she'd imposed a shape and order to the poem, and then she'd rewritten the entire thing on the inside of a clean pizza box. Nearly all the other poets at the slam had memorized their poems, but while she had most of hers committed to memory, it was a long piece and the pizza box contributed something to her recitation. She wasn't sure what, but she'd won the prize.

She should be strutting and preening. She should be psyched about viewing her star turn in Rick's movie, which he was about to screen for family members in this mini-theater on the sixth floor of the TV studio building. But she was melancholy, and she took a seat near the front of the room, slid her feet out of her sandals, and propped them on the edge of the chair's cushions so she could wrap her arms around her legs and rest her chin on her knees. It felt good, curling up like that, folding in on herself.

Her family left her alone, thank God. They must have chalked up her uncommunicativeness to nerves about her performance in the movie. Most of them swarmed around Rick, who wore his pretentious lens on its cord around his neck and who, after editing the film and adding music and voice-overs to the soundtrack, had finally shaved off his flimsy goatee. Uncle Jay hovered near Rick, his chest puffed up and his smile threatening to reshape his cheeks permanently as he kvelled over the accomplishment of his son, the auteur. Wendy flitted about, overseeing an ice chest that contained several bottles of champagne she and Uncle Jay had brought for a post-screening toast. Aunt Martha, Uncle Jay's first wife and Rick's mother, attached herself to Susie's mother. She looked less proud than apprehensive, but then Aunt Martha didn't do positive emotions very well.

Grandma Ida was already settled into her seat at the center of the front row. She stared at the blank screen, her lips pressed together in an expression of vague malice, apparently prepared to dislike the movie. Julia and Joffe schmoozed with Adam and his spindly ballerina girlfriend, whose legs were so disproportionately long they seemed to emanate from just below her armpits.

Susie tuned them all out, sat by herself, and sulked.

Her misery was her own fault. After the poetry slam last night, when she and Anna had returned to their neighborhood, she'd begged Anna to walk with her to Avenue B and 4th. She'd been avoiding that corner for two weeks, but at half past midnight, she figured the odds of running into Casey there were negligible. The store he'd rented for his new shop was dark, and a corrugated metal gate had been rolled down and locked in place to protect the glass display windows, so she couldn't peek inside. Above the gate a new sign hung: "Casey's," in large green block letters, and "Gourmet Breads" in smaller italic letters underneath.

Merely seeing his name was enough to throw her into a tailspin.

She didn't like the person she'd become. Even though this dark mood had spawned several other really cool poems, she'd liked herself much better when limericks had flowed easily from her word processor, and she'd enjoyed excellent sex on a regular basis, and her biggest dilemma was which Heat-'N'-Eat entrée to bring home for supper. She'd liked herself better when she'd been fantasizing about piloting an eighteen-wheeler across the continent, and analyzing cheesy martial arts films, and living her life as if adulthood and responsibility were light-years away, in some other galaxy.

They weren't. They were here, right beneath her feet in New York City. Casey had tried to get her to understand that, but she'd panicked and fled, and now that she'd finally acknowledged the truth it was too late.

"Okay, let's get started," Rick announced. "I've only got this room for an hour."

"I take it the movie isn't that long," Julia murmured somewhere behind Susie. She heard people shuffling around, the hinges of the purple chairs squeaking as people took their seats. Her left foot jiggled but she refused to pivot in her chair and meet anyone else's gaze.

Julia and Joffe planted themselves directly behind her. When Joffe whispered to Julia that someone ought to advise Wendy to buy her blouses one size bigger, Susie heard him without having to strain. She also heard Julia's hissed response—that he shouldn't be looking so closely at her uncle's wife's bosom, and Joffe's defense—that avoiding looking at Wendy's bosom was like avoiding the smell of French fries in a McDonald's. "It's just there," he explained. "You can't escape it."

Julia whispered that he ought to avoid French fries, too, because they were high in fat and salt. Joffe whispered that if she was going to turn into a nag, he might call the wedding off. Julia whispered, "Just try it, buddy," and Joffe laughed.

Susie slouched lower in her chair.

Someone dimmed the lights. Rick settled into a front-row seat a few chairs down from Grandma Ida and grinned.

The screen glowed blue, then went black, then slowly, gradually warmed to orange as atonal tinkles of sound filled the room like wind chimes. The orange brightened, revealing the curved edge of a planet—earth, if Susie wasn't mistaken.

A voice—Rick's, not hers—narrated: "Billions of years ago, life emerged from the Primordial Soup. Today, soup is as important to life as it was then—except that now we eat it rather than slither out of it. Soup is what we make of it. Soup is what we put into it. Once we eat it, we're souped up.

"Soup."

The screen filled with towering white letters spelling "Bloom's Soup."

"What the hell...?" Julia whispered to Joffe, who promptly shushed her.

The camera zoomed in like a rocket entering the earth's atmosphere, searching for a landing strip on the east coast of the North American continent. Music swelled as towering letters filled the screen: "A Film By Rick Bloom." From another part of the screening room Susie heard her mother remark, "Someone seems pretty full of himself."

The camera zoomed in further as trees and houses and roads became decipherable. The lonely caw of a seagull resounded. The zoom stopped on a close-up of Linus lying on beach sand. Susie's toes appeared at the top of the screen, but someone not aware of what they were might take them for smooth pink shells. Her voice took over the narration: "You know that expression, 'You are what you eat'? Well, that's kind of ironic, because I'm a Bloom and when I was growing up, I didn't eat much Bloom's food. I do now, though." The camera inched back, then panned up Susie's body. She looked wan and somber, the sea breeze tossing her hair and her eyes squinting from the glare of the sun bouncing off the white sand. "They don't sell lobster at Bloom's," she said, gesturing toward Linus at her feet. "It's not kosher."

"That's right," Grandma Ida announced into the darkness. "Lobster, it's *trayf.* I never in my life ate it. Or pork."

"I eat lobster, but I'm not a lobster," Susie said on camera. "So who knows? Maybe that old saying isn't true."

"You eat lobster?" Grandma Ida peered in Susie's direction. Even though Susie refused to look back at her, she felt Grandma Ida's disapproving stare. "It's *trayf!*"

"What does she mean, *trayf?*" came an unfamiliar female voice. Adam's ballerina, probably.

"This is supposed to be an infomercial," Julia muttered.

"Ah, but it's so much more," Joffe muttered back, then chuckled. Susie didn't hear any laughter from Julia.

The camera veered away from Susie to a wide shot of the ocean—that good old Primordial Soup. Susie felt as if the woman speaking on the beach was a stranger. The filming seemed so long ago, especially those scenes in Revere. Of course she didn't recognize the sun rising over the rim of the earth and the camera zooming in—stock footage Rick must have added in the editing room. But the scenes she appeared in—and the film cut to another such scene, this one featuring her surrounded by a potato field—who had she been then?

Someone afraid to admit she wanted a home. Someone who didn't even know what home was.

"Thank God she's talking about knishes," Julia grunted. "We actually sell them in the store."

"I've eaten knishes!" Wendy cried out, obviously proud of herself.

"That's a nice line, about how potatoes hug us from the inside," Joffe commented.

"*Oy*, with the lobster again," Grandma Ida commented as the camera filmed Linus standing in his original place, perched on a crumbling concrete pedestal at the side of the road. If Grandma Ida learned that Rick had left a hundred dollars in cash on that pedestal, she'd probably have a stroke.

"I don't get it," Wendy said in a stage whisper that resonated through the room. "Why does he keep showing that ugly thing?"

"How can you say a lobster is ugly?" Uncle Jay argued. "You order lobsters in restaurants all the time."

"To eat, not to look at."

"Shh!" Martha silenced them.

Scenes unreeled before Susie. A syncopated drumbeat accompanied the section Rick had taped in downtown Boston. Susie was dwarfed by the skyscrapers just beyond Quincy Market. The downtown Boston footage faded into a night shot in which the skyscraper windows twinkled like stars. Susie was sure she'd seen that scene at the start of a TV show based in Boston. She hoped Rick knew what he was doing when it came to filching shots from other shows. Were copyright issues involved?

"How is this going to get people to come to Bloom's?" Julia asked in a low voice.

"Beats me," Joffe answered.

"I gave him twenty-five thousand dollars to make an infomercial."

"It's not bad for twenty-five thousand dollars."

"Easy for you to say. It didn't come out of your ad budget."

The *Bloom's Bulletin* was paid for out of the ad budget, too. Susie wondered idly whether she would get laid off because Rick's movie had devoured twenty-five thousand dollars and wasn't a proper infomercial.

The drumbeat drifted off, replaced by a lilting flute. There she was, sitting on the cabin's porch steps at Pine Haven. There she was, talking about white bread and home. There she was, looking wistful and wise. What acting! She deserved an Oscar.

The camera panned to a vista of the pond—without Linus in it, thank God. "Sometimes you just have to stop and think about what matters," she said in a voice-over. When had she spoken those words? When had she become so tritely profound?

At last Rick's voice rejoined the soundtrack, along with a lilting Klezmer clarinet. "Bloom's," he said. "It's about food. It's about life. It's about who we are and what we eat and why it matters." The screen faded to black and titles began to scroll: A Film By Rick Bloom. Directed By Rick Bloom. Produced By Rick Bloom. Edited By Rick Bloom. Sound Production By Rick Bloom. Cameraman: Rick Bloom. Written by Rick Bloom and Susie Bloom. Starring Susie Bloom. Narrator: Rick Bloom.

"The phrase 'vanity production' comes to mind," Julia commented dryly, her words nearly drowned out by enthusiastic if solitary applause from further back in the room. Wendy, probably.

"*Oy,*" Susie's mother said.

"I don't get it," Grandma Ida added. "What's with the lobster? Lobster's *trayf.*"

"It's a leitmotif," Rick explained, rising from his seat as the lights came up. He looked close to ecstatic. "It's a metaphor, Grandma. This movie is about the primordial—"

"Soup, I know, I understand. But what kind of soup doesn't have *knedlach* in it, or at least matzo balls? What is it, borscht? Lobster bisque we don't sell at Bloom's."

"I was talking about the primordial urges within us all," Rick explained calmly. "The innate yearning to eat the food our ancestors ate. That was in the narration. The lobster is like some prehistoric—"

"Primordial, okay," Grandma Ida cut him off. "It's a big red fish inside a shell. It looks like a bug."

Susie kept her face forward. She didn't have to see her relatives to know who was talking.

"I think it's brilliant," Aunt Martha declared. "The allegorical through-line was magnificently handled."

"I think it could work," Uncle Jay added with a little less certainty. "We can buy some cheap time on cable, I can hype the movie on the web site, we'll put it on YouTube. It'll generate interest. Bloom's is a patron of the arts. I like that."

"It was supposed to be an infomercial," Julia reminded him.

"So Rick approached the subject with some originality."

"And wit," Aunt Martha chimed in. "Astonishing wit."

"Bloom's got mentioned a lot in it. How many times does Bloom's get mentioned, Rick?" Uncle Jay asked.

Rick shrugged. "I never counted."

"A lot," Uncle Jay insisted. "We can broadcast this the way PBS broadcasts Masterpiece Theater, you know, with the British voice intoning that this broadcast was made possible by some oil company. Only we say, 'This film was made possible by the generous contributions of Bloom's.'"

"Masterpiece Theater," Martha echoed. "For once we agree, Jay. This movie is a masterpiece."

Susie wasn't sure what she herself thought of the movie, other than that it wandered, just as she herself had wandered through Maine and Boston and the Catskills, just as her thoughts had been wandering ever since Casey had asked her to move in with him. Just as her heart had been wandering from fear to love to regret.

"I thought it was good, but it could have used a little more action," came a voice from the back of the screening room—a voice that didn't belong to any of her relatives. Susie almost jumped out of her seat. And out of her skin.

What the hell was Casey doing here?

"You think so?" Rick asked.

"A little Jackie Chan-style action," Casey said. "Maybe a kick-boxing scene between Susie and the lobster."

Linus would have won any bout with Susie, hands down. Or claws down. Was that what Casey wanted? For Susie to get beaten to a pulp by a fake lobster?

She stood and spun around. Casey lounged against the wall at the back of the room, his hands in the pockets of his khaki cargo slacks and a clean white T-shirt reading "Casey's Gourmet Breads" covering his chest. His hair hung in loose blond waves around his face, and his gaze zeroed in on her. He smiled.

He had plenty to smile about. He was opening a new business, he had something good going with the Halle babe, and he was probably spending his spare time teaching Linus all the taekwondo moves he knew.

Who'd told him about this private screening, anyway? It was supposed to be for family only.

She glared at Rick, who seemed not the least bit startled by Casey's presence. A glance at Julia indicated that she also wasn't surprised by his invasion of a Bloom gathering. Grandma Ida squinted at Casey as if uncertain where she knew him from, Sondra scowled and Uncle Jay appeared too elated by his son's cinematic feat to care. Wendy was busy setting up disposable plastic champagne flutes on the lid of the cooler chest.

Susie turned back to Julia, who smiled apologetically and answered her unasked question. "He asked if he could come. I checked with Rick, and he said he thought it would be a good idea."

"A good idea?" Susie snapped. "This screening was for family. Casey doesn't belong here,"

"I'm not so sure of that. Go talk to him." Julia reached over the back of Susie's seat and gave her a nudge. "He's so knowledgeable about kick-boxing."

Susie flinched. She couldn't recall the last time her sister had teased her, but it had been a while. She'd been so moody lately, Julia must have been afraid to push her too far.

Now Julia was pushing her literally. Another nudge, and Susie had to walk away from Julia just to escape her prodding fingers. Walking away from Julia meant walking toward Casey, but Susie didn't see any alternative.

At the rear of the room, Casey took her arm. She deftly wriggled free of his clasp but left the room with him. She felt her mother's glare following her. The possibility that her leaving with Casey would piss her mother off made her feel marginally better.

She halted outside the door, but Casey kept walking, and Susie reluctantly continued behind him, even though she felt ridiculous trailing after him like a loyal dog. "Where are we going?" she asked tensely.

"I want to show you something."

"Maybe I don't want to see it."

"I think you do."

Damn it, she did. Just watching his graceful strides, observing the sexy contours of his butt and the confident swing of his arms, made her eager to see whatever he wanted to show her.

He reached the elevator and pressed the button. He had hands big enough to palm a basketball, big enough to knead dough, twist it into bagel circles, and toss it into boiling water. Hands big enough to cradle her hips. She loved his hands—hands that were undoubtedly bringing another woman great pleasure these days.

"Why are we doing this?" she asked.

The elevator arrived and Casey motioned with his chin for her to enter ahead of him. Once the doors slid shut, he lobbed back a question. "Why did you leave me that lobster?"

"Okay, so that was stupid of me." Perhaps a quick confession would put an end to this game.

No such luck. "Why did you do it? You're not a stupid person."

"I told you—I had no room for it in my apartment," she said, which was the truth. "Rick had no room for it in his apartment, either. My mother has room for it in her apartment, but it doesn't match her décor. And Grandma Ida would never allow it in her apartment, because it's *trayf.*"

The elevator thudded to a stop on the ground floor. Casey took her elbow again, and she didn't shrug her arm loose this time. She felt that he was her gravity, and if he wasn't holding her she would spin away into the ozone.

"So you arrived at my door at close to midnight and dumped it on me?" He ushered her down the main corridor while he talked. "It didn't occur to you to leave it on the sidewalk? Someone would have picked it up if you had."

He was going to embarrass her until she spilled the truth. With a sigh, she said, "I wanted to see you. I'd had some insights while Rick and I were roaming around New England making the movie, and I thought maybe I could share them with you. I didn't know you'd be hosting a party at that hour."

"It wasn't a party," he said, guiding her through the door and out onto the sidewalk. She blinked in the heavy afternoon light, and staggered slightly when he released her arm. He stepped to the curb and waved at every cab he saw until one pulled over. "Get in," he told Susie as he opened the door.

She ought to have resisted, or suffered a twinge of apprehension. But this was turning out to be an interesting adventure, so she went with it. "Where are we going?" she asked.

"You'll see." He got in next to her, struggling to fit his lanky legs into the narrow space, then gave the driver an address on Avenue B.

His store, she guessed. Well, she'd wanted to check it out last night. Today the metal gate would be open. Casey would rub her nose in the reality that he was about to ruin her neighborhood by opening his new shop there. Its existence in the East Village would act as a constant reminder of everything she'd lost. She could have been married to the famous bread chef, but no, she'd turned him down because she'd wanted her freedom, and now he would be the toast of the town, and his bread would be the toasted of the town. He'd probably appear on the cover of *Gotham Magazine*, with Halle hanging all over him. Joffe could write a story about his wonderful business triumph.

"The movie wasn't bad," he remarked as the cab headed down Broadway, dodging cars with the flare of a stunt driver on a slalom course. "I don't know how much good it'll do for Bloom's, but the allegory worked."

"What allegory?"

"Stone Soup. Bloom's Soup. You take nothing, add good food to it, and wind up with something. You take a situation where people don't realize what they have, and you give them exactly what they have, and they realize what they have is actually valuable."

"You saw that in the movie?"

"It was all there," he said.

She pondered his analysis. Maybe it *was* all there. She just hadn't been looking for it. She'd been too busy thinking she looked pale, or worrying that Linus was upstaging her—hell, she'd been upstaged by the collapsing cabin. She'd been upstaged by a potato field. Preoccupied by how well she was coming across, she'd forgotten to pay attention to the overall theme.

"I don't think my sister wanted an allegory."

"She can work it out with Rick. It's not your problem."

That much was true. Her problem was that Casey had abducted her and was dragging her downtown to his store. Her bigger problem was that sitting in the cab's rear seat with him turned her on, and he didn't love her anymore.

The cab dropped them off at Avenue B and 4th. Casey paid while Susie stood on the corner, her arms folded and her gaze deliberately angled across the street so she wouldn't see the "Casey's Gourmet Breads" sign. Once the cab pulled back into the traffic flow, Casey clamped his hand over Susie's shoulder and propelled her along the sidewalk to his store. The sun glared off the front panes, making it impossible to see inside.

He unlocked the door and urged her in ahead of him. The place smelled like flour and dust and disinfectant, not a bad smell but not as good as it would smell once the place was filled with fresh loaves and rolls. She briefly took in the shelves, the display cases, the front counter and the industrial ovens in back, and then Casey rotated her to face Linus.

The six-foot lobster stood front and center, his claws outstretched, a chef's toque perched on his shell head, drooping slightly over one antenna, and a linen apron tied around his midsection. The apron's bib featured the same writing as Casey's T-shirt. "What do you think?" Casey asked.

She wasn't sure what she thought—other than that Linus looked kind of cute in a chef's toque and apron.

She shifted her gaze from the lobster to survey the store again. The cash register appeared old—Casey would need to replace it. The linoleum floor had been washed enough times to imply that whatever scuffs and stains remained imbedded in its surface were permanent. The shelves were attractive—polished hardwood. Matching hardwood bins lined the front of the counter, beneath which was a glass showcase.

She turned back to Linus. He looked perfect standing there in his baker's costume.

"This is good," she said, gesturing toward Linus. "He didn't really match your apartment's décor, either."

"You don't mind my using him here?"

"Why should I mind? I gave him to you. He's yours."

"He just seems...I don't know. At home here. Like he belongs."

Susie nodded. Linus looked the way she wanted to feel: at home here. Like she belonged.

She realized that Casey hadn't removed his hand from her shoulder. Instead, he tightened his grip and turned her to face him. "Look, Susie—"

"The other night..." Her words tumbled on top of his, and she silenced herself.

"The other night...?"

"No—you go first."

"No, you."

She sighed. "The other night, I went to your apartment because—well, like I said, I had some insights. Also,

I had the van for the night, because Buck-a-Truck didn't open until eight a.m. so I couldn't return it, and I couldn't find a parking space, so I figured, what the hell."

Casey nodded, as if this all made perfect sense.

"But I know you've gotten on with your life—as you should." Her voice wavered slightly and she swallowed. Being a grown-up entailed taking grown-up positions on things, making grown-up pronouncements, accepting grown-up conclusions. "I mean, opening your own business. Leaving Bloom's. Everything."

"Everything?"

"Don't make me say it," she snapped, then went ahead and said it. "You're seeing someone. I don't blame you. She's gorgeous."

Something flickered in his expression, but with only the afternoon sunlight slanting through the front windows to illuminate his face, Susie couldn't interpret it.

"All right," she continued bravely. "I don't want to be bitchy, but she's got the most awful laugh I've ever heard. Other than that—"

"She likes bad knock-knock jokes, too," Casey told her.

Was he going to give Susie a complete inventory of the woman's pluses and minuses? "It's your choice, Casey. You want bad knock-knock jokes in your life?"

"No." His hand relented on her shoulder, his fingers curving gently. "I don't want bad knock-knock jokes in my life. I don't even want good knock-knock jokes in my life."

"I suggest you take that up with her," Susie said, feeling enormously grown-up.

"There's nothing going on between Eva and me," he said. "LaShonna tried to set us up, but it didn't click. At least not for me."

"Because of the knock-knock jokes?"

"And also because I didn't want to have to start wearing condoms again."

Susie jabbed him in the stomach. He recoiled slightly, but laughed. Evidently her best poke felt like a tickle. In a kickboxing bout, Linus would beat her senseless before the first round ended.

Susie didn't mind her lack of boxing potential. She was too delighted to learn that Casey hadn't slept with Halle. Or Eva, if that was her name. It hadn't clicked for him.

Hope gave her courage. "I love you, Casey," she said. "I don't want to get married—I mean, not yet. Marriage seems so...*adult*." She could be only so grown-up, after all. "But if that's what it takes, I'm willing to try."

"You're willing to try marriage? What does that mean? You'll give it a three-month run and then decide whether to renew?"

She poked him again. "Come on, Casey! I'm laying everything bare here, and you're giving me shit."

He pulled her close, so close she could no longer poke him. "I wish you would lay everything bare," he murmured before hitting her with one of his nuclear-powered kisses—his lips, his tongue, his arms closing tight around her, his body spreading its heat to her, his hands cradling her hips just the way she loved it. "But there's too much window glass," he groaned after breaking the kiss and dragging a ragged breath into his lungs. "Besides, my father'll be here soon. He's putting in some new outlets for me and making sure the wiring can handle updated equipment." He brushed a lighter kiss on her mouth, then pulled back and peered into her eyes, as if searching for her soul. "I love you, too, Susie. Let's not get married."

"Really?" Joy spiraled through her. "You don't want to marry me?"

"I tried that route and you disappeared."

"I don't want to disappear. I realized while I was away that I like home. I mean, home is important. It's essential. I wrote a long, wonderful poem about it. This is my home. This city. This neighborhood." *Your arms are my home,* she thought, but saying that would be way too corny.

"Yeah." Casey glanced toward the front windows, then turned back to her. "Speaking of this neighborhood, I'm thinking of finding a place to live around here. I'll have to be in the shop by four a.m. to get the ovens up and running. Commuting in from Queens would be a pain in the ass. You know of any apartments in the area?"

"Mine isn't big enough, plus Anna and Caitlin live there."

"I was thinking of my own place. Close to yours, so you could drop by without having to rent a van and not find a parking space, or whatever."

"I could drop by a lot," Susie suggested. Now that he'd taken marriage off the table, she yearned to put something back on the table. "Like, often enough to keep a toothbrush by your sink. If that's okay with you, of course," she added, aware that when he'd withdrawn the marriage proposal he might have been negating the whole living-together idea.

"Yeah." He nodded and gave her a lazy, bedroom-eyed smile. "Yeah, I'd really like to have your toothbrush by my sink."

A tap of metal against glass caught their attention. On the other side of the glass front door stood a tall, silver-haired man who looked like a slightly beefier, older version of Casey. Casey opened it and the man entered. "Wow! Nice place!" He peered around. "I think you're nuts, but when has that ever stopped you? What the heck is that? A lobster?"

"Yes." Evidently Casey saw no need to explain. "Dad, this is Susie Bloom. Susie, my father, Keenan Gordon."

"Hey, Mr. Gordon." Meeting Casey's father seemed almost as serious as getting married. Susie felt exceedingly mature as she extended her hand.

"Susie Bloom, huh?" Casey's father shook her hand, then tossed Casey a look. "The ex-boss's daughter, right?" he whispered, although she had no trouble hearing him.

"The ex-boss's sister," Casey corrected him.

"Is she going to help us set this place up?"

"I hope so," Casey said, including Susie in his gaze.

"Just tell me what you want me to do," she said, then winked at Casey. "And maybe I'll do it."

The Bloom's Bulletin
Written and edited by
Susie Bloom

In search of connubial bliss
Bloom's president found happiness.
Our own Julia Bloom
And her wonderful groom
Sealed their vows with a passionate kiss.
(So when can we hope for a bris?)

Welcome to the October 7th edition of the *Bloom's Bulletin*. In the spring a man's fancy turns to love, but early this autumn, the Bloom family—and the Bloom's family—turned love into a fancy wedding. In a ceremony high above the city on the roof of the Bloom Building, Bloom's president Julia Bloom exchanged vows with journalist Ronald Joffe. The roof was transformed into a paradise of greenery, with philodendron vines and multi-colored roses adorning the huge tent erected on the roof. The tent proved unnecessary, thanks to the dry, balmy weather, so the walls were tied up and the night invited in. Rabbi Avram Kopelstein performed the ceremony under a traditional Jewish *chuppa*, or canopy, the poles of which were held by Neil and Rick Bloom, both cousins of the bride, father of the groom Norman Joffe and family friend and Bloom's accountant Myron Finkel. Prayers were recited, Ron and Julia sipped wine from a goblet, Ron stomped on the glass to shouts of *L'chaim* and *Mazel Tov*, and the writer/editor of this publication gained a brother-in-law.

"We originally considered holding the wedding in Grandma Ida's apartment," Julia said. "But if we'd done that, we would have had to whittle our guest list down. We had so much room on the roof, we were able to invite everyone who works at Bloom's. They're all a part of our family." This would explain the rare early closing of Bloom's at three p.m. on the day of the wedding, as employees were sent home early to prepare for the party.

Buffet tables were heaped high with delicious edibles provided by Bloom's catering service. Everyone loved the succulent roast beef, steamed fresh vegetables, salads and pastries. Among the biggest hits were the potato "latkettes" and the tiny marzipan fruits decorating the pastry table.

Julia's uncle, Jacob Bloom, escorted her down the aisle. The groom was attended by his brother, Ira Joffe, and Adam Bloom, the bride's brother, served as usher. *Bulletin* writer/editor Susie Bloom (that would be me) was the maid of honor, and everyone remarked that salmon pink was a flattering color on her. Music was provided by harpist Jocelyn Bennett and flautist Errol Stack and by Herschel Katz and the Klezmer Cats.

The party lasted late into the night. The newlyweds are spending their honeymoon sailing in the Florida Keys, a trip arranged by cousin Neil Bloom, who runs a sailboat charter company. While Julia is enjoying the tropical breezes in Florida, Bloom's is under the capable management of her mother, Sondra Bloom, who said of her eldest child's wedding, "It was a lovely affair, even if it wasn't at the Plaza."

Speaking of which... Bloom's has set up a bridal registry. Sondra Bloom will be available to work with brides-and-grooms-to-be on registering food items, gift baskets and must-have appliances from our kitchenware department. Before you send out the invitations, register!

Wedding, schmedding—what's on sale this week? Lots of wonderful items, including some of our most popular kitchen gadgets. Check out the garlic presses, melon ballers, and top-of-the-line electric can openers on the second floor. Also, pickled everything: pickled tomatoes, pickled beets, pickled artichokes and just plain pickles—sours, halfs and garlic dills. Don't get yourself in a pickle! Get a pickle into you!

Employees Profile: At the wedding atop the Bloom Building, many Bloom's employees were polled on their ideas of love, home and food. Most agreed that a wedding pretty much encompassed all three necessities. "You get married for love—if you're smart," Bloom's cheese department manager Albert Medina opined. "If you're not so smart, well, you must be stupid."

"Home is a lot better if you've got someone waiting for you there," cashier Lois Schickel said. "To me, home is where you go to when you don't want to be alone."

"Food?" Helen Wacklin, Bloom's office administrator mused. "I guess the best definition for that is Bloom's."

"Home is a place in your heart," insisted Casey Gordon, owner of Casey's Gourmet Breads in the East

Village and also Bloom's chief bagel supplier. "If you're looking for home, your heart will tell you when you've found it."

Wise Words from Bloom's founder Ida Bloom: "You want to have a wedding in your apartment? Don't be *meshugge.* Have it somewhere else."

o

Acknowledgements

Thanks to Beverley Sotolov and Dianne Moggy for encouraging me to write another Bloom family story, and everyone at the Story Plant for allowing me to share the Blooms with readers. And mostly to the Bloom family, for taking over my imagination and my life.

About the Author

Judith Arnold is the bestselling, award-winning author of more than one hundred novels and several plays. A New York native, she lives with her husband near Boston in a house with four guitars, three pianos, a violin, a kazoo, a balalaika, and a set of bongo drums. She treasures good books, good music, good chocolate, and good wine—although she will settle for mediocre wine if good wine isn't available. You can learn more about her at her website: www.juditharnold.com.